❧ HELP FOR ❧
THE HAUNTED

HELP FOR THE HAUNTED

A Decade of Vera Van Slyke Ghostly Mysteries

by
TIM PRASIL

BROM BONES BOOKS

This book was originally published by Emby Press in 2015 with the same title. This edition is slightly modified, hopefully in a good way.

ISBN: 1-948084-02-3
ISBN-13: 978-1-948084-02-4

DEDICATION

This book is dedicated to Bill Balcer,
who always enjoyed a ghost story—
but who did not live quite long enough to read these.

CONTENTS

INTRODUCTION

Vera Van Slyke (1868-1941) was a paradox. On the one hand, she earned a living as a journalist in the era of the great muckrakers, gaining some distinction in this career by being a foe to Spiritualist mediums. She even published a book on the topic, *Spirits Shouldn't Sneeze: A Decade of Defrauding Mediums* (1901). On the other hand, she was a ghost hunter, fully convinced that spirits of the dead lingered among the living. This part of her life is the focus of the book you are about to read.

Van Slyke's investigations into hauntings were chronicled by my great-grandaunt, Lida. (My immigrant ancestor's birth name was Ludmila Prášilová, her Anglicized name was Lucille Parsell, and then she took her husband's surname, Bergson. For simplicity's sake, I identify her by her pet name: Lida.) She first met Van Slyke in 1899 and was employed as the journalist's personal assistant within a year. An avid reader, Lida chronicled their supernatural cases in lengths and detail that suggest she had an eye on possible magazine and/or book publication. However, I've been unable to discover any publication history, which is surprising because of the interesting subject matter and because they were written in an era of widespread reading. The pieces were also written in English, not in her first language, Czech. Lida's command of English no doubt resulted from her arriving in the U.S. at an early age.

There isn't room here to recount how the manuscripts, stored haphazardly in a wooden box intended to display seed packets, passed through the Prasil family to finally come into my possession. Let me just note that my organizing and editing of the chronicles have been very educational. At times, what appeared to be errors turned out to be historically accurate. Pittsburgh, for example, was spelled without the final "h" for several years, and the song I knew as *"Jimmy* Crack Corn" was sung as *"Jim* Crack Corn" by an earlier generation.

This raises the question of how much of Lida's narratives constitutes reliable history versus imaginative fiction. Harry Houdini, of course, was a real person who appears in one chronicle. A bit of research has also revealed two more actual people: a mariner named Henry Thorn Lord, who had served as second mate on a ship called the *Junior,* and a coroner for Cook County named Peter M. Hoffman. The Internet has facilitated confirmation for the rounded corners of Stickney House as well as the tragedies at Fort Pitt and Fort Dearborn. Several other details can be verified, too.

On the other hand, Lida took some liberties. For instance, I can find no Tadcaster, Massachusetts, on any map. Her reason for sidetracking identification of the church in that town might be the same one that explains her openly evading the name of another church, one in Arkansas—she didn't wish to cast aspersions on these congregations. In addition, some fabrication might be attributed to the pitfalls of Lida recalling events that had happened roughly ten years earlier, a matter that I return to in my Postscript.

As to my great-grandaunt presenting the ghosts and other supernatural manifestations as completely *real,* I can only bid readers to follow their own convictions. Even if her chronicles of the remarkable Vera Van Slyke are deemed by some readers to be little more than, say, a mix of detective and supernatural fiction, it is heartening to see them finally made available for the public. My editorial changes have been minimal, but even so, I accept full blame for any glaring historical anachronisms, especially in the language.

Let me close by soliciting help in locating a copy of Van Slyke's *Spirits Shouldn't Sneeze,* the book that sparked the affection between ghost hunter and assistant. Despite extensive searching, I've never found a copy of this volume. Still, I hope that someone somewhere will find a dusty copy packed away in an attic or on a shelf at an out-of-the-way used book store. If you're so lucky, please contact me. I'll make it worth your while. Although the scarcity of this book suggests it was unsuccessful in terms of sales, it was *very* successful in sowing a friendship between my ancestor Lida and her employer, Vera.

It also succeeded in launching a fascinating series of ghostly investigations.

THE MINISTER'S UNVEILING
(1899)

Ghosts might enter here without affrighting us.

— Nathaniel Hawthorne

At first, I was not certain if Vera Van Slyke had taken pity on me—or was taking advantage of me.

We had met in Boston in December of 1899. Vera was a journalist devoted to flushing out corruption and laying bare the truth. She crusaded alongside Ida Tarbell, Lincoln Steffans, Jacob Riis, and Nellie Bly. However, Vera specialized in unmasking a particular *kind* of dishonesty. She attended séances. There, in the dark, she sat and surveyed as would an owl. She waited until she could prove that the writing on the slate exhibited signs of the psychic's own spelling and not that of some entity guiding that psychic's hand. The hovering image of the deceased was simply a photo framed with phosphorous-soaked gauze. The ethereal voice came from a very corporeal confederate. Vera Van Slyke sat patiently, ready to prove once again her reputation for yanking the sheets off fraudulent spirits and unveiling the deceptions of the Spiritualist mediums behind them.

I, at the time, was a Spiritualist medium. Only seventeen years old, I had already developed a persona befitting the role. Inspired by Madame Blavatsky, the famous Russian psychic, I wore the most flamboyant of Eastern European fashions. I spoke with an accent untraceable beyond *Slavic*. I introduced myself with the name Ludmila Prášilová. Once hired, I worked myself

5

into a trance and then contacted the spirits of children who had died of whooping cough, husbands crushed in manufacturing accidents, and beloved grandmothers who had reached the end of rich, full lives. My fee was slightly above reasonable.

In that winter of 1899, my tricks came under the piercing brown eyes of Vera Van Slyke. Immediately after she exposed me, however, I pled my case. Her triumph melted into sympathy when I explained *my own mother* had sent me down this path. A squint of caution remained in Vera's eyes. Still, when I dropped the accent and reintroduced myself as Lucille Parsell, she offered me the chance to help her with a project she was starting. She hoped to write a book revealing the secrets of my trade.

Confession is good for the soul, according to the popular adage. I told myself that, instead of fooling those aching to be fooled, I could help them muster the strength for facing the truth. I accepted the opportunity to do something noble instead of remaining a pawn in a game of chicanery. It was the chance to free myself from the grip of my mother, whose motives seemed too narrow to include what was best for her daughter.

I did not know Vera's motives.

•

A few days after our dreadful introduction to one another, I arrived at Vera's hotel. She took my coat, and I sat down on what might have been a very comfortable chair if the subject of discussion had been anything else. She had said that this would be the beginning of a series of interviews. However, Vera surprised me with a new plan and a very new timbre to our relationship.

Initially, she stood with a hand resting on the back of the chair across from mine. Physically, Vera's most striking characteristic was her height. I would have estimated it to be an inch or two below six feet. Her hair was stubbornly wavy— frizzy, one could say—and mostly auburn. Its streaks of gray might or might not have been premature, given that her age could have been anywhere between the low-thirties and the mid-fifties. Settling on any figure more precise was made impossible by her face, which was pleasant but without any particularly distinctive features. There were no wrinkles around the eyes or sagging jowl to suggest the passage of years. If Vera's face revealed anything at all, the somewhat thick brows, somewhat thin lips, and somewhat square jaw implied a frank and stalwart quality that some might ascribe to a man.

Next, Vera presented me with an astonishing invitation. "There is a report," she said, "that the ghost of a *Puritan* minister is haunting a *Catholic* confessional just a few towns to the north. Care to go investigate?"

"I—I'm," I stammered. "Uhm, I'm—"

"Now, *that* hardly answers my question." A teasing glee shone in those brown eyes of hers. "Let me explain." She looked upward, placed her palms together, and began. "Ever since I was a child, I've *adored* ghost stories. This passion led to my interest in you Spiritualists. I've made sure that those who know me *also* know about this fascination of mine. Moments before you arrived, one of my associates who'd heard I was in Boston informed me of the situation regarding the ghostly Puritan minister."

"In a—haunting a Catholic church? A *Puritan?*" I felt as if I were dismounting a horse to discover myself stepping into a rowboat.

"Troubling, isn't it? One hardly gets more Protestant than a Puritan minister! Why, the Church of England first formed as a protest against Rome, and then the Puritans protested against the Church of England! What's he doing *there?* Aren't you curious?"

"Well, I'm—I'm—"

"Please, don't start that again, dear! If we leave now, we can catch the train up to Tadcaster. After lunch, of course. Lunch before ghosts, I always say!"

Later, I learned that *not* missing lunch is one of Vera's topmost priorities. At this point in time, though, I was giggling far too much to refuse her offer. She scurried to fetch my coat, and we were on our way.

•

While Massachusetts towns such as Concord and Lexington were bravely marching into histories of the Revolutionary War, Tadcaster seems to have been sitting in a cabin, absorbed in scripture while puffing on a clay pipe. In the subsequent century, like so many other New England towns, this one's small farms had given way to large factories. When the Gossamer Lace and Drapery Company built its manufactory in Tadcaster, it lured to town a flock of Irish and Italian workers. To serve their souls, Saint Brigid's arose. The church's simple wood and whitewash exterior shone beautifully amid freshly fallen snow.

Vera halted us on the church's shoveled walkway. "Would you happen to know how one addresses a Catholic clergyman?"

I watched a puff of my breath appear and vanish before I offered, "Politely?"

"No, I mean in terms of title. Not 'Reverend.' Not 'Your Grace.' Certainly not 'Rabbi'."

"Ah! Start with *Father*, then fill in the last name."

"*Father!* I knew that!" She resumed walking. "Now that I think of it, it's puzzling how rarely ghosts inhabit religious locales. Oh, you hear of them lurking around churchyard burial grounds and such. But those never turn out to be authentic."

"Authentic? Are you implying you've encountered *real* ghosts?"

"Well, yes. Those stories I told you at lunch. Those were real ghosts."

"I thought they were just—*ghost* stories!"

"Well. Yes. Exactly."

This time, I halted us. "Are we not here to *debunk* this story? Do you mean to say that you travel around exposing mediums and psychics—people who summon *spirits*—and all the while, you actually believe in *ghosts?*"

"It's charming how often I'm asked about that," she laughed. "It's not really a contradiction. I know that Spiritualists are frauds because, well, ghosts are like *cats*. They're real, but they hardly come when called. They act of their own accord. My aim is to coax ghosts into *moving on* from the places they haunt, not draw them *closer!*"

She dragged me forward by my elbow.

We found the church unlocked. Once inside, while kicking the snow from our feet, we turned to one another. A mumble had sounded. The same voice continued from within the sanctuary. Vera charged ahead, barely noticing as I blessed myself at the fount.

The mumbling vanished once we were both within, and Vera angled her head almost as if an echo might indicate the direction from which it had come. She looked at me with a raised eyebrow, and stealing forward, she pointed to the sanctuary's solitary confessional. Wide ribbons had been draped to bar the doors on either end, doors that would otherwise welcome the penitent.

"I'm confused, Lucille." Vera's voice resonated in the vacant chapel. "I expected only two stalls, one for the priest hearing confessions and one for those who confess. Why *three* compartments?"

"The priest sits in the middle and hears confessions from either side."

"I see. Efficiency is *everywhere* these days!"

I was about to reply when another voice spoke.

"Might *I* be of assistance, ladies?"

A short and wizened priest arose among the back pews. He moved with the slow struggle of advanced age. Indeed, his bald and spotted scalp confirmed he was a man of many years. The shock of his unexpected ascension passed once he chuckled.

"Apologies," he continued. "Seems the only way Mr. and Mrs. Trigilio can keep their twins quiet during mass is by supplying the boys with taffy. I fear I might need some kind of tool to remove the stuff. You wouldn't happen to have a scraper, would you?"

"I regret that we do not, Father," Vera said as she brushed by me. "We are following up on reports of a haunted confessional. I knew nothing about the taffy dilemma." She moved so rapidly toward the priest that I believe I saw him flinch.

Still, he shook her hand warmly. "Ah, yes. The confessional. Now, that's an enigma. That is a strange, strange—but excuse me! I'm Father O'Neil."

We introduced ourselves, and the priest ushered us to the pew closest to the enigmatic confessional. I saw that the two ribbons tacked across the doors were so aged that their scarlet color had faded to pink.

"Our doors are always unlocked," the priest began. "Tadcaster's safe enough, and some of the parishioners like to come in to pray after late shifts and whatnot. One of the factory men first heard the ghost. He claims he had stepped in one night to rest from tromping home though the snow. Sitting about where we are, he heard a voice call out from the confessional."

Vera scrutinized the structure before asking, "What did the voice say?"

"I can only paraphrase. It was something like: 'You, who tarry there. Come! Come and speaketh to me of thy sins.' Now, the worker assumed the voice was *mine,* though he couldn't fathom why I'd be up that late. He replied, 'I've nothing to confess, Father.' But the voice persisted! Of course, the Puritans could be rather headstrong." Father O'Neil touched the side of his nose as he added, "You can ask the *witches* about that!"

Vera was too engrossed in ghosts to entertain witches. "How is it you're convinced this voice emanates from a *Puritan?*"

"At first, it was his manner of speaking—'prithee' and 'goodman' and 'forsooth.'"

A bit shyly, I inquired, "And secondly?"

"Secondly, he *said* as much. Several of us have encountered him now, and he's rather a chatty, old macaw. He's even introduced himself! Said his name is the Reverend Mr. Dimmesdale."

Vera's eyebrows raised. "Dimmesdale? Isn't that a character in that novel? You know the one. *The Purloined Letter.*"

"*The Scarlet Letter,*" I quietly corrected her.

"That's it," she nodded. "By James Fennimore—"

"Nathaniel Hawthorne," I said quickly.

Vera snickered. "I'm not very strong with names."

Father O'Neil nodded. "We had considered that. However, one of our well-read parishioners pointed out that Hawthorne used to find his characters' names by wandering 'round old cemeteries in Concord and Salem and Marblehead. We decided this might be the ghost of one of those very same Puritans whose headstone Hawthorne had seen."

"I can see water running along that canal," Vera agreed. She had a variety of such sayings, I would learn. She continued, "More to the point, you say that he's chatty. Could, perhaps, I go in and speak with him even now?"

"Unfortunately, he seems to follow no set schedule. In fact, he's appeared a few times as I was listening to confessions! That by itself is unsettling, but to make matters worse, he's had the gumption to ask the penitent for clarification on specifics!"

"Sat in on confessions, has he? That *is* awfully brash," Vera commented. "This explains those ribbons barring the confessional, I assume."

"Indeed so. I've written the Bishop for guidance." The priest rubbed his bony fingers. "As yet, he's only advised me to keep the sacramental wine sacramental."

Vera nodded with sympathy. "I had hoped we were hearing the ghost's voice when we first entered. Was there someone else here?"

Father O'Neil chuckled. "No. You see—well, I hope you can understand. The voice you heard was my own."

Seeing the priest fidget, I attempted to relieve his embarrassment. "I'm certain most people talk to themselves from time to time."

"They do, no doubt." He chuckled again, but this time, it sounded less natural. "But I was not speaking to myself. I was speaking to Thalia, my daughter." He smiled weakly and stared at the crucifix hanging behind the altar.

Vera slowly rested two fingers against her jaw before she whispered, "But I understood that you *priests*—that there are certain *vows* that priests—"

I intervened. "Did you have a family before you joined the order?"

Father O'Neil scratched his cheek while explaining. "No. No, but a part of me very much wishes that I had. And to calm that longing, once upon a time, I invented Thalia. For the better part of my long life, my daughter has remained a young girl. She keeps me company, you see."

We shared a moment of silence. Finally, Vera broke it.

"And is young Thalia with us now?" she asked warily.

"She generally flits away when more *tangible* company arrives."

"Then you are to be commended for having reared a dutiful daughter, sir," I said.

"How charming," Vera added, though her eyebrows were contracted. "For the moment, though, let's return to the less welcome spirit. The one who intrudes during confessions! You say he follows no set schedule? How would you feel if Miss Parsell and I camped out here tonight on the chance that, at some point, he might appear?"

I was taken aback by Vera's suggestion. After all, one likes to be consulted before being included in plans to spend the night in a church on the chance that a nosey, Puritan ghost might stop by for a chat. At the same time, one hardly *declines* such a proposal. Father O'Neil was reluctant. He cited the risks posed by having two women stay there overnight unprotected, and he added the risks posed to the church, given that we were strangers. However, when Vera declared that she might be able to rid his church of the ghost, his permission was granted—and gratefully so.

•

Apparently, such adventures were nothing new to Vera Van Slyke. She secured us several blankets for our overnight watch. We then had supper, after which she inquired where we might purchase a few bottles of beer to bring with us. She had quite a taste for beer, I learned, a fact I found both intriguing and worrisome, given my agreement to share quarters with her until morning. Had this woman fallen prey to the reputed evils of alcohol?

I suddenly remembered my mother's suggestion that we sidestep Vera's defrauding our séance business by simply fleeing to Europe and resuming it there. Averting adversity is a routine maneuver among Spiritualist mediums. Though I had firmly rejected my mother's plan, I could resort to some quick evasion should Vera prove to be undesirable company.

We located the drinking establishment that had been recommended by our waiter, a tavern known simply as Gable's. I had never before entered such a place, though I had peeked into some on occasion. As such, I was only a bit distressed by the dingy, pungent confines we discovered. No patrons were present just then, but a red-haired gentleman behind the bar looked up from his game of solitaire. Presumably, this was Mr. Gable himself. He greeted us—two women without male escorts—with a straightforward smirk. Vera seemed oblivious to the greeting. I, however, came close to mirroring that smirk upon seeing that the man's thick, carroty moustache was caked with enough wax that I feared the repercussions of his leaning over a flame.

After transacting her business, Vera engaged the likely proprietor in what appeared to be local gossip. She asked what he had heard about the reported ghost at St. Brigid's. Vera's purchase of beer, it seemed, was a calculated part of her investigation. Furthermore, as soon became clear, interrogating the local tavern-owner about the *ghost* was not her main intent.

"Oh, I've heard plenty about the Pryin' Puritan," replied the mustachioed man. "That's the name we've given 'im—least, those of us who worship down the street."

"You're not Catholic, then?" Vera affirmed more than asked.

"Congregationalist, ma'am!" he declared proudly. "Myself, I don't put much stock into reports of ghosts. I'm of a mind that holding to Popish ways makes those folk susceptible to all kinds of wild notions."

Vera nodded. "We spoke with Father O'Neil about the manifestation just this afternoon. Do you think he might be laundering only the front of his shirt?"

The barman blinked hard.

"Bending the truth?" I translated. It struck me as amusing that I was already catching onto Vera's colorful twists of language.

"Oh heavens, no!" he exclaimed. "Why, Father O'Neil's one of the mos' plainspoken and forthright men in town! No, ma'am, I would not doubt what Father O'Neil says!"

"Really?" Vera pressed him. "You *do* know about his imaginary daughter, yes?"

"Thalia? Sure, I know about Thalia. Father O'Neil never misleads folks about Thalia. He's the first to explain that he simply wishes he coulda become a priest *and* had a child. Perfectly understandable! Him talking to Thalia might give the impression he's a bit touched in the head, but having a pretend daughter is what keeps Father O'Neil a right reg'lar fella. Truth is, I take to *him* more warmly than to my own minister!" The barman twitched. "Now, don't you ladies go spreadin' that last bit 'round town, if you please."

Vera turned to me, and a gleam came to her eye. She thanked the gentleman. She then took the top blanket I was holding, fashioned it into a sack for the beer bottles, and slung them over her shoulder. Her wordless exit from the tavern indicated it was time to proceed to the next chapter of this ghostly mystery.

•

The lone Franklin stove in St. Brigid's was not enough to keep us from wrapping ourselves tightly within our borrowed blankets. Like the snow that blew against the tall windows, our conversation appeared, disappeared, and reappeared.

At one point, Vera offered me a bottle of beer as she opened one for herself.

Rather than refuse her courtesy, I reminisced aloud. "My father drank beer. I enjoyed the smell of it. I'm not sure how he would feel about *me* drinking one. And in a *church*, no less!"

Vera snickered. She then quietly asked, "Do we know — where he — *is?*"

"There's nothing shameful to it," I replied with a grin. "He passed away when I was still a girl."

"Leaving you to your *mother*, I guess."

"Yes. To my mother."

I then changed my mind about accepting the beer. Vera opened a bottle for me, and I mustered the courage to take a swig. The taste was not what I had expected. Far from pleasant but *tolerable*. My reaction must have shown on my face.

"It's an acquired taste," she assured me. "Am I right in assuming that, after your father died, your mother needed to find a way to support the two of you? And were there any other children?"

"No other children. Only me." I took another swallow of beer. I stood up and began to pace. It was to counteract the cold, I told myself.

"When did the Spiritualism racket start?"

"Oh, right away," I sighed. I stared at a stained-glass window, so wrong looking with darkness behind it instead of the morning sun. "Another medium contacted my mother shortly after my father's death. She — my mother — was too bright to be bamboozled. Yet she was *fascinated* by the audacity this medium showed for coming to her so soon after her husband's funeral." I took another swallow of beer, a rather substantial one.

"As this is your *first* beer," said Vera, "you might want to take your time—"

"But she played along," I interrupted. "My mother played along because she wanted to learn the tricks! So that she could do the *same!*" I put my hand up against the confessional for support.

"Could another explanation possibly—"

"She started grooming *me* for the job when I turned *twelve!*" I had more beer. "Just *twelve* years old, mind you! People *believe* children, after all. That, and I spoke English better than she could."

"Oh! Was she an immigrant, or was it just that—"

"Yes, an immigrant. As was my father. As was *I!* We arrived in America when I was five."

"From where?" Vera had learned to keep her questions brief.

"Prague. Bohemia." I sipped some beer. "I fear I've misled you about something, Miss Van Slyke. Do you remember the name I used at the séance you attended?"

"Yes. Yes, I do. Wasn't it Lucretia Papadopoulos?"

"Ludmila Prášilová."

"Oh dear. Why can't more people have names like Father O'Neil? Easily remembered! '*Oh, kneel* at the altar,' said *O'Neil* at the altar." Vera gave me a wink.

Instead of being amused, I swirled my beer bottle a few times. I then drank down a great mouthful. Once I had finished, I noticed the church pews were beginning to teeter just a bit, all slowly swaying in unison like a silent choir. I paid no mind to it, though. I had something I was determined to say.

"Ludmila Prášilová is my *real* name. I made up Lucille Parsell to introduce myself when my mother wasn't around."

"Ah! So you made a *lie* out of telling the *truth.* Most interesting!"

I knew that I had heard those words spoken aloud. I also knew Vera's lips *hadn't* moved.

And yet there was nobody else with us. Nobody else *physically* with us.

I looked at the bottle of beer in my hand, as if it had voiced the comment. However, when Vera slowly rose from the pew—letting her blankets drop to the floor—I followed the aim of her eyes directly to the confessional.

The voice, I realized, had come from there.

Vera glanced at me twice before straightening herself to her full, impressive height. She then carefully asked, "Am I addressing the Reverend Mr. Doltendale?"

"Dimmesdale!" I hissed.

"Dimmesdale?"

"Yes," said the voice from within. "Pray, do continue with thy tale. Tell me, that I might determine thy penance. What preceded your deceiving—with *truth*? Fine artistry lieth within the scene."

"The *scene?*" I asked. "Did you say 'the *scene*'?"

Vera and I shared a look of confusion. She opened the first door to the confessional. The compartment was empty.

"No, not *scene* but *sin*," replied the phantom. "Fine artistry within the *sin*, I had intended to say."

Vera nodded to me and then crept to the priest's door in the middle. She spun back. She nodded again. I realized this was her way of prompting me to continue the discussion.

"Uhm, uhm—" I sputtered. "Uh—"

Vera gave me a stern look. She then slowly opened the door to the priest's compartment. There was nothing visible *there*, either.

"Well," I resumed, "I—I *fooled* people. I fooled them into thinking I could communicate with spirits. You wouldn't understand, I don't think."

"Why sayeth you thus?"

Vera moved to the alternate compartment on the far side of the confessional.

"Well, Spiritualist séances are only half a century old," I answered. "We understood that you were one of the Puritans. Certainly, you would not have known about the subject in your—uhm."

I froze. An image flashed in my mind of a centuries-old body moldering in a crumbling coffin.

"In my *lifetime?*" the voice offered.

The last compartment's door was so arranged in that, once Vera opened it, I was unable to see if any specter were visible. However, the slump of her shoulders told me there was not.

"Nonetheless," continued the invisible minister, "I am familiar with your Spiritualism—as I am with your Mesmerism and Transcendentalism. Many are the schools of thought that grow from our longing to prove that we are *more* than can be explained by empirical science."

"Excuse me, sir," said Vera as she walked back. "You did not sound much like a Puritan just then." She took on the very same face that she had worn when we first met. It is a look that I can only describe with the words: predatory patience.

Vera Van Slyke was about to trap a fraud.

"Could you tell us something of your life?" she asked. "Your earlier *mortal* life, I mean?"

"I can. T'was the year of our Lord 1630 that I journeyed from England's shore to plant the seed of Christ's most shining society in the King's colony."

"By way of Holland, if I'm not mistaken."

"Those were members of Bradford's passage. I was among the greater number who followed with Winthrop."

"So you know the history, Reverend. But what about literature?"

"I am well versed in Scripture, as befits one of my calling."

"*And* you know about Spiritualism and other matters of *this* century, so you have said," Vera persisted. "I wonder if you know about novels. There is one in particular that features a fellow with the very same name as yours—the Reverend Mr.

Dimmesdale. This fine work of literature is titled *The Scarlet Letter.*"

She looked to me, and I nodded to assure her she had said the title correctly.

No words came from the confessional. Vera went back inside the first compartment to examine the lattice between it and the priest's chamber. The church remained silent. She drew back, looked at me, and shrugged.

We both *jolted* when the voice cried, "You *know* about *The Scarlet Letter?* You *know* about my Arthur Dimmesdale?"

Vera asked slowly, "Is he *your* Arthur Dimmesdale?"

There was a hesitation before the voice admitted, "He was born of my pen. And of my heart. As were Hester Prynne and little Pearl. And even Roger Chillingsworth."

I could not refrain from asking the obvious. "Are you Nathaniel Hawthorne?"

"I confess I am, though my charade was not nearly as clever as your own, young Miss. I merely spoke with the voice of one of my invented persons. It's hardly as artful as feigning to be *myself.* Can a sin be secret if it's unfurled before all? I wish to hear more. This might make a wondrous allegory!"

"Is that why you're *here?* In this *confessional?*" asked Vera. "Are you gathering material for your stories?"

"I had gained some little knowledge concerning the Sacrament of Confession during my residence in Italy. I remained an outsider, though, before passing here. Had I experienced confessionals from the *inside,* my tales and romances could have restocked the Library of Alexandria! This Protestant notion of intimate communion between God and the individual—it leads to so many sins left unspoken! I took exactly *that* as my subject matter."

I clasped my hand over my mouth to keep from laughing. Vera's clenched lips showed that she, too, was stifling her amusement.

"But," Vera began. She paused. She tried again. "But how did you discover this place? How is it that you can speak to us so easily?"

"There was a violet light that drew me toward it. It wavers and dims, brightens and disperses as oil on waves. I heard voices emanating from this light. The faces beyond it are perceptible only occasionally. It must be no less than a breach between the two great realms! I have no explanation as to what causes it."

"I'm not able to see *you*," said Vera, "but you say you are able to see *us*?"

"It is less *seeing* and more *reading* once the skin has been shed and one becomes more ethereal. For instance, as I face you, I sense a Dutch name. Van Slyke, is it?"

I heard myself blurt out, *"But is there comfort and happiness there?"* I had assured so many mourners that there *is*, perhaps I needed to know how accurately—or inaccurately—I had led them.

"And when I face *you*, young Miss," Mr. Hawthorne said softly, "I perceive an injured fawn. But to answer your plea, imagine a life much like what you've led. Yet without a need for sleep. Without a need to eat. Growing neither old nor sick. Imagine the freedom to pursue your deepest avocations without the barrage of complications that exist in your physical realm."

"So you are continuing to write, Mr. Hawthorne?" Vera asked.

"More prolifically than ever before possible. Yet *this* place. This church! What grand inspiration! The easing of conflict that occurs in the spirit realm takes its toll on crafting a gripping story. I fear that Mr. Irving has grown quite lackadaisical in *his* writing."

"Mr. *Washington* Irving?" I asked.

"The same."

"Ooo!" Vera waved her hand as if signaling to take the floor. "Have you met—*oh*, what's his name? Hamlet! And Juliet!" She looked at me with wide eyes.

"William Shakespeare?" Mr. Hawthorne said with a laugh. "Well, I met the person who wrote the plays we *accredit* to Shakespeare."

"So it's not who we think?" I inquired, enchanted by the prospect.

"She's not even English," answered Mr. Hawthorne. "But did I hear earlier that *my own* works are still known in your realm? Can that be correct?"

"Oh yes," replied Vera. "Your works sit in any library of merit, both in the United States and abroad. In fact, some of your works are starting to become required reading in our schools."

"That is—very heartening to hear. *Very* heartening. We authors invest so much to achieve immortality through our scribbling. Like a bellows spewing air at a forge, we thrust our souls onto paper with the dream that we might continue to be read for some slip of time after our passing. It is simultaneously tragic and comic, this *dream* of immortality."

"If I might request a special favor," I said. "I wonder, sir, if— if you might deliver a message for me. To my father."

There was no immediate response.

I clarified my request. "He would have passed over about a decade ago. He is a Czech man, my father. His name is *František Prášil.*"

"*Prášilová,* I think you mean," said Vera.

"No, that's for women!" I scolded.

"Different surnames for men and women? Now, you're just being *cruel* to me!"

I had barely heard her. The confessional was starting to blur. I remember becoming afraid that *crying* would only muffle my message, even though I had very little idea what that message should be.

Still, no response came from the confessional.

Vera stepped beside me and took my hand gently into her own. She continued to let the silence do the explaining.

At last, she confirmed, "Mr. Hawthorne has gone now, my dear."

•

"Guilt!" shouted Vera.

We were on the train back to Boston. I had noticed that she was drifting repeatedly into a state of deep concentration. After a few attempts to learn the subject of her preoccupation, I had decided to let her be.

"That word is a promising start to an interesting sentence," I teased.

"It fits with each of my earlier experiences that proved to involve genuine ghosts. Guilt! Think of it, Lucille. What does one find highly intensified in a Catholic confessional?"

"Guilt?"

"Guilt! I theorize that the emotion of guilt, when concentrated in a given physical space, acts as a knife that slices wide those breaches between this and the spirit realm. Mr. Hawthorne claimed a violet light drew him to the breach hovering in Saint Brigid's. *Violet,* say our scientists, is on the extreme edge of visibility! Could it somehow mark a passage between ours and the *invisible* world?"

"I can see water running along that canal," I said with a grin.

Vera merely nodded. "The key was that business with Father O'Neil's imaginary daughter, Ophelia—"

"Thalia."

"That business with Thalia. Talking to imaginary people is a habit most adults would labor to keep secret. Yet the good Father admits it so easily that he suffers almost no guilt about it! It becomes an admirable thing, even an example to others. I must write to him! He has a congregation of working men, and all they need do is relocate the confessional! That is, if Mr. Hawthorne returns at all."

"Is there reason to think he might not?"

"I suspect his motive for lingering at that breach was not just to gather confessions as future story ideas. I think he wanted to know if his *past* stories still garner interest in the world he left behind."

"That does account for his sudden disappearance. Perhaps *that* motive was so very secret, he was unaware of it himself."

"Very astute. But this prospect of guilt opening doorways between the dimensions—I must consult my books. Catherine Crowe especially. Yes, remind me to do that, won't you, once our business in Boston is complete, and we arrive back home in New York?"

I must have made a perplexed expression because I saw Vera cock her head. "I consider *Chicago* home," I explained, "not New York. I understood that we would finish the interviews regarding the tricks of Spiritualism, and then I would return to Chicago to find *honest* work. I know the stockyards there offer certain opportunities to young women in predicaments such as mine."

Vera looked in several directions before finally settling on the passing scenery. "Chicago," she whispered. "I think so much more sharply when there's someone to keep me on course. I hadn't even asked about your home, had I?"

The feeling was that of walking away from a friendly dog, unsure if it belongs to someone in the neighborhood or is lost. I rapidly resumed our prior discussion. "But your theory about guilt seems a sound one, based on what I saw in Tadcaster."

Vera looked back at me with renewed vigor. "And yet it's absolutely mad, isn't it? Tell me, what *is* your reaction to what you saw in Tadcaster? Wasn't it exciting?"

"Definitely exciting. And yet—you know what?"

She raised her eyebrows.

"I thought it would be more *frightening!* Ghosts and hauntings! Aren't they supposed to be frightening?"

"Sometimes, they are *very* frightening, my dear. It's something like eating at a French restaurant. One mutters something from the menu with no idea at all of what will be served. Often, these cases are less about confronting hobgoblins and more about solving riddles. More about unveiling those secrets kept *very* secret."

I smiled. "Along with Father O'Neil, *you* seem to be the only one involved in this adventure without any secrets kept very secret."

Vera shook her head slowly. "We *all* have secrets, Lucille. *All* of us have secrets." A moment of melancholy took shape in her brown eyes. It vanished instantly, though, and she continued, "I must ask you! The associate of mine who informed me of the ghost in Tadcaster—his *primary* reason for calling was to deliver an invitation to his New Year's ball. You and I shall finish our interviews and then begin the year 1900 with a lavish farewell to one another. Say you'll accompany me! Oh, *do!*"

Much as the witches had learned how headstrong the Puritans could be, I had learned that Vera Van Slyke was rarely refused. I nodded with a smile.

"Oh, and by the way," she chuckled, "it's a *masquerade* ball."

THE GHOST OF BANQUO'S GHOST (1900)

Glendower: I can call spirits from the vasty deep.
Hotspur: Why, so can I; or so can any man:
But will they come when you do call for them?

— *Henry IV, Part One*

Vera Van Slyke's exposé on the séance held at the Morley mansion appeared in newspapers across the U.S. and into Canada. I was relieved that the article left me unnamed, since it laid bare my fraudulence as a Spiritualist medium at that same séance. I very much hoped I would likewise remain anonymous in Vera's subsequent book exposing the tricks of my trade. Eager to atone for that life of pretense, I had divulged many secrets to her for the book.

During the interviews, however, Vera invited me along on an investigation of a ghost purported to be haunting a church—a ghost that proved to be entirely real! After the interviews regarding my *counterfeit* psychic powers and the adventure with the *genuine* ghost, Vera and I promised we would keep in touch via letters. She left Boston to return to New York City, and I went to my hometown of Chicago.

As so often happens, no letters were sent either way.

By August of 1900, I had secured a position on the sales floor of Mandel Brothers, the popular department store on State Street. It had become my routine to eat my lunch in a backroom of this large establishment. One day, a woman who I recognized as one of the managers' wives joined me there. She had come to while away a bit of time with a newspaper. The woman had not introduced herself, and I was keeping quiet, as a humble sales clerk ought.

"It's a stunt!" the manager's wife snorted, giving the newspaper a good shake.

I had just taken a bite of my apple and could not reply. Instead, I angled my head and looked inquisitive, feeling something like a puppy.

She pointed to the headline: "SPECTER CREATES SPECTACLE AT SCEPTER!" Still chewing, I knit my eyebrows and leaned forward. The fine print was too far away to read.

She must have understood. "Oh, there's supposed to be a *ghost* tossing things around at the Scepter Theatre. Ask me, it's a stunt to sell tickets! *Shakespeare,* after all. The play's not the thing folks will go to see. They'll go to catch sight of that *ghost!*"

"Shakespeare?" I asked after swallowing. "I once heard that Shakespeare's works weren't written by the person who we typically—"

"All I know about Shakespeare," the woman interrupted, "is men dress up like women and women like men! Maybe *some* consider that fine art, but give *me* an old-fashioned minstrel show, if you please!"

"What does it say about the ghost?" I asked. My view of ghosts had changed considerably during the investigation in Boston.

"They claim it dropped a crossbar or whatever they use to hang backdrops. Almost crushed an actor." She flung the newspaper to the table and exited the room. "Ghosts in a Shakespeare play now," the woman muttered on her way out.

I examined the article quickly. The very last line read: "A lady investigator of similar hauntings has been summoned from New York." Though no specific lady was mentioned, I am fairly certain that I spoke the three segments of her name out loud.

"Vera. Van. *Slyke!*"

•

After work, I found that the lake breeze was cool enough to make a late-summer stroll from downtown to the Scepter Theatre an inviting one. Ticket prices there were beyond my current salary, but I knew the location. I found one of the stage doors unlocked. Technicians or possibly actors in street dress paid little attention to me as I walked amid curtains and ropes, hoping to find the audience seating area. Instead, I wandered under the glaring lights of Stage Left. Shading my eyes, I scanned the dark rows upon rows of seating.

"Well, it's high time *you* arrived!" This came echoing from above.

I recognized the voice and was excited to spot Vera's tall figure waving at me from the first balcony. She stood beside someone, so I raised my palm to her and began to wind my way down from the stage, along the aisle, and up the stairs. Once I had arrived, Vera made the gentleman wait while we embraced.

"Oh, I think you're going to enjoy this one!" she said with a grin. "Apparently, there are some very odd goings-on here, as Mr. Haddock had been telling me just now."

"A pleasure to meet you," he said, half-bowing to me. "But my name is Chester *Paddock*. Not Haddock."

"Terribly sorry," said Vera quickly. "I'm practicing a new system to remember names, you see. As the play's director, you act much like the captain of a *ship*—a ship at *sea*—searching for *fish*—and perhaps finding *haddock*—which, of course, rhymes with *Paddock*. I haven't quite mastered the system yet."

We all chuckled courteously.

"Do go on with what you were saying, Mr. Paddock," I said. "I'm certain Vera will fill me in afterward."

I admit that I hadn't known what to expect of a theatrical director, but Mr. Chester Paddock was unexpectedly *ordinary*. His hair was sparse, and he held a pair of spectacles in his hand. His suit was a solid gray, the collar slightly crooked. Perhaps his most distinctive feature was the trace of a drawl, one suggestive of a childhood spent close to the Mason-Dixon line.

"Well, I was just telling Miss Van Slyke that this production was intended to feature the final performance of the great Luther Arnold Weber. I believe this would have been his *fifth* final performance, but as it turns out, he died of heart trouble while we were still in rehearsal. I figure if anyone were haunting the place, it would be him."

"Would he have a particular reason to return *here?*" I asked. I shrunk back, fearing that I had entered the discussion too quickly. Neither Vera nor Mr. Paddock seemed irked.

"Mr.—*Paddock,*" said Vera with a nod to the director, "was explaining that Luther Arnold Weber took his acting very seriously. If he agreed to a role, he veritably *became* that character, insisting that the audience deserves no less."

"And he expected no less from everyone else in the cast and crew," added Mr. Paddock. "He was not an easy man to get along with, but one had to admire his dedication. That sense of commitment is why I think he's come back from grave!"

Vera shook her head slowly. "The manifestations, however, suggest otherwise."

I opened my mouth to speak but caught myself.

Vera must have noticed this. She explained, "We *appear* to be dealing with what Catherine Crowe describes as a *poltergeist,* a term she takes from the Germans. These are not spirits clinging to the physical realm. Instead, a poltergeist is more like a phantom ball of mischief that bounces in all directions. It knocks things over, shatters bottles, hurls vases, and generally makes a nuisance of itself."

"This production has seen a *lot* of such activity," Mr. Paddock added.

I could not hold back. "But this activity hadn't begun until *after* the death of your lead actor, correct?"

Mr. Paddock nodded and shrugged. "In fact, it almost *killed* his replacement. One of the battens—uh, a batten is a heavy pipe that holds up a backdrop—one of these fell just as Luther's replacement was walking beneath it. Never heard of such a thing."

Vera received permission to speak with the actor who was to step into the role left open by Mr. Weber's demise. On our way to the make-up room, I told her about my current position as sales clerk, and she informed me that her book about the deceptions of Spiritualism was in its final stages. It felt as if no time at all had passed. However, this mood was derailed the moment she asked what might have seemed like a very simple question.

"Why did you not introduce yourself to Mr. Paddock?" she asked me.

"Oh," I replied, "I assumed you had told him who I was as I was coming to join you."

"I see, my dear. I see."

I halted us both. With some hesitation, she pivoted toward me. I required a moment.

At last, I said, "Why hadn't you written to let me know you were coming to Chicago?"

She jerked her head away and avoided eye contact. "Well! It all worked out, didn't it? Here you *are!*"

I sighed deeply. "You don't remember my name, do you?"

She pressed her lips tightly together before hypothesizing aloud, "I remember the initial G."

"Lucille Parsell. There's no G at all, is there now?"

"Ah, but you went by *another* name when conducting séances, did you not?" She bit her lip.

I hissed, "Ludmila *Prášilová*! Again, not a G to be found *anywhere!*"

"I'm not very strong with names," she confessed quietly, her head slowly listing to the starboard side. "At times, I think I would be wise to hire a personal assistant. Are you *happy* as a sales clerk?"

I refused to answer and, instead, grabbed her by the elbow to resume our walk.

Once we had located the make-up room, we found the actor who had narrowly avoided being crushed. His name was Reginald Caber, and he came closer to my mental picture of a theatrical professional. His hair was blonde and longish, and his chin was strong and cleft. A script sat between him and a long line of mirrors. These mirrors, I noted, were lit with electrical bulbs rather than gas flames. Curiously, rather than reposition his chair, Mr. Caber spoke to our reflections in his mirror. This inspired us to do the same in return.

After we had exchanged introductions, Vera began the interview. "I've been developing a theory that a concentration of the emotion *guilt* weakens the borders between the physical and spirit realms. Can you think of anyone involved with the show who suffers from a guilty conscience?"

Mr. Caber laughed with startling volume. "Why, it's the Scottish play, isn't it? It *drips* with guilt—to the point of hallucination! Macbeth, who murders King Duncan, claims to see a floating dagger. Lady Macbeth, who shames her husband into committing the deed, thinks she cannot wash the blood from her hands. The play is a deep *study* of guilt."

"Lucille, what do *you* think?" Vera asked. "Is it possible, Lucille, that stage-acted guilt could work in the same supernatural manner as *true* guilt? Do you suppose—Lucille?"

"I'm not certain, *Vera*," I spit back, still warm from our skirmish over her forgetting my name. "Perhaps, *Vera*, a play about guilt reminds those involved of their own reasons for feeling that emotion, *Vera!*"

She reacted to my taunts by slumping her shoulders. She turned to Mr. Caber's reflection and said, "I know others working on the play have witnessed objects flying and falling. However, have any of these others been *endangered* by the phenomenon?"

"If they have, I am unaware of it."

I heard myself mutter, "You know, Sherlock Holmes never forgets Dr. Watson's name."

Vera turned slowly to me. "I don't know who Sir Lockholms is, my dear."

Only then did I realize that Vera's forgetting my name was not due to any ill will. She simply had certain limitations along with her remarkable attributes. With some poetic justice, I regretted venting my spite. I felt—in a word—*guilty.*

Vera turned back to Mr. Caber's image in the mirror. "Do you think the falling backdrop support was actually *intended* to hit you?"

"If I believed it wasn't a complete coincidence, I would now be speaking to a police detective rather than to yourself. Those battens are heavy enough to *kill.* There's some talk that it's the ghost of Luther Arnold Weber, that he's angry about my taking his role. But I knew Luther. He was a consummate thespian. The overall production is what mattered to him, and he's hardly in a position now to do a better job than me at playing the lead."

"Has anyone claimed to have heard any voices?" asked Vera. "Of course, I mean *disembodied* voices."

"I don't recall anyone mentioning spirit voices."

"This brings us back to the poltergeist theory. Thank you so much, sir. I do sincerely wish that, should any bones be injured, it is your leg and not your spine."

Mr. Caber shifted from Vera's reflection to peer at mine as if seeking clarification on her last statement.

"She means to say 'Break a leg' in the theatrical sense," I assured him.

He nodded and rose from his chair to signal farewell. He then returned to studying his lines. Vera and I were almost out the door when she turned back.

"One last question, sir—a very informal one. Could you recommend a local establishment where I might purchase some beer?"

I remembered that, during our previous investigation, Vera had shown a taste for beer. In fact, I had sampled my first bottle of it with her.

Still looking at us by way of the mirror, Mr. Caber replied, "I'm most sorry, but I am not a drinking man. I know there are taverns in the neighborhood, but I would not be able to tell you which one is preferable over the other."

Exactly then, one of the electrical bulbs burst *loudly!* Its glass was spewed across the table and floor. I grabbed Vera's arm. *Another* bulb popped, and Mr. Caber almost fell backward in his chair. As if a giant fist holding a giant hammer were sweeping across the room, the line of remaining bulbs exploded in rapid succession. The room plunged into darkness, though the hall light remained steady.

"Are you still with us, sir!" Vera shouted. "Speak to me, Mr. Carter!"

I did not correct Vera but instead waited for a reply from the darkness. The dashing actor's image slowly came into view as he walked toward us. Rather than appearing heroic, though—he was quivering.

•

The electrical lights bursting stirred a good deal of hubbub. Once it settled, Vera asked Mr. Paddock if he knew of someplace to buy beer. He mentioned The Foiled Gelding, a nearby public house where many of the theater personnel ate and drank. He assured us that two unaccompanied women would be treated respectfully there.

Once arrived at this pub, we selected a nook away from the boisterous activity. Vera traced the grain of the dark-stained table with her finger. She kept glancing up at me as if reluctant to speak her mind.

"What is it?" I inquired, reaching my hand to her arm.

"I should have written," she lamented. "It's all this travel. People flitting in and out of my life. At times, I consider settling down and forming more lasting friendships. But I know that a highly ritualized life would put me into a stupor. Which should I choose? A stupor—or chaos? It's why I think a personal assistant might be of value. Tell me, *are* you happy in your current position?"

I reflected before saying, "Things could be worse. I was so intent on leaving the Spiritualism racket behind that I was ready to go to work in the stockyards! It was an old friend who helped me find less *bloody* work. I should have written to you, as well."

"I am not lying when I say I had a hunch we would meet here. I *did* remember that you live in Chicago. Maybe the hunch sprang from that."

We smiled. I was not fully prepared for the sudden shift in topics, though.

"That actor has a problem with alcohol! He drinks more brutal stuff than beer, I tell you!"

"Oh, uhm—Reginald Caber? But didn't he claim he *isn't* a drinker at all? Could you smell it on his breath?"

"I can believe that an actor might avoid drink altogether. *Barely* believe it. Nonetheless, one who works around *other* actors—yet who cannot even name a local drinking establishment—must surely be lying. Let me remind you how easily the other fellow, that drab director—"

"Mr. Paddock," I clarified.

"How easily *he* recommended this pub. Now, let's tip a paint can, and see what picture takes shape, shall we?"

Vera's interesting expressions gave some glimmer of the operations of her mental facilities. I noticed next that, when forming a theory, she had no problem remembering names.

"Let's say we *are* dealing with the spirit of the late Luther Arnold Weber. The 'consummate thespian,' Mr. Caber called him." Vera placed two fingers against the side of her jaw. "What if our ghost *knew* of his replacement's drinking—knew that it threatened the production? Could Weber be trying to scare him off?"

I began to see the picture forming in the spilled paint. I suggested, "By *posing* as a poltergeist?"

"He *is* an actor, after all," Vera said. "His manifestations seem to be closing in on Mr. Caber. We witnessed as much!"

"And even if the guilt evoked by the play cannot explain how Weber is able to reach across from the spirit realm, it might be that Mr. Caber's secret drinking causes him terrible shame."

"Very astute. I hadn't considered that. But where does this leave us?"

"Perhaps Mr. Caber needs careful watching," I suggested.

Vera was too meditative to notice that our food and beverages were now being set before us. She concluded, *"Watching,* I think, is key. This drama needs more *watching."*

●

After our meal, we returned to the theater. As the production was behind schedule due to the death of its lead actor, additional rehearsals were being held each evening. Mr. Paddock had invited Vera to attend her choice of rehearsals in the hope that she might observe something useful.

Unfortunately, we promptly learned that this evening's rehearsal was delayed due to trouble with a witch's cauldron. Vera used the time to hunt down the production's leading lady.

"If she plays Mr. Caber's wife," Vera explained, "it's possible she'll have an insight into his offstage life."

The playbill listed the actress playing Lady Macbeth as Josephine LaFrance. Despite the Gallic cast of her name, the woman's offstage accent attested to her being from someplace closer than even Quebec. We found her in a dressing room. Wearing a wig that cascaded with russet waves, Miss LaFrance stood on a stool while her lavish costume was being refitted to better accommodate her grand figure.

Without reserve, Vera marched toward the actress and offered her hand. "Mrs. Macbeth," she jested, "my name is Vera Van Slyke. I've been asked to eliminate whatever has been haunting this show. And I'm being ably assisted by this pretty miss, Lucille—uhm."

Stopping at the door, I chuckled. "Lucille *Parsell."*

"No need to be *noyvous,* Lucy," said the actress. "C'mon in. Don't let the dress fool ya. I only put on airs to pay my rent. Vera, is it? So ya here to evict our ghost, ay?"

After shaking hands with Miss LaFrance, Vera turned to the woman doing the tailoring. Holding pins in her mouth, she was a petite woman with a dark complexion and deftly controlled hair. Vera also offered her hand to this seamstress, who had to bunch the folds of the dress into one hand before returning the salutation.

"That's Mary, my dressuh," noted Miss LaFrance before declaring, "But, so's we're cleah, *I'm* the very foyst to've had a brush wit' that ghost."

Vera considered the actress a moment. "Now, I've heard that accent before. On some of the more colorful streets of New York City, if I'm not mistaken."

"Are *you* from New Yawk, too?" she shouted. "Yeah, it takes a local ear to catch my accent."

The dresser and I shared a look of curbed amusement.

Vera replied, "I grew up in a small town quite a way up the Hudson, but I moved to Manhattan as soon as I was able."

Miss LaFrance grinned slightly. "Yeah, Manhattan's nice. But ya asked about my brush wit' the ghost. It was when I'm tellin' Macbeth how to kill the king, if mem'ry soyves."

Vera's eyebrows rose. "So the actor *now* playing Macbeth was near you, correct?" She turned to wink at me.

"Yeah, Reggie was there. But *I'm* the very foyst to've spotted the bottle come rollin' onstage. I went ahead, recitin' my lines, figurin' one of the stagehands knocked it off the props table."

"What kind of a bottle was it?" Vera inquired.

"Oh, the old sort. *Clay,* I think. A porter or someone carries it in a later scene. But *I'm* recitin' my lines, when in come this bottle. It rolls. It stops. It rolls. It stops and rolls and stops. Like some baby playin' wit' a ball!"

"Intriguing," Vera stated. "And then?"

"Well. Well, once the bottle'd stopped that thoyd time, it stopped *dead!* Absolutely *dead!*"

After a hesitation, Vera looked back at me and shrugged. This was apparently the extent of the manifestation.

Removing the pins from her mouth, Mary added, "We've had *more* scary things happen since. Other props flung and dashed onstage. Strangeness offstage, too."

"I s'pose that's true, Mary," said the actress, who then checked her seams. "But I'm the very *foyst* to've had a brush wit' the ghost."

After a quick smirk, Mary licked her thumb and ran it along the seam. She next patted Miss LaFrance's back and the actress stepped down from her stool.

Vera stated, "Thank you kindly for your help. It's always useful to hear about the earliest manifestation—uh, from the very *first* witness. Mary, may I now speak with you about those later manifestations?" She turned to Miss LaFrance. "We can move if you'd like a private spot to concentrate on your lines."

After glancing between Vera and Mary, the actress replied, "Nah, we'll be startin' soon. The cast needs me to give 'em a stimulatin' speech beforehand." She straightened her costume, bid Vera and me luck with the investigation, and exited.

The rest of us found seats. Vera began her interview, and I strained to detect what she might be garnering from Mary's account of objects tipping, skidding, and crashing inexplicably.

At one point, Mary interrupted to say, "I hear they're calling places. If you ladies want to watch the rehearsal, you best be going. I do hope that I've helped a little, though."

"You've helped very much, my dear." Vera again shook the woman's hand. "Putting what you've told me in order and placing it *after* that minor event Miss LaFrance described, I am now of a mind that our ghost is, in fact, *improving* at being a poltergeist."

"Do you mean—what—what *do* you mean?" I stuttered.

Mary explained it. "You mean he's *rehearsing?*"

Vera nodded and replied, "Well phrased."

•

Finding our way back to the seating area, Vera and I treated ourselves to the front row. There was something about Vera's demeanor, perhaps a leisurely lean, that suggested her interview with Mary and Miss LaFrance had settled the mystery she had been hired to solve. Even so, her silence suggested she was waiting for one concluding piece of evidence.

Settling myself in my seat, I asked, "Do you attend many theatrical productions?"

"Well, you recall that I *aaaam* from New York City, my dear," she said, mimicking a snobbish tone. "As such, I am *haaardly* convinced that I'm attending a theatrical production right *nooooow.*"

Our giggles earned us a stern expression from Mr. Paddock. I had never seen a production of *Macbeth* previously. Its mixture of witchcraft and politics was very much at odds with the melodramas and musical reviews I could afford. Miss LaFrance's earlier dialect was expertly disguised, and in fact, she was a truly riveting actress.

More germane to the haunting, though, I began to comprehend why Mr. Caber described the play as a deep study of guilt.

It was the third act. A feast was being held for Banquo, though Macbeth had had that guest of honor murdered. Whispering, Vera asked if I had spotted any evidence of Mr. Caber furtively imbibing. I had not. I was leaning over to her ear, intending to suggest that we move to positions backstage.

Instead, I yelped *loudly,* much to Vera's anguish.

With no visible hands to account for it, one of the pewter dinner plates and its matching goblet had risen from a table. They were then hovering about two feet in the air. None of the actors were positioned to see it. However, once I managed to raise a trembling finger to point, Vera saw the impossibility that I saw.

She immediately stood, shouting, "I advise the actors to quickly depart—"

But the plate and goblet were now flying in different directions! As had happened with the electrical light bulbs, the *next* dinner setting—and the *next* and the *next*—went hurtling across the stage! The actors scurried to crouch behind chairs or shields or whatever else the props and set afforded. Only Mr. Caber remained standing. He looked around as if dazed.

And then he wiggled. He wiggled as if performing a comic rendition of a South American dance. At last, he grabbed around behind himself. It was too late, though, for a silver flask was slowly levitating above him, a flask that apparently had been hidden in the back of his costume. It ascended of its *own* accord to a position between its owner and the audience seats. Mr. Paddock had now rushed up onto the stage. He froze there. Along with all the other witnesses, he fell under the immobilizing spell of the floating flask.

Our bewitchment crumbled, though, because of something incongruous. It was Mr. Caber's loud laugh, the same guffaw we had heard in the make-up room. It was not one of those laughs that curiously burst from someone alarmed, however. It was a *drunken* laugh.

"Is this a *flagon* I see before me?" he jested. He then jumped to snatch the flask, but the invisible agent yanked it away from him.

I turned to Vera. Her eyes were fixed on the scene, but a twist in her lips and a sigh told me that she was sorry her theory had been proven correct.

As it turned out, she had a final surprise awaiting her.

"I have a strong notion," she announced loudly, "that what I had taken to be a poltergeist is, in fact, the spirit of Luther Arnold Weber. He's come to ensure a successful production of his last scheduled play by showing that your new lead actor might not be in the best condition to remember his lines."

At that very point, the flask dropped to the floor with a resounding clang.

"Nonsense!" shouted Reginald Caber, as much to the entire company as to Vera. He ran to retrieve the fallen flask. "This is exactly what I need to carry me through this performance! Have I slurred? Have I missed my mark? Chester! Chester, tell me if I've in *any* way hurt the—Chester? What are you staring at?"

Mr. Paddock slowly took the flask from Mr. Caber. The director was scrutinizing the polished canteen while chewing on the inside of his cheek. He said, "Miss Van Slyke? You say Luther is back among us?"

"That is my belief," she replied.

"And he can make things float. And move? Without wires?"

"He appears to have perfected that talent now."

"Luther!" Mr. Paddock said decisively, though he said it into the air. "You've passed the audition! I'm re-casting you in the role of Banquo's ghost! We'll also need you to work the dagger at the start of Act Two."

The theater and everyone within it were starkly silent. Even Vera was dumbstruck.

"Granted, it's not the lead," the director continued. "But you were always far more concerned with the production overall than your own place in it. And rest assured, Luther, you'll get *top* billing. This will—again—be your *final* performance!"

"*He'll* get top billing? A *dead* man?" Mr. Caber scolded as much as inquired. He reached out for his flask.

Mr. Paddock pulled it back. "We'll assign a guard to Reginald here. We'll use Malcolm's entire *army,* if need be, to prevent him from drinking!"

Mr. Caber continued to hold his hand out for the flask, looking something like Romeo expressing his longing for Juliet on her balcony. Suddenly, the actor's hand drooped. Next, his posture altogether drooped, too.

Vera crossed her arms. She gave me the look of someone who had relinquished any control over her horse now that it had caught scent of the barn.

"Luther?" shouted Mr. Paddock. "Luther, give us a sign if you accept the role. You know you'll pack the house! It will be a finale *unprecedented* in the history of Drama!"

It seems that even an actor who cared more about the audience than his own reviews could not dismiss such an accolade. One of the tossed plates rose from the floor—and then another plate—and then a goblet. The three items hovered only a moment before the incorporeal Luther Arnold Weber began to juggle them. In fact, the seasoned showman juggled them admirably. The company of actors, still looking rather stunned, slowly began to applaud.

•

Naturally, this production of the play was controversial from Opening Night through the end of its run. Mr. Paddock had informed the press that the late Luther Arnold Weber would be featured in the role of Banquo's ghost, and no one else in the show denied this. Nonetheless, critics were divided: some found the idea delightfully true to the *spirit* of Shakespeare's tale while others decried it as preposterous. One local magician claimed he would debunk the production's astounding effects by reproducing them in his own act. He never did.

After the production had completed its schedule, no poltergeist-like activity was reported to linger at the Scepter Theatre. Needless to say, *other* ghosts have since been spotted or heard or felt. It is a theater, after all.

Vera's involvement with the Scepter, however, ended after that evening she had revealed the ghost's identity and the motives behind the haunting. She decided to remain a while in Chicago, a city she said held certain charms. One evening, we shared another dinner at The Foiled Gelding.

"Won't you come back with me to New York?" she asked as we were finishing our beers. "You would make a fine assistant. And I can promise you far grander adventures than one finds even in retail sales!"

"Tempting," I replied. "However, my years as a medium still clamor in my head. I yearn for a break from all types of spirits— phony, authentic, *and* theatrical. It's nice to have time to catch up on my reading. Still, who knows what the future might present? I *am* only eighteen years old, you know."

"Didn't you say you were *seventeen?*"

"That was in Boston. Last year."

"Ah!" Vera's brown eyes drifted to her napkin. "Try as I might, I have no hunches that we'll ever get together again."

"Perhaps that's for the best. Didn't Macbeth lose his head for acting on a hunch? Albeit, a very *strong* hunch."

My attempt at wit seemed lost on Vera. She looked at me with a blinking squint.

I clarified, "Macbeth was the character in the play. The play *Macbeth.*"

"Oh, yes, dear. I know that. *Sometimes*, I remember names." With a thoughtful tilt to her head, Vera then gave me a very direct look. Her silence suggested that, perhaps, she was experiencing a hunch at that very moment. She reached out and touched my arm.

"Yes. Sometimes, I remember names—Dr. Watson."

SKITTERING HOLES
(1900)

Occasionally, it is said, phantom music, by way of warning, is heard just before death, instances of which are numerous.

— T. F. Thiselton Dyer

After investigating the haunting of a production of *Macbeth*, Vera Van Slyke remained in Chicago. "I've only visited this city once before," she explained. "That was back in '93, and I'd spent all of my time at your World's Fair. I really cannot tell how much the place has changed these seven years."

Once my shift on the sales floor at Mandel Brothers Department Store had finished, I took Vera to see some of the local sites. Riding the elevated rail barely interested her. She was noticeably bored by the Home Insurance and Rand McNally Buildings, so-called "skyscrapers" girded with steel. Even the Masonic Temple—the world's *tallest* building—did nothing to stifle her yawns.

"You seem weary," I conceded.

"*All* cities are turning into these mad dioramas of the Alps constructed with giant boxes," she replied. "I'd like to see less of the rectangular Chicago. Show me the city's tapers and twists. Its zigzagging cakewalk rather than its stiff box steps. Lucille, don't *your* people have something called the polka? Show me where Chicago dances the polka!"

"*My* people?" I replied. "Well, I could take you to Pilsen. That's the Czech neighborhood, where I grew up. Say, I could introduce

43

you to my děda—my Grandpa David! He knows a lot about Chicago from playing with bands and giving music lessons all over the city." I saw interest ignite in Vera's brown eyes. "Sadly, he's been slowing down with age. I must warn you, his finances have forced him into one of Pilsen's cheaper rooming houses."

"My newspaper work has taken me to the grisliest slums of New York, my dear. I won't be shocked. But you say he's a musician?"

"My, yes! My děda can play almost any instrument at all! He was a marvel to me as I was growing up. And he granted me refuge during my darker days. In fact, Grandpa David sheltered me when I came back to Chicago after—well, after Boston."

"This Grandpa David—he is your—your *mother's* father—perhaps?"

Vera's hesitations, I had little doubt, stemmed from knowing that the topic of my mother was an unhealed wound. Since Boston, my mother and I scarcely had communicated at all. For the first time, I wondered if Vera might feel accountable for this split, since her journalistic crusade against Spiritualist frauds had ended my career conducting séances. My mother, who had acted as my manager, had proposed we simply move on to Europe. However, I was unable to continue leading that counterfeit life *anywhere.*

"David's not my real grandfather," I said, avoiding discussion of my mother. "He lived across the hall when I was a child. I guess he's actually just a dear, dear friend."

"Then I must meet this important historical personage!" Vera declared with a nod of finality.

•

As we climbed to the third floor of Grandpa David's rooming house, the late-August heat seemed to weigh heavier with each step. We knocked on his door, but by then I was nearly certain that he would be out at his favorite park, enjoying the cooling air of evening.

On the way there, I told Vera, "David grew up in Josefov, the Jewish quarter of Prague. He told me that feeling restricted to

Josefov as a boy is what inspired him to journey to the Land of Liberty."

"Is he a Jew, then, your grandfather? *Honorary* grandfather, let's say."

"Yes, he is." I stopped abruptly. "I know some people have a dislike of Jews. But—do *you?*"

"Oh, not at all, my dear," she said reassuringly. "No, not a dislike of *Jews.*"

I did not grasp what was implied by the last part of Vera's statement. Pleased with the first part, though, I continued. "In fact, he's been speaking a lot about Josefov lately. I worry that growing old has him feeling restricted again."

Vera appeared pensive until we found Grandpa David. He was sharing a bench and some crackers with a squirrel. I pointed to him, and Vera rushed before me.

"I see your friend finds it warm enough to carry his fur coat *behind* him," she shouted. "Or is the fur coat behind him carrying your *friend?*"

Even at a distance, I could tell from Grandpa David's hanging jaw that Vera had served him too much English all at once. He then spotted me and turned back to bow at Vera. The squirrel, in the meantime, scampered up the nearest tree and shook its tail as if we had soiled that fur coat.

Seeing Grandpa David struggling up from the bench, I trotted to him. We embraced.

"So!" he said, "You come lookin' for me, or is dis a happenstance?"

"We came looking," I answered. "My friend here is visiting Chicago, and I wanted her to meet you. May I present Miss Vera Van Slyke? Vera, please meet Mr. David Gans."

Vera offered her hand. Grandpa David took it, glancing over at me as if shaking hands with a *woman* was an unfamiliar novelty.

"May we join you, Mr. Gans?" asked Vera. "Gans! Now, *that's* a name worth remembering!" She gave me a wink.

Grandpa David lowered himself down again with a groan and a grin. Vera and I sat on either side. I reminded him of how I had met Vera, emphasizing that she had facilitated the end of my career as a Spiritualist medium.

"No good could haf come from such a life," he said to Vera. "I am happy dat you give Lída a good spankin'."

I clarified that Lída is a pet name for Ludmila, my Czech name, and Vera then burst out laughing at the idea of having spanked me. Her delight seemed to put Grandpa David at ease. We spoke of his life as a musician with symphonic orchestras back in Bohemia and with traveling bands here in the Great Lakes region. As the sun dipped below the surrounding buildings, the conversation drifted back to Vera's life as a reporter.

"Maybe dis job is a help to dose being taken advantage—but still you want to become someone's wife one day, yeh?"

Vera winced. "Well, that's not entirely up to *me*, now is it?"

"True," Grandpa David responded, "but *God* has an awfully lot of responsibilities."

Vera knit her eyebrows. "Oh, by saying 'not up to me,' I meant that I'm not certain any *man* would be willing to allow his wife to continue earning her own—"

I cleared my throat.

"*Yes!*" Vera said instantly. "Yes, God certainly *does* have many duties. Yes, indeed."

"And tell me more of dis business wit' ghosts. In a playhouse, I can belief it—but in a *confessional?* Is askin' for trouble, dat!"

"Well, as Lucille probably explained to you, that ghost was *actually—*"

Vera stopped speaking. Grandpa David had pivoted toward me and was cupping my cheek in his hand.

"*Lucille,*" he repeated. "Lucille Parsell, my little American. Maybe one day you become Ludmila Prášilová again, yeh? Don't never forget your fadder. Now, your *modder?* Dat's a bad bushel of berries. But I interrupt."

"Quite all right," Vera said.

"And here I interrupt again! Miss Van Slyke, what you tell me about little spots dat *glow!* What's more, dey glow *purple!* Almost like—like—" He turned to me to say, "Malé svatozáře?"

"Little halos?" I offered.

"Like little, purple halos. You can see into dem almost like dey're holes! But holes burned wit' purple embers. So hard to say wit' English! Dey skip across deh floor and up deh walls almost like vermin. Don't seem natural, so maybe—supernatural?"

"Vera! The violet light!" I said.

She slowly turned to scrutinize a random patch of grass. Finally, Vera responded, "Mr. Hawthorne—the ghost in the confessional, Mr. Gans—he claimed to see a violet light that marked a breach between his spirit world and ours. He described it as moving like oil beading on water. *We* were unable to see it, however. Where have *you* encountered these purple holes that skitter along surfaces?"

"Up in my room at night. I play my oboe in deh dark wit' deh orchestra."

Vera's head twitched. "An orchestra? In your *room?*"

She looked to me for a translation, but I could only raise my eyebrows and shoulders. Suddenly, Grandpa David laughed, patting us both on our hands.

"Help me up, Lída," he said. "By deh time I hobble home, it will be dark. I show you deh orchestra in my room. And dose crazy purple holes."

•

A pang came to my chest each time I saw Grandpa David's current residence. As he lit the gas lamp—the landlord being too miserly to convert to electricity—I saw what struck me as a prison cell. He had a cot to sleep on, two crates to use as table and chair, and another crate to hold some cheese, bread, and a few onions. The other side of the room was not quite so barren. There was a wooden chair he told me was for his music students, though I had never met any. In separate cases were a violin, a trumpet, and an oboe. He had sold all of his other instruments.

There was also something I had never seen before. It was a machine topped with a large cone that looked like the nearly opened flower of a gigantic, metal lily.

"Dědo!" I shouted. "When did—*how* did you manage to get a gramophone?"

"Isn't she a beauty?" he replied. "A Lit'uanian lost his job in Packin'town. He sell it to me. I try and help deh family."

"Ale to muselo *stát peněz*, dědo!" I cried.

He cocked his head toward our English-speaking guest before replying, "I find a way to affort it. And it come wit' nice music! We talk later, yeh? For now, I gif you a concert."

Grandpa David took the room's only chair, leaving the two women to the crates. This caused Vera to wink at me, showing that she understood that it was merely his custom. Our host explained how, at night, he turned off the gas due to the heat, sat in the dark, and played along with the gramophone. Occasionally, he would explore harmonies never intended by the composers.

"It was Brahms' *Concerto for Violin*. In deh second movement, dere's a solo for oboe. Adagio! Nice and slow. I play along on my *own* oboe, but—forgive me, Mr. Brahms—I play it like a *duet!* I demonstrate. Lída, you crank deh gizmo, yeh?"

He located the record, and I prepared to play it while he twisted together the sections of his oboe. Pointing, he indicated that Vera was to manage the gaslight. The recording began. Grandpa David nodded to Vera, and the room filled with darkness.

Nothing happened at first. Grandpa David's accompaniment was soothing and, at times, a bit daring. And then there came a flicker of *violet light!* It had appeared as spots throughout the room. It vanished. Some moments later, it reappeared. It lingered just long enough to discern what Grandpa David had meant by "holes." Imagine dozens of small jellyfish rimmed with purplish florescence, the glow gradually dimming into empty centers. *Little halos* began to make sense.

The next flash lasted longer, and I saw Vera grab some sort of stick and thrust it before her.

Grandpa David then stopped playing. "Lída, stop deh record. And Miss Van Slyke, deh lights please."

Vera lit the gas lamp before explaining, "There was a larger hole *floating* just about here." She waved her hand in a particular spot in the air. "To see what might happen, I managed to poke into it with—"

She lifted what turned out to be a violin bow, which must have been the closest object at hand. We gazed at the *end* of the bow, the part that Vera had poked through the larger hole. This half appeared to have turned to *glass. Crystal clear *glass!* I gasped as Vera touched the crystalized part of the bow. Before our eyes, it crumbled to dust! The string draped downward, and we saw that the remaining half was unaffected. It was still solid wood.

Vera turned to us with wide eyes. Grandpa David attempted to rise from his chair, but he was unable, and I was too distracted by the half bow in Vera's hand to think of helping him.

At last, he ended our silence. "It don't work when deh same notes are played on a violin or a trumpet. It's deh—it's deh two *oboes* togedder is my tinkin'. And only when it's B-flat played wit' high G." He reached out for the bow.

Vera crossed the room to hand it to him. "Of course, I shall purchase a new one for you, Mr. Gans. Were I to also buy another oboe, do you think that we would be able to reproduce this effect for a *longer* period? By playing those same two notes on two oboes?"

"Don't see why not," he answered. He then blew on the violin bow where it had disintegrated.

A cloud of shimmering dust drifted down from it.

•

The next morning, Grandpa David seemed almost giddy when we collected him for our trip to the music shop. Such a trip would have been too expensive for him in a taxi and too exhausting for him to walk. Not nearly as giddy was the young clerk at the shop to whom Vera started speaking. She has a habit of formulating her theories by explaining them aloud. The clerk was obliged to listen to our encounter with the violet holes without betraying any sign that he very likely fancied us victims of opium mania.

"As such," Vera continued her lecture, "tonight we shall play a B-flat on one oboe and a high G on the other. That harmony, combined with the unique timbre of the oboes, somehow illuminates what I suspect are ruptures between the physical and spirit realms. *Sustain* those notes, and perhaps we shall be granted a frame whose picture is nothing less than the Great Beyond!"

The clerk wrapped the new violin bow in paper. He then did something unexpected, especially given that he had barely spoken up to this point. He inquired calmly, "Do you need any help conducting this experiment?"

Vera, Grandpa David, and I looked back and forth at one other. As if choreographed, we then all turned to the clerk.

"I once attended a séance," he explained, "and a spirit spoke through a megaphone that levitated right there before me. I've been a believer ever since."

Vera drew in her lips tightly. She then sighed and explained, "No, your speaking megaphone was poppycock. As Lucille here will attest, the Spiritualists rely solely on clever parlor tricks such as that one. Ghosts, I assure you, do *not* come when called. Nonetheless, you are a *seeker*, and it might prove useful to have another able body in the room."

Grandpa David agreed to let him join us. We were then formally introduced to the clerk, Mr. Eric Bergson. He preferred we call him Rick. He had blue eyes, which glanced at me more than once. He also had a chip in the corner of his front tooth that made his bashful smile all the more boyish. Despite this youthful cast, I imagined he was a bit older than me, perhaps twenty years of age.

That afternoon, the first breezes of autumn air had migrated from Canada, and by evening, the three flights up to Grandpa David's room were not so oppressive. I was pleased to think that his cell would be more tolerable for at least a couple of months.

As usual, my děda assumed the rank of king once we were all assembled in his room. He assigned Rick to stand at one side of the room with the new oboe while, with his old one, he claimed his throne on the other side. I knew Vera thought herself best qualified to conduct this experiment, and her clenched fists conveyed her frustration. Nonetheless, the arrangement freed her to examine any glowing holes at will.

I was given no assignment. I decided I could best assist by restraining Vera should she venture too closely to any of the mysterious holes. After all, the crystalized violin bow had proven that we were embarking on a dangerous operation.

Vera then took me very much by surprise when she announced, "We have some time before the room is adequately dark. May I ask that the two *younger* members of our team step out into the hall for a moment while I discuss a delicate point with Mr. Gans? With *your* approval, of course, sir."

Grandpa David tilted his head, shrugged, and nodded. Rick walked to the door and held it open for me. Just before I stepped out, I looked back at Vera. She averted her eyes until the door was shut between us. Now, it is true that Vera *is* older than me. Were one to guess at her exact age, one would likely flail helplessly in a range between her early thirties and her mid-fifties. Still, her banishing me to the hallway — with a near stranger, no less — stirred both anger and hurt in me. What had Grandpa David to share with *her* that he ought not share with *me?*

I curtly grinned at Rick. The chipped-tooth smile he returned suddenly looked less boyish and more oafish. I noticed he still held the new oboe, and then I noticed that this oboe ended with a detachable section that splayed out into a bell.

"Did you know," I said softly, "that those floating megaphones used by Spiritualists both amplify and *funnel* sound? You simply flip it over, put the smaller part to your ear, and sounds are channeled into a neat stream." I pointed to end piece of his oboe.

"I *did* know that," he whispered. He then looked at the oboe — and back at me.

Rick Bergson, it appeared, was not one for subtlety.

I put a finger to my chin before saying, "I wonder if we might see if we could make that happen with the end piece of this oboe. We might test it on, oh, let's say this door! And the conversation occurring behind it!" I blinked twice with wide eyes.

Rick was a trusting soul, but he was no oaf. Sneering at me, he firmly twisted the bell section from the oboe and dropped it into my hand. He then walked to the far end of the hall to stare through a dirty window, his arms crossed.

Despite his apparent disapproval, I gingerly placed the wide end of the bell against the door and listened through the narrow end. I had already suspected that Vera would be asking about *guilt,* that emotion lurking behind both of our investigations of ghosts. She had theorized that concentrated guilt punctures the skin between the physical and spirit realms. I, however, could not imagine that Grandpa David would have done *anything* to cause him to feel excessively guilty.

And I was not able to tie this metaphysical theory to the muffled conversation I heard. Not at first, that is.

"... but Josefov is no longer dere," Grandpa David said. "I read reports dat it has been torn down for deh new, modern Prague. Prague, dey say, is to become anodder Paris."

"Even as far away as that," Vera lamented. "We cannot escape this modernization."

"Besides, I want to be buried in America!"

When I heard this, I shook. Why were they talking about where my děda would be *buried?* I pressed my ear closer to the oboe bell.

"Your allegiance to this nation is enviable, Mr. Gans. At times, I find it difficult to feel like an American myself."

"*No!* How come you don't feel American? Your name is Dutch, yeh? For a long time, dey been comin' over. When *your* family arrive from Europe?"

"My—my *grandfather* was the immigrant," Vera said. There was a quaver in her voice. "It was a fair time before the war. The Civil War, I mean, not this last fistfight with Spain."

"Your grandmodder don't come wit' him?"

"No. No, she had already *arrived,* let us say. But that's a story for another time. Tell me more about why approaching the end of your life causes you to feel *guilty.* Are there secrets back in the Old World perhaps? Or did you do something unsavory here?"

"I make some mistakes like any man. But deh shame, Miss Van Slyke, it's not what *was.* It's what's *to come.* I sit and tink—how should dis life of mine end? Slow and sad? 'Lento' as deh composers put it? Dat's no good. So maybe I—maybe I conduct deh concerto a bit different. Yeh?"

"I'm sorry, Mr. Gans. I don't understand."

"Maybe I conduct deh end of deh concerto 'allegro.' *Quicker.* You see now?"

"Ah!" Vera replied. "Yes, I see. But speeding things along, as it were, must conflict with your religious views."

"You don't got to be a Jew to know it's a sin to take your own life. So what I do? What I *do?* Dis is somet'ing I cannot talk about wit' Ludmila—your Lucille. Is good you put her in deh hall. You take care of—"

I pulled my ear away from the oboe bell quickly. As gently as I could, I removed that black funnel away from the door. What I first took to be a fly on my cheek became a tear when I brushed it away. I rushed over to Rick while I still had the voice to ask that he let the others know that I had changed my mind. They did not need me for the experiment, I explained as I handed back the end piece of the oboe. I could not manage to say anything more.

And I barely remember rushing down the three flights of stairs.

•

The first day of my new position as personal assistant to Vera Van Slyke began on October 1, 1900. She had taken lodgings at the Hotel Manitou, which would serve as her home and office. "Chicago is a fine base for a journalist," she had said. "And centrally located for our investigations into hauntings. I shall think of the move from New York as my immigration to America!"

Still, as she let me through the door on that first day, she smiled with her lips but not with her eyes. In fact, her eyes were looking everywhere other than at me.

I asked quietly, "Is there a problem? You haven't—have you changed your mind? About my assisting you?"

There was a moment before she must have realized what I had meant, and this is when she looked at me. She looked at me softly. "No, dear! The position is still very much yours. I would like you to sit down, though. We have never discussed that second time we saw the skittering holes at your Grandpa—what was his name again?"

"David."

"Of course. Mr. David Gans. I do remember his *last* name."

I swallowed before adding, "Again, I am very sorry for disappearing the way I did."

"And Mr. Gans and I were as sorry that you had heard our little discussion."

"You *knew* that I'd been listening? Did that music store clerk tattle on me?"

"I'm afraid it was your disappearance that tattled on you. More to the point is what we discovered that evening. Come in and take a seat."

I entered Vera's new lodgings pensively. Since the evening of my well-punished eavesdropping, I had gone to visit Grandpa David more than once. We had avoided any talk of his contemplating suicide. I could not have suffered it. Instead, he mentioned that he and Rick had struck up a friendship of sorts. Mostly, Grandpa David and I discussed Vera's decision to make Chicago her new home. And her offer to hire me as an assistant.

However, the last time I had gone to visit him, he was not in his room. Nor was he at his favorite park. It made my heart race, but his neighbors told me that nothing seemed amiss in terms of any sounds. Or any smells.

Taking the chair Vera had offered, I asked, "Were you able to preserve the violet lights that night?"

"We were. The sustained B-flat and high G did the trick! It allowed us to see that the many small holes hovered first near solid surfaces but then launched themselves to drift toward a wobbling, floating center hole. Very hard to describe, as Mr. Gans had mentioned."

Vera squinted a moment. She then pulled over another chair for herself.

"We found that this center hole was growing," she resumed. "That first night, when I poked the violin bow into it, it was roughly the size of, oh, let's say a chicken. The second night, however, the hole was more the size of a sack of potatoes."

"It's a bit early to be thinking about lunch, Vera," I said. I was laboring to present a cheery disposition.

"Lunch? Ah, you know me too well. But my point is that the hole was *growing*. Growing each day, it seems, as Mr. Gans wrestled with a decision that was piercing him with guilt."

I felt the tears building again, and Vera reached across to take my hand.

"I received a letter," she said. "I am not exactly certain when. It more or less simply *appeared* on my table. I am a bit more certain that it is written in *Czech*. Do you suppose you might take a look at it for me?"

Vera led me toward a dining area. Toward the table there. Toward a shimmering sheet of glass upon that table. As I neared it, I saw that the glass was far thinner than any I have ever seen. As thin as paper! Without words, Vera indicated that I was to bend down and look at the sheet from a particular angle.

There was fine etching on this impossibly slender pane. It was handwriting. I had to twist my head to various positions to make out the simple sentence written there:

$$Hudba\ je\ tady\ nebeská.$$

I stood up straight. "It says, 'The music here is divine'."

Vera stepped beside me. Almost whispering, she explained, "I spoke with that clerk from the music store yesterday. He confirmed my suspicions. Without my knowledge, the two of them met a *third* evening. Mr. Gans had said nothing to prepare the clerk for what would happen." She stopped and appeared as if she were struggling to find the right words.

I helped her finish. "I know what happened. By then, the hole in the center of the room was larger still. And my děda struggled out of his chair. And he hobbled, didn't he? He hobbled *through* that hole. Didn't he?" I blinked hard.

"The way the young clerk described it, Mr. Gans *marched* through that hole. He marched, holding his oboe bravely before him and sustaining his single note."

Could such an act be deemed suicide? I had no answer. Clearly, by delivering the letter to Vera, he wanted *her* to see what could be accomplished from the Other Side. Yet the letter's language indicated that it had been written for *me.* Again, I bent over it, bringing my trembling fingers to my lips.

As Vera pulled me back, a single tear fell. It fell—shattering that letter into a cloud of shimmering dust.

DARK AND DIRTY CORNERS
(1901)

All houses wherein men have lived and died
Are haunted houses.

— Henry Wadsworth Longfellow

"Me? Conduct a *genuine* séance? There's no such thing!" scolded Vera Van Slyke. "Did any of you bother to *read* my book?" She raised and shook her copy of *Spirits Shouldn't Sneeze: A Decade of Defrauding Mediums,* which had been released to the public a month earlier. Vera then slammed the book onto the top of the parlor piano beside her, using such force that the strings knelled.

Each member of the Nunda Psychical Research Society—they were only three in number—responded differently to Vera's sharp inquiry. Mrs. Constance Haase, in whose parlor we had assembled, straightened her posture and crossed her arms. She was a middle-aged widow whose weathered face and hands were offset by a dignified dress and smart jewelry. The contrast told of the financial climb achieved by her generation, the progeny of those white settlers who had first plowed the Illinois prairie. Constance's only child, Peter, answered Vera's question with a snort, one which joined earlier derisive snickers at the society's proceedings. It seemed the fourteen-year-old's interest in the psychical had been maternally mandated. The remaining member was Dr. Philip Kling, a neighbor and the only member who slumped with shame. Earlier, treating Vera and me to lunch after collecting us at the train depot, he mentioned that he had moved from the heart of Baltimore to the hinterland of Chicago two years earlier. This comment, though made offhandedly, lingered with me because the doctor appeared to be about fifty years of age—an odd age for such a significant change in one's professional life.

After shifting in her seat, Mrs. Haase retorted, "The invitation to speak to our society was intended to be an opportunity for you to *tell* us about your book, Miss Van Slyke. *That,* I remind you, is why we *paid* for your passage here."

Vera looked down at me with raised eyebrows and tight lips. Feeling small in my chair, I lifted and dropped my shoulders.

"Kindly forgive my tone," Vera enunciated carefully. "The train ride from the city, though barely *fifty miles,* seems to have frazzled my nerves. I am only too pleased to describe my book to your little—uhm, to your *esteemed* society."

Wincing, I tilted my head sideways to remind Vera to be polite. She pursed her lips, adjusted her cuff, and straightened her stance. Only then did Vera begin her recitation.

"I begin my book by describing one of my favored methods of *defrauding* Spiritualist mediums during séances. You see, when I was a bit younger than Master Peter here, I assisted my father in his candle-making shop. To create interesting fragrances, he experimented by adding flowers and other flora to the wax. But he was a chandler, not a botanist. In one of his trials, he mistook ragweed for immature goldenrod, and the results were unexpected. Almost anyone standing near the lit candle would be induced to *sneeze* upon breathing the fumes."

Master Peter laughed heartily at the prospect of such a candle. He then mimicked a sneeze, his thick, black hair breaking free from the oil intended to tame it.

Vera winked at the boy before continuing. "Years later, I tinkered with that recipe to make the candles even *more* effective! I intended to use their flames to illuminate the dark machinations of mediums. The fumes, after all, rise *over* the heads of those seated but are inhaled by anyone—anyone *living,* that is—wandering just beyond that ring of sitters. In this way, I was able to expose the mediums' confederates who were masquerading as spirits of the dearly departed. Thus my title: *Spirits Shouldn't Sneeze.*"

At this point, Dr. Kling joined the boy's merriment. I believe I also saw the ends of Mrs. Haase's mouth curl, if only slightly.

"So you see," said Vera, "I am very far from qualified to *conduct* a séance for you. I'm afraid you'll have to find some other party to contact the late Mrs.—what was the woman's name?"

Together, Mrs. Haase and I answered, "Mrs. Stickney."

Dr. Kling cleared his throat before saying, "I fear I'm to blame for having invited you, Miss Van Slyke. I serve as the voice of scientific skepticism in our little club here, and I might have misrepresented your book a bit." He turned to Mrs. Haase. "For once, I wanted to hear someone agree with my *own* view."

As her son tittered, Mrs. Haase uncrossed her arms.

"But poor Mrs. Stickney!" the widow pleaded. "I'm hardly the only one in this village who's heard her crying in that strange house. And Peter, tell our guests about the phantom child you saw through the house's window! I think it's George Junior come back from the grave!"

Vera spun to the boy, who became mute under her gaze. She next turned to me with her eyebrows raised again. She, too, appeared to be struck speechless.

I took the initiative. "You hadn't mentioned any ghostly manifestations to us. You'd only said that, while living, the Stickneys had built a house specially designed for séances. That's why you think Mrs. Stickney would be a willing spirit for us to contact, you said."

"Well," Mrs. Haase replied with a glance toward Dr. Kling, "I had been *informed* your book concerns Spiritualism, not ghosts. I was *about* to explain that I'd hoped to contact Mrs. Stickney to see if she still grieved for the loss of her boy, George Junior. I'm convinced that's why she had been drawn to séances—to check up on him in the next world. But now that she's gone, too, it seems she and George Junior *both* haunt that house!"

Dr. Kling amended, "George Stickney Junior was the couple's first born and the very first person to receive a Christian burial in Nunda Township. He died in the log cabin where they lived before having their brick house constructed."

"Dear me," Vera sighed. She took a spot on the sofa beside the widow. "You people ought to learn more about those you invite into your home. I'm sorry to disappoint you, Dr. Kling, but while I share your skepticism regarding our ability to *summon* spirits, I am very certain that some souls either remain in—or return to—our physical realm."

Mrs. Haase gently reached out and touched Vera's arm. "You mean to say that you believe in ghosts?"

"With great surety," Vera attested.

Dr. Kling quietly laced his fingers and placed them upon his lap. As quietly, young Peter did the same.

Vera resumed, "Now, tell me more about this house the Stickneys built for séances. You say it has *rounded* corners?"

"That's right," replied Mrs. Haase with a gleam now in her eye. "It must have been the wife's idea! I'm sure of that. Her name was Sylvia, and she was the medium. Yes, the Stickneys are well remembered for conducting séances on regular occasions, inviting people from all over. The rounded corners were designed to facilitate those séances, you see. I'm hoping you can explain the rationale, Miss Van Slyke. Is communication with spirits hindered by ordinary corners?"

"Spirits *caught* in corners?" Vera pondered aloud.

"That was the thinking half a century ago," Mrs. Haase explained. "During the dawn of Spiritualism."

Vera replied, "I've researched Spiritualism in all of its phases, and I'm afraid I've *never* come across anything about spirits getting caught in corners. Have you ever heard of this, Lucille?"

My previous involvement in the Spiritualism business continued to be a source of some discomfort, but I freely admitted that I had never encountered this belief.

Vera resumed, "There *is* a house back in New York whose builder claimed he had been guided in its construction *by spirits.* I'd once planned on investigating the place, but my usual ruses failed me. I was only able to see the structure from the outside. To be sure, the corners there *are* rounded!"

"You must mean the Timothy Brown house in Georgetown," I added. "Many Spiritualist meetings have occurred there. I wonder if the Stickneys followed Brown's building plan. He built his spirit house about the time of the Civil War, I believe. I know it was at *some* point in the 1860s. Do you happen to know when the Stickneys built theirs?"

"Quite a bit *earlier,* I'm afraid," Dr. Kling answered. "1849, in fact. I've studied that house as if it were one of my patients. The brickwork itself is done with curved corners, and that suggests they're part of the original plan."

Vera stood again, retaking her lecturer's position. "1849 is a problem. You see, the Fox sisters first went around claiming their toe-cracking trick was a form of spirit communication in *1848.* And, while they did open up a floodgate for the Spiritualism movement, it's doubtful those waters spread all the way to Illinois in just a single year."

The widow Haase crossed her arms again.

And, again, Dr. Kling cleared his throat. "You're not the first to inform our society of that problem."

The widow countered, "The Fox Sisters were *also* from the state of New York. And George Stickney moved here *from* the state of *New York!*"

"In 1835," Dr. Kling added calmly. "He was the very first pioneer here. According to a book on local history, Sylvia arrived in 1838, so she wouldn't have known anything about Spiritualism even if the round corners *were* her—"

"They would have kept in touch with relatives back east!" Mrs. Haase insisted.

"But Constance," the doctor implored. "Designing a house to accommodate a religion only one year old is a bit much to—"

"Belief in the afterlife hardly *began* in 1848! And there was more to the start of Spiritualism than two sisters pulling a prank. Swedenborg and Mesmer and Andrew Jackson Davis had *many* followers beforehand, and—and—*and* none of this explains the woman's cries heard coming from that *empty* house!"

"*And* I saw that ghost boy!" Peter said, reminding us he could do more than snicker. "Through one of the windows, I did!"

"*And* a bear on the path doesn't mean the library is closed!" Vera added, punctuating her point with a snap of her fingers.

The rest of us sat motionless with individualized expressions of befuddlement. I knew Vera had created a metaphor. I could not unravel its meaning, however.

"Let's go learn what's haunting that house!" she clarified.

Only then did we stand to retrieve our hats and outerwear.

•

Rather than bother to hitch the horses, we agreed to stroll the mile or so to the house with round corners. Vera told me to bring our two oboes. These odd-sounding instruments traveled with us regularly since our discovery that playing two particular notes on them simultaneously creates a vibration that shifts any ruptures between the spiritual and physical realms into the violet edge of the visible spectrum. Vera explained this principle—and her theory that such inter-dimensional ruptures are caused by extreme guilt— as the five of us wandered toward the house.

"If," Vera said pensively, "the spirit of Mrs. Stickney is suffering terrible guilt over the death of her first-born son, it's possible she—or she *and* that son—remain in contact with this side. Before we can learn their reason for doing so, checking for holes between the dimensions can show us if such contact is possible in the first place."

"Well," Dr. Kling muttered, "these violet holes are something I would very much like to witness. I hope your oboes are loud, though. The house is vacant, but it's also locked. You'll probably be stuck examining it from the outside."

"That *is* discouraging," Vera said. "To tell the truth, if we can't go inside, I'm a bit more concerned about those rain clouds returning."

We looked upward. The blotches of gray across the sky reminded me that Vera and I had passed through some spring showers during our train ride from Chicago. The humid, country air was aromatic, but I noticed mud clumping on my shoes. Peter must have had his eye on me. He briskly strutted beside me, grinning confidently and tapping an umbrella to assure me I would be kept protected. At this point, he offered his arm in a gentlemanly fashion. Only then did it occur to me that I was close to five years his senior. As I accepted his courtesy, I concealed my amusement that those years seemed to matter far more to me than to him.

"Though Mrs. Haase is not fond of it," the doctor resumed, "I have a theory of my own regarding those rounded corners."

As I stepped closer to hear the theory, Peter stayed at my side. His mother, on the other hand, marched resolutely ahead of us.

"Have you ever seen a *round* barn, Miss Van Slyke? A few have found their way out here from the East."

"George Washington had a round barn!" Peter announced with more volume than necessary.

"Good job, Pete," Dr. Kling said. "But so did a sect of Christians. They were called the Shakers by those who knew about them mostly for their zealous dancing. Rumors spread about these people, the way rumors do. One was about how they believed evil spirits hide in corners. That was how outsiders explained why the Shakers favored *round* barns over traditional ones. No corners? No evil spirits!"

Vera nodded. "It's a widespread superstition. I once asked a good friend why the roofs of many Chinese homes end with upturned eaves. It seems they're designed to protect the home from dark spirits! You see, when in China, hobgoblins can only travel in a straight line."

Vera and the doctor chuckled. Peter, however, silently guided me by the arm in a slightly different direction.

"That book on local history I mentioned says that old George Stickney worked for a time in the lumber trade before heading west. What if he picked up a few ideas about construction and adapted the idea of round barns when designing his mansion on the prairie?"

Tugging my escort back toward the main group, I said, "So, are you suggesting that, instead of *welcoming* spirits, the Stickneys might have been trying to *banish* them?"

Before Dr. Kling could respond, Mrs. Haase spun around.

"Then why did they have so many *séances?*" she howled.

With the languor of pulling on an old sock, the doctor replied, "As I've asked many times before, how do we know if they had any séances at all? Are there any records of them holding—"

"Everyone around here *says so!* Everyone around here has *always* said so! *You* wouldn't know about that! But *I* was born here! I don't need any book to teach me local history! I know about Mrs. Stickney's grief for her child from those who remember her!"

As if more interested in the case than in our hostess's agitation, Vera asked, "Do they say she felt that grief until her own death?"

"They do indeed!" Mrs. Haase asserted. "Folks tried to convince Sylvia that she wasn't to blame for the boy's illness—that *no one* could have kept a log cabin hygienic. But she was a very contrary woman on that topic. *Very* contrary. The more folks said she wasn't at fault, the more she said she was. And when *more* of her children died afterward, well, that only deepened the wound of losing George Junior."

I submitted, "Could it be that there was an important detail about the death that she never confessed? If she felt such persistent guilt, I mean."

I shouldn't have implied that a mother could have been responsible for her own child's death. I shouldn't have said that with Peter so close beside us. No one spoke. The only sound was the suction of our shoes pulling up from the wet, deeply rutted road.

After a time, I attempted to pave our path by changing the subject. "Dr. Kling, you'd mentioned you came here from Baltimore a couple years back. May I ask what motivated you to do so?"

"Ah. That. Well. Don't all city doctors dream about moving their practices to the country one day? My 'one day' arrived, I guess. But look up ahead. We'll be able to see the Stickney house once we're around those trees."

Vera stretched and stooped like a child anxiously awaiting the circus parade. I had been in her employ for almost a full year at this point, but she still frequently surprised me. Upon our first glimpse of the house, Vera began to giggle and even to leap over puddles to get closer to it!

She called back us, "I *do* love a haunted house! And this one looks like a haunted *doll's* house, doesn't it?"

The tan-brick structure *did* have a playful quality to it. It was symmetrical with an arched doorway between a pair of arched windows. On the floor above, a balcony doorway was flanked by a two parallel windows—again, each of them arched. Bookending the doors and windows were the gently curved corners. From a distance, the house looked like the six-dotted side of a giant's well-rolled die. As we approached, though, I saw how the curved corners were limited to the vertical junctions of the walls. With an ornate overhang, the roof sat flatly upon the four walls as if it were the lid of a tall tin of fancy candies.

Vera was the first to reach the front door. Mrs. Haase joined her next, placing her fists on her hips as if claiming ownership. With Peter still faithfully at my side, I mentioned to Dr. Kling how sorry I would be to miss seeing the *inside* of this architectural wonder.

"I'll get you inside, Lucy!" the boy shouted. "Here, Doc, take the umbrella!"

Dr. Kling barely managed to catch the umbrella flung to him. The boy charged around the curved corner to the back of the building. We strolled toward the porch.

"He's a fourteen-year-old boy," Dr. Kling explained with his soft voice.

"Yes," I agreed. "He was informing me of exactly that on the way over."

•

Peter's fourteen-year-old face appeared as the front door opened. I turned to see Mrs. Haase's eyes narrow and her neck muscles distend. A tense trial between mother and son ensued. The accused pleaded that locking doors but *not windows* made the absentee owner's intentions ambiguous. In the end, the matriarchal judge conceded to the verdict put forth by the jury of her guests: we were justified in exploring the unoccupied house, given the reports of intruders within it.

Passing through the entry hall and entering the front room, I felt my mood suddenly sink into cold, turbid waters. Though it was afternoon, the overcast sky made the rooms gloomy, underscoring their echoing emptiness. There was a strong smell of dust and disuse. Still, it was the curvatures at the meetings of wall-to-wall and wall-to-ceiling that, I think, especially created an atmosphere of misgiving.

The curves in the corners looked like solid-plaster spider webs made by human hands.

"Let's prepare the oboes, Lucille," Vera said somberly.

Apparently, her disposition had clouded as quickly as mine.

"Peter? At what window did you see the ghostly boy?"

Peter fiddled with his lower lip. "Uhm, I—I don't—it was upstairs, I guess."

Vera nodded. "If we don't discover any holes down here, we'll try up there. I ask you all to remain perfectly motionless during this procedure. The holes have proven to be dangerous. Doctor, perhaps you can ensure that Peter does not forget this?"

The doctor agreed. The society ambled back to the entry hall as if they had read unflattering reviews of the musical duo about to perform. I had to correct Vera's fingering on her instrument before she sounded the B-flat. I joined her with a high G.

Almost immediately, I *halted!* I pulled the oboe from Vera's lips—but she, too, had stopped blowing. The sound I thought came from her oboe was, in truth, Mrs. Haase *shrieking*. I saw the widow throw her arms around Dr. Kling, burying her face into his chest. With one arm around her back, the doctor used his other to yank the boy against them.

All of that had happened in an instant. It had happened because, upon our sounding the two notes, the room had glowed with *more* violet holes floating and coalescing in the air than I had seen even in pitch-blackness.

"What the devil *were* those?" the doctor rasped. His eyes searched the room. Keeping a firm grip on Peter's shirt, he rubbed Mrs. Haase's back. "Are we *safe* here?"

Vera nervously wet her lips before speaking. "The holes are—they're only dangerous when shifted into the, uh, visible spectrum. We are safe from them now. Safe from the holes, yes, but—but, so far as you know, the manifestations have only been a woman's cries and a boy standing at a window? Is that correct?"

The two Haases took a moment before they stepped away from Dr. Kling. Peter looked around with his mouth open but a smile forming in his cheeks. He nodded. The widow also affirmed that no other manifestations were known before she shuddered and then anxiously adjusted her hat and necklace.

"I have no reason to think that there's danger, then," declared Vera. "Nonetheless, we should investigate quickly. We don't want to be caught here should a heavy rain come. Dr. Kling? I trust you're a little less skeptical now than you were a minute ago."

With a bewildered grin, the doctor conceded with a bow.

"Excellent. You'll often find matches and a candle or lantern at the top of a cellar stairway. Would you mind seeing if that's the case here? If so, please perform your best medical examination of what's below."

He turned to the widow. With a nod, she granted him leave, and the doctor strode bravely in the wrong direction. Taking a different approach, he disappeared.

Vera next addressed the widow. "With your permission, Mrs. Haase, I'd like Master Peter to help Miss Parsell here determine the room where he saw the child spirit. I assure you that Lucille has blossomed into a very reliable asset to my investigations, and we need to see if anything can explain why the manifestation occurred where it did."

His mother agreed to the arrangement, making Peter significantly more enthusiastic than myself. This time, I politely declined the offer of his arm as we walked to the staircase. At the top, we crept toward the first room. I looked inside to see that it was completely vacant. Checking to be certain we were out of his mother's hearing, I called Peter closer.

"Now, did you really see the phantom boy through one of the windows—or did you see him while you were *inside* this house?"

At first, Peter fidgeted with the buttons on his shirt. He next tried to smooth his raven hair. Finally, he confessed, "Inside this house."

"Why did you come inside?" I asked, now guiding him back to the hallway.

"I told Lizzie Rosenthal I could get her in. She's from school. She said she'd heard the house once belonged to witches, and she wanted to see inside it." Peter smirked and pointed ahead of us. "We kissed in that room over there. Would you like to go there?"

"Only if that's where you saw the ghost," I said firmly. *"Where* did you see it?"

Peter's eyes drifted to the side, settling on a particular door. He said, "We—we probably should go back downstairs now. I, uh—I don't think the ghost will be here anymore."

I noticed his face had gone blank. After taking a few steps toward the door that his gaze had indicated, I looked back. Peter remained exactly where he was with the same lack of expression.

"I'm not fibbing," he said. "I think the ghost probably left. And you probably don't want to open that door."

"You'd best not try to scare me, Peter. Believe me, I've seen ghosts far more frightening than this one." Of course, given that I actually had no clue what I might encounter, I was mostly fibbing.

"We probably shouldn't—I'm going back to the staircase," Peter said, though he remained fixed in the same spot.

I inched a few more steps toward the door. I turned back and waved for him to join me.

"*You're* the ghost hunter," he said, refusing to budge.

I surveyed the door. "I'm the ghost hunter's *assistant.*" Taking a deep breath, I grasped and twisted and pushed the knob.

If the two manifestations had occurred separately, I would have seized Peter and hauled him back to the others. What probably kept me in place, though, was the confusion of hearing a woman crying—it was somewhere else in the house—at the very same moment as I saw the back of a boy in that room. He stood in the corner. *Embedded* in the corner because of the plaster curvature. The phantom was sharing the same physical space as that rounded corner.

As I say, the apparition in combination with the distant crying had halted me physically. Emotionally, though, I felt a whirlpool of both pity and fear. Only half-intentionally, I approached the only half-visible ghost of the boy. His size showed that he was a year or two above the age of walking. Amid a collision of impulses within me—fleeing, fascination, failure at my assignment—I managed to walk toward the ghost, step by unsteady step.

"George Junior?" I whispered. "Georgie?"

My heart sank when the child twisted around. Like dingy paper, the skin around his eye sockets was crinkled and gray. His mouth hung open, a swollen tongue barely kept inside it. His head lolled to one side—then forward and to the other side. He appeared unable to control the aim of his eyes.

I stopped. The tiny boy, suffering from some horrifying disease, appeared to sense this. With terrible struggle, he turned to face the corner again. A soft splash beside my foot made me think a fresh rain must have come. But, no, I would have noticed any damage to the ceiling. It had been my own tear.

And as my eyes blurred, the vision before me faded.

I then found myself staring out of the room's arched window. I didn't know how I had gotten there from the center of the room. Nor how much time had passed. I dimly felt that some commotion had occurred on the floor below, but it was Peter's voice that snapped me back to full awareness.

"Come on, Lucy. They want us to go back downstairs." Despite his previous immobility, Peter had entered this haunted room to fetch me.

I gave my arm to my young protector.

•

While I had been upstairs, learning a secret and encountering a ghost, Vera had done the same on the ground floor. She provided details of this part of the investigation while she and I were on the train back to Chicago.

Vera had little patience for those who put stock in Spiritualism, so finding herself alone with Mrs. Haase was a bit like the teetotaler sitting next to the bartender at Intermission. Rather than chat, Vera gingerly touched the tantalizing webs between the walls.

"I can explain," said Mrs. Haase, "the reason you saw me hurl myself at Dr. Kling when those holes—those bizarre *holes* appeared out of nowhere. You're probably wondering about my reaction, Miss Van Slyke."

"I *observed* it."

Tapping her fingertips together, the widow continued, "The doctor and I have a perplexing friendship. If 'friendship' is even the appropriate term. When our visits aren't medical, they're—well, they're *psychical*. My, how we bicker over séances, clairvoyance, prophetic dreams—you name it."

"I also observed that."

Mrs. Haase leaned back against one of the walls. "And yet our Psychical Research Society has lasted over a year! And, in all that time, it's only had the same three members." She laughed. "Only *three* of us, and we call ourselves a *society.*"

Vera refrained from saying that she had observed this as well.

"I'm convinced, Miss Van Slyke, that Dr. Kling is an unbeliever who wishes to believe. Why else would he keep coming to my house to debate these topics? If he had any *other* interest in my company—some interest in my company beyond the occult, if you see my meaning—he's never dropped even a single hint of it."

Vera turned in time to see Mrs. Haase's cheeks redden. She asked, "At what point in history has it not been the *woman's* burden to drop the first hint?"

Still blushing, the widow laughed again. "I've tried. Oh, how I've tried. But the best I've managed is to tell him that Peter's of an age when he needs a masculine hand in his supervision. Of course, that's more an understatement than an overture. Let me tell you, if his father were still alive, that scamp wouldn't be climbing through windows simply because they're unlocked! The consequences would be stiff! *Very* stiff! You know, Miss Van Slyke, I often wonder if I'm disappointing Peter's father in how I'm raising his boy."

Vera put her hand on Mrs. Haase's arm. "You say the doctor is an unbeliever who wishes to believe. Could it be that you're the reverse? A believer who wishes to *unbelieve?*"

The widow snickered, sounding much like Peter. "Whatever do you mean?"

"Do you worry about your late husband's reaction if you were to drop a hint in Dr. Kling's direction? Do you wonder if the dead keep watch over the living? That's a notion I've always found to be as unnerving as it is comforting."

After a long pause, Mrs. Haase grinned. She stated plainly, "You are very observant, Vera."

It was shortly afterward when the two *jolted!* A quavering wail of some other woman had stabbed through the musty air. Vera told me that she first heard it coming from the adjacent room, one that probably had been used for dining. She charged into that room. The wail then seemed to come from the parlor she had just left. She ran back! The widow, too frightened to have joined Vera, reported that the moans had come from the dining room the *entire* time.

Meanwhile, Dr. Kling raced up from the cellar, thinking the crying might have come from one of the three women in our group. As soon as he reached the top stair, however, he said he heard the sobbing coming from deep *within* the cellar. Vera and he next investigated the other first-floor rooms and confirmed that—no matter which one they entered—the ghostly wailing continually sounded from some *nearby* room.

All of sudden, Vera shouted, *"Tell us why you cry so!"* Hearing no answer, she ran to a central location. *"What is it that pains you?"*

Regardless of their location, each of the three living beings on the first floor heard an answer come from a different, adjacent room.

That answer was: *"Heeeee thooooought heeee wassssss baaaaaad."*

Vera shouted, *"Who thought he was bad?"*

No answer was returned. The manifestation had ended.

Vera sent word that Peter and I were to rejoin the group.

•

Once I had described my sighting upstairs and the others had related their *sounding* downstairs, Vera put two fingers to the side of her jaw. She paced for ten or twelve minutes. I knew that remaining silent was the best form of assistance, and the others must have recognized this, too.

At last, Vera raised a finger. "A pioneer's life affords scant opportunity for tending to the bedridden. Even the mother of a dying child has a myriad of chores that must be performed to ensure that the healthy survive. What if Mrs. Stickney hadn't been able to attend to George Junior at the moment of his death? What if she found his dead body in the position that Lucille describes?"

"Facing the corner?" Dr. Kling said with his tone of gentle skepticism. "Why would he be facing the corner?"

Reverently, Vera responded, "Perhaps it takes another mother to answer that."

Yet it was Peter, not his mother, who explained it. With the same blank stare I had seen upstairs, the boy repeated what the ghost of Mrs. Stickney had communicated: "He thought he was bad."

Vera nodded. "George Junior might well have considered his sickness a type of punishment, be it a punishment like those he'd heard about in Sunday School or simply one inflicted upon him by his parents. What if, in his last moments of life, he attempted to atone for whatever had brought on this punishment in the only way that he knew how?"

Mrs. Haase clutched her son. Dr. Kling, seeing this, stepped toward her and placed his hand on her shoulder.

"Even more awful, imagine the guilt of the mother. She might have left only so long as it takes to collect some eggs! But she finds her deceased son out of his bed and crumpled in a corner." Vera sighed. "Of course, I'm stitching together this history from very few scraps of evidence."

"Sometimes, it's the *cure* that proves the disease," the doctor offered. "What do you suggest we do to alleviate Sylvia Stickney's anguish?"

"We've seen that she can communicate with us. We must get her to re-manifest!"

"But Vera?" I interjected. "Wouldn't that be the same as summoning a spirit?"

"Oh, believe me! We're going to hold a séance unlike any you've seen before! And it begins with this handsome lad right here!" Vera ruffled Peter's already wild hair before adding, "I must ask a favor of you, Prudence."

Perhaps I was still too dazed from my experience upstairs to quickly correct my employer.

"Do you mean me?" asked Mrs. Haase. "My name is *Constance.*"

"Ah! I'm not very strong with—" Vera began. She then muttered to herself, "Constance Kling. Now, wouldn't *that* be a steadfast name?"

I glimpsed the widow and the doctor turn very slowly toward one another.

"I must ask a favor of you, Constance. I need your son to run outside and come back in, tracking as much *mud* across the floor as only a country boy can. In fact, I need additional volunteers to do exactly the same."

Peter's eyes brightened. He spun to face his mother and bounced in place as he awaited a decision. His mother knit her brow and glanced back at Dr. Kling. A shrug was apparently the best advice he could offer. She nodded her consent.

As swift as a rabbit, Peter darted out the front door.

The rest of us followed. Muddy patches were easily found in the unattended yard, and being outside of the house again seemed to act as a tonic. Soon, we were all gleefully stomping around and returning to the halls of the house to stomp again, creating a terrible mess.

While the others continued, I pulled Vera aside to discreetly ask if she truly thought this would induce Mrs. Stickney to reappear, if only audibly.

"Look what we're doing to the woman's *home!*" Vera answered with no discretion at all. "How could she *not* reappear? There's a more difficult question, though. Is the son a ghost *independently*—or is he only the ghost that haunts the *mother's* ghost?"

"I don't follow."

"The boy died in the log cabin, not here. Why would his spirit be bound to this place?"

"Are you saying that what I witnessed upstairs might have been a manifestation of the *mother?*"

"Yes. Of that which haunts her. You've been with me long enough to know that, in most cases, a ghost haunts the living—because something haunts the ghost."

Perhaps these very words rather than the mud tracks account for the sorrowful Mrs. Stickney's return at that moment. We heard her warbling cries in the next room over, and my first inclination was to rush there. A tug on my sleeve, though, reminded me that this would be fruitless.

Quickly, Vera instructed me, "Tell our hostess to wait outside, but have the doctor join us. He's likely to comprehend this treatment."

"And Peter?"

"Bring him in, too. He'll leave with a better understanding of motherhood."

I soon returned with the two gentlemen, leaving the widow at the open front door. Despite the disembodied sobs that seemed to come from all around us, we followed Vera's voice. Once we found her, we were witness to one of the most disturbing ghost layings on record.

"Mrs. Stickney!" Vera shouted with a harsh timbre. "Sylvia Stickney? You were a *terrible* mother! How *dare* you ignore your dying child?"

My first thought was that my employer had become possessed by a demon, and I saw Dr. Kling's face blanch. Both of us mustered enough trust in Vera, though, to not restrain her. Meanwhile, with the wisdom of youth, Peter cowered behind the doctor and me.

Vera gesticulated dramatically as she continued. "Poor George Junior! He thought you were punishing him for getting sick! That innocent child you let die all alone! All *alone!* For shame, Sylvia—for *shame!*"

The ghostly wailing grew fiercer, either from painful repentance or from furious indignation!

Dr. Kling whispered, "Of course!" He then stepped forward to yell, "A *terrible* mother! What a mistake to allow you near your newborn baby! It should have been swept away to an orphanage!"

The cries rose even louder! It sounded as if the bereaved woman were attempting to form words but the anguish—or was it outrage?—was too powerful. I felt Peter, who was crouched behind me, sticking his head through the bend of my arm for a view.

Vera and the doctor continued their tirade of reprimand until, at long last, the spirit of Mrs. Sylvia Stickney found just enough composure to speak.

"Nooooo! Noooo, I'm not to blammmmme! I never accused himmmmm. I never chastissssed! I! Am! Not! To blammmmmmme!"

An electric crackling then swept from one room to the next, down each hall and along every staircase. As it surged around me, I felt a sharp tingling, as if thousands of pins had flicked my skin. Like lightning, the rush of splintery ether had come and gone.

After catching our breath, we wandered to the front, where Mrs. Haase greeted Peter with an abundance of hugs and kisses. He was duly humiliated, but the adults understood that the mother had heard everything. After finding spots on the porch to sit down, each one of us found a different way to describe what we had witnessed inside. Despite these differences, it clearly had been the same phenomenon.

"I sense she's *gone*," the widow exclaimed. "I felt it at the door! Her business here is complete. She's moved on from this world. Never to return!"

Afterward, on the train, Vera explained to me how Mrs. Haase might have been speaking as much about her own late husband as about Sylvia Stickney. On that front porch, though, the vigilant ghost hunter had something else to say.

"Several months without any manifestations will have to pass before we can confirm our success. If it turns out we've completed the task, *you* are to thank, Constance. You're the one who gave me the key when you described our ghost as being a contrary, *very* contrary, woman when it came to the death of her first born. I merely applied a bit of psychology to coax her into seeing that she truly *wasn't* to blame at all."

Dr. Kling had the final word on Vera's treatment. "Psychology in *reverse*," he said.

•

At Vera's request, Dr. Kling sent a report several months later. She read it in her office at the Hotel Manitou, summarizing its key points aloud. She was too pleased for me to mention that, as her secretarial assistant, I had already read the letter in full.

"No reports of sobbing women or sickly children," Vera stated, "even from the house's new occupants. Rumors continue to roam, but the good doctor finds no evidence to support any of them. Not even for the cow that got loose on the Stickney property and came back with the power of speech—albeit, very limited." She looked up from the page with a smirk.

"It appears you were successful, then," I concluded. "Except for the cow perhaps."

"Far be it from me to muzzle ol' Bessie, my dear." Vera flipped the letter's top page. "And yet he continues. Hmm, it seems young Peter has developed yet *another* theory for the rounded corners. When the Nunda Psychical Research Society returned to clean up our mud, the boy realized how easy it was to mop a floor without any tight corners."

"Corners *are* the most grueling spots to clean," I agreed.

"Though Mrs. Haase adheres to the idea that the corners were built to accommodate séances, the doctor says he can't dismiss Peter's hunch that those corners were simply meant to facilitate housekeeping. He adds that the same principle is used in the sick wards at Johns Hopkins Hospital to minimize germs." Vera set her head at a contemplative angle.

Adding to the mystery, I mentioned, "I've since read about those round barns that Dr. Kling had mentioned. Some promote them as being more structurally stable than traditional barns. Do you suppose the Stickneys' design grew from their worries about living in tornado territory?"

Vera mumbled, "But both of these new theories are so—disappointingly practical."

"Isn't there more to the letter? He doesn't mention any changes in affection between himself and the widow. Or *does* he?"

Vera glared at me. "You read it, didn't you!"

I shrugged. "Sadly, I saw no comments on that topic. But he *does* go on to delicately suggest why he moved from Baltimore to the prairie. I wonder what you think of his change of heart regarding ghosts."

Her eyes widened, and she returned to the letter. "He found our experience at the Stickney house 'revivifying.' Curious choice of words. He explains that working in the sanitarium ward of Johns Hopkins back east had made him a sullen and doubt-filled man. Some of his patients—insensate ones—seemed to have lost all trace of their souls. No cure for them. Living bodies without—" She looked up at me.

"Living bodies without *ghosts*," I said. "It's an even more frightening prospect than ghosts without living bodies, don't you think? Could that be why he made such a major move?"

Vera put down the letter. Nodding, she commented, "But, as you say, it's grueling work to clean up those dark and dirty corners."

A BURDEN THAT BURNS
(1902)

A poor ghost, who all his life had befooled himself with lies,
may in Hades bethink himself, come to a sounder judgment,
see his miserableness and seek deliverance from it.

— Irys Heffner

Typically, Vera Van Slyke's investigations of ghostly spots
came about either because of serendipity or reputation. One of her
many acquaintances might hear of a supernatural disturbance and
then contact her. Vera might read a newspaper article about an
otherworldly manifestation. An employee of a haunted theater
might have worked previously at another theater that had engaged
Vera to handle its own supernatural disturbance. Unfortunately,
this manner of happening upon cases led to lengthy periods of *not*
exploring her special interest.

After one particularly long interval of feeling imprisoned by
the mundane, she placed an advertisement in prominent
newspapers across the country. It read as follows:

HELP FOR THE HAUNTED
Ghostly visitations occur when
emotional distress ruptures the
membrane between the corporeal
and ethereal realms. Such ruptures can be confirmed through a
technique involving harmonic resonance. V. Van Slyke specializes in

the investigation and resolution of supernatural disturbances. Send a full description of the situation to the Hotel Manitou, Chicago, Ills. Will travel. References provided upon request.

Subsequently, about once a week, we would receive a correspondence from someone claiming to be seeing or hearing a ghost. One harried correspondent even claimed to be *smelling* a ghost! As she did with this malodorous specter, Vera judiciously avoided performing many investigations and, instead, sent her best advice by return post.

However, in April of 1902, one letter slipped through her wall of wariness. I should say it *seared* through that wall in that the letter told of a series of inexplicable fires. Mr. J. Horace Ritchie, the correspondent, detailed his efforts to erect a building in Pittsburg. However, the land he had purchased for the project came with an unfortunate legacy. Originally, the site was intended to house a livery. Once the stables had been completed, they were lost to a blaze ignited by no traceable spark. The next landlord had attempted to build a barrel manufactory there. The building lasted only two weeks before being consumed by flames. Mr. Ritchie then took ownership. Though built more of brick than wood, the structure he had erected was likewise destroyed by an inexplicable inferno.

Summarizing the letter for Vera, I explained, "Despite becoming victim to this series of fires himself, Mr. Ritchie attempted to rebuild. Yet *another* fire devastated the nearly completed building. On both occasions, the brickwork was charred beyond use."

"That suggests a terribly *hot* fire," Vera said, picking up the letter opener and idly spinning it. "It sounds almost as if a *curse* lingers over the spot. Oh, but curses are hokum! Take your *family* curses. Any livestock breeder can tell you the truth behind them. Let's call it 'marrying too close home'."

"But this is not a family curse," I responded. "It appears to be grounded in—well, in the *ground* itself."

"Alleged curses on a house or even a plot of land can have any number of geological explanations. These fires might result from some sort of gas escaping from deep below the surface. High concentrations of sulfur in the soil. Even some old Pennsylvania farmer resorting to *arson* to thwart the encroachment of the city!" She swiped the letter opener back and forth to enact that farmer's battle.

"Mr. Ritchie says that he hired a geologist to analyze the terrain—to no avail. He adds that other businesses have built successfully on adjacent properties."

"That certainly is curious. But not in an especially *ghostly* way." The letter opener drooped in Vera's hand. "And all the way to Pittsburg? I wonder if it would be worth our time and trouble."

Enclosed with the letter was a bank note, which I handed to Vera. "This is *half* of the payment Mr. Ritchie is offering us."

Vera stared at the slip of paper for a moment. She blinked repeatedly and then stared several more moments. At last, she said, "I haven't been back east in quite a while. It'll be nice to see a few peaks and valleys again."

•

Mr. Ritchie met us at the train station. He was one of those men whose freshly trimmed beard, handsome walking stick, and opal tiepin told of his financial success. At the same time, any feelings of intimidation were averted by his gleeful smile and attentive manner. His assistant took command of transferring our luggage to the hotel. I saw Vera fidget at the sight of someone else assuming control. Of course, she remained as cordial as she could. This task became much easier for her when Mr. Ritchie announced he would treat us to lunch at one of Pittsburg's finer eateries.

"Never let the shadows of ghost hunting darken a radiant lunch!" Vera jested. "That has become my guiding principle, Mr. Richards."

On the trip to the restaurant, I quietly whispered to Vera that our client's name was *Ritchie,* not *Richards.*

"Are you sure?" she whispered back. "That seems so informal."

Perhaps being in the company of women induced Mr. Ritchie to delay our discussion of business until the end of the meal. I noticed he stopped eating altogether when Vera ordered a beer upon clearing her plate. It was not to be his only surprise.

"Of course, I would like to examine the property," Vera said once her beer arrived. "And it should be at dusk or afterward."

"That can be arranged," replied Mr. Ritchie. "However, both of the fires that occurred during my possession of the land began during *daylight* hours."

"Useful information perhaps," Vera said, "but not germane to our method of identifying breaches between the physical and spiritual realms. Our first step is to ensure that we have something supernatural here." She took a swig of beer.

"You have a method," he asked, "to *ensure* the activity is supernatural?"

Forgetting to dab the foam from her lip, Vera leaned forward. "If I had any logical way to explain it, I would surely write all the details into a scientific article for publication! It involves two oboes, one playing B-flat while the other plays a high G! This exact combination of timbres and tones allows the living to see the violet light that the departed can see. This purplish glow marks the edges of holes between our respective dimensions."

One of Mr. Ritchie's eyebrows rose.

"Are you doubtful, sir?" I asked. "I can vouch for the method."

Our client sat back in his chair. He lifted a finger before responding. "In my correspondence, I mentioned that I run a cable and wire business. However, did you notice that I never mentioned what I hope to manufacture at the new factory, the one that keeps burning down? I avoided it out of fear that *you* would be the doubtful ones. Surely, you have both heard of telephones, yes?"

We nodded. A smile gleamed through his dark beard.

"Imagine them assembled in such a way—and in such mass numbers—that people from *all* levels in society could enjoy such devices! Not just one in every town! *One in every home!* My colleagues mock me for investing in such a plan. One has even proclaimed the two fires to be a sign from on high, a portent that my scheme is doomed. No, I am not *doubtful*, Miss Parsell. *Enchanted* is the better word to describe how I feel about the wonders of this new century. And I would be thrilled if you would allow me to witness this business with the oboes."

Mr. Ritchie followed his request with a laugh. Nonetheless, I believe I saw him wince slightly when Vera answered it by raising her beer to him.

•

That evening, shortly before sunset, the three of us gathered at the plot of land in question. The damage of the last fire had been mostly cleared. Lingering scents of it, however, swirled among the breeze. It was an odd smell, curiously out-of-season—like an autumn leaf fire among the spring blossoms. A few blackened bricks and a pile of partly charred timber also remained. Vera examined them, glancing at me with pursed lips as if to suggest she had no notion of what she sought.

"I'm sorry that I neglected to bring you both chairs," Mr. Ritchie said.

"Chairs?" Vera scanned the premises as she spoke. "Miss Parsell and I shall have to wander a good deal, sounding our oboes in search of the violet holes."

"But thank you kindly for the thought, sir," I added. Tempering Vera's practicality with politeness had become second nature to me.

In fact, Mr. Ritchie began directing his conversation to *me* as we watched the red sun sinking. "We're close to where the Monongahela and Allegheny Rivers merge into the Ohio. We're likely to get a bit of a fog as the air cools. I've got a couple of blankets in the coach. Do let me know if you'd like me to fetch them for you ladies."

I thanked him again while Vera silently strolled off, presumably searching for something worth finding. I sensed that Mr. Ritchie found Vera off-putting. This was often the case with those who met her, men in particular. I suggested we go ahead and light the lanterns we had waiting as the sun had now touched the horizon.

Once dark enough, Vera returned to tell us it was time. We had performed the procedure enough to know that she would play B-flat on one oboe while I sustained a high G on another. As crickets began to chirp and stars began to twinkle, we roamed across the property, calling out our harmonious whine. Despite this drone, our client followed behind us faithfully. Being without an instrument to blow allowed him to more easily twist his head in various directions, seeking the luminescent haloes.

At least a full hour had passed without result. As Mr. Ritchie had predicted, a chilly fog had developed. In addition, my breathing revealed my exhaustion, and I saw that Vera was in the same state. Finally, she touched my arm to indicate it was time to stop.

Vera turned around and said, "While your problem *might* be a supernatural one, Mr. Ritchie, it appears to be beyond our knowledge to investigate it further. We've seen no glowing circles. I assume that, even from your vantage point, neither have you?"

Mr. Ritchie's shoulders slumped. "Sadly, the closest thing to glowing circles that I saw was that swarm of fireflies."

I began to say, "I'm terribly sorry that we weren't able to—"

"*Swarm* of fireflies?" Vera interrupted. "As a girl, I was quite adept at catching fireflies. Unless those in New York State are very different from those here in Pennsylvania, fireflies do not *swarm.*"

"I wouldn't know what else to call it," Mr. Ritchie replied. "I only glimpsed them briefly, but their glow was decidedly not violet."

"It is unfortunate," I resumed, "that our efforts proved—"

"Fireflies *swarming,*" Vera pondered aloud. "What color *was* the glow?"

"The typical yellowish gold. And the shape was the typical single dot, not a circle. I would have mentioned it otherwise."

After a brief hesitation, I inhaled and then said, "Unless Vera believes we should investi—"

"We should investigate this further," she declared. "If we don't, it will nag at me all the way back to Chicago. Where did you see these fireflies, sir?"

He pointed, and Vera pulled me by the elbow in that direction. Once we arrived, she nodded. With renewed vigor, she bellowed her B-flat. I managed to draw in enough air to resume my high G. Mr. Ritchie surveyed the area and then suddenly pointed again. This time, I also saw the deep yellow lights—but they glowed only so long as we played our two notes. Those were no *fireflies!*

Vera warned Mr. Ritchie against getting too close. She then resumed playing her oboe and led us toward them. The points of light slowly grew into wobbling circles. Vera began trotting, somehow continuing to blow her oboe. I did my best to follow, and Mr. Ritchie charged before us. When he had gotten several yards ahead, he spun around.

"It's a *mix!*" he shouted. "Violet rings splotched with yellow! Up close, it's a dingy, almost sickly yellow! But it still overpowers the violet, especially at a distance! I can't see the stars through them—only empty darkness! Come quickly! They're *enchanting!*"

•

Riding Mr. Ritchie's private coach back to the hotel, Vera reminded him that the phenomenon we had witnessed resulted, not from ghosts themselves, but from strong feelings of guilt. When intense, this emotion opens passageways to the spiritual dimension, permitting ghostly interaction but not ensuring it. She cautioned that the fires might not have a supernatural source. Instead, she suspected an arsonist was at work, and we should seek one riddled by guilt.

"Good gracious," Mr. Ritchie bemoaned. "Why might someone want to keep that *one* plot of land open? Is there—is some poor soul *buried* there? I can imagine a man, one who committed a crime of passion, being now driven to commit *further* crimes! Forgive me, ladies, but perhaps a man murdered his own *wife!*" He shuddered.

Vera stared out the coach window. "To discover the roost," she said, "it's better to follow the whole flock than to try to focus on a single bird."

In response to Mr. Ritchie's knit brow, I clarified, "General speculation can guide us. Overly *specific* speculation can mislead us." I saw him nod. "Do you happen to know, sir, how much time passed between the burning of the livery and the destruction of your own buildings?"

Vera continued to watch the passing scenery, but I noticed she turned her ear slightly toward us.

"Believe me," Mr. Ritchie answered, "I've had these fires well researched. They've been occurring for more than a decade. The liveryman held onto the land several years, hoping to rebuild. He was unable to raise the funds, though, and eventually sold it to the barrel man. After *that* fire, the reputation of the place made selling difficult. Plenty of other land nearby for sale, after all. I've had ownership for a bit more than two years now."

I continued, "Could guilt drive someone to commit arson for more than a decade? I suppose so, but the pangs of guilt do generally subside with time."

"Those punctures between the dimensions," said Mr. Ritchie, turning to Vera, "do *they* also subside? The mix of purple and yellow reminded me of a bruise healing."

Vera glanced at Mr. Ritchie. "That we do not know," she said. "But I believe Lucille is suggesting that the source of the fire is on the spiritual side rather than the physical. Let's put our remorseful arsonist aside for a moment. Did your research include what had been done with the land *prior* to that first known fire, the one that destroyed the livery?"

"I'm afraid not. I only know that, long ago, Fort Pitt stood nearby." He smiled at the sudden tilt of my head. "Yes, it was named for same man for whom Pittsburg is named. The fort itself vanished long ago, but it played a key role in the English securing the region from the Indians not long before the Revolutionary War. The French had originally built a fort there, but that had been destroyed in *their* battle with the English. I don't wish to alarm you, but quite a lot of blood was shed on those grounds."

"Alarming, to be sure," I said, "but please go on."

"I don't know the details. I can only recall the outlines from a series of articles written by a local history buff named Vitellius Berry. How's *that* for a moniker? Miss Van Slyke, you'll be interested to know he's some kind of editor at the newspaper that ran the articles. I'll be sure to send over his workplace address by tomorrow morning. I must warn you, though, this Berry's a bit of a character."

"How so?" asked Vera.

"Well, he leads a campaign to restore the original spelling of Pittsburg." Mr. Ritchie laughed. "He feels that pinning the 'h' back onto the end honors our forebears. Personally, I think the new spelling looks more modern—more *efficient.*"

"Indeed, it does," I commented.

Vera grinned at us both, though not in a very convincing way. She then silently watched the scenery again until we arrived at the hotel.

•

The next morning, a note from Mr. Ritchie guided us to the offices of *The Pittsburg Daily Canvas.* Once arrived, we were told that Vitellius Berry could usually be found in the archives room in the cellar. Indeed, we discovered him blissfully cracking pecans while confirming facts amid dusty, dimly lit shelves filled with past issues of the newspaper. Mr. Berry was a small man, whose high voice and high forehead somehow seemed perfectly suited to the high stacks of local history wherein he dwelled.

As soon as Vera introduced herself as a journalist from Chicago, the two acted like childhood sweethearts reunited. He spoke of his envy of the great newspapers in Chicago. She suggested he consider relocating there. He insisted he could never leave his home. If she could leave New York City, Vera retorted, he could leave Pittsburg. Mr. Berry regretted he was too old. She called that nonsense, adding that his face glowed with the gusto of youth. He blushed. She told him he was blushing. They giggled together.

Finally, Vera noticed me waiting. She said, "I neglected to introduce my personal assistant, Lucille Parsell. Now, uh, Lucille? What was it we came to ask Mr. Berry?"

"If he knew of any history of the general region where Fort Pitt stood that might pertain to a series of fires," I reminded her. "Especially any old, unsolved crimes."

Vera turned toward Mr. Berry, who remained quiet. His eyes slowly drifted to the left. His head began to lean to the right. It occurred to me that he might be about to faint, but I was unable to anticipate which direction he might fall.

He then suddenly restored his posture. "You mean those two fires that occurred on the property purchased by J. Horace Ritchie, I venture. Yes, that land *is* near where Fort Pitt stood. But—but a *connection* between the two? Fort Pitt didn't burn. It *decayed*. And—and how would an unsolved crime figure in?"

Vera recounted what we knew. In telling the story, she also mentioned that, though we were familiar with violet-edged holes being produced by strong guilt, we had never before seen them tainted by yellow splotches.

"Yellow splotches?" Mr. Berry thrust his tongue out between his lips, just enough to taste the air. He appeared to be unsure if he approved of its flavor.

"How was it Mr. Ritchie described them?" Vera asked me.

"I believe he called them a *dingy* yellow. He used the word *sickly*, too."

Still tasting the air, Mr. Berry repeated his exercise in counterbalance. His eyes went left, and his head went right. Vera looked at me and nodded excitedly to show that she thought we were on the brink of an important revelation. I fear I must have expressed greater trepidation regarding this man who lurked in history's cellar.

Mr. Berry again snapped upright. "Francis Parkman! In one of his better books, he writes about the efforts of the English to protect Fort Pitt from Indian attack. There were *letters.* Letters written in the 1760s. Letters passed between Colonel Henry Bouquet and Sir Jeffery Amherst, Commander-in-Chief."

"You're able to *remember* those names?" Vera marveled. "More importantly, what has this to do with the color yellow?"

"No!" Mr. Berry shouted. "Not the *yellow!* The *sickly* yellow! In these letters, Bouquet and Amherst discuss ways to combat the Delawares and neighboring tribes by infecting blankets—blankets they would offer to the enemy—*after* they were infected." And there he stopped.

Vera turned to me, silently seeking clarification.

All I could do was to ask, "Blankets infected with *what,* Mr. Berry?"

"Smallpox," he answered. "Bouquet and Amherst discussed using smallpox as a weapon to kill the Indian warriors."

Vera cleared her throat before adding, "Along with their women."

"*And* their children," I said.

Mr. Berry said, "One can see *that* as a crime, I venture! A crime of *war!* Parkman suggests as much in his book. But—but he also makes it clear that Bouquet and Amherst saw it as merely clearing the woods of ferocious beasts. Wolves or bears."

"So the two officers would not have suffered any guilt over infecting their adversaries with a deadly disease?" Vera inquired.

Mr. Berry nodded. "But—but the letters only speak of them entertaining the idea, not actually going through with it."

"Even if they had," I mentioned, "who would have felt guilty about it? Certainly, not the victims."

"There might be nothing here. Forgetting the color's association with sickliness, Mr. Berry, do any other crimes come to mind that might pertain to our investigation? Possibly something more recent?"

I feared he would repeat his routine of moving his eyes and head in opposite directions, but after a momentary glare, Mr. Berry told us that nothing came to mind. He offered to look into the matter, however.

"You are a kind man, sir," Vera said with uncharacteristic graciousness. "Nonetheless, I wonder if you might remind me of that author you mentioned. I do so like being thorough about such matters."

"I'm exactly the same way, Miss Van Slyke! Let me jot down his name along with the book's title for you. Or—or I could lend you *my* copy! It's not the kind of book one finds on the shelf of a corner shop, I venture."

A lingering smile passed between the two of them. I chose to wait in the hallway until they had finished their transaction.

•

On our third afternoon in Pittsburg, Vera arranged for another experiment to be performed on the property where the series of fires had occurred. Mr. Ritchie was in attendance, but he appeared a tad discomforted when Vera informed him that Mr. Berry would also be joining us. She assured our client that the historian might prove to be of assistance, adding that his help had already been vital in the development of the theory she wished to test. She raised Mr. Berry's copy of Francis Parkman's *The Conspiracy of Pontiac and the Indian War after the Conquest of Canada* as if it were evidence in court.

"I regret to inform you, Mr. Ritchie, that this tract of land harbors a terrible secret. I take you back to July of 1763." She opened the volume to a bookmarked page. "In addition to being under threat of Indian attack, smallpox broke out at Fort Pitt. Sir Jeffery Amherst wrote to Colonel Henry Bouquet, and in his postscript asks if they could devise a way—and I quote—'to send the Small Pox among those disaffected tribes of Indians'."

Mr. Ritchie's expression remained rigid. However, his neck muscles clenched, and he swallowed hard.

Vera continued, "The Colonel wrote back to say that he would attempt the plan, adding that he would — again I quote — 'take care not to get the disease myself.' Now, pay close attention to the very next line. Bouquet says that 'it is a pity to expose good men against them.' In other words, he would order his soldiers to collect and deliver the blankets. Here, I think, we see the root of those dimensional ruptures!"

"The guilt!" a high voice exclaimed. "It was Bouquet's!"

The three of us spun around to see that Mr. Berry had quietly joined us. His enthusiastic grin quickly fell.

"Apologies," he muttered. "I didn't wish to interrupt, Miss Van Slyke. But — but that *is* your theory, I venture. That Bouquet executed the plan. That he became wracked by guilt when his soldiers contracted the disease lurking in the blankets they had been ordered to deliver."

Vera tilted her head. "The thought actually hadn't occurred to me. Very astute, but it doesn't account for the fires. No, to explain the guilt, one must explain the burning."

"The blankets," said Mr. Ritchie. "It's common practice to *burn* infected blankets. But who would have felt *guilty* burning blankets infected with small pox?"

Vera looked at all three of us, one by one.

She then explained, "The soldiers! The soldiers commanded to deliver them to the enemy." She nodded slowly and then held up the history book. "The plan was 'detestable' and 'shameful,' according to our author. Those poor soldiers probably thought the same, especially given that it put their lives at risk!"

"And — and yet, doesn't Parkman say that smallpox did indeed spread through the Indian tribes?" Mr. Berry gently took the book from Vera and turned to the next page. He read, "'There is no direct evidence that Bouquet carried into effect the shameful plan of infecting the Indians though, a few months after, the smallpox was known to have made havoc of the tribes of the Ohio.'"

Vera retorted, "Exactly why we proceed on a *theory*. Perhaps some blankets *were* delivered. Perhaps whatever had brought smallpox to Fort Pitt also brought it to those tribes. But we must account for both the guilt *and* the fires. Now, how does one burn blankets? Can you heap them up into a pile and drop a match on them?"

"Precisely so," said Mr. Berry with a confident bow.

Mr. Ritchie rolled his eyes before saying, "Blankets *smother* fires. To burn one, it must be exposed to plenty of oxygen. It helps to hang it over something, almost like drying laundry."

"And something to hang it over appeared each time construction began," Vera said. "Let me show you how it works. Mr. Berry, would you kindly help me stack some of those salvaged timbers? We'll need to arrange them with gaps to ensure airflow. I'm hoping our ghosts will find them of use."

Mr. Ritchie took a step to join them, but I tugged his sleeve. He seemed to understand the meaning of my nod toward Vera and Mr. Berry.

As we watched them work, Mr. Ritchie asked me, "Do you really think the ghosts have been waiting for close to a century and a half to reenact their disobeying orders?"

"A crime concealed can fester," I told him. "The yellow splotches might be a symptom of this. And, if I've learned anything from my time spent with Vera—uh, Miss Van Slyke—it is that ghosts manifest in a *multitude* of ways. Some are fully conscious beings, but other hauntings seem more like echoes. Traumatic events echoing over and over in the very place they originally occurred."

"I see. I do see. But how does one *end* such an echo?" His brow rippled. "Will I *never* be allowed to build my telephone factory?"

I grinned at his comment. "Think of it as someone using a telephone to share some dire news, but no one at the other end responds. The telephone user tries and tries and tries. Sometimes, the way to end such an echo—is simply to *listen* to it."

Like a bud opening, Mr. Ritchie's look of worry transformed into his more familiar expression of enchantment. He laughed and shook his head. This same jubilance remained until we went over to examine what Vera and Mr. Berry had cobbled together. It struck me as a makeshift corral for no more than three or four chickens. Very lackadaisical chickens, too, since the waist-high stack of timbers was held together only by its own weight.

However, it was solid enough to remain standing as we stared at it.

We waited.

And the wait was not a long one. A gasp from Vera drew our attention. She pointed to a wisp of smoke rising from one of the boards. Mr. Berry spotted the next thin plume, and I signaled yet another. Mr. Ritchie's search for the next one was thwarted when Vera drew our attention. She pointed to a spot where a flame had erupted, small but *growing*. Nothing visible could explain what had started the fire. New flames began to spot all along the timbers. They spread and flared. In no more than five minutes, the entire construction was ablaze.

Vera began to roam. She looked neither at the fire nor at anyone *in the flesh*. Instead, she looked up, over, and all about. Clearly unsure of where to face, she began to speak loudly. "You are recognized! We know about the plan to bring blankets to the Indians!"

Vera jumped back when a sudden burst of flame roared. Now, she seemed to be back among the living as she looked at me with wide eyes.

"Gentlemen," she stated matter-of-factly, "would one of you be so kind as to smother the ember that has started to burn my assistant's skirt? I've grown very fond of her."

The bearded man rushed to his knees beside me and, slapping the material in front of my calf, extinguished a fiery-orange oval enlarging there. I hadn't noticed the danger until Vera's mention of it. Rather than thank my rescuer, I stared at him. I felt him walk me backward a few steps. As if hypnotized, I then swiveled my gaze back to Vera.

Again facing random spaces, she resumed addressing the spirits. "We know those blankets were infected with smallpox!"

The flames flared higher and roared louder. One of the timbers fell and rolled a short way.

"Yes, we also know you *burned* the blankets instead of delivering them, disobeying orders!"

Suddenly, one side of the corral tumbled over as if it had been kicked. Vera had to lurch to the side, and Mr. Ritchie ran over to protect her. At the same moment, Mr. Berry scurried away, spinning back to face us once he was several yards from the flames.

I found myself unable to move at all. Despite my being a yard or two from the fire, its heat *felt* like hellish hands against my face. Vera glanced around with wide eyes. She wet her lips over and over, appearing lost in indecision. She must have summoned self-control, though, because she attempted to step forward. Mr. Ritchie quickly put a hand on her shoulder to prevent her from doing so. She gently removed his hand, holding it long enough to give him a pat of gratitude. She then turned back to the fire, stepping even closer to it.

"*And* we know that the orders you disobeyed—the action you were *commanded* to take—were *unworthy* of any soldier serving in His Majesty's military! We know that you followed a higher, nobler authority in burning those blankets! We know your choice was either to betray your *commander* or betray your *conscience.* And you made the better decision!"

Suddenly, I felt the heat against my face vanish. It was as if I had blundered into a spider's web covered with cool dew. Startled by the sensation, I realized I had raised my arms to ward off that moist web.

Vera concluded, "*That* is how we will tell your story!"

As if a mighty gust of wind had charged through or a torrent of water had gushed down, the flames suddenly disappeared. They were instantly extinguished, but neither wind nor water could explain it. Except for those that had already fallen, many of the boards remained stacked and balanced. Nothing *physical* had put out that fire.

Smoke still rose from the wood, though, and its pungency acted as a smelling salt, fully restoring my ability to move. I stepped beside Vera. As we stared at the ashes, listening to the cooling wood crackle, Mr. Ritchie touched our arms. The three of us glanced at one another but remained speechless. I barely noticed Mr. Berry slowly rejoin the group. He was hunched over, either from fear of what he had seen—or from shame for having fled.

At long last, Mr. Ritchie spoke. "Miss Van Slyke? May I buy you a beer?"

•

On the train back to Chicago, I asked Vera if she was convinced it would be safe for Mr. Ritchie to build on the land now.

"We won't know the answer to that until after construction is complete. *He* certainly seemed persuaded we had earned that second bank note," she said with a smirk. Switching to a squint, she then added, "But what is it you *truly* want to ask me?"

I chuckled. Vera had gotten to know me quite well. I wondered if our friendship *allowed* me to ask what I wanted, or if it was the very reason I should *not* ask it. I stammered, "Now—now, if you'd rather not speak of it, I'll understand. I'll understand completely! About that Mr. Berry. Mr. Vitellius Berry. I know that, at the fire, we saw a rather unmanly side of him."

Vera smiled more with her eyes than her lips. "Well, he had no vested interest in the situation. Putting distance between himself and that weird blaze was far more sensible than what *we* did, you know!"

"That's a charming way to see it. But afterward—at the tavern—" I took a deep breath. "When he asked if you would inquire about editorial opportunities in Chicago for him, why did you change your mind and discourage him from pursuing such a change? You do realize, I trust, that he wasn't actually asking about *editorial* possibilities."

Vera looked down, feigning interest in her fingernails. "I suspected that might've been the case," she said softly. "But I'd only met the man the day before! Can you blame me for telling him he was better off staying in Pittsburg? Besides, a historian could prove useful to a ghost investigator, as he did this time. It's likely he and I will be seeing each other again in the future." She peeked up at me and put a finger against her lips as if to stifle the grin growing there.

"Why, Vera Van Slyke!" I gasped. "I believe you're *blushing!*"

We giggled.

AN UNANCHORED MAN
(1903)

'Sir, in my heart there was a kind of fighting
That would not let me sleep; methought, I lay
Worse than the mutines in the bilboes.'

— *Hamlet*

The breadth of a book would be needed to properly recount the investigation of the Morley mansion haunting. Undoubtedly, it was the most complex and dangerous case that I shared with Vera Van Slyke to that date, which was October of 1903. In the wake of this adventure, however, Vera and I had an experience that, while less complicated, far better illustrates the remarkable *expanse* of the spirit dimension. As we were in Boston, we decided to take advantage of our nearness to Cape Cod and devote a week to relaxation. Few tourists remained in the seaside town of Granger, and I imagined its unoccupied beach would provide me with a tranquil setting for reading. True to her nature, Vera was more interested in the seafood—and the beer.

"I'm hoping we might hunt down some of this town's music, too," she said as we unpacked our bags in the hotel room. "These maritime towns are filled with local musicians who play rousing sea shanties and melancholy airs. It must be the Irish blood in me that explains my affection for such music."

Playfully, I grabbed a bedpost and steadied myself against it. "Mercy—I'm *shocked!*" I jested. "You've let slip something about your family!"

Vera tilted her head and stared. She then turned to me. "Have I never mentioned that my mother was Irish?"

I grinned. "Not in the four years that I've known you."

She resumed transferring her clothes to a dresser drawer. "About as Irish as they come, I'd say! As a young girl, she left County Sligo, fleeing the Great Famine. Met my father in upstate New York. At bedtime, she used to sing me the old songs."

"That's very sweet," I said, sitting on the edge of the bed. "Not everyone has a mother like that. Did she also tell you those ghost stories you said you loved as a girl?"

"You might think so, given how the Irish love a spooky yarn. But, no, I found those on my own. In fact, my mother admonished me regularly about what she called 'yar pookas an' yar bahnshees'."

I chuckled. "I shouldn't have brought it up. We're here to get *away* from our pookas and our banshees for a while."

Once unpacking was finished, we asked the hotel clerk where we might find some musical entertainment for the evening. We had missed the last of a series of band concerts held on the town common, he said. Scratching his neck, he added that amateur musicians sometimes gathered to imbibe and play together at a waterfront tavern called Scully's. The clerk suddenly straightened his posture and clarified that we should go there only if accompanied by men. He insisted that it was no place for two women traveling alone.

"*Two* women traveling *alone*, sir," snarled Vera, "is an error in basic mathematics! *Scully*, if I'm not mistaken, is an Irish name, suggesting this tavern is exactly the type of place I have in mind. You will write down the address, thank you kindly!"

Bowing in penitence, the clerk obeyed orders.

•

That evening, I learned the hotel clerk might have been doing the honorable thing by cautioning us against this establishment. It was located in a section of town rarely revealed to tourists, an area where the buildings gasped for paint and the railroad tracks beside them choked on high weeds. The tavern's interior was almost as unwelcoming. Granted, the darkly stained walls and the crisscrossed oars hanging on them had a certain rustic charm. Still, the few conversations being held by patrons ceased as we looked for a place to sit. We were silently observed as we chose one of the few tables in the place. Most of the customers sat upon stools along the bar, and they continued to gawk at us in that formation.

"What can I get you, ladies?" called the bartender. He was a burly man with a heavy, black beard. Nonetheless, his dapper vest and collar showed that he was no brute.

"Bring us two of your finest beers please," Vera returned. "Let's see if you New Englanders can brew an ale that's as hearty as the ones back in Chicago." She winked at me.

I very much hoped that Vera's friendly challenge would be received as more *friendly* than *challenge*. The bartender grinned, and the other patrons began to lose interest in us. I noticed then that one elderly gentleman had paid us no mind at all. He sat by himself at a rear table, facing the back wall. His sparse, white hair and lopsided slouch were the only bits of information he was divulging about himself.

"My brother runs cargo through Chicago," explained the barman with a fine, baritone voice. As he delivered our beers, he added, "Prefers the lakes to the oceans. He was always the dainty tea cup of the family, you see." His smirk revealed that he had accepted Vera's invitation to a verbal fencing match.

"I *do* see," Vera returned. "However, this establishment was recommended, not for what I would *see,* but for what I might *hear.* Is it true that there's a chance of some music being played at some point?"

"Oh, you flatter me! It's not often I get asked to take my concertina off the wall. If you're lucky, a few of my regulars will play louder on their own instruments. But none of them have arrived just yet."

The gentleman then introduced himself as Scully. It was a nickname he gave himself after—as he phrased it—"demolishing some very fine Harvard boys in a sculling race one weekend in Cambridge." When Vera inquired about his true name, he introduced himself as Marcelo Silva. I chuckled at Vera's pursed lips when Mr. Silva explained his ancestors had sailed from Portugal, not the Emerald Island.

"And as we're so cozy with one another now," Mr. Silva continued, "may I ask what brings you two landlubbers to the east?"

Perhaps I had been too eager to join in the conversation. "We came to investigate certain reports in Boston," I told him.

Mr. Silva cocked his head. "Reports about what?"

One by one, the patrons at the bar began to turn back to us, and I noticed Vera sigh.

In a flurry, I searched for a way to avoid the very subject that Vera and I had come here to escape. "Oh, uh. We. Well. We— investigate hauntings. Ghosts and that." I winced.

When I reopened my eyes, I was met with the blank faces and undivided attention of everyone at the bar. Indeed, Mr. Silva pulled over a chair and sat down. With a grin, Vera shrugged. I knew that I would have to relate the whole story of the haunting of the Morley mansion. Truth be told, I rather enjoyed the intrigue I stirred in my audience, who inched closer and closer during my narrative. The stupefied silence following my finale was more gratifying than applause. I had even managed to get a few backward glances from the elderly man so determined to avoid being disturbed.

Though there was much debate over the veracity of my tale, Vera and I became the guests of honor. We were treated to more beers than I care to admit. Once the bartender's musical "regulars" arrived, we were granted an evening of rousing sea shanties and melancholy airs. The small crowd escorted us safely back to our hotel, much to the consternation of the same desk clerk who had regretted ever mentioning the place to us.

•

The following morning, I awoke with a headache. Vera suggested we enjoy some ocean air, and we went to the shore fronting the hotel. She wandered off to seek low-tide treasures while I remained sitting on the hotel veranda to read. My novel, though, turned out to be frustratingly jumbled and broody. A young man with dreams of going to sea finds work on a whaler, one whose capricious captain is driven by extracting revenge against the sea beast who lost him his leg. Instead, I had been hoping for swashbuckling pirates in pursuit of hidden jewels. My eyes drifted from the pages to the waves.

And I *jolted* when a scratchy voice blasted beside me.

"What potions have I drunk of Siren tears," snarled a white-bearded man. Though he chortled, his scarcity of teeth failed to add much whimsy to the odd comment.

First, I realized that the reference to a siren had been directed to me. Next, I recognized the man from his sideways slouch. He stood as if he were a sack of grain that someone had barely managed to balance upright.

I said, "You startled me, sir! Aren't you the—uh—the *gentlemen* who drank alone—uhm—who was with us at Scully's last evening?"

He nodded. "That was myself, missy—but there's no need to be startled," he said, the soft *r* in his last word revealing a strong New England accent. "I'm not much for manners, I s'pose. It's just—I'm curious about that experience ya spoke of. The ghosts there in Boston. I come by to tell ya—that is—I wanted ya to know—" He stopped there and suddenly looked down at his boots.

As he was not sitting down, I thought it best to join him standing. I asked, "To know *what*, sir?"

He looked up, and my new position allowed me to see that his eyes were dim with age. The dark, deep-wrinkled frames around those eyes implied it was not *time* but *experience* that accounted for his state of physical collapse.

"To know that I believe ya. I believe that ya tangled with ghosts up there." He nodded again. "I believe because I myself have ghosts. The marauders come *charging* through my cottage some nights. Lately, it's been *all* nights, and that's why ya found me out among folks. Drive me out of my own bed, they do! I come looking to see if ya got some incantation or such to send 'em back into the sea." Slowly, he nodded yet again.

Something about his demeanor gave me a chill. I snapped shut my book, startling myself again in the process. "Well, the woman you saw me with last night is the one to consult. She's the expert. I simply assist." I smiled as best I could.

I waved and called to Vera, perhaps with more urgency than was polite. She waved back and began to tromp through the sand toward us. I was both dismayed and pleased that she did not take the time to put her shoes back on her feet.

The man beside me rubbed his pocked nose and then looked down at his boots again. He muttered, "I ain't like that fella in your tale of the mansion. I ain't a millionaire."

The obviousness of this fact evoked a pang of sympathy in me. "You needn't worry about paying us. If Miss Van Slyke feels she can help, she will do so. My name is Lucille Parsell. And how shall I introduce you?"

Once Vera arrived, I introduced her to Captain Henry Thorn Lord. I glimpsed her lips tighten instantly upon hearing his professional title. Rigidly, she offered her hand. She then remained silent. As the captain seemed unpracticed in social amenities, I told Vera what little I knew about his haunted cottage. I emphasized how his ghosts *charged* around the place, even chasing him out, and I suggested to Vera that this might be our first chance to witness what Catherine Crowe terms a poltergeist in her famous guide to ghosts.

"Well, then," Vera replied, "the case is certainly of interest. Shall we discuss the details over lunch? I'm told there's a lovely restaurant just across the—"

"I ain't hungry," Captain Lord interrupted bluntly. These were the first words he spoke to her. Clearly, he was unaware of the danger of keeping Vera Van Slyke from her lunch.

She merely raised her eyebrows, however. After slowly smoothing one of those eyebrows with her little finger, Vera said,

"We can as easily begin our inquiry here." She sat down on the veranda railing.

I considered resuming my seat, but as the captain remained standing, I felt I should, too. Though it was entirely likely that our new client's refusal of lunch was more a matter of finance than appetite, his unapologetic manner had been nonetheless disconcerting. I discreetly slid closer to Vera.

"Lucille says your ghosts charge through your cottage? Are they visible, then?"

"No, can't see 'em. But ya feel 'em shaking the floor like one of those earthquakes out on the West Coast. Knock the lamps over, they do, and shake the dust from the rafters. Even a chain of trolling hooks I had fixed firm above my fireplace come down!"

"And this occurs randomly rather than, say, only on windy nights?" asked Vera.

"Ain't a single natch'ral explanation for it," the captain lamented. "As I asked the missy here, I'm hoping ya have a spell to drive 'em back to the sea. I'm fond of the little cottage. Think of it as my final port and that."

"There are no magical spells for evicting ghosts, Mr. Lord, but we might be able to help you. I have one pivotal question, though. Throughout your sailing career, were you primarily a fisherman — or did you transport cargo? If the latter, was your cargo ever of *African* origin and sold at *auction?*"

Despite our time together, Vera still managed to befuddle me with some of the initial questions she asked our clients. Regardless, they frequently came to pertain directly to the heart of the haunting. In fact, this question clearly held particular meaning for Captain Lord. For the first time, he looked directly into Vera's eyes.

"I know full well what ya're asking, madam. I'm an old man, but surely ya don't think me old enough to have imported *slaves* from Africa! I'd wager a month's salary ya haven't even a notion when such practice was deemed *illegal!*"

"1808," Vera returned with a brittle tone. "Of course, *smuggling* followed after that. But I was referring to shipping slaves from, say,

Virginia down to Louisiana, a practice that ended roughly forty years ago. Seamen generally begin their careers as young men, Mr. Lord—and you are clearly a man who's seen at least seven decades go by."

A sneer came to the captain's grisly face. "Sure enough, back during my apprentice days, I bunked with those who had sailed on slavers. From the very start, though, I worked solely on *fishing* boats, madam!" His hand was rising and taking the form of a fist. "It's a chain of *trolling hooks* I said fell from my wall—no chain of *manacles*, madam!" He struck his fist into his palm.

Though my breath stopped and my neck clenched, Vera remained calm. She merely stared back into Captain Lord's glaring eyes.

"As such, we shall take your case, Mr. Lord," she said at last. "Lucille and I will visit you this evening if you jot down the location for us. Come, we'll find paper and pen inside the lobby."

The captain complied with Vera's instructions and departed without another word.

•

Vera and I lunched at the Granger Galley, a cozy eatery whose tablecloths and drapes were embroidered with seashells and sandpipers. The black-haired proprietress put down her newspaper with a smile, laughing at our being her only customers since the *one* at breakfast. The menu, which changed daily, was confined to a chalkboard. Vera ordered the cod, and I surrendered to the scent of chowder wafting from the kitchen.

I also surrendered to a nagging curiosity once our hostess left us alone. "1808," I began, "I didn't know that bringing slaves from Africa was outlawed at such an early date."

"You wouldn't have need to know such a thing," Vera replied a bit snappishly.

"And you *do?*"

Vera looked back at the chalkboard before saying, "I should have asked if I could get lemon with my cod."

I took a less leisurely approach. "Why did you ask Captain Lord if he had been involved in the slave trade?"

"Oh, the usual matter about guilt," she replied, turning back in my general direction. "Guilt and ghosts swirl together in all of our cases. I wondered if our ancient mariner might be reflecting back over his life. What *other* past sins might stab at the conscience of a seaman of his generation?" She snatched the saltshaker to examine it more closely.

"I doubt that someone engaged in slavery is capable of feeling much guilt about it. Your question was so distinctive that I wonder if it might have sprung from your *own* concerns." I watched my friend pour a small amount of salt into her palm and taste it. It was my turn to be snappish. "Come now, Vera, it's a *saltshaker*. Tip it, and *salt* comes out."

She inhaled deeply, returned the shaker to its place, and exhaled slowly. "There is a reason that I so seldom speak of my family. Yes. You are correct about the question having less to do with this sea captain. More to do with—with my own concerns."

This was a side of Vera that I had rarely witnessed. I spoke with greater compassion than I think I had ever shown her previously. "Vera, you and I have been through quite a lot together. Don't you know that I—"

She cut me off, confessing, "My grandfather was a sea captain, too. He shipped slaves on that route between Virginia and Louisiana. A shameful thing, and it seems to have clouded my questioning of this fellow. I've never been at ease around men of his profession, but he claims to be a different sort of sailor. A fisherman. So let us not be weepy women, and instead consider this business of ghostly 'marauders' with clear heads."

Despite her quick evasion, I considered this one of the most intimate moments I had ever shared with Vera. Of course, I strongly suspected there was *more* to this family history than she was telling. However, as she once said, a crack in the egg today can, with time, become a roasted goose.

"He said something curious," Vera continued. "He said he wished we could magically drive these ghosts *back to the sea.* Yet nothing else in his story suggested they would have *come* from there. Why does he fancy these to be *briny* ghosts?"

"Crew members lost while hauling in the catch?" I offered.

"No guilt in that."

"But if they served him well?"

"These men have a way of hardening to the risks involved. Even those on the Great Lakes are far from *dainty tea cups,* despite what Mr. Scully suggested. Or—what was his name?"

"Mr. Silva," I answered. The image of this hefty, affable gentleman inspired an idea I knew Vera might not like. "It occurs to me that Mr. Silva knows this town—and probably Captain Lord—far better than we do. And the captain—did he strike you as a bit *unsavory?* Might it be wise—or *warranted*—to ask Mr. Silva to accompany—"

Vera again interrupted, "Mr. Silva strikes me as a man who would be game for some ghost hunting. It's a small town. Quite likely, this woman fixing our meal would know how we can contact him and extend the invitation."

"As our thank-you for the music last evening?" I added.

Vera winked. "Yes! Of course! For the *music,*" so she said.

•

Indeed, the restaurateur knew how we could reach Mr. Silva during the day. He promptly informed us he could easily find a substitute bartender and would be delighted to join our investigation. The captain's cottage was in a lonely spot, Mr. Silva explained, and the way to it was too rough for a buggy. He gave us the option of, in his words, "surf or saddle." Vera and I both eagerly chose his rowing us rather than our riding horses. We met at the wharf an hour before dusk.

The sea was calm during our short voyage, but Vera and I huddled against one another for warmth. We distracted ourselves from the cold air by engaging our companion in conversation. Before long, Mr. Silva recounted a romance about the woman who convinced him to leave the sea behind. The story ended as a tragedy, though, when he spoke of her succumbing to diphtheria just a year or so before its antitoxin became widely known.

"I take comfort in the notion that she's now an angel," Mr. Silva concluded, letting the oars drift. He then resumed rowing more vigorously. "On the other hand, I *refuse* to think of her as a ghost. I confess, ladies, that I'm a bit of a skeptic when it comes to the dead rattling chains or carrying their heads tucked underneath their arms."

"Certainly, the woman you describe awaits you in heaven," I said. "But the *magnitude* of the afterlife is very much a mystery—perhaps especially to those of us who investigate it! I'm inclined to think that there's room enough there for both angels *and* ghosts."

"Quite true," Vera affirmed. "The sheer variety of ghosts we've encountered suggests almost unlimited possibilities in the spirit realm. For example, prior to this case, I'd never heard of ghosts that *stampede!* On this topic, Mr.—uhm, let's say I call you *Scully*—what do you know about our client? Is there anything in Mr. Lord's past that might plague him now with a guilty conscience?"

"I know nothing about his past. All I know is that doing business with him is like scraping barnacles. Takes determination! At times, he'll tense his muscles as if he's readying to throw a punch. Always walks off before he does so, though. That seems like a sign of a man trying to do the *right* thing."

"Or hoping to not repeat a past crime?" Vera suggested.

I worried that Vera's ill feelings toward sea captains might incline her to make unfair judgments. I attempted to change the subject. "The captain mentioned that he had trolling hooks draped above his mantle. This struck me as odd, but I'm a landlubber, as you say, Mr. Silva. *Is* that odd?"

He laughed. "Wish I could blame you landlubbers for that, Miss Parsell, but we do it ourselves, too. Funny thing, turning tools of the sailing trades into decorations. Lighthouses, anchors, even buoys and lobster traps. The old skipper is likely trying to put a smidgeon of beauty in his life by hanging that line of hooks in his parlor. Kind of like a strand of garland."

"Well," I said, "that somehow makes him seem even lonelier. More sympathetic."

I feared Vera might disagree with this comment. However, she peacefully surveyed the passing shore for the rest of our ride. The town had given way to untamed coastline, and the few leaves remaining on the scattered trees blazed a bloody red as the sun was beginning to touch the treetops. In this ruddy and slanted light, I recognized Captain Lord's lopsided figure waiting for us on a pier in the distance.

It was the very same moment that I felt the hard prod of my own foolishness. "Good heavens, Vera!" I cried. "The oboes! I forgot the *oboes!*"

Vera glanced rapidly around the boat before saying, "Well, this is unfortunate. But don't let it upset you, my dear. We *both* forgot the oboes. Understandably so. We came to Cape Cod for leisure, not for work."

"Oboes?" Mr. Silva inquired. "Should I have brought along my concertina?"

Vera explained, "The oboes help to confirm that we're dealing with the supernatural. Nonetheless, should Mr. Lord's ghosts come charging, no doubt *that* will serve as ample evidence. It *is* sad you didn't bring your concertina, though. We might have to spend quite a while waiting for something to happen."

My chagrin over the oboes had eased by the time we reached the pier, though being back in the company of Captain Lord produced a feeling worse still. All without uttering a word, he caught the rope thrown by Mr. Silva, secured the boat, and helped Vera and me out. The sandy slope up to the cottage was long, and I noticed that the path had been outlined with driftwood. Clearly, the reclusive captain did have a sense of décor, humble though it was.

The cottage was well-weathered but picturesque. The moment we stepped inside, Vera halted. She grasped my arm.

"The oboes are expendable," she said, "but now we've lost our bartender!"

True enough, our escort was no longer with us. Vera shot a cold glance at the captain before she turned to check outside. I tilted my head and grinned at our host. He resumed his habit of examining his footwear. Pardoning myself, I quickly joined Vera.

Mr. Silva was a few yards off the path, standing in a patch of grassy sand beside the cottage. "Spotted something unusual over here!" he called to us. "It's a fluke!"

"This entire case is the *result* of a fluke," Vera said as she strolled to the spot.

"I mean a whale fluke! Well, the *marks* of one—or maybe of a *few*," Mr. Silva said. "An easy way to tell whales from fish is the hind flippers. On fish, they go up-and-down like a rudder. On whales, they're flat as a pancake, and they're called flukes. They would leave a print looking very much like this." He waved us closer and then squatted down.

Though the fading light made them difficult to discern, winding impressions were scattered in the sand. Mr. Silva used his hands and arms to show the lengths of each print, and there surely did seem to be a single pattern to each.

Captain Lord came toward us, revealing the difficulty he had walking in sand. He scolded, "The ghosts strike *within* the cottage!"

"Of course," replied Mr. Silva. "But have you noticed these prints? I was just saying they resemble the marks beached whales would make. Same prints left by those blackfish that beached themselves."

"Black*fish?*" I asked.

"They're a kind of whale, despite the name. A whole school of them were stranded on a beach not too far from here just last year."

"Aw, ya're talking like a lunatic!" returned the captain. "The tide don't come this far for 'em to have left such marks. And where are the carcasses? Or the *stench?*"

"I'm not saying they *are* actual fluke prints," Mr. Silva insisted. "I'm saying there's a *resemblance!*"

Vera pressed two fingers against the side of her jaw. She wandered off a few steps, apparently to contemplate what this meant.

"Come help me build a fire, son," said Captain Lord, assuming an unexpectedly congenial tone. "The night brings a mighty chill this time of year."

As the gentlemen and I started for the door again, Vera remained where she was, gazing at the prints in the sand. I called to her, but it seemed as if my words flittered like moths. Finally, she turned to me. She dropped her fingers slowly from her jaw and then ambled back to the cottage door.

If Vera were theorizing in the direction that I suspected she might be, we were likely to have a difficult time ahead of us—not just in dealing with stampeding spirits—but also in convincing our companions of the origins of those spirits.

The interior of the captain's cottage was spare but not uncomfortable. A patchwork of burlap squares did the work of a rug. A magazine illustration of a medieval castle was tacked to the wall, an ancient fortress curiously at odds with this nautical surrounding. A broken flowerpot on the single, small table revealed how the captain's attempt to beautify the place had been dashed by his supernatural intruders. I noticed the chain of large fishhooks glimmering above the fire the men built. The flames grew, and the various signs of loneliness were cast into shadow as the four faces there now became highlighted.

Vera requested that a lantern be set beside the door, explaining it might prove useful should we need to flee the violent manifestation. With that in place, we gathered chairs by the hearth. Either out of deference or discomfort, Captain Lord sat on a stool several feet removed from the warmth of the fireplace. Leaning against the wall, he lit a pipe, which I suspected was his means to avoid conversation.

Vera also remained silent. Mr. Silva and I chatted about how whales, being mammals, suckle their young and surface in order to breathe. We meandered through other topics: oboes and concertinas, the novel that had disappointed me that morning, and the linguistic nuances distinguishing New England from the Middle West. As often occurs in such situations, there was a moment of quiet during which we all stared into the fire.

"Whales that *beached* themselves?"

Vera asked this as a casual rejoinder to some topic just discussed, but at least an *hour* had passed since Mr. Silva had mentioned the beached blackfish when describing those curious prints in the sand. It took a moment before our new friend grasped her meaning. Luckily, his sails caught wind, and he moved forward.

"Ah, yes! Last year! A whole school stranded itself onshore. The oddest thing, but there's a long history of these beachings. The poor creatures come close to the shoals, probably to feed, and the tide goes out, leaving them to perish onshore. It's almost as if they forget they belong in the sea."

"And yet I once heard whales described as intelligent creatures," Vera commented.

"Now, that's the very *thing* of it!" Mr. Silva exclaimed.

Vera quickly raised a finger to her lips, bidding Mr. Silva to hush. She pointed to Captain Lord, who had extinguished his pipe and was now dozing against the wall. As he had endured several restless nights, it seemed best that we let him sleep. Mr. Silva turned from that direction back to Vera with a smile and a nod.

"That's the very thing of it," he repeated in a whisper. "Whales *are* smart. I've heard tell of a crew who harpooned a bull, which then sounded. Once it resurfaced, they discovered that a cow alongside it had *bitten* on the rope to free her mate. And one of my regulars at the bar swears they're clairvoyant! If one whale is under attack, others somehow know it and either flee or even *come to its aid!*"

"Might this response be the result of the attacked whale thrashing and splashing in the water?" Vera asked, keeping her own voice quiet.

Mr. Silva moved his head from side to side. "The others will sometimes be too far away to hear any splashing. If it's any sound at all, more likely it's the *singing* of the whales."

"Whales are very smart indeed if they've mastered the art of song," I said, suspecting that Mr. Silva might be making sport of us.

"Not singing in *that* sense exactly," he replied. "It's more of a deep-base warble. I've heard it described it as the groan of Goliath as he fell."

Exactly then, as if cued by a symphony conductor, the poker leaning against the fireplace began to clatter. We noticed that the bricks supporting it were vibrating. The rattling poker suddenly fell with a clang. The three of us could only look at one another dumbly.

Our attention was then pulled toward a new sound. Captain Lord began to mutter inarticulately, though every other sign told us he remained sleeping.

"As I had expected," Vera said softly as she rose from her chair, "something haunts this old salt in his dreams as well as in his cottage. Something shameful enough to rupture the membrane between the physical and spirit dimensions. Lucille, would you light the lantern by the door? And wait there!"

As I stood, I felt the unsteady vibrations in my feet. Mr. Silva then rose, and he must have felt the tremors also. He steadied himself against the bricks of the fireplace. The chain of trolling hooks started to shudder and shake. All of a sudden, it *slipped*—but Mr. Silva managed to safely catch the chain before it struck the floor.

Obviously exhausted, Captain Lord continued in his disturbed slumber. He grumbled some words that sounded like a hound attempting to speak.

"You might stand by the door, too, Scully," Vera said. She stepped gingerly to the captain and then glanced back at us both. "Lucille? The lantern? By the door?"

I had forgotten my task, mesmerized by the quaking cottage. With a gasp, I rushed to the door. Shaken by fear as much as by the floor, I managed to lift the glass chimney, light the wick, and replace the chimney without dropping the lantern. Allowing a glass lantern—one lit and filled with oil—to break on the floor would, of course, be disastrous. Holding it firmly, I was now free to see that Vera was kneeling down beside Captain Lord.

"What is it? What do you see?" she asked him. Despite supporting herself by pressing a hand against the wall, she still lurched each time the cottage shook.

The spindly chair that had been Mr. Silva's suddenly tipped over. After stepping toward it, presumably to set it upright, he waved it off and moved behind Vera. My eye caught the magazine illustration tacked to the wall, the incongruous medieval scene. Something had swiped it into the air, leaving the tack behind. Not even a mighty castle could withstand the convulsions assailing this frail cottage.

Our host continued to growl in the grip of his nightmare.

"Tell us, you old sinner!" Vera demanded. "What stalks you in your dreams?"

The captain barked a string of words that were only slightly coherent.

Vera twisted to Mr. Silva, saying, "Was that *'I'll not have another Junior on my hands'?*" She spun back to the captain. "Did you have a *son?* Are you ashamed of having *another* son?"

The tremors were growing in power now. Clumps of dust and dirt fell from the pine beams overhead. I spotted what appeared to be a bend in one of those supports. Stepping closer, I raised the lantern to it. Through the falling debris, I glimpsed a *crack* in the timber. It split apart for a mere instant as the quaking became stronger.

"Vera?" I coughed more than articulated. "Vera? We'd better go now. This beam doesn't look right."

Without turning to me, she shouted, "It's *vital* that we discover the source of guilt before we can attend to the manifestation!"

But the volume of her voice was just enough to rouse the captain. He blinked hard while his eyes darted amid the rocking furniture. "Not again!" he moaned. "Are they back *again?*"

Something invisible slammed against one of the legs of the table, forcing that leg inward. The flowerpot upon it slid off, smashing on the floor. Another fierce blow collapsed the table altogether!

I squinted to see that the gap in the ceiling beam was now split *further.* It gaped like the cruel grin of a toothless devil. "I *insist* that we leave now!" I shrieked. "We might be *crushed!*"

Vera and Mr. Silva turned from me to look at one another. Without a word, they both grabbed Captain Lord by his arms and dragged him toward the door. I felt an impulse to shove my way before them, but somehow, feeling the lantern in my hand reminded me to do the nobler thing. I ushered them through the door first.

And I was barely outside when I heard Vera calling.

"Lucille, quickly! The lantern!" She was running to the spot where Mr. Silva had found the curious prints in the sand.

I left Mr. Silva supporting the rattled captain and rushed to Vera's side. There, we saw what I can only describe as flashes of wide, wet canvas being slapped fiercely against the ground. The images remained visible only for the duration of each strike, and they were occurring at unpredictable points. Vera pulled me backward. One of the heavy slaps could easily have come down upon our legs.

At a safe distance, we were able to observe that each slap left the imprint of a blackfish's fluke.

Vera wrapped her arm around mine and said close to my ear, "Thar be whales here!"

"*Beached* whales," I said. "The *ghosts* of beached whales—struggling to swim forward! But they're held in place. Why? Why would they be held in place? They're *spirits!*"

"Guilt, I fear. The intense guilt hovering around this place has pierced holes between their realm and our physical one. It's acting like a net. Come, dear, we *must* discover what haunts this man!"

Vera had to pull me away from the vision of the flukes, away from the revelation that *whales survive death!* She dragged me back to where the two men had taken refuge from the haunted cottage. The phantoms struggling to swim beyond this structure continued their clamoring. A loud crash of glass caught our attention, and the moonlight revealed that a side window had shattered outward.

"There's no time to waste—you must tell us what wrongs you've committed in the past, Mr. Lord!" Vera entreated the captain. "In your nightmare, you spoke of not having another Junior. Did you disavow a son or do something *worse* to him?"

The lopsided captain teetered and almost lost his balance, but Mr. Silva caught him. The old man swatted at the air, silently demanding to be allowed to stand on his own. Mr. Silva took a step back. The captain then steadied himself and turned toward Vera. It appeared to take him a moment to focus on her face.

"What do ya accuse me of, fool woman? I've had no children! The Junior is a *ship!* A ship long gone. I served as second mate on her back in '57."

"Did you commit some crime onboard that ship? You must confess it, or the ghosts will continue their attack on your cottage!"

"The crime was committed against *me!* Mutiny, it was! *Murdered* Captain Mellon—and threatened to do the same to the first officer and myself! But the fiends reckoned they needed us to navigate 'em to Cape Howe. Kept me in irons with my wounds festering! There's your crime, woman!"

Mr. Silva stepped forward. "These mutineers—do you think *they* might be the ones ransacking the cottage?" He was asking anyone able to answer.

Vera began to pace. "No. No, the ghosts aren't human. You were right, Scully, about the prints over there. They were made by beached whales. We just observed a manifestation of them. The cottage happens to be in their way. They're struggling to get through it."

Mr. Silva slowly faced the spot where he had discovered the prints. His jaw hung open a moment. He then dashed to that place where we had witnessed the blurs of flukes.

Meanwhile, Captain Lord sidled toward Vera and glared closely into her eyes. "Lunacy, woman!" he spit at her. "Ghosts of *whales? A* whale is a *soulless* beast! These ghosts are the conniving crewmembers I made examples of! No, madam, I made certain there'd be no mutiny aboard any ship *I* captained! At the earliest signs, I let the men know how *I* dealt with disobedience!"

A piercing, agonized squeal sounded from within the cottage. I remembered the ceiling beam that was giving way to the poundings, and I pictured it twisting in two. The walls were now beginning to rock erratically.

"Tell me *how* you made examples of these crew members!" Vera demanded. "You say those men are the ghosts—the ghosts you wanted driven *back into the sea?* What did—what did you—" She was unable to utter the words.

I stepped forward. "Captain Lord, did you throw those men *overboard?* Men who showed *any* sign of disobedience? Was *that* your way to prevent mutiny?"

"I'll not be accused by *women!*" the captain shrieked. "It's *those* men who've come back! It's *them,* I tell ya! I had doubts if I'd done right by 'em—but this *proves* they were wicked! Wicked and now cursed to roam the earth! And now they've found me to destroy what little I have! I'll not abide such insolence! Not from *them,* and certainly not from the likes of *women!*"

At this, the captain shoved Vera out of his way. As if frozen in my own nightmare, I watched my dear friend hit the ground. Not until I saw her begin to roll and push herself upright did I regain the cognizance to assist her.

"Scully, *stop* him!" Vera shouted. She pointed toward the cottage door, struggling to keep her arm poised. "We must bring him to justice!"

Captain Lord had managed to stagger back inside the cottage. Mr. Silva, clearly overwhelmed by all he was seeing, came running to *us*. He knelt down beside Vera, putting his arm around her waist to lift her.

"Don't bother with *me*," she moaned. "That wretched sea captain confessed to tossing men overboard to prevent mutiny. There needs to an inquest! A trial to see if his actions are defensible!"

"There might not be time," I said, staring at the cottage.

My meaning became clear when another shrill squeal pierced the air, a portent of what was about to happen. A major section of the roof collapsed with a thunderous crash and a whirlwind of debris.

Shielding his eyes, Mr. Silva charged into what remained of the cottage, despite protests from Vera and myself. I stooped down beside Vera, hiding my face against her neck. I could hear that the quakes and strikes continued—but gradually the clamor diminished. The ghosts of the whales, it seemed, were freeing themselves of the dimensional net and swimming forward.

I pulled my head back. "Does this mean he's—is Captain Lord—dead?"

Vera put her hand gently to my cheek.

Mr. Silva emerged from the wreckage with the captain limp in his arms. Vera and I helped each other up and rushed over to examine the old man's condition. There were no signs of life. The captain did *not* appear to have been crushed, though, despite some streaks of blood on his face. Subsequent medical reports confirmed what we had suspected.

Captain Henry Thorn Lord had expired from an overstrained heart.

•

"I submit that it was the long, dark shadow of what he had done to those sailors that had taken a toll on his heart," Vera said. "His past finally caught up with him, so to speak."

Mr. Silva set a beer before her. After a wearisome day of official interrogation and, ultimately, official exoneration, we were hoping to regain our composure at Scully's bar before the regulars arrived.

"That is sensible, Vera" I said. "However, I see the captain as a man *driven* to monstrous acts. A man ensuring he'd never again suffer as he had on the *Junior*. His attempts to beautify his cottage, meager as they were, suggest a deeply buried decency. Why else would there have been any guilt? And what do *you* think, Scully?"

He stroked his dark beard. "I think what stopped the old skipper's heart was your idea that his ghosts were *whales.*" He paused and then added, "If whales they were."

Vera's eyebrows shot upward. "Did you not *see* the flukes striking the ground? I know they lasted only an instant, but Lucille and I both saw them!"

"I didn't have the lantern, remember. I don't know *what* I saw. Something, I guess. I certainly can't explain the invisible assault on the cottage." A smirk peeked through that beard. "Ghostly whales caught between dimensions—now, *that's* a remarkable notion."

Mr. Silva moved to the far end of the bar, where he picked up a towel and began to wipe the insides of a line of beer glasses. The fact that these glasses were not wet implied he needed a moment alone.

I leaned toward Vera. "He's grappling with an afterlife that's large enough to include angels—*and* ghosts—*and* whales. It takes a while to accustom oneself to such expansion. But what I still grapple with is why Captain Lord stirred such disdain in you. Yes, he reminded you of your grandfather, so let me rephrase the question. Why does your *grandfather* stir such disdain in you?"

Vera ran a finger around the rim of her beer glass. "His transporting slaves—especially transporting them to the deep South—isn't enough?" she asked. "I realize my grandfather was simply following one school of thought during the era in which he lived. But would you have me ignore the tenement owner who preys on struggling immigrants because others our own era do the same?"

Journalists, I reminded myself, prefer to *ask* the questions. Nonetheless, I persevered. "When Captain Lord spoke of not having another Junior, you assumed he meant a son. There is certainly logic in that. Yet you also asked if he *disavowed* his son or did something *worse*. Why might that have come to your mind?"

Vera slid her beer forward a bit and gazed in its direction.

I continued, "I ask because, if the captain reminded you of your grandfather—I mean to say—and I sincerely hope I'm not being too bold. But—well, just as our understanding of the afterlife has been expanded on this trip, I wonder if we might *expand* our friendship, too. If only a bit."

Without turning to me, Vera stated, "My grandfather never acknowledged his son. He acted as if my father had never been born at all." She reached for her glass but then withdrew her hands and folded them on her lap.

I took her nearest hand and held it a moment. "Vera," I said gently, "such neglect is *atrocious*. Perhaps beyond forgiveness even! Why would a *father*—how could *any* parent ignore a child that way? Were you ever told a reason?"

Vera glanced at me. She pulled her hand back, but it was so that she could caress my cheek. She replied, "Be it one's understanding of the afterlife—or of friendship—it takes a while to accustom oneself to such expansion."

Vera and I sat at the bar patiently. We waited until the musicians arrived. Once they were prepared to play, we asked to hear some melancholy airs but suggested that any rousing sea shanties be postponed for another evening.

To honor the passing of the captain, so we said.

SHADOWS CAST
FROM BEHIND ME
(1904)

In these days of rapid transit and the electric telegraph, needs there a ghost to tell us that our great-grandfather, or a rich relative, died the night before?

— L.J. Vance

Lest these chronicles of Vera Van Slyke's investigations into supernatural troubles create the impression that she devoted her time to little else, permit me to correct that misperception. Her daily life was filled with reporting on a range of earthbound topics, from suffering in the slums to extravagance among the elite. An example from the summer of 1904 nicely illustrates the point. 40,000 members of the meatpacking union went on strike across the nation, but Chicago especially felt the tremors of the walkout. From July to September, the span of the labor dispute, Vera's journalistic duties made her as familiar with the boardroom negotiators as with many of the workingmen's families.

She was so engrossed in the strike that she barely noticed *other* events that were occurring in the meanwhile. One such event was the anniversary of our second ghost hunting adventure. We were dining at The Foiled Gelding, a public house we had discovered during that case and had since claimed as our special spot.

"Do you realize," I asked her as my Salisbury steak arrived, "that it's been *four years* since you and I investigated the haunting at the Scepter Theatre's production of *Macbeth?* Imagine that. *Four years!*"

"Ah, yes. The Scepter case." She stared at the plate being placed before her almost as if it were her very first encounter with veal. "The ghost of an actor *acting* like a poltergeist, wasn't it? How long ago was that?"

I paused before repeating, "Four years. I was still very new at the ghost hunting business back then."

"Unskilled labor," Vera said, cutting into her meat. "That's what started this strike! Tell me, are *you* still on strike? From your *mother,* I mean. You were during that case, as I recall." She stabbed a bit of veal with her fork and then paused to look at me.

"W-well," I stammered, "in a fashion, I'm—I suppose I *am* still on strike from my mother. True enough, when we were performing séances, she was management and I was labor. Still, I prefer to think that I had *quit* the Spiritualist profession."

"Ah, but you cannot quit your *mother,*" Vera declared. "How have negotiations between you two been going since? You so seldom speak of her."

I was suddenly struck by the fact that I was very much like Vera in my reluctance to discuss family history. "Well," I said, "isn't that the pot calling the kettle black?"

Vera paused from chewing. She tilted her head. "Black?" She straightened her head. "My mother was *Irish.* I'm sure I've mentioned this." She returned to chewing.

I saw that I was competing with the meatpackers for her thoughts. "Well, fine. Yes, you're certainly right that I rarely speak of my mother. After you exposed us in Boston and I decided 'go on strike,' as you say, my mother and I had a bit of a row. I came back to Chicago to find respectable work. She decided to step into the role of psychic medium, eventually seeking her prey in Europe. In her last letter, she said she'd given up swindling and planned to settle with relatives back in

Bohemia. Traveled full circle, as it were. I wrote to tell her of my change of address, but I haven't heard from her since."

It then dawned on me that at least *four months* had passed since I had moved into a new rooming house. Probably *twice* that span had passed since I had heard from my mother. Shame prevented me from divulging this information to Vera.

It might not have mattered if I had.

"Among the strikers," she said, "the Bohemians seem to be a very stubborn—uhm, *resolute* bunch. Perhaps that's a Czech trait, one that accounts for the rift between you and your mother."

I grinned at the thought. "I consider myself much more an American than a Czech. Especially since I moved out of the Pilsen neighborhood. Remember, I left Bohemia when I was five. I'm *twenty-two* now."

"*Twenty-two!*" she teased. "A veritable *spinster!*"

Though I chuckled at first, I had that peculiar feeling of being Vera's echo again. Whether being so was desirable or not became a moot point when our lunch was interrupted by a young gentleman.

"I beg your pardon, ladies," he said, bowing. "I won't disturb your meal, but I had to say hello and to ask if you still explore the supernatural."

Vera looked at the intruder with one eyebrow raised threateningly. I noticed his sandy hair and his blue eyes. I didn't recognize the face, though, until I saw the chipped tooth at the front of his smile.

"Good heavens, Vera, it's Rick Bergson!" I exclaimed. "This was the young man who helped us discover how to illuminate the ruptures between here and the spirit realm. It was just *after* the Scepter case! Don't you remember? The music store clerk? He played one of the oboes. My Grandpa David played the other."

Vera relaxed her eyebrow like a castle guard lowering his weapon. "Of course! Why, Rick Bergson! I'd almost forgotten your name! We've used the B-flat and high G on many of our ghost hunts! How long has it been since we all made that discovery together?"

"Why, it must be close to three years!" Mr. Bergson replied, now beaming.

"*Four,* actually," I muttered.

The moustache that Mr. Bergson had grown sometime over those years, grown with only modest success, reminded me that he had originally impressed me as being a bit naïve, even dull-witted. Much can change over four years, however, so I decided to give him a fresh chance. Besides, I found a certain, hard-to-define charm in his light hair and eyes combined with the nicked tooth.

"If you haven't eaten yet, Mr. Bergson, perhaps you would care to join us," I blurted out without reflecting on Vera's wishes and barely on my own. I heard myself add, "We've only now started our own meals."

Vera heartily endorsed the invitation, and after the customary parley, we were sharing our table with the hair, eyes, and distinctive tooth of Mr. Eric Bergson. The conversation covered many topics, though Vera repeatedly navigated it back to the meatpackers' strike. Mr. Bergson, we learned, had come from the wheat fields of Nebraska, joining thousands of others to seek employment in the growing cities. A cousin helped him find a clerkship at the music shop where we had met him, and since that time, he had advanced in position by proving that profits could be gained by offering customers a wide selection of player-piano rolls. He was infatuated with such novel forms of mechanical entertainment. In fact, at one point, he asked if Vera and I would accompany him to enjoy one of Thomas Edison's latest sensations, the Vitascope.

"It's only recently become practical in terms of profits," explained Mr. Bergson. "You both already know about Edison's Kinetoscope, I'm sure. But instead of having to hunch over and watch a motion picture by yourself, his Vitascope projects it onto a large screen. A group of people can see the show together!"

Vera sneered. "Kinetoscope! Vitascope! *Phooeyscope!* The Wizard of Menlo Park did well with the electric light bulb, but it's come time to cut off his magic wand!" She punctuated her suggestion with a slash of her dinner knife.

Mr. Bergson opened his eyes wide. "I take it, then, that you'd rather *not* join me, Miss Van Slyke?" He glanced at me, touching his moustache to stifle a chuckle.

"Should I ever *wish,*" snarled Vera, "to observe a man *sneeze* or a woman *pirouette* or even a couple *kiss,* I am quite sure I can do so *without* the loss of even *one* coin!"

"I understand," our friend conceded, placing his hands together almost as if in prayer. "But those short scenes from life are starting to be replaced by full stories. Wild-west adventures, for example, or comedies. I see great promise in our new forms of entertainment."

I was impressed with Mr. Bergson's confident reply. Vera had a way of unsettling some men, but she did not dampen the enthusiasm this man felt for motion pictures. It inspired me to attempt something slightly daring.

"I think *I* might enjoy seeing one of these Vitascope stories with you, Mr. Bergson."

This time, Vera raised her eyebrow at *me.* "Is that so, my dear?" she asked a bit snappishly. "Then by all means go! Modern, thoroughly American ladies such as *yourself* require no chaperone!" She put down her knife with such suddenness that it clanged against her plate.

I glanced to ensure that no damage had been done to the dinnerware. I next asked slowly, "So you won't feel neglected if I accompany Mr. Bergson some evening?"

Vera snorted. "Not in the *slightest!* I'm your employer, Lucille. True, I'm also your friend. But I am decidedly *not* your mother. *Go!* Perhaps you'll be so bewitched by this Vitascope that you'll come back and change my mind. But for *now,* I'm far too busy with the meatpackers' strike." Despite her words, she pursed her lips and scowled at her glass of beer.

There was a moment of silence.

Finally, Mr. Bergson said, "Well, I must say—I take pleasure in having had *no* say whatsoever in this new arrangement." He lifted his glass and bowed to us both.

I laughed at his light-hearted handling our oversight. Vera, on the other hand, merely shook out her napkin and avoided eye contact.

I confess that I felt some satisfaction in discovering a way in which I differed from her.

•

In hindsight, I see that Vera's hollow support of my accepting Mr. Bergson's invitation was perfectly natural. When I wasn't working as her assistant, I spent more time with books than with suitors. As such, she had a central role in my life—as I think I had in hers. No, she certainly wasn't my mother. She was more like an aunt, albeit a decidedly *eccentric* aunt. With this in mind, it becomes understandable that she would have jumbled feelings about my betrayal regarding her opposition to the Vitascope.

Hindsight also tends to cast a golden hue over those days shortly before the rise of the nickelodeon. The Vitascope was in a backroom of an arcade that, along with several Kinetoscope machines, offered a variety of music-making devices. I fondly recall one that displayed a tall case of hanging bells, and these dozen or so chimes would mechanically perform a melody whenever a coin was inserted. Mr. Bergson claimed to share my delight in it, but I wonder now if he had been more amused by *my* enchantment with the machine.

"I'm glad you like the music," said my escort, "but I wonder if the inventor knew that his contraption plays a *funeral* march. It's a movement from Beethoven's 'Piano Sonata Number Twelve,' I think. Of course, it's usually played with more *tears* and fewer *gears.*"

Giggling, I placed both my hands beside one cheek. Melodramatically, I wailed, "I can't help but imagine that—somewhere—an automaton has *sprung* its last *spring.*"

Mr. Bergson's laughter exposed his chipped tooth, which was steadily increasing in adorability. "I see they're letting in folks for the next Vitascope show. Shall we?" He offered his arm as if we were heading into a formal dinner.

I was hesitant to let go of that arm after we had entered the backroom. Though I hadn't known what I would find there, I did not expect the room to be so compact. The Vitascope stood close against one wall, and a framed screen hung opposite to it. There was barely room enough for the twenty or so patrons. We shuffled and squeezed next to one another, new odors compounding with those of previous audiences. Cigar smoke floated amid oily fumes from the Vitascope projector.

And the room then went dark. The projector began to growl. The drama it displayed involved an asylum inmate who fancies himself to be Napoleon. He escapes his chamber and is chased by the institution's aids. The lunatic leads them through forest and field, ultimately returning to the very cell in which he started. I saw the novelty of this new kind of enacted storytelling in its unique use of settings, which transcended those of the conventional stage. For example, at one point, the faux Napoleon and his pursuers cross what is obviously an *authentic* brook, rousing a laugh when one the actors topples into the water. That and a bit camera trickery were of some interest. However, the story itself struck me as being, in a word, *trivial.* I worried that Mr. Bergson's hopes regarding the future of motion pictures might be misguided. I did not mention this to him, of course.

I was imagining my having to tell Vera that she probably had been right to snub the Vitatscope. But something very *unexpected* happened.

The film came to an end, and the operator failed to shut off the intensely bright bulb that had projected this modern-day shadow play. I continued to face the screen, and a flash of searing light assailed my eyes almost as if steam had exploded into my face. I was dazed!

And yet, *beyond the light*, I saw colors.

And then *shapes!*

There were leafy greens surrounding a river, the cloud-dappled blue sky reflected on its surface. I saw a chestnut-hued duck bobbing beside a bend in the stream, and I ran across the grass-patched earth for a closer look. As I neared the duck, I realized there was something odd about how its head drooped below the water. Stumbling, I came to see that the bird must have *drowned*, perhaps snagged in the roots of the tree that clawed into this curve in the river. And yet the duck *wobbled!* Creeping closer now, I saw under the surface of the crystal water. Two or three ebony turtles, yellow speckles on their heads, were swimming *beneath* the duck, rocking it with their heads.

I realized that those dark turtles were nipping at and devouring the flesh of that poor, pretty duck. The sight made me woozy and almost sick. It was as if the blood drained down from my head, taking control of my muscles with it. The desecrated bird blurred, and I felt myself slump forward.

Forward into the *same* river as those hungry reptiles!

A gush of cold water enwrapped me, reviving my sight. There were mud and vegetation on the bottom of the stream, and over them came a dancing, contorted shadow. Whoever was casting that shadow snatched me up and carried me back to the riverbank. There, I saw a boy, maybe nine or ten years old, not the person who had rescued me. That cruel boy was guffawing at me, offering no assistance at all.

I was spun so that my face pressed beside my rescuer's neck, and I heard stern words fired at the boy. The sharp voice then became soothing. "Lída," it cooed. "Lída, Lída."

The vibrant yet disturbing scene faded. I was back at the arcade, supported in Mr. Bergson's arms. Strangers were staring at me, jabbering.

"Clear the way!" Mr. Bergson shouted. He then whispered to me, "Let's get you outside for some air."

Cognizance slowly returned once I was seated on the front staircase of a neighboring tenement house. Suddenly, I pulled myself away from Mr. Bergson. His arms flew back as if he had been caught committing a crime. Automatically, I placed my hand on his shoulder to assure him he had done no wrong.

Confused by how glowing streetlamps and moving cabs had entered the arcade's small backroom, I muttered, "What happened?"

"I was hoping *you* knew," Mr. Bergson replied. "The film ended, but the fellow running the projector wasn't around to stop it. The screen went white, and next I know, you had collapsed against me! I guess you fainted."

"*Fainted?*" I protested. "I've never fainted in my—well. No, that's not true. I fainted once when I was a little girl. That—that's what I *saw!* On the *screen!* Beyond the light, I saw the time I *fainted* as a little girl!"

"*Beyond* the light?"

"That's the only way I can explain it. It was a memory of when I saw some turtles nibbling at the floating body of a duck. I don't know how it had died, but when I realized that the duck wasn't really alive—that the turtles were making it bob up and down—I—I was only about three or four years old. It was back in Bohemia."

"That's a gruesome sight for a girl so tiny. I still remember a day back in Nebraska when my pa and I came across a rattlesnake. All he had at hand was a shovel and—well, yeah. What else did you see?"

I rested my hand on his arm as I recounted the scene to him. The shadowy figure from behind rescuing me. The mean boy being chastised for laughing at me. The comforting words of affection.

"That figure behind me," I realized aloud, "it must have been my *father!* I wonder if this—this *vision* was influenced by his presence in some way. Ever since I first began ghost hunting with Vera, I've hoped that *somehow* my father's spirit would find a way to contact me."

"Oh, so he's—" Mr. Bergson uttered, doing his best to stay balanced upon my bouncing train of thought. "I suppose he *is*, if he's a spirit now. Maybe we should go see Miss Van Slyke. Have you two dealt with this kind of thing before?"

"No. She thinks the only people who have visions are—well."

Mr. Bergson nodded. "Like the fellow who thought he was Napoleon?"

I nodded, too. "Let's not tell Vera just yet. But do you know what? Oh, you'll be convinced I *am* a lunatic if I say it."

"Go on." He placed his hand over the one I had on his arm. *"Say* it."

"I want to try it *again!* I want to find out if I can see my father! Maybe he was trying to tell me something! The only thing I heard was 'Lída' repeated in my ear. Such a soft voice." I saw Mr. Bergson cock his head. "Lída is a pet name for Ludmila. That's my Czech name."

"I see," Mr. Bergson stated. "Sure, let's try it again *another* evening. For *now*, though, I think it'd be good for you to get some rest. Are you strong enough to stand?"

Though disappointed, I knew this was a wise plan. I consented and let Mr. Bergson help me to my feet. Once standing, though—I *froze.* I stared into his eyes. If that didn't frighten him, he should have been by how tightly I began squeezing his arms.

"The boy," I said. "Rick, you know the boy who laughed at me in the vision?"

"Yeah," he returned with a glimmer of a smile, "what about him, *Lida?"*

Barely noticing our newfound familiarity, I took a step backward. I looked at the street. At the staircase railing. At the light above the door beside us. I then slowly turned back to Rick's eyes.

"I'm fairly certain," I explained, "that I have a *brother!*"

•

Rick was busy at the music store each evening until the following week. I contemplated returning to the arcade by myself to see if I could evoke the vision again. However, the fear of fainting alone slightly outweighed the hope of communicating with my father once again. I yearned to discuss the matter with Vera, but I was dissuaded by her skepticism toward visions and her preoccupation with the meatpackers' strike.

At last, Rick became available. Our return to the arcade, I fear, was less a matter of him escorting me and more one of me tugging him. We spoke with the gentleman responsible for the Vitascope projector, a Mr. Jenkins. He was a friendly old soldier, whose wrinkled face was aptly complimented by his rumpled suit.

Between showings, Rick introduced us and inquired how we might persuade him to let the film run through so that the bare light could strike the screen again.

"Oh, *that,*" Mr. Jenkins responded. "I know that light's terrible on the eyes, and I 'pologize for putting the lady through that pain. See, this here job is the same over and over and *over.* Sometimes, it gets so a man hankers to wet his whistle. Now, I know it's wrong to imbibe while on duty, but I'm a man of some years. I got aches, and the whiskey eases the pain. 'Medicinal' they call it. Mostly, the aches are in my legs, right around the knees." He then pointed to the specific areas of discomfort.

"I'm sorry to hear about your pain, sir," I said, "but I'm not sure you're understanding us. We would like you to *let the film run through* so that I'll be exposed to that glaring light."

The projectionist scratched his chin. "You ain't complaining about my slip, then?"

"Quite the opposite," I assured him. "We would like you to *repeat* your slip!"

"We *enjoy* the glaring light," Rick added encouragingly.

Mr. Jenkins appeared to give this proposition serious consideration. Unfortunately, he decided against it. "Oh, *no,* that's like looking right at the sun. Not a smart thing to look at the sun for long. Burns the eyes! I know some things about that. I was here when the Great Fire swept through this city in '71. That was a calamitous thing. Some say it was started by a cow kicking over a lantern. I suppose that's as likely an explanation as any, but I honestly haven't looked into it. So I tell you that as secondhand."

Rick adjusted his tie. "But we don't want to *stare* at the light on the screen. We only want to — well, yes, I guess we *do* want to stare at the light." He fidgeted with his moustache.

"That's a fine moustache you're raising there, young man. You'll want to wax it regular. But not with candle wax. They got special wax at the barber's. I'm good friends with my barber. He has the same first name as mine. *Charles.* Common enough name, but still, knowing your barber shares your first name — well, it's a comfort."

That is when the irony of Mr. Jenkins struck me: a projectionist who could not maintain focus.

I opted for a new tactic. "You mentioned earlier, sir, that you wet your whistle to ease the pain in your knees. I wonder if you might recommend a beverage for — uhm, for my dear *husband* here. I'm afraid that he was raised by *teetotalers.*"

Mr. Jenkins's jaw dropped. He turned to Rick and swung his head in pity.

"Yes," I lamented, "teetotalers from *Nebraska.* Why, the poor rube can't tell a fine, aged Scotch from castor oil. Won't you give him the wisdom of your experience?"

Finally, Mr. Jenkins showed he understood by shutting his eyes halfway and sniffing. He then guided Rick a few paces to a quiet corner for a private conference. Rick glowered with revenge at me for a moment, but the wink that followed assured my future safety.

When the consultation had adjourned, Mr. Jenkins patted Rick's back. As they returned, I heard Rick assuring him that sharing a bottle was the least he could do to show appreciation. The projectionist then informed us that he had to start his next exhibition. Rick left to purchase the recommended elixir from down the street.

I was left alone, feeling grateful for the result of my stunt but also guilty for having resorted to it. That is when I realized that *my own guilt*—the very emotion that punctures the wall between this and the spirit dimensions—accounted for my vision the previous evening. Ever since my discussion with Vera about having gone "on strike" against my mother, I had been troubled by the notion that I was an unforgiving daughter. After we immigrated and my father died, my mother found herself in a terrible dilemma: a woman who could barely speak English having to fend for herself and her twelve-year-old daughter.

To be sure, it was poor judgment to force that daughter into the role of Spiritualist medium in order to survive. But survive we did.

On the other hand, if my hunch were correct about having an older brother left behind in Europe, he would have been approximately fifteen years old when my father died. That's a fair age to start contributing to the family income. Why hadn't my mother sent for her son? It's not unusual for immigrant family members to arrive over time, the earlier ones laying the foundation or calling for the later ones when needed.

Perhaps, I had no brother at all. Why wouldn't I have been *told* about him? Or *had* I been told but was too young at the time to remember it? And did my tender age explain why *I* was brought to America instead of my brother? Was my father trying to communicate some answers, utilizing the dimensional ruptures caused by my own guilt? My frantic reflection persisted until Rick returned, a bottle concealed in his suit pocket.

"May we hurry?" I implored. "Unless this experiment works, I'm going to be hounded by a hundred unanswered questions—and possibly by a team of asylum workers right afterward!"

We waited for the start of the next show, and when admitted, Rick discreetly passed the bottle to Mr. Jenkins. The audience wandered into place with a sluggishness that stirred a nasty thought—during a meatpackers' strike, what is done with the cattle corralled into the stockyards? Such was my impatient state of mind. In fact, I cannot recall the plot of this new motion picture, since I was preoccupied with hoping that Mr. Jenkins would forget to stop the projector after the film ran its course.

However, he disappointed us the first time.

"May we see it again?" Rick asked Mr. Jenkins.

The old man scratched his chin, peered to the left and to the right, and then patted Rick's shoulder.

We watched the motion picture again. It probably lasted fewer than ten full minutes, yet I shifted from one leg to the other in anticipation of it finishing.

Again, Mr. Jenkins managed to shut down the light precisely when the show reached its conclusion.

"I best make sure he's wetting his whistle," Rick said. "Maybe I'll ask about the projector and see if I can make sure the timing goes wrong."

Rick was proving to be my hero, an idea that replaced the less noble ones in my mind as I endured yet *another* viewing of the motion picture. It told its story *exactly* as it had before, coming to *exactly* the same conclusion.

And *exactly* as with the first two showings, no bare light filled the screen!

The crowd began to wander out of the room. I turned around to watch Rick chat with Mr. Jenkins about the machine. They pointed at its various parts. Mr. Jenkins was explaining the operation while also pulling Rick's hands away from the equipment. Suddenly, Rick turned a switch.

The projector's blinding light gushed directly over my face.

I was underwater. I glimpsed the wavering plants at the bottom of the river. Pushing against the mud, I caught sight of the turtles fleeing. Wisps of blood swirled from the duck's submerged wounds.

Then the shadow cast from behind me appeared. I felt myself taken up by strong arms and carried back to the riverbank. There, again, was the laughing boy. His resemblance to my family was now unmistakable.

Only when I heard the gentle "Lída—Lída, Lída" did I experience that odd sensation of *fathoming* that one is *dreaming*. Very vaguely, I knew that becoming aware that one is dreaming usually *ends* the dream itself. Nonetheless, I managed to summon forth my will. I pulled my head away from my rescuer's neck to identify who held me.

The glaring white light closed to a pinpoint and then vanished. Rick's face was the first thing I discerned in the now dim room. He was standing in front of me, and I *faced* him. This meant that I hadn't fainted this time. Instead, I had remained upright, staring into the light in some sort of trance state.

I struggled to say, "It—it was my—*mother*. Not my father. My *mother* was the one who saved me after I had fallen into the river. I saw it all again. The bobbing duck. The turtles. But, Rick, was it my mother who was trying to contact me? To tell me— what? That she had only wanted to *protect* me? But, if it was her contacting me from the other side, that would mean that she's— *dead*."

Rick took my hand, and I leaned my forehead against his chest.

"Given what you said about how you and your mother parted ways," he whispered "the notion that she wanted to tell you she was only trying to protect you—well, that's a real sweet way to make sense of all this. But maybe we're not intended to know for sure if this is a message or just a memory."

Then came a voice from beside me. I turned my head to see who was speaking, and the man there repeated himself.

"Lída?"

In the weak light, I recognized the man beside me to be my *father*.

•

"I wish I had a picture of my father to show how striking the resemblance truly is! The same wavy, brown hair. The same deep lines branching toward his temples when he smiles. And the same *nose!* Twice the nose of any Irishman!" I joshed.

Chuckling, Vera turned to my brother as if to see how my father must have appeared at about the age when I was born. František Prášil, son of the *late* František Prášil, grinned shyly. It was the evening immediately following our mysterious reunion. Once again, Vera and I were at The Foiled Gelding, but this time my *brother* was sharing our table. The three of us were waiting for our beers to settle. In addition, Rick had yet to arrive after working late at the music store.

"How do you account for all of this, Vera?" I asked. "How do you explain that scene from my childhood that I saw *beyond* the light? Was it mere happenstance that my brother was in the same room? Does it weaken your opposition to visions even a bit?"

"Oh," Vera replied, "I wouldn't call what you experienced a *vision* per se. I have a simpler theory. Hmm, perhaps not so *very* simple. First, though, I must ask about your mother's death. Was it sudden, František?"

"No, not shudden," he answered. "She know she dying, and dat's reason she come back to Bohemia." He tapped his heart and nodded at me.

I wasn't sure if that meant my mother had suffered from heart problems or if she longed to die in her homeland. Perhaps, there was no difference. I nodded back.

František continued, "She come talk vit' me. She push on me to emigrate. I am then already thinking to emigrate. Many of ush already talking, 'Go to America! No more outshiders to boss ush around!' Not too hard to push me over to leave Bohemia!" He smiled.

Vera next asked, "Did your mother push you to come to *Chicago* specifically to find Lucille?"

Seeing him squint at me, I clarified, "I'm called Lucille here. Did you come to Chicago to find *me?*"

"Yesh, yesh! Before she die, she tell me Lída liff in Cheecago. And many Czechs, too. I am trained to bootcher meat, but I never count on big shtrike at shtockyards! Inshtead, I do find job at Novak's Bootcher Shop. Nice shop. Friendly neighbors. I ask many people, but I do not find Lída. I never exshpect to find her in deh *arcade!*"

"I had sent a letter with my new address, but František says it didn't arrive before he left. If it arrived at all."

"Well," said Vera to my brother, "you're a saint for traveling so far to be with your sister."

František vigorously shook his head from side to side and then thumbed his chest. "Not shaint! *Freethinker!*" He laughed.

Vera laughed with him. "A tree holds up two of its branches to the heavens to show gratitude. It *thrusts* up one branch in exasperation. And *all* the rest are raised to ask questions."

When František went suddenly quiet, I speculated aloud, "I think he doesn't know 'exasperation' just yet. He's still learning English."

"If he's learning *English,* I imagine he knows exasperation very, very well." Vera lifted her glass to František.

He gladly returned the gesture. I knew that shifting my position to face Vera would be enough to remind her to continue her theorizing.

"Where was I? Oh, yes. As we know, ghosts tend to be spirits who are reluctant to leave this world behind. As such, Step One of my theory involves your late mother's spirit following František here to America, almost like a guardian angel. Her doing so is especially understandable, given how her *first* journey here had come to such dire ends."

"The death of my father," I said quietly.

"And troubles with her daughter, too," Vera reminded me. "Now, many immigrants—those still among the living, I mean—are new to English. Being so, they enjoy watching motion pictures. The stories are pantomimes, after all. But if motion pictures ever learn to *speak*, and I read that Edison is contemplating the creation of such a monster—well, my point is that it's only logical that your brother frequented the Vitascope once he arrived. That's Step Two."

I was distracted for a moment by František gazing at Vera, his elbow on the table and his chin in his palm. The angle of his head expressed incomprehension, but his stare was a study in fascination. Vera cleared her throat, and I snapped back to attention.

"Step *Three*," she asserted, "involves the guilt you felt regarding the rift between you and your mother. That guilt pierced the dimensional membrane, allowing for communication. No doubt, your late mother would have tried to communicate regardless of the place. In fact, she might have attempted to do so previously. However, you were 'on strike.' Negotiations were at a standstill! That bright light of the projector, I suspect, worked to burst through the barriers you had erected against her. And so she seized her one opportunity at the arcade!" Vera paused to take a sip of her beer.

I had to admit that her theory seemed sound, given what we know about interactions between the dimensions. Still, I found one key point downright disturbing. "Are you suggesting, then, that ghosts can—that they can reach into our *minds?*"

"They *can* and *do* on occasion. Some attribute it to telepathy. Even Mark Twain, usually the steadfast skeptic, wrote an essay inspired by his own experiences with it. He called it 'mental telegraphy.' In truth, it's all merely ghosts going about their business."

"Gracious, it makes me wonder how often what we deem coincidence isn't coincidental at all. But I like your theory, Vera.

It harmonizes the logical and the mystifying in the same manner that you bring to all of our supernatural cases."

Vera crinkled the bridge of her nose. "There remains at least one problem, though. František? Do you know why Lucille—uh, why *Lida* here wouldn't remember your parents ever speaking of having left you behind in Bohemia?"

František paused a moment. I assumed it was to make sure he understood the question. However, instead of answering Vera, he turned to me.

He wet his lips before saying, "Our fadder we share. *My* mudder—*she* die giving birt' to me. My *new* mudder—*your* mudder—she vas not happy vit' me."

I felt the old anger against my mother begin to rise again.

Perhaps sensing this shift in the tide, František added, "My fault, zough! *My* fault! Vhen I'm a boy, I'm like deh fox—alvays stealing deh cheekins. Alvays making trouble. Dey say besht to put me with Uncle Anton in deh mountains. Better place than Prague for deh fox to run."

Vera suggested, "I imagine your father must've spoken of him, but you were so young when your father died, why *would* you recall this?"

Facing my brother, I scolded, "But why did my mother go to *you*, then? After I refused to play the medium any longer—after she abandoned the role herself—what was her *next* scheme? *She* was the sly fox, František, not *you!* Did she convince you to emigrate simply to get you out of her way?" I suddenly feared my brother might think I was angry with him rather than with my mother.

František stared at me a long time, his brow furrowed and the mirth drained from his eyes. He wet his lips, but he did not speak.

"I wonder if he knows about your past as a medium," Vera stated quietly. She then slid her chair closer to mine. "Your poor mother had made serious mistakes with her own daughter. Her stepson was all she had left. She went to him because she didn't want *you* to be without any family at all. It was her dying wish."

I felt myself awash in family history. I sat very still, struggling to keep from crying.

It's disheartening to think back on that moment now. I remember worrying that Rick would arrive and see me in tears, *sobbing* after he had already seen me in such extreme states. I was concerned with the impression I would make on a young man when I *should* have been dwelling on my dying mother's selfless wish. The memory kindles shame in me to this very day. A tenacious ghost.

František must have seen my tight-pressed lips and hard-blinking eyes. His response was to gently introduce a new topic. "Miss Van Shlyke? In my old country, it ish regular for women to drink deh beer. But not *here* in my new country. Are you drinking deh beer because of my Lída here? No, I must learn—because of *Lucille* here?"

"Just the reverse," Vera said with a chuckle. "I introduced *her* to beer! That was during our very first ghost investigation, wasn't it, Lucille?" She sipped from her glass.

"Yes, our very first. But may I ask something? Please, both of you? Call me *Lída.* Lucille Parsell was a name I chose to raise a wall between my mother and myself. To deny that I was her daughter. But I think I'm beginning to realize that you cannot *quit* your mother. You can *never* quit your mother." I gave Vera a sidelong glance and a weak grin.

She replied with a bit of foam on her lip. "I shall do my best to call you Lida, my dear. However, as I believe I've mentioned once or twice, I'm not very strong with names. And, by my count, this is your *third!*"

Joining the merrier tone, František said, "At deh shop, dey call me Frank! Ish good American name, yeah? You both call me Frank, too, yeah?"

The three of us toasted to names new and old.

At the same time, I sensed something about to happen. Perhaps I caught it in my companions' eyes. Perhaps I glimpsed a reflection in my glass or even a shadow on the wall across from me. Regardless, I knew without looking that Mr. Eric Bergson had arrived from the music shop and was now walking to our table.

"And here's Rick," I announced before turning around to see him there.

HOUDINI SLEPT HERE
(1905)

Scrooge then remembered to have heard that ghosts in haunted houses were described as dragging chains.

— Charles Dickens

Vera Van Slyke and I were in her office at the Hotel Manitou. We were in the midst of reducing the large number magazines she had accumulated over the years, weeding an unbound garden of articles about topics both natural and supernatural. The latter prompted me to ask Vera why she never wrote about her investigations into ghostly phenomenon. Her skills in the publishing field, I reasoned, would likely lead to a profitable return on such chronicles.

"Harry Escott is the reason," Vera said. "I've mentioned Harry, yes?"

"Your mentor in the field of occultism." I had heard several of Vera's tales about this fascinating gentleman, who had passed away before I met her. In my mind, he shimmered with the radiance of legend.

"Yes, my mentor. Early in his career, he had granted permission to an aspiring writer to pen a couple of his experiences. That writer took the liberty of presenting both cases as if recorded by Harry himself, perhaps for the dramatic effect that goes with firsthand accounts of the supernatural. They were published in this manner. Published in a magazine of some prominence!"

Vera took a moment to locate and then hand me a recent copy of *Harper's Monthly,* showing that the journal still thrived. I checked this specific issue's date and added it to the keep pile.

Often preferring the past to the present, Vera sat down to reminisce. "You see, spectral encounters are *better* related by a reporter who brings some objectivity to the subject. By impersonating Harry himself, the writer inadvertently prompted many readers to view my mentor either as a liar or a lunatic." She put two fingers to the side of her jaw, her usual pose for contemplation. "I imagine that allowing that fellow to mention Harry's penchant for opium—entirely accurate, mind you—only worsened the portrait."

"Your Mr. Escott," I replied, "learned a painful lesson in becoming a public figure."

"And passed it along to me decades later," Vera added. "You know, if I hadn't been so young when I knew him, *I* could have written some of Harry's exploits from the perspective of his assistant. One day, I ought to do exactly that."

"A Dr. Watson to his Sherlock Holmes," I suggested. This time, I spotted and lifted a copy of *Collier's,* which ran Arthur Conan Doyle's popular series. "Were the great detective to tell his *own* stories, he might be seen as a braggart prone to wild exaggeration."

She nodded. "Were *my own* ghost investigations put to paper, it would be better for *you* to be holding the pen." She chuckled at the notion.

I was a stung by her reaction to the prospect of my chronicling our cases. I was quite an avid reader, and once or twice, I had considered fashioning a story of my own. Rather than defend myself, though, I tossed the copy of *Collier's* onto the rubbish pile and continued working silently.

"Besides," Vera resumed, "there are the reputations of our *clients* to respect."

This final comment is well illustrated by a case we handled for another man named Harry. Attempting to mask our client's identity would be foolhardy, since this magician is internationally recognized for escaping from handcuffs, padlocked chains or trunks, and almost any other kind of restraint. Many years will have to pass before readers no longer recognize the personage known as Harry Houdini.

In 1905, however, most Americans probably would have had trouble distinguishing *Houdini* from *spaghetti*, both being new attractions here at the time. Though Vera and I had enjoyed the Italian noodles, neither of us had heard of the showman. Nonetheless, Mr. Houdini had heard of Vera Van Slyke.

"It's your book about the tricks of Spiritualist mediums that brings me here, Miss Van Slyke," he explained as he sat down in the parlor at the Manitou. Mr. Houdini bore the trace of a central European accent, much like the voices in the Chicago neighborhood of my youth. Though possibly half a foot shorter than Vera, his vibrant presence very likely would have dwarfed hers were they ever to share, say, a lecture stage. At the same time, I remember that his habit of parting his hair in the middle made his head look almost humorously flat on top.

"You've read *Spirits Shouldn't Sneeze?* That's odd," Vera replied. "I've reached a far larger readership by authoring a short newspaper advertisement."

He grinned. "Ah, you must mean your offer to help the haunted! Yes, you see, I've studied you carefully before coming here. Your defrauding mediums with one hand while *allegedly* exorcizing ghosts with the other makes you the very person to consult in regard to my dilemma."

I saw Vera's lips tighten with the magician's suggestion that her dealings with the supernatural were dishonest. However, she allowed him to continue.

He laced his fingers together. "My dilemma might be compared to that of a poacher trapped in a tree by the dogs of the country squire. Imagine the squire himself holding off his dogs and demanding *money* from the poacher. Now, replace that squire with a Spiritualist medium named Alexander Lavelle. And replace the dogs with—a *ghost!* A ghost that Lavelle claims will *haunt* me if I don't pay him a considerable fee!"

Vera picked up a pair of scissors from her desk. She worked the blades as she said, "Lida, you were among those I interviewed for that book. Are mediums capable of commanding ghosts to do their bidding?"

Despite my sudden blush at having my former profession exposed, I stated evenly, "Oh, mediums are capable of doing anything their clients *believe* they can do."

"*Ghosts,*" insisted Vera, "perceive things far too clearly to be so easily led. This, Mr. Houdini, is also why ghosts seldom attend *magic* shows."

The magician glanced between Vera and me with a twinkle in his eye. He then admitted, "Forgive my speaking facetiously. I had to see how you would react to the case as it is being presented to me. Needless to say, I'm being flimflammed! But, you see, I *have* been caught poaching in a manner of speaking. And this Lavelle fellow claims he gets his information about my crime from the world beyond. Either I pay him—or he embarrasses me publically, thereby advancing his own career. The situation must be handled gingerly. Like picking a lock with a horsehair."

"Occasionally, a lock is better opened with an iron mallet," Vera responded, setting down the scissors. "Please *openly* tell us the details of your crime. I haven't time for horsehairs."

The magician collected his thoughts before speaking. "As the last century came to a close and after years of my traveling with circuses and medicine shows, I finally broke onto the vaudeville stage. Success can misguide a young man on the road, and I've always been, let me call it, *vigorous. Physically* vigorous. I pray I do not shock you fine ladies, but I made the mistake of associating with a certain redheaded dancer. And this is despite the fact that— despite my being *married* at the time."

Vera and I both shifted in our chairs.

Mr. Houdini continued, "The dalliance with the dancer was short-lived. After it had ended, Bess—she's my wife—and I decided that an extended tour through Europe might bring my career to fruition. That is where we have spent the last several years."

Vera raised her finger. "The showgirl, I presume, was left behind stateside?"

"Correct, Miss Van Slyke. But then we *returned* stateside. I had experienced great fortune in Europe, which left me with, well—a great fortune. I'm no Astor, mind you, but I suppose I could have been less public about my new wealth. For instance, it's no secret that I purchased a *couple* of houses. One is a summerhouse in Connecticut. The other is a modest mansion in New York City."

"A *modest* mansion?" said Vera with a chuckle. "Those are words seldom put together."

"Has she contacted you?" I inquired. "The redheaded dancer, I mean."

"Not directly. No, not directly." Mr. Houdini lifted a valise he had beside his feet. From it, he withdrew a photograph, which he then handed to Vera.

Vera perused the photograph before passing it to me. It displayed a gentleman who wore an eye patch, crouching forward in a wooden chair. The tips of his fingers were pressing his temples. Above and to the side of him floated the face of a woman—a woman without a body! A gossamer material encircled her head. On the wall behind them hung a certificate of some kind, perhaps a college diploma. That certificate showed *through* the floating head and the delicate substance that surrounded it.

Vera sighed heavily. "It's dumbfounding that these are still being passed off as authentic. If you read my book, sir, you know I devote a chapter to how such 'proof positive' of psychic powers is manufactured. Two exposures. The medium and the camera remain perfectly still for both. The spirit comes in for just *one* exposure, dressed in black except for whatever fluff serves as ectoplasm and, of course, her face. The officious certificate in the background is a novel touch. It's usually a vase of flowers."

Mr. Houdini again peered into his valise. "I was quite ready to accept the photograph as a fake. However, it was accompanied by this." He handed Vera a newspaper clipping.

Again, after Vera had inspected the item, she passed it to me. It was a death notice for a woman named Dolly Dunwiddle. According to the description, the deceased had been a dancer who died at the age of 29 years. No cause of death was provided.

"Am I to understand," Vera said, "that this unfortunate woman is the redheaded showgirl with whom you were *vigorous* prior to your European tour?"

A look of sincere sorrow descended across Mr. Houdini's face. "The very same," he mumbled. "And that most certainly *is* her face floating in the photograph. Lavelle informs me that her spirit contacted him after Dolly—after she had—had committed *suicide.*" Mr. Houdini slumped in his chair and let his gaze drift to the side.

Vera then clapped her hands together very loudly. There was a joyful grimace on her face. Mr. Houdini's eyes darted from her to me and back to her. I had some idea of what Vera was thinking.

"A hoax coupled with a hoax!" I exclaimed. As soon as I heard my words, I realized I should have shown greater sympathy to our guest.

Vera explained, "There are many items submitted to newspapers that good editors will carefully check before publishing. However, a death notice is not among them. Who would run a false report of a death, after all? Oh, I imagine it's been done. Perhaps to escape the law. But this is as fraudulent as that certificate in your ghost photograph, Mr. Houdini. If you were fooled by it, we can blame your being dazed by the claim that this woman from your past took her own life."

"But *were* you fooled by it?" I asked, noticing the twinkle returning to Mr. Houdini's eye.

He shrugged, casting off his pretense of sorrow with as much disregard as a dog shakes rainwater onto whoever is nearby. "No, I was not fooled," he admitted. At this point, however, the magician folded his arms. He next began to bite his thumbnail.

Vera asked, "Is there something more? Something not as easily explained?"

Mr. Houdini slowly nodded. Though this man was proving himself to be as talented an actor as a magician, my intuition told me that we were now seeing him *genuinely* seeking Vera's expertise.

He spoke solemnly. "At night, when Bess is asleep beside me, I've started to hear *whispers.* They started shortly after the photograph and death notice arrived. The whispers *might* be products of my own conscience, I suppose. But can one's conscience actually articulate words? If so, how can they seem to come at varying distances? At first, the whispers are about five or six feet away, barely perceptible. Suddenly, they'll be an *inch or less* from my ear! That's when I *jolt!* That's when I worry I'll wake Bess! And that's when I fear that Bess will hear the whispers, too!"

"A difficult trick, to be sure," Vera mused aloud. "Assuming this Miss Dumwooden—"

"Dunwiddle," I corrected.

"Miss Dunwiddle is still alive," she continued, "I imagine it would be *her* voice that speaks to you at night?"

"The whispers are so quiet that I'm unable to tell if they come from a woman or a man. I've scrutinized the bedroom from top to bottom for an explanation. A hidden telephone of some kind. A pipe. Perhaps echoes through the chimney! To my shame, I haven't a clue how those whispers are being produced!"

"Curious," Vera responded. "And what do the whispers tell you?"

Mr. Houdini faced Vera a long time before saying, "One thing. Only one thing. The voice bids me, *'Tell her I'm sorry for what I did.'* Only that, over and over. *'Tell her I'm sorry for what I did.'*"

•

Along with a persuasive promise of payment and a trip to New York City, Mr. Houdini provided us with two tickets to his performance at the Colonial Theatre on Broadway. We attended the show on the same day that we had arrived from Chicago. Despite the ladies who levitated, the feats of mental telepathy, and the escapes from tight coils of chains, Vera kept a sharp eye on the audience. I assumed she was hoping to spot, if not Dolly Dunwiddle, then at least Alexander Lavelle. I knew that his happening to be in attendance at this show would be an astonishing coincidence. However, he *would* be easily recognized, given his eye patch.

As it turned out, when the houselights rose at Intermission, Vera explained, "I figured I might catch sight of some of my old newspaper cronies. Silly of me, isn't it? To think that New York has been poised and waiting these four years for my return?"

I smiled at both of our faulty assumptions. "Well," I stated, "as this show illustrates, humanity is ever eager to believe in the unlikely."

I felt as if my comment had encapsulated an ageless truth. However, before Intermission was over, my companion had bumped into not one but *two* of her former professional colleagues. Such was life with Vera Van Slyke.

The band called the audience back to its seats for the second half of the entertainment.

Vera leaned toward my ear. "Do you mind letting our client know we've arrived? Slip backstage after the show, and tell him that we're prepared to investigate his ghostly whispers at his discretion. I'd do it myself, but I've been invited out for beers with a couple of my old news-hounds."

"Yes, of course," I answered as the curtain rose. "I mean, *no.* No, I don't mind. Yes, you should go reacquaint yourself with your friends." As the audience applauded Mr. Houdini's return, I felt myself suddenly discomforted. Was I to find my way back to our hotel on my own? Had Vera forgotten that I was a stranger in New York? I chose to blame my suddenly sour mood on the fatigue from our long trip.

These sentiments only worsened during a long wait to speak with our client after his finale. I was jostled this way and that by shouting stagehands and saucy showgirls. However, once I was admitted to his dressing room, Mr. Houdini greeting me with refreshing congeniality.

"Miss Parsell!" he hailed. "How wonderful to see you again! But where is Miss Van Slyke? Resting at the hotel?"

"I fear she was shanghaied by a roving crew of newspaper reporters," I replied with a grin. "She says that your performance was superb, however, and she looks forward to beginning the investigation."

Mr. Houdini dragged a chair over and offered it with a grand flourish, as if he were displaying one of his magical cabinets.

"Oh, thank you," I told him, "but I'm only here to notify you of our arrival and to tell you that we stand ready with our duplicate photograph and death notice."

"Wonderful!" he cheered. "Tell me, who posed as the medium and the ghost?"

"A friend of mine named Rick Bergson served as the psychic. I assumed the role of the ghost myself. You see, I have some previous experience in the ectoplasm business."

"Yes, I recall Miss Van Slyke mentioning that," he said, nodding to the chair. "I must confess I also did a stint as one of these blasted Spiritualists."

"Did you?" I realized my sour mood had passed, and I accepted the chair.

"Now, what was the name used for the obituary notice?"

"The dearly departed was named Lucille Parsell. A bit of significance in *that*, but much like our having once conducting séances, that tale should be kept under lock and key."

"I know some things about unfastening locks," the magician quipped as he scooted his chair closer to mine.

"Speaking of *names*," I scolded with a smirk, "*Houdini* sounds suspiciously like a stage name. Is it your real name?"

He laughed with the bit of a blush. "I was born with the name Erich Weiss."

"I see. And *where* were you born?"

"Appleton, Wisconsin."

"Odd. I thought I heard the trace of an accent in your speech. An accent from much further away than Wisconsin."

"Ah, well." He leaned forward. "Perhaps these several years in Europe have me sounding a bit like my parents. They came from Budapest."

"That's a fine explanation," I conceded. I had an inkling that I might be witnessing yet another of the magician's tricks, but I saw no reason to dwell upon it. "I'm originally from Prague. Say, during your stay in Europe, did you happen to visit—oh, but listen to me blather. I'm sure you'll want to return home after your strenuous performance."

Mr. Houdini scooted his chair still closer to me. "As it happens, I'm in no rush to return home." His eyes drifted sidelong. "You see, in order that you and Miss Van Slyke will be able to freely perform your investigation, I invented a reason for my wife and the rest of my family to stay in our Connecticut home for a few days. This means I'll be sleeping alone tonight." He returned his gaze to me. "I do so hate to sleep alone."

He then gently took my hand into his own.

Perhaps my response could be attributed to his physical proximity. Or to my fatigue from the long trip. Or to my earlier sourness. Regardless of the cause, after reclaiming my hand as my own, I squinted at Mr. Houdini a moment.

I then inquired, "Has anyone ever told you that parting your hair in the middle makes your head look almost perfectly *flat?*"

His brow furrowed. He leaned back in his chair. "I must say that this is the first time I've heard that. You don't think it makes me look distinguished?"

"It makes me wonder how many books you could balance up there," I answered.

Mr. Houdini crossed his legs. "Perhaps I could make that part of my show."

"Oh, would you listen to me?" I giggled. "It *has* been a long trip, hasn't it? Your idea about resting at the hotel is a very wise one. Thank you for suggesting it." I giggled again as I rose from my chair.

Without shaking my hand, Mr. Houdini escorted me to the door. We curtly arranged a time when Vera and I could conduct our investigation of his bedroom. I found my own way out of the theater. Though I also made the trip back to the hotel alone, I admit that I allowed another few giggles to sneak out from time to time.

•

The next evening, Vera and I went to our client's "modest mansion" in a neighborhood called Harlem. It was an area of the growing city that real estate speculators had eyed with great hope. Vera was pleased by this but less so by the many other changes that had happened in New York during her absence. She mentioned that the subway train, which had been completed the previous year, could carry us to Harlem. She seemed wary about such a mode of travel, though.

I insisted we ride the new subway! Subsequently, I found the ride to be a thrilling one.

"We shall never do *that* again," Vera declared once we'd returned to street level. "I prefer a *private* coffin when I'm buried, thank you—and a far more *stationary* one!"

After we had arrived at the Houdini residence, our host greeted Vera with the cheerfulness he had shown me the previous evening. He was standoffish toward me, though, often aiming his responses to *my* conversation at Vera instead of me. I became even more quiet than usual.

Before long, he was taking us to the room where he had heard the mysterious whispers. He granted us entry with one of his grand gestures that seemed better suited for the stage. The boudoir was ornately furnished, and its walls were decorated with memorabilia from our client's predecessors in the profession of illusions. The scent of rose water wafted from Mrs. Houdini's vanity.

"I sleep on this side of the bed," Mr. Houdini commented as his hands circled above one of the pillows, "and so the whispers must come from this vicinity."

Vera nodded as she found a spot to place her satchel. I put our two black oboe cases beside it.

Our host continued, "Rest assured that I am very much intrigued by your procedures. However, I am sorry to say that I won't be joining you during your investigation. A new book has arrived, you see. One that has traveled far to meet me." He bowed.

"By all means, attend to your book," Vera replied. She had already begun scanning the corners and crannies of the room. "But I do have one question. What is your usual bedtime? If the lights going out in this room act as a signal to someone waiting outside, I'll want to recreate that with the hope that the whispers will appear." She returned to her examination.

"On nights when I have no show, I generally go to bed around 10:30. Bess does, that is. Sometimes, I'll stay up later, but I don't turn the lights back on, of course." Mr. Houdini glanced at me and then quickly diverted his eyes. Next, he added, "I very much hope you can tell me all that you discovered tomorrow morning. Shall we plan on sharing breakfast?"

Vera spun from looking behind a dresser to face our client. "Not *lunch?*" she implored. "Can't we plan on *lunch?*"

I attempted to explain Vera's plea by saying, "We're likely to be very tired tomorrow morning."

Without turning to me at all, Mr. Houdini smiled at Vera. "Lunch, then. Should there be even the smallest emergency, I can be found in the library or, later, in my mother's bedroom. I'll be sleeping in her bed tonight." He bid us good luck and closed the door behind himself.

Vera put a finger behind her ear and froze, as if listening to Mr. Houdini's fading footsteps. She then asked, "Regarding last evening, my dear—did the gruff bull stomp his hoof at the frisky calf who wanted to play?"

I pursed my lips at my place in the metaphor. "The gruff bull *did* have to change the topic of discussion a bit abruptly at one point," I explained.

"I must tell you something, Lida," Vera said as she began feeling above the doorframes in search of a clue. "In the years we've spent together, I've watched you blossom into womanhood. You've gone about it all wrong, becoming as pretty as you have. Pretty women are virtually indistinguishable from one another."

I helped myself to the vanity chair. "If only you had met me earlier, Vera. Perhaps, your influence would have made me as unique as yourself."

This time, Vera pursed her lips. She appeared to be reviewing my comment for any traces of slander. I decided to grant the jury a recess regarding it. Following her instructions from previous investigations, I remained silent as Vera proceeded to check behind the furniture and pictures, under the carpets and mattress, and along the woodwork and windows. She even tapped on walls, listening for hollow spots. Finally, she looked at me and shrugged.

Sitting on the side of the bed, Vera said, "I forgot to ask you about your afternoon trip to see Lady Liberty. Does the grand girl appear very different from the last time you saw her?"

"Of course, she does," I asserted. "I saw her from the *other* side this time! Oh, Vera, it's heartbreaking that you lived so many years in this city and have never been to the Statue of Liberty!"

"Yes, yes. One day." Her eyes brightened. "But I *did* find some interesting evidence at City Hall this afternoon! Or, rather, a *lack* of evidence! There is no death certificate available for our redheaded dancer."

"You checked the name I had written down for you?"

"Repeatedly."

"Well, then, that suggests that Miss Dunwiddle still walks among the living!"

"And she is very likely Mr. Lavelle's source of information regarding her unsavory liaison with our client. Making matters worse, I also discovered that, while Mr. Houdini was betraying his wife, *Mrs.* Dunwiddle was betraying her husband!"

"Gracious! You found a marriage certificate?"

"I found a *death* certificate." Vera crossed to where we had placed our belongings and pulled a notebook out of her satchel. After flipping a few pages, she read, "It was dated 1902, *after* Mr. Houdini left for Europe. Mr. Eugene Dunwiddle—spouse of Dolly Dunwiddle—was a sword-swallower who died of internal injuries. A hazard of the trade, I suppose, but still a grisly end for poor Eugene! I deliberately didn't mention it to our client."

"You also didn't mention that we might now be dealing with an *actual* ghost," I remarked. "Well, this puts us back on familiar ground. Shall I take out the oboes? It's dark enough now."

Vera nodded. I retrieved our oboe cases, and we assembled the two musical instruments. We next extinguished the lights. Vera sounded a sustained B-flat on her oboe, and I droned a high G on mine. This exact timbre and harmony creates vibrations that illuminate any breaches between the physical and spirit realms. The illumination appears as a violet glow, the color that science confirms wavers on the precipice of visibility. Though we played the B-flat and high G in about as many spots as the room afforded, not a single violet-edged, wobbling hole appeared.

Vera signaled for me to stop playing. In the moonlight coming through the window, she returned to the side of the bed, where she rested two fingers on her jaw. "No *violet* equals no dimensional *ruptures,*" she pondered aloud. "No *ruptures* equals no *guilt* in the room—or, at least, no guilt powerful enough to *cause* the ruptures." Snapping upright, she protested, "But this makes no sense at all! No guilt? Remind me what the ghost says."

"According to Mr. Houdini, it whispers, 'Tell her I'm sorry for what I did.' And nothing more."

"He confessed his marital infidelity to us! And yet the man feels no remorse? Even when disembodied whispers imply that his wife there *beside* him deserves an apology? I am flabbergasted!"

Not knowing what else to say, I suggested, "Perhaps all that's left to us is to bring back the lights and wait until 10:30. Only then can we hope to trick anyone spying on the house into initiating the whispers."

"We *must* do exactly that, my dear! This pudding gets thicker the more it's stirred!"

Once sufficient time had passed with the lights up, Vera dragged the vanity chair close to the head of the bed, where Mr. Houdini indicated he had heard the phenomenon. She sat there. I then extinguished the last light and assumed my post on the edge of the bed. Toward the end of the first hour of maintaining our watch—or, rather, our *listen*—I began to feel my head drooping. Sometime during the second hour, I began to slouch backward more than once. Vera pinched me on the arm each time to bring me back to soldierly attention. As on our previous outings, I was astounded by Vera's ability to remain sharp and virtually motionless through a long night of ghost hunting.

Eventually, all sounds coming from other rooms in the house passed away. Even the slow approach and departure of hooves on the street became infrequent. I hadn't realized that my eyelids had been closed for some time when they snapped open at the sound of a *thud!* I turned quickly toward Vera.

Though the moonlight had now passed, I discerned her shadowy figure raise a hand, cueing me to remain still. With the grace of a creeping cat, she rose from her chair and moved toward the center of the room. She pointed to the door, indicating that the sound had originated from beyond it. Then came another *thud!* This time, it was followed closely by the creaks of bedsprings in the distance and then footfalls rushing down the hall toward us. A gentle yet impatient rapping sounded on the bedroom door itself.

"Are you still there, Miss Van Slyke?" hissed the voice of Mr. Houdini through the door. "I heard the whispers! The *whispers* again! But how could they have known that I'd switched rooms? Miss Van Slyke, how could they have known where I'd *be?*"

•

On the ride to confront our adversary, Mr. Lavelle, Vera glared out the coach window while persistently tapping her chin.

Mr. Houdini leaned toward her and said softly, "Not to worry, Miss Van Slyke. True, you weren't unable to explain what mechanism accounts for the whispers. If I understand what you explained earlier, though, you've shown there was no aperture, no channel—no *medium,* if you will—for those whispers to have come from the spirit world."

Vera continued to look out at the passing buildings. *"Medium* is the right word in this case," she snarled, "since Lavelle might go so far as to claim that you *yourself* are unconsciously a psychic sensitive. *That,* then, can explain the whispers."

I submitted, "But we also have our photograph and obituary notice to show that Lavelle's are as phony."

Vera rested her hand on my arm. "Helpful but not conclusive. Many a Spiritualist has claimed that *faking* what they do fails to *disprove* what they do. Any of us can put on a false moustache, a pair of pince-nez, and a Rough Rider's hat, but that doesn't mean that Theodore Roosevelt isn't actually our President."

Mr. Houdini chuckled. He leaned back and began to straighten the cuffs of his shirt and coat. He said, "Remember that Lavelle has never mentioned the whispers. It's possible he has no knowledge of them. Even if he does, I'll wager he's counting far too much on that ace up his sleeve, given your findings."

Vera turned suddenly to our client. "And, since we only have a queen up *our* sleeve, it is *vitally* important that none of us mention the ghostly whisperer! Are we thoroughly understood on this point?"

Mr. Houdini chuckled again.

"Are we *clear* on this point?" Vera reiterated pointedly.

Our client resumed attending to the correctness of his cuffs. I saw Vera's eyes narrow as she stared at him. She remained silent until, with that familiar flourish of his hand, the magician let us know that we had arrived at Mr. Lavelle's brownstone.

After Mr. Houdini introduced Vera and me as a pair of psychical researchers from Chicago, Mr. Lavelle escorted us to his parlor. I immediately recognized features of the room as being tailored for séances. The center table, for instance, had a top that extended farther on one end than the other. Applying one's elbows to that longer side, one could easily rock the entire table. In addition, rather than a door or open entryway to the next room, there hung a dark, heavy curtain. It granted a confederate covert passage once the room goes dark.

"Would you ladies prefer coffee or tea?" asked Mr. Lavelle with a cloying smile. He was a gangly man with dark hair. His most noticeable feature was that eye patch we had first seen in the fake photograph. I assumed it was a mere affectation, designed to imply that the wearer's restricted vision in *this* world must surely have sharpened his insight into the world *beyond.*

Not until our refreshment arrived did Mr. Lavelle commence the transaction. "Let's discuss the proposal that brings us together. Sir, are you prepared to pay the $1000 I mentioned in my letters? I assure you that I could earn *more* by going to the press with the story that the late Mrs. Dunwiddle told me. It has both scandal *and* the supernatural! And reporters these days are so very vulturous when it comes to either of those." He resumed his honeyed smile.

"There is no such word as 'vulturous'," Vera stated blandly.

After tilting his head, he asked, "Are you sure?"

"I ought to be. I'm a reporter."

Mr. Lavelle licked some of the honey off of his lips.

Our client interceded. "But to answer the question about your proposal—as it seems we're not calling it *blackmail*—I absolutely refuse to pay you so much as a wooden nickel. You see, I am fully prepared to respond to your chicanery with a bit of my own. Miss Van Slyke, would you care to present our counter-proposal?"

"Yes, thank you," she replied. "As regards your photograph, does your good eye allow you to recognize the dearly departed in this portrait of our own making?"

I passed our photograph to Mr. Lavelle. His good eye shot up and down between my face and the picture several times before he managed to reconstruct his smile.

"But, of course, we also—I mean, *I* also have the newspaper notice of Mrs. Dunwiddle's death to confirm that the woman in *my* photo is no longer living."

"Ah, yes, the death notice," Vera said. "Now, not everyone is strong with names, sir. But do you recall the name of the pretty miss beside me now? You were introduced only moments ago."

I passed our newspaper clipping to him.

Mr. Lavelle stared some time at the clipping before reading aloud, "Lucille Parsell. The pretty miss." He then cleared his throat and continued to stare downward at the clipping.

I took the opportunity to discreetly tap the arms of Vera and Mr. Houdini. Upon gaining their notice, I cocked my head in the direction of the curtain. My intent was to signal that Mr. Lavelle was most likely not acting alone. My two companions nodded.

I assumed they were likewise recognizing that the man before us lacked the cunning to have devised this scheme by himself. Indeed, I reconsidered his eye patch. No longer did I see it as an indication of sophisticated subterfuge. Instead, it suggested congenital clumsiness.

As if cracking a whip, Mr. Houdini snatched Mr. Lavelle's attention with a sudden guffaw. "Those were both schoolboy tricks! But I confess I haven't a clue as to how you managed to create those spooky whispers in my house. And to perform them night after night! In different rooms yet! Remarkable!"

Slowly, Vera pivoted her head to our client, narrowing her eyes into the same scowl that she had given him in the coach.

Mr. Lavelle blinked his eye several times. "Did you say *whispers?* Dolly—er, Mrs. Dunwiddle didn't tell me—or, I mean, the *spirit* of Mrs. Dunwiddle didn't tell me about any whispers!"

Mr. Houdini continued, "I won't ask you to divulge your secret, of course, but do let me compliment you. *That* trick, sir, was pure genius—if indeed it were a trick at all! I called in these ghost hunters, hoping to reveal some physical explanation for the whispers. Miss Van Slyke, in your opinion, *was* there a trick at work here?"

Vera sighed while accepting her role in the playlet being directed by our client. Standing, she recited, "I was unable to expose any mechanism or any other *physical* means whereby the whispers might have been produced." She then curtseyed and resumed her seat.

Exactly then, the curtain behind Mr. Lavelle rippled.

The magician very likely noticed this and proceeded, "But I never quite understood the meaning of the message being whispered. Lavelle, if it was really you, please clarify what was being said? Being said *over* and *over!*"

The medium's mouth hung open a moment. Sounding like a teased child, he whined, "What *was* being said?"

Mr. Houdini fiddled his fingers as if casting a spell. He intoned, *"Tell her I'm sorry for what I did.* Only that each time. Never anything else. *Tell her I'm sorry for what I did."*

Suddenly, a woman burst through the curtain. Her entrance was indeed startling. However, I do not believe that any of us were surprised by the color of her hair.

"Now, what the devil does *that* mean?" demanded the redhead. "What would *Eugene* have done that he needed to apologize to *me* for?" After putting her hands firmly on her hips, she peered around if slowly realizing there were strangers in the room.

Mr. Houdini stood up to announce, "Ladies, allow me to present the late Dolly Dunwiddle." Though a devious smirk had come to his mouth, he abstained from making the customary grand flourish with his hand.

In unison, Vera and I also rose.

Mr. Lavelle finally did, too. He whimpered, "I—I don't understand. Dolly, you said Eugene was your husband. But he died, you said. And now these whispers! So—so was there *really* a ghost?"

"Imbecile!" Mrs. Dunwiddle groaned, punctuating her statement with a wallop to the back of Mr. Lavelle's head. "If it wasn't a trick, then it *must* have been Eugene's ghost! He told me at the hospital that I would be punished for how I treated him. That my punishment would come from the next world!"

Mr. Houdini gestured for Vera and me to head to the door before him. However, Mrs. Dunwiddle interrupted.

"But, Harry, why would Eugene ask *you* to apologize to *me*? If *either* of us had a reason to—but—but what did *he* do behind *my* back?" The flushed face of the red-haired woman suddenly paled. She clapped her hand over her mouth and froze. She might have been sensing a digestive problem on the rise. Another possibility is she recognized that Mr. Houdini had duped her.

"*That* seems to be a secret known only by those beyond the Veil," Mr. Houdini said decisively. "Mr. Lavelle, as Dolly's spirit has apparently reconciled with her body, I think it best that we bid you farewell. But I thank you, sir. You've inspired me to expose you Spiritualists far more vigorously in the future than I have today."

Mr. Lavelle stumbled as he dumbly accompanied us to the door. We left the widow Dunwiddle in her state of nervous befuddlement, a condition that was likely to haunt her for a long time to come.

•

"Please confirm *three* of my suspicions, my dear," Vera said.

We were back in our hotel. We had taken a room among the top floors of the Seville, one of New York's newest and tallest hotels. Vera was unbuttoning and unhooking a few of the tighter spots of her apparel, not to change outfits but to relax after a vexing day.

"If any of those suspicions concern the resurrection of Dolly Dunwiddle," I replied, "I think you should have asked Mr. Houdini while you had the chance during our return trip. Very likely, *he's* the only one who can divulge what occurred behind the scenes of this afternoon's matinee performance."

"I don't believe that man would have ever told us the truth. But I will grant that he certainly has a talent for escaping all *kinds* of chains!"

I smiled. "Yes, but I feel like we were little more than tools concealed for that escape. Handsomely *paid* tools, mind you. Nonetheless, let's discuss your three suspicions."

"First, we never heard the ghostly whispers that brought us here. Indeed, I highly doubt that Houdini ever heard them. No, we were called upon to bring the veneer of validation to the ghost. The fact that we traveled so far to investigate the whispers gives that ghost a certain—a certain *weight,* doesn't it?"

"The illusion thereof," I amended.

"Yet *how* did Houdini know that the red-headed dancer would so quickly assume the whispers came from her late husband? Did he even know that Eugene Dunwiddle was dead?" Vera began to pace. "This brings me to my second suspicion. Did the man simply perform the medium's standard ruse? The one in which he claims he's been contacted by a spirit who has unfinished business with the poor patsy?"

"I think so," I said. "The safer method is for the medium to say that he has been contacted by a spirit who loved the patsy very much. Almost everybody will think of some deceased friend or relative who fits the bill. That's when many will take out their money to hear more. Mr. Houdini probably deduced that Dolly was involved in the scheme, given Lavelle's—limited vision, let's call it. So he simply held up an empty sheet. He knew Dolly well enough to predict that she would fill that sheet with whatever ghost was lingering in the back of her mind."

Vera stopped pacing. She crossed her arms and raised them to lean upon the window frame beside her. Outside, the sky over the city was a darkening orange.

"The last mystery," she said, "is the lack of any ruptures between the dimensions. The lack of a ghost is one thing. Every ghost hunter expects to come up empty handed now and again. But the lack of *guilt!* Our not finding any violet holes in that bedroom where the sinner sleeps with the woman he sinned against—why, I can barely form a theory! On the one side, did his guilt simply evaporate with the passage of time? Or, on the other, did it so plague him that he often slept in another room?" Vera tapped a finger against the windowpane.

I walked over to her. We had an impressive view of the metropolis and of the multitude of lights that, one by one, were appearing before us.

"Do you remember telling me about the writer who ruined the public reputation of your mentor, Harry Escott?" I saw Vera nod, or rather, I saw her reflection in the window. "I suspect Harry Houdini *refuses* to meet a similar fate. He retains complete control over his public portraiture and, indeed, paints that picture himself. I wonder, though, if he doesn't paint himself in a style that is very much—" I paused to think of the best word.

"Romanticized?" Vera offered.

"Exactly. And, in romanticizing how *others* see him, perhaps our magician has himself become fooled by his own larger-than-life image. That, then, saves him from any feelings of guilt. Any merely *human* feelings of guilt."

Vera smiled. Using the window as a mirror, she straightened a strand of her stubbornly wavy hair. She then stepped back to make a dramatic, sweeping gesture to the humanity beyond the window.

"And *that*, my dear, is a magic trick we *all* perform!" she concluded.

GHOSTS AND
OTHER IMMIGRANTS
(1905)

The joys of boyish days come thronging back like sheeted ghosts, to haunt the chambers of memory, and affright the heart with the thought of the wild hopes it once cherished, and of the tomb which engulfed them.

— P., *Yale Literary Magazine*

"There's someone you must meet," announced Vera Van Slyke, "someone with a story about a ghost I think you'll find intriguing—if a bit *unnerving.*"

This was the morning after we had completed our adventure with the spirited escape-artist, the artless Spiritualist, and the artificial spirit. We had decided to spend an additional day or two in New York City so that Vera could visit with some of her former acquaintances. At this particular moment, we had just left the Hotel Seville and were strolling through Madison Square Park.

Vera paused upon confronting the curiously wedge-shaped structure nicknamed the Flatiron Building. With her lip curled in disdain, she commented, "I see that, in my absence, they've taken to building skyscrapers out of *cheese.*"

"Someone with a ghost story, you say?" I reminded her.

"That's right," Vera resumed. "I first met the gentleman, oh, a good twenty years ago. Harry Escott was still alive—and still mentoring me in the field of Occultism. We found ourselves on a case in San Francisco."

"San Francisco!" I exclaimed. "I knew you and Mr. Escott travelled together. I didn't know you both had crossed the entire continent, though!"

"Yes, he was always one for exploring, be it the territory *beyond* or simply the next territory over." Vera sighed. "It was always a joy to travel with Harry. People must've thought I was his granddaughter, given the difference in our ages. Despite his snowy-white beard, though, he was as lively as—ah, but I've already told you all about him. And here comes an available cab."

As we boarded the coach, Vera gave the driver an address on Mott Street, adding that he should look for a fishmonger's shop. My employer often settled into a meditative state during cab rides, perhaps the steady rhythm of horse hooves having a slightly hypnotic influence on her. She gazed out the window, sometimes smiling but without explaining why.

"Are you remembering your travels with Harry Escott?" I inquired gently. "Vera?"

It took a few tugs before she drew her attention back into the coach. "Oh. Oh, no. I was just remembering these streets. It seems I'm homesick. Tell me, dear, how would you feel about living in New York?"

"It's an exhilarating city. However, if you're asking if I'd be willing to move here from Chicago, I'd have to decline."

"Ah! You wouldn't want to leave Rich Burglar? That can't be right. Burglars are rarely rich."

"Rick Bergson is his name. It's true that he is *one* factor keeping me there. He and I have become very close. However—" I wriggled. "You know, I've sat in more comfortable cabs!"

Vera rested her hand on my arm.

I nodded and began to rearrange the folds of my skirt for no real purpose. I explained, "Rick's been speaking of heading out west, too. He says he's climbed as high as he can at the music shop, and he'd like to seek his fortune up in Alaska. My own fault, I suppose. I made the mistake of introducing him to the tales of Jack London."

Vera remained silent. With sudden enthusiasm, she then inquired, "You know what the frog did after it jumped to another lily pad, don't you?"

Still fiddling with my skirt, I muttered, "I hope it didn't get swallowed by a heron."

"It jumped back to the *same* lily pad it had left! And most people *are* frogs, you know."

We traded grins. Vera gradually drifted back to gazing through her window, and I through my own.

•

It took the driver announcing our arrival to shake us from of our moods. Vera led me to a shop whose sign shouted "FRESH FISH" above and mentioned "Wou Sankwei, Proprietor" below. I next spotted smaller signs written in both English and Chinese. The clothing of passersby caught my eye: dark wools made drab by their contrast to crimson, teal, and lavender silks. Finally, the faces and spoken exchange of the cart vendors and many of their customers confirmed that I was in New York's Chinatown.

I stood still a moment to appreciate the scene.

Vera stopped abruptly. "I know some people have a dislike of the Chinese. But do *you?*"

"No, no!" I replied. "It's just that, when you told the driver that the address belonged to a fishmonger—well, I imagined your friend might be Jewish. It was silly of me."

Vera tilted her head. "Not silly. Jews eat fish, don't they? Come along."

We walked into the fish shop. Following the clamor of commerce outside, this establishment seemed like a library. Perhaps the impression came from the fact that the solitary salesclerk was reading. He sat as if frozen among the ice-filled cases of cod, haddock, and clams. I noticed a section for farther-ranging tastes: octopus, shrimp, and shark. A bell jingled as Vera pushed the door closed behind us.

Continuing to stare at his book, the clerk raised one finger. "If you would please let me finish this last paragraph?" he said.

Vera sauntered toward him. "Shall I guess? A book on Astronomy?"

The fishmonger lifted his head, letting the book's pages flip of their own accord. Glee seemed to rise from his lips to his eyes and even to his brow. "Vera Van Slyke!" he cheered as he rushed from behind the counter.

Only then did I realize that he was Chinese. His accent rang more of Canton, Ohio, than the Canton Provence. Indeed, from his haircut to his collarless shirt with the sleeves rolled up, the gentleman served as solid evidence against those who hold that his race is incapable of Americanization. Even his hefty build confirmed that he was succeeding here.

The two joined hands, communicating with their eyes. Until that moment, I'd had scant opportunity to closely observe an Oriental face. What I noticed most about this one were the deep crinkles splaying from the outer ends of his eyes. Among them, on each side of his face, a longer line fell almost straight down like a trail of tears. As I waited, I thought about the smiles and sorrows etched on faces around the world.

I waited some more.

And there I waited—glancing at various fish.

At last, I cleared my throat. "If I may ask, was Vera correct about the book?"

Chuckling, Vera introduced me to Mr. Wou Sankwei, whose name I recognized as the shopkeeper. She made a special point to clarify that he should be addressed as Mr. Wou. Her mental facility for recalling names, I noted, follows a system beyond scientific explanation.

Mr. Wou bowed. "Regarding the book, is Vera *ever* wrong? It's titled *Journey to the Planet Mars,* only recently published. And if you wonder why I'm so interested in the stars and the planets, Miss Parsell, let me point out that I was born in the Celestial Empire."

I sincerely *endeavored* to laugh convincingly.

"Oh dear, Vera," he said, "that's still not funny, is it?"

"And it never will be, Sankwei," she teased. "It is true, though, that Mr. Wou is an immigrant like yourself, Lida."

He turned to me and said, "Oh?"

"I was born in Prague," I explained, "but my family came over when I was very young."

He shrugged. *"Everybody's* an immigrant these days, especially in *this* city! Ah, but *I* immigrated to the U.S. *twice!"*

Vera grabbed Mr. Wou's arm. "That's a story better told some other time. I promised Lida that you would tell her about how we met. The story of Representative Clancy."

"Oh, *that* story, huh? It's a humdinger, Miss Parsell. But this place smells of fish. Would either of you be interested in going to— *lunch?"* He spun to Vera, crossed his arms, and cocked his head with a mock expression of curiosity. "Either *one* of you?"

With a mock expression of *innocence,* Vera placed two fingers against the side of her jaw. "Oh, I might be persuaded," she replied with a smirk.

"It's my contention that, when Vera was a baby, she was fed exclusively at noontime," I joshed. "But, Mr. Wou, aren't you here alone? What if a customer comes?"

"Not to worry, not to worry," he said, gesturing for us to lead the way. Mr. Wou then added, "Later this afternoon, I'll have many customers. But *now,* I have Vera Van Slyke."

•

After we had settled at a restaurant down the block, Vera eagerly ordered a dish that combined pork and noodles. Mr. Wou ordered a meal I could not pronounce. Following my companions' advice, I was very pleased with chicken mixed with rice and nuts. However, I quickly realized that using chopsticks was a form of Practical Geometry better left to mathematicians smarter than myself.

Once our meals arrived, Vera opened the conversation. "What we now know about ghost sightings, Sankwei, might have changed how we handled the Clancy investigation."

Mr. Wou nodded while chewing.

Vera continued, "Strong feelings of guilt are always present. The guilt can originate on either side of the veil, but that particular emotion *rips* through the veil itself. Only then can inhabitants from the next world find ways to make themselves known in our own."

"And they find a variety of ways to do so!" I added.

Mr. Wou gave Vera a glance before replying to me, "That they do, Miss Parsell. That they do. Now, regarding Representative Clancy."

The two took turns recounting the story. Vera began, but almost as if rehearsed, she stopped at points to let Mr. Wou narrate. From time to time, he would pass the pen back to her, so to speak. It seemed that recalling the strange experience depended on their *shared* memory of it.

The tale they told covered nearly a lifetime of years and miles. Vera explained that, to fully grasp Mr. Clancy's story, we needed to return to the middle of the last century. Barely old enough to do so, James Francis Clancy bid his family farewell and fled Ireland's Great Famine. Landing on the American shore, he led the kind of life that Horatio Alger would put into novels: Mr. Clancy worked hard, he seized opportunities, and he educated himself on the political system of his adopted nation. After defending the Union cause in the early 1860s, the immigrant's zealous ambition drew him away from the smokestacks of the East to the redwoods of the West. In San Francisco, he climbed to political prominence during the 1870s.

After he had become well-established in the Paris of the West, Mr. Clancy's aversion to slavery, which he had garnered during the Civil War, was reignited as opposition to the coolie system of contracted labor. Mr. Wou explained that the coolie system afforded many Chinese men passage to America in exchange for an agreed number of years spent digging mines, laying railroads, or plowing farms. The arrangement often led to bosses making abusive demands upon their contract-bound workers.

In Mr. Clancy's mind, the blame for this promising system turning corrupt went, not only to the people who benefitted from it, but also to those who suffered under it. As Vera lamented, the twists in some human hearts make contempt for slavery tally with contempt for the slave himself. And Mr. Clancy was far from alone in this sentiment. The rungs in his ladder of success were comprised of his drafting or, at least, supporting a series of city, state, and finally national laws restricting the freedoms of Chinese newcomers. These legal prohibitions made Representative Clancy a champion among the voting majority—which was decidedly not Chinese.

•

Sometime around 1885, however, Mr. Clancy's lodge brothers began to notice changes in their friend. For example, he was seen taking most of his meals on Sacramento Street, which Mr. Wou explained was called Tongyan gaai—meaning Street of the Chinese—by the residents there. Concern was also stirred among the lodge members after the Representative left behind an issue of the local newspaper *Chung Sai Yat Po.* In fact, there were reports that Mr. Clancy was learning to read the Cantonese language with remarkable speed.

Changes in Mr. Clancy's behavior at home also had pulses fluttering. The butler claimed that his employer often wore clothing he had purchased during his many rambles through the Chinese Quarter, especially a red robe decorated with cranes. The maid added that Mr. Clancy once asked if she thought he could grow a queue, the long braid that some Chinese men wear down their backs. Speechless, the timid maid could only point at what little remained of the Irishman's curly, ginger-colored hair.

Whenever his lodge brothers alluded to or even boldly addressed the changes to the man himself, Mr. Clancy shrugged and scoffed, insisting that the ways of the Chinese had been a part of his daily life as long as he could remember. When this claim was challenged—when it was contrasted to his Irish origins and especially to his history of legislation aimed *against* the Chinese— Mr. Clancy became dismissive or downright angry. Worried that their political friend might have become a victim of ghostly possession or perhaps some form of pagan sorcery, his cronies decided to find a detective with expertise in the extraordinary.

Harry Escott was summoned. Mr. Clancy's biographical and domestic details were collected during the initial inquiry, Vera at Mr. Escott's side to keep notes. Mr. Wou then joined the investigation to serve as an interpreter. He was also directed to discreetly follow Mr. Clancy during his forays through the Chinese District.

"I had a *wonderful* time playing detective!" exclaimed Mr. Wou. "During the day, I earned a living as a bookkeeper. Very dull work. Back in China, I had boyhood dreams of skipping across the great green waves as a fisherman. Sadly, such a career would have been too lowly for one of my family. That is what I was taught. But do you see? All these years later in America, I've found a way to *combine* bookkeeping with fish! And I am content." Mr. Wou's smile accented the crinkles of his eyes.

"If only everyone could be as content," I replied, an image of Rick at the music shop flashing through my mind. "But how did Mr. Escott meet you? Why did he go to a *bookkeeper* for detective work?"

Mr. Wou turned to Vera and raised his eyebrows. Vera nodded in reply. Again, they had spoken without words.

Grinning weakly at me, Mr. Wou explained, "Mr. Escott stopped me on the street one day to ask if I knew where he could purchase *opium*. Vera has mentioned his unfortunate habit, yes? Well, some white people think that all Chinese either frequent opium dens or, at least, can provide you with an address for one. I made it *very* clear to Mr. Escott that I could *not* help him. And I think *that's* the very reason he offered me the job!"

"Indulging in opium was Harry's only vice," Vera interjected. "He claimed it helped him transcend the physical, making him more sensitive to manifestations from the afterworld. Who knows? I *can* say that, in the end, Harry was correct in sensing there was no possession or sorcery happening with Clancy. True, the man's apparent reversal in feelings toward the Chinese *was* very strange, but he seemed very at ease with the paradox. There was no battle for control of his body. In fact, at first, Harry wondered if the matter were otherwordly at all."

"To help decide if it was or not," said Mr. Wou, "Mr. Escott and Mr. Clancy's lodge brothers hatched a scheme to look for signs of the supernatural. The lodge building had areas for reading newspapers and playing cards. It also served drinks and provided a few overnight rooms. The plan involved the lodge brothers getting Mr. Clancy drunk on the following Saturday evening and persuading him to spend the night in the one of their beds."

Vera explained, "Harry would then sneak into Clancy's room to scout for spectral evidence. A chilly draft, for instance, or an electrical crackling sound that Harry said he often heard in the presence of ghosts. Everything went perfectly to plan."

"But then there was a problem," Mr. Wou stated, his finger raised. He glanced at Vera.

Vera glanced at Mr. Wou. She leaned forward to peer deeply into my eyes.

"At some point over the night," said she.

"Harry Escott *disappeared!*" said he.

•

"Please don't tell me Mr. Escott went off to locate an opium den!" I exclaimed. "Is that why he disappeared from his secret watch over Mr. Clancy?"

Mr. Wou pivoted in his chair to face Vera. He cocked his head in my direction and then nodded. Vera grinned and slowly nodded in reply.

"We had hoped you would assume something much more *mystical* had occurred, my dear," Vera answered, "but yes, that is exactly what happened. Harry went in search of opium. Of course, neither Sankwei nor I had been invited to join Harry that night. The lodge was for men only." Vera must have seen Mr. Wou tap his finger two times before she clarified, "For *white* men only, that is. However, one of the lodge brothers reported Harry's disappearance to me at our hotel early the following morning."

Mr. Wou explained, "It was Sunday, my day off of work, so I was pleased when Vera contacted me. We decided that, until Mr. Escott returned, we might try our own simple scheme. It would not have been very *politic* for Mr. Clancy to attend church, given the scarlet taint in his eyes and the devilish throb in his head. Vera and I waited outside the lodge to see where he might go instead. When he finally appeared, we discovered that he was walking toward the waterfront, perhaps for some sea air. Now, it had been easy for *me* to follow Mr. Clancy around *Chinatown* without being noticed."

"But Sankwei walking along the wharves with a white woman as tall as myself," Vera laughed, "well, that was considerably more conspicuous. At one point, Mr. Clancy sat down on a crate. There, he shouted, *'Is there something you wish to ask me?'* The dairy cow had spotted the two thirsty kittens stalking her! Taking flight seemed foolhardy, so we meandered up to the Representative. I sat down on the crate on his left side."

"And I sat on his right side," Mr. Wou explained.

Their duet resumed. Vera, I was told, pretended to be a bashful admirer who recognized Mr. Clancy's face from newspaper articles and campaign posters. Mr. Wou was presented as her house servant. Luckily, when Mr. Clancy asked which voting precinct Vera called home, Mr. Wou answered for her. Rubbing his temples, the recuperating politician thanked Vera for her support and requested she tell her father to vote for him in the next election. He then waved them both off.

"Is it true that that you're originally from Ireland, Mr. Clancy?" Vera cried, anxious to extend the meeting. "My *mother* immigrated from Ireland!"

He either smiled or winced. "A daughter of the old sod, was she? I see something of my own mother in your auburn hair, sweetie. Your complexion is duskier, though. Hers was alabaster. Oh my, I can still see my poor ma returning from the potato fields, the River Erne rolling along behind her. But there I go again, meandering through the past. You and your boy here really ought to be running—"

"Is your mother still living, sir?" asked Mr. Wou, sensing Vera's plan.

Mr. Clancy turned to his right. He then did something quite unexpected. It took Mr. Wou a moment to realize it, but Vera heard it immediately.

"I sincerely *hope* she is still living," he answered.

However, on that crate on that wharf on that Sunday morning, Representative Clancy spoke his answer in *perfect Cantonese.*

Inspired by a glimmer of a hunch, Mr. Wou then asked in the same language, "What—what did she *look* like, if you don't mind my asking?"

Mr. Clancy now chuckled as he continued in Cantonese. "Her face was not as white as a magistrate's wife, of course, but that was because my mother worked under the sun. I remember her thick hair flying wild like a flock of sable birds when we harvested our family's crops."

Vera and Mr. Wou both leaned forward to look at each other with furrowed brows and gaping mouths.

"What crops did you grow?" asked Mr. Wou in his native language.

In kind, Mr. Clancy answered, "Rice, sugar cane, sweet potatoes, and litchi. The typical crops for farms on the Pearl River."

Sitting suddenly upright, Vera cleared her throat and asked, "Where did you grow up, Mr. Clancy—in what town?"

"Enniskillen—in County Fermanagh," he said to his left in English.

Mr. Wou asked, "In which village does your family remain?"

"Kaiping—in the Guangdong Province," he replied to his right in Cantonese. An edge of impatience was starting to slice through his voice. Facing forward and again rubbing his temples, he resumed his English. "Please! I woke up with a bad headache, and I really must ask you both to let me rest."

"Certainly. Of course, sir," Vera apologized. "But you mentioned you've been 'meandering through the past' lately. Have you been thinking a lot about Ireland?"

175

The sudden slump of Mr. Clancy's body might have indicated exasperation or, possibly, regret. He responded softly, "I have, indeed. My mother recently passed away, you see, and I told myself that I was too busy to travel so far to attend her funeral. I have five brothers and sisters still in Ireland. I've been thinking that, when *my* time comes, it would be nice to be buried among my people."

"Did you leave many siblings behind in China?" asked Mr. Wou in Cantonese.

Mr. Clancy slumped to the right and answered in the same language. "A brother named Ming and a sister named Mai. Our father is deceased, so our mother depends upon her children for an income. I plan to send back money, of course—if I am *ever* permitted to leave the wooden house! But until then, I thank you for your interest, and I bid you to enjoy a pleasant stroll, though I am very sorry I cannot join you." He bowed.

Standing, Mr. Wou returned the bow. "It has been an honor to meet you, sir. I am foolish. Could you remind me of your name?"

Though the question had been asked in casual Cantonese, the answer came back in stiff English.

"James Francis Clancy, boy! Now, don't make me lose my *temper!*"

Vera then jumped off the crate. Unsure of whether to bow or curtsy, she wished Mr. Clancy a quick recovery from his headache. As the two walked away, each step accelerating with urgency, they struggled against the urge to holler in astonishment.

Once beyond earshot of the man—or the *dual* man—she had left behind, Vera demanded, "You *must* tell me what he said when he was speaking Chinese!"

Mr. Wou supported himself against the nearest wall. He recounted how, for each reminiscence of Ireland that Mr. Clancy had related, he offered a mirror memory of his past in China. The auburn-haired mother in Enniskillen, and the sable-haired one in Kaiping. The respective crops and rivers. The deceased mother, the deceased father. The brothers and sisters left behind.

Vera waited until her breath became more regular. She pondered what this meant. Finally, she threw up her hands and confessed, "I don't know what to make of it! Come, we'll have to see if Harry is back at the hotel now. He'll be able to sort it out for us."

"Fine, but let's make one stop first. It's just down there at the Pacific Mail wharf. I need to ask a few questions at the *muk uk* there.

Vera stared at him.

"Sorry," responded Mr. Wou. "It means *wooden house.* It's where Chinese immigrants are detained to see if they qualify for admittance."

"I see. A sort of Castle Garden of the West?"

Mr. Wou inhaled deeply and exhaled slowly. "Since the Chinese Exclusion Act was passed a few years back, very few of us are allowed to enter. It can take *weeks* before decisions are made. And there can be *hundreds* waiting. The living conditions there— well, let me say that, based on what I've read, European immigrants passing through Castle Garden don't—I, uh—I mean to say—" He retracted his lips tightly.

"You don't have to say it, Sankwei," said Vera pensively. *"Muk uk* is most assuredly *not* the Castle Garden of the West."

The two shared a silence that conveyed more than speaking.

•

Looking unexpectedly refreshed, Harry Escott was in the lobby when Vera and Mr. Wou returned. They found a private corner. The two younger detectives reported on the amazing encounter they had had with Representative Clancy less than an hour earlier. Mr. Escott listened attentively, his eyes drifting slightly to the side as he mentally arranged and rearranged these additional facts.

"It's *not* two personalities vying for control," Mr. Wou stated.

"Rather," Vera clarified, "it's one man with two sets of *memories.* Memories that are recalled along similar paths. Two rivers merging into one."

"One river from Ireland," said Mr. Wou, "the other from China. Next, we went to the immigrant detention station on the

Pacific Mail wharf. I asked if anyone there knew of a detainee who had left a brother named Ming, a sister named Mai, and a mother behind in Kaiping. There's a deaconess who visits regularly, and she said that a man named Hom Hing fit that description. But he had *died* over a month ago."

"About when the changes in Clancy started to be noticed," Mr. Escott commented, stroking his white beard.

Mr. Wou continued, "The deaconess also said that fresh air and better food might have done Mr. Hom a world of good. Who knows? As he was dying, however, he had spoken of wanting to meet with those responsible for making immigration so difficult for the Chinese. According to Mr. Hom, there was too much distance between the Chinese and the white Americans, both seeing the other as barbaric devils. He said that, if the politicians spoke with some of the detainees—if they heard one or two of the immigrants' stories—their views would change." Mr. Wou put two fingers to his jaw as he added, "But the poor man never had the chance to meet with any of the politicians."

"Or *did* he?" Mr. Escott stood and began to stroll in small circles. "It all *fits!* It fits with my experience of last night. Shankwei, one of my earliest encounters with a ghost helps to illustrate what I think is occurring *here.* That ghost couldn't rest until his last will and testament were uncovered and his daughter awarded her inheritance. I could *see*—but not *hear*—the ghost, forcing him to communicate with symbols. Specifically, he displayed a pot of tulips! Enough of a clue for me to eventually find the papers he regretted having hidden so well! Now, the ghost and I might've used *speech* had there been much greater *magnetic rapport* between us! Etheric vibrations! One soul harmonizing with another! When the magnetic rapport is strong—well, sir, *that's* when things get interesting!"

Mr. Escott was too engaged with his own theory to notice the slight rise in one of Mr. Wou's eyebrows. Vera, however, sensed his skepticism and had to repress a giggle as her enthusiastic mentor continued.

"Last night, in Clancy's room, I experienced no cold draft or electric crackling. After a couple of hours, though, I jumped when a ghostly figure came *through* the wall and drifted toward the man's sleeping body. The ghost appeared like glowing gauze, so to speak, through which its outlines were visible. It hovered beside the bed for a long time, finally bending down over Clancy, head to head. This is when I observed a most peculiar phenomenon, one I've never before witnessed! Imagine luminous strands of spider web shooting from the ghost's head and attaching to Clancy's. I should have tried to intercept, but I was too entranced—too *perplexed*—to do so. Who am I fooling? I was too *stunned* to do so. Especially when discreet colors began to flow along the strands!"

"*Colors?*" Vera exclaimed. "What—were there any colors in particular?"

"I saw reds and greens," Harry replied, "and violets and yellows and blues. The colors mixed and separated along the various strands. The magnetic rapport between the two must have been *tremendously* strong for such a thing to happen! It was obviously strong enough for the ghost to have located Mr. Clancy even though he was sleeping in an entirely *different* area of town!"

Out of the corner of her eye, Vera saw Mr. Wou slowly nod. She felt he was becoming a bit more convinced of Mr. Escott's theory.

The snow-bearded man supported himself against the back of his chair. "Based on what you two have told me, the stream of colors must have been some manifestation of the memories this Chinese detainee was sharing with our Mr. Clancy. Was the ghost acting on his final wishes to communicate his background to those who had barred him from entering the country? Sankwei, have you ever heard of anything like this? Is it found in Oriental ghost lore?"

"I've *never* come across anything like *this!*" Mr. Wou answered. "I doubt it's Chinese. Or from any *other* nation."

Vera submitted, "Perhaps, it originates from immigration itself."

Mr. Escott sat down again and leaned forward. "It was the sheer *attraction* of the luminous colors, I think, that pulled me out of my paralyzed state. I struggled up and managed to inch toward the ghost. Reaching out, I grabbed its shoulder! It's the kind of blunder a *novice* would make!" The seasoned student of the Occult then held up his palm to reveal a constellation of small blisters.

"Oh, Harry!" Vera cried. "Shouldn't that be bandaged?"

He scanned his wounds. "Aw, they'll heal on their own. The physical touch of the ghost was superficial. The emotional touch went considerably deeper."

"The *emotional* touch?" Mr. Wou said an instant before Vera did.

Mr. Escott crossed his legs and squinted at the carpet a fair time before lifting his head. "Hard to find the right words. A feeling— not of loneliness but of *disconnection.* Not isolation but *vagrancy.* A dreadful feeling, and it compelled me to go out and find some opium. In fact, the emotion I felt when I touched that ghost is the *opposite* of what comes of opium. The exact opposite of that *boundless* feeling of existence, when we seem to have points of contact with the *whole* universe! Do you understand?"

"The late-at-night feeling one has during a long train trip," Vera said.

"Or when simply staring up at the stars," added Mr. Wou. "In fact, that's about when I started to become interested in Astrology, Miss Parsell."

In a blink of the eye, San Francisco became New York. The mid-1880s leaped to 1905. I saw that my companions had cleaned their plates. Mine was only half so. Nonetheless, my *ears* had feasted on a hearty meal.

"Harry had a good idea of what was happening to Mr. Clancy," Vera explained, "but he really had no clue what could be done to remedy it."

Mr. Wou said, "He told the lodge brothers who had hired him that, once the late Hom Hing had finished relating his autobiography, the ghostly visits would end. Mr. Escott speculated that the Chinese Irishman would then gradually return to normal, safe from the spectral influence that had deposited its own memories into another man's mind."

"Harry explained that it was the strong magnetic rapport between the two," said Vera.

"The harmony between their life experiences," Mr. Wou interjected.

"That accounted for the phenomenon," Vera concluded. "But let me interrupt the tale by saying that Representative Clancy's *guilt* about missing his mother's funeral—indeed, his dwelling on having left his family behind during the famine years—had torn open the passage between the living immigrant and the ghostly one."

"We understand that now, and it guides our own investigations," I stated. "However, Mr. Escott set his sights more on what he called the 'magnetic rapport' between the ghost and the haunted, correct?"

"Exactly," said Vera. "Harry was a brilliant ghost hunter, I must say."

"And yet he was mistaken about one part of the case," Mr. Wou added. "He assumed that Mr. Clancy's Chinese memories would fade. But they didn't fade. They amalgamated with the Representative's past. And, Miss Parsell, do you remember that Mr. Clancy had been drifting toward the decision to be buried in Ireland?"

I nodded, thrilled by the prospect of an epilogue.

"Well, that urge only grew with time," Vera said. "However, instead of purchasing passage that would take him to the Atlantic and then on to the Port of Belfast, Clancy's ticket carried him across the Pacific to the Port of Hong Kong. This would have been in the late 1890s. Do you happen to know what was happening in China during the late 1890s?"

I had to think hard. "Wasn't it the Boxer Rebellion?"

"Specifically, yes," Mr. Wou replied. "More generally, there was an expulsion of anything Western—anything not Chinese—

starting with commercial trade and ending with missionary work. So you can imagine the reaction when a freckled, elderly man named James Francis Clancy declared that he wished to enter the country to be buried on his ancestral homeland. He was judged to be senile and ordered to return to the U.S. The newspapers used the incident as proof that the foreign devils feel no concern for their elders, a sign of the moral decay prominent among the white race of the West."

I thought about the ghost of Hom Hing. I thought about good intentions versus revenge. I thought about how, in some cases, good intentions might be inseparable from revenge.

Mr. Wou continued, "I had returned to China by this time. Vera and I had agreed to keep in touch by letter. I wrote to explain what I had read in the Chinese papers."

"And I had become a journalist here in New York. I turned to my professional connections to discover what next became of Representative Clancy. But it was as if he had vanished somewhere on the Pacific. Perhaps, he found another route to Kaiping. Maybe he decided Enniskillen would serve as well." Vera shrugged.

"Sadly," Mr. Wou concluded, "not all mysteries end with a solution."

•

We visited with Mr. Wou once more before leaving New York. I took advantage of the opportunity to write down the details of the case for future reference. I explained that it was my duty as Vera's assistant, though she herself claimed there was no need for it. Perhaps my real reason for wanting to remember the story was the growing movement to restrict immigration from all across Asia and well into Eastern and Southern Europe. I was thankful that my brother had joined me from Prague the previous year.

The time had come for us to leave Vera's beloved city and return to Chicago. Our train departed Grand Central Station fairly late in the evening, and our compartment came with pull-down bunk beds. Though it was not yet our usual bedtime, we changed into our nightgowns. Vera climbed into the top bed as I settled into the bottom one.

We rocked with the clatter of the rails. A narrow gap beside my pillow let me watch the starlit landscape pass. After about half an hour, the bed springs above me revealed that Vera was still awake.

I began to pester her for even more of the particulars of the investigation. "Vera? Before you go to sleep, may I ask about Mr. Wou's claim to have immigrated *twice?* His first time was to San Francisco, where he worked as a bookkeeper, I assume."

"That's right." Vera shifted to the outer edge so that I could hear her more easily. "There's another sad story there. Like Clancy, Sankwei first came to the U.S. when he was barely a man. Even so, his family arranged for him to be married before he left. The bride stayed behind, so that Sankwei could make a comfortable home for them both. It had taken him a good many years, during which he had joined our investigation. Finally, Sankwei sent for her. Unfortunately, his poor wife was simply unable to make the adjustment to San Francisco. There was some trouble, and Sankwei decided it would best for them both to return to China."

After some contemplation, I asked, "But, then, at some point he came back for a *second* time, correct?"

"Yes. To New York. To open the fish shop." The springs in Vera's bed creaked slowly.

"Oh, dear," I said softly. "Had his wife passed away?"

She sniffled before answering. "No."

"So he—does he still have a wife in China?"

"Yes. A wife. In China." There was a pause followed by another sniffle. "Given your predicament with that young man you've grown so fond of—his talk of leaving you for Alaska—I thought it best to avoid any conversation about Sankwei's two immigrations."

I thought I heard a quaver in Vera's voice, but it might have been due to the vibrating train car. What sounded like a whimper might have been the whine of a nearby coupling. I wondered if Vera had some reason to avoid the subject of Mr. Wou's second immigration other than my predicament with Rick Bergson. If so, she was keeping it private.

"Thank you for safeguarding me," I murmured. Hoping to end the discussion, I added, "Mr. Wou couldn't readapt to life in China any better than his wife could adapt to life here, I suppose."

"No, no! It's not *that*," Vera exclaimed. Her face appeared over the edge to peer down at me. "His study of the planets has taught Sankwei to think of himself a resident of Earth, not of any one country. He could live *anywhere*, I imagine."

I pulled myself sideways to look up at her. "Then why did he leave China a *second* time—even though he had to leave his wife behind *again?*"

"Well, you see, Sankwei began to reconsider his obligations to his family," Vera said. "He married because his family had wished him to marry. He became a bookkeeper because of family honor. Perhaps his exposure to the American self-made man—the very ideal that inspired Clancy's success—truly had *decayed* Sankwei's morals, as the Chinese newspapers would paint it. He decided to return to America to become a fishmonger."

"But why go all the way to New York?" I asked. "The Chinese eat fish, don't they? And so do San Franciscans for that matter."

"Ah, well," Vera uttered. "Why all the way to New York?"

As the springs of her bed squeaked, she withdrew from sight. There was a pause. I wondered if she might have drifted to sleep.

Barely loud enough to be heard, Vera finally said, "Perhaps that is best attributed to—*magnetic rapport.*"

I remained very still. I began to think about mysteries gone unsolved. About stories gone untold. About feelings of disconnection and vagrancy, and how we seek ways to soothe them.

Eventually, I rolled onto my side to watch the dark landscape passing by us. Above it, the distant stars shone brilliantly.

VAMPIRE PARTICLES
(1906)

He come on moonlight rays as elemental dust.

— Bram Stoker

"According to this gentleman," I told Vera Van Slyke, *"you're a gentleman."* I handed her a letter addressed to Mr. Vernon Van Slyke.

Glancing over the correspondence, she replied, "One might expect greater precision from a *coroner."* She looked up and winked at me.

"Oh, that's far from the strangest part of the letter," I warned.

Vera's smirk was replaced by a blank expression. She placed two fingers to her jaw as she leaned back to read.

Peter M. Hoffman, coroner of Cook County, explained that his office had been tasked with explaining three deaths of a highly peculiar nature. A possible fourth victim was still being investigated. In each confirmed case, termination of life was preceded by—as Mr. Hoffman termed it—"manic vitality," which he defined as "an exuberant and indefatigable expenditure of energy on such activities as dance, sport, drink, and less sanctioned forms of pleasure seeking."

Vera looked up from the letter. "Does he mean these three people *enjoyed* themselves to death?"

"He says each man died with a smile on his face," I responded.

After another blank stare, Vera returned to Mr. Hoffman's letter.

The coroner surmised that the condition was somehow related to the employment of the victims. All three of the confirmed dead men—Cyril Hughes, Donny Reynolds, and Carl Hanacek—worked side-by-side for the Illinois Tunnel Company. The man still being sought was their co-worker. This firm had been organized to dig passageways deep below downtown Chicago, the tunnels designed for transporting freight, coal, and mail, thereby easing congested street-level traffic. The four men had performed the initial digging and finishing work before another shift lined the tunnel with concrete. Sometimes, their work had taken them as far as forty feet below the surface.

"Forty feet *underground*," Vera muttered. "Must the sun of ingenuity forever be eclipsed by the moon of *lunacy?*" She began to sneer at the letter.

Fearing that the deaths might have resulted from some unknown gas or other substance better left buried, Mr. Hoffman presented his findings to the city council charged with overseeing the tunnel project. The coroner argued that informing the public of the early symptoms might prevent future tragedies and that the digging should stop until more information was gathered. The councilmen, however, unanimously insisted that the public *not* be alerted to the danger. Mass panic was likely to result, they insisted. The digging, they amended, would continue. Mr. Hoffman suspected that the council was more concerned with its own reputation than with the public good.

"This Hoffman seems like a well-intentioned fellow," Vera murmured as she turned the page over.

Seeking the assistance of a courageous journalist, Mr. Hoffman had been told that "Vernon Van Slyke" was known among local reporters for being both daring *and* otherwise well-qualified in dealing with strange phenomena. The three deaths certainly counted as *strange.* The coroner ended his letter with an urgent request to meet, suggesting a time and location that would allow an examination of the tunnel where Hughes, Reynolds, and Hanacek had worked together before losing their lives. In a postscript, he clarified that the tunnel had been lined with concrete and no workers since had shown any symptoms of the deadly "manic vitality."

Vera carefully placed the letter down on her desk. "Jot a note in reply," she instructed me. "Say that I'll gladly meet with him as he suggests. If at all possible, don't indicate that I'm a woman. I'd love to see his face when *I* arrive in my most frilly and feathery hat."

With a snicker, I said, "I'll do my best, sir."

•

Mr. Hoffman was not amused when Vera and I arrived at the meeting place. It was the basement of an office building in the northeast quadrant of downtown Chicago. The man's stout build, bristly moustache, and darting eyes somehow made him look as if he were hunting big game instead of tracking clues of an undiscovered disease.

After introductions, Vera explained, "Though you erred slightly with the name, rest assured that you contacted the correct reporter for the job."

The coroner crossed his arms. He grumbled, "As I explained in my letter, I'm *defying* a council of Chicago politicians by sharing this information with the press. With all due respect, Miss Van Slyke, I need a reporter who won't crumble and cry once the news hits the streets—and the councilmen hit the ceiling!"

Vera narrowed her eyes. "I neither crumbled nor cried back in New York, sir, when my articles time and again exposed the corruption of Tammany Hall. Now, I applaud you for fighting for the public good, but you do *no* good when you assume that my sex makes me too feeble to do the very same! Need I mention the fortitude of Jane Addams? Need I mention the steel of Clara Barton? Need I mention—"

"You need not *scold* me!" Mr. Hoffman snapped. "I was simply being *cautious*. Understand, I'm putting my own political career in jeopardy here! Coroners *are* elected officials, you know! And I plan to advance to *sheriff* one day!"

The two glared at each another. Again, I thought of big game. Specifically, I imagined a bull elephant confronting a lioness.

Feeling a bit like a young gazelle, I submitted, "Perhaps, we could discuss this further while seeing where the men were working before their symptoms appeared."

"Perhaps, that would be time better spent," Vera added.

"Perhaps—that makes sense," Mr. Hoffman conceded.

We then rode the elevator down to the tunnels. We were guided by a smudge-faced employee of the Illinois Tunnel Company whose observable disinterest in us implied he had duties he considered much more important. Once we stepped out of the elevator, we saw that the tunnels were roughly six feet wide and seven or eight feet high. Cables hung along the top, and twin rails, smaller than typical train tracks, lined the bottom. As we walked the first stretch of tunnel, I was surprised by how well ventilated and nicely illuminated the tunnels were. However, the concrete walls were egg-shaped instead of rectangular. This curvature created the sensation of walking along the intestines of an industrial behemoth.

The only sounds were the grumbles of machinery at some inestimable distance and our own footfalls beneath us. Vera and Mr. Hoffman were still not speaking, and neither was our guide.

Timidly, I asked, "Do either of you gentlemen happen to know when this tunneling project began?" The echo of my voice was unsettling.

"1899," stated our guide bluntly. He then used his thumb to indicate that we were to turn the corner.

As we turned, I began to wonder why Vera wasn't leading the inquiry. To fill the silence, I resumed, "I've lived in Chicago a long time. How is it that I've never heard of these tunnels?"

Mr. Hoffman spoke. "The operation's been designed to be as unobtrusive as possible, since the goal is to ease street traffic instead of hindering it. It's quite an amazing feat of engineering, and the city hopes to boast about it once it's complete. I imagine that's why they don't want any unflattering publicity in the meantime." With a sneer, he added, "Your New York might be transporting *people* in its subway, Miss Van Slyke, but Chicago hopes that these tracks for transporting *freight* underground will serve as a model for the world."

As if in reply, Vera coughed twice.

Suddenly, I remembered the trip to New York that Vera and I had made the previous year. We had ridden in the subway for our very first time, and Vera compared the experience to traveling in a speeding *casket*. She had insisted she would *never* ride another subway. As it had been then, her face now was very pale. Though the tunnels were cool, beads of perspiration covered her brow. She was breathing heavily through open lips. I touched her arm, and she jerked away from me. Immediately afterward, though, she gave me a weak smile.

My first impulse was to ask if we might rest to let Vera regain her composure. But I knew she was determined to prove to Mr. Hoffman that a lady reporter could be just as courageous as a male one. I continued to walk silently, pondering the fact that neither Jane Adams nor Clara Barton had ever ventured through gargantuan intestines forty feet underground.

I then realized that *I* would have to lead the investigation.

"If I may ask another question," I began, "can you tell us more about the symptoms the three victims exhibited before dying, Mr. Hoffman? In your letter, you only mention that they exerted a lot of energy on dance and sport and such."

The coroner nodded. "Never heard of anything like it before. Hughes' and Hanacek's widows said their husbands had stopped sleeping altogether in favor of any kind of excitement they could find. They found *Hughes'* body in West Side Park. The Cubs hadn't played there for days, and his footprints showed he'd been running around the bases for what must've been *hours!* It took three cops to pull *Hanacek* out of Lake Michigan. Said he wanted to swim up to Milwaukee to hear his favorite polka band, but he died while struggling to stay out of a straightjacket. Reynolds' mother said her son had always been a homebody before he died at Freiberg's

Dance Hall from—well, let's just say from too much *activity* with the, uh, the *barmaids* who work there."

"Yes, I—I think I understand," I stuttered.

"Medically speaking," the coroner continued, "they overtaxed their hearts and kidneys. Like a steam engine exploding."

"How long did the symptoms last," I asked.

"*Three* days from when the men's womenfolk first noticed changes in their behavior. That's how we worked out the spot where they were probably working when it first hit them. It was close to *here,* wasn't it?"

Our guide nodded and pointed to a spot not too far ahead.

As we walked the final few yards, I glanced at Vera. Despite the sickly sheen on her face, she began to carefully examine the concrete ceiling, which was low enough for her to touch.

She coughed again but managed to ask, "What's above?"

Mr. Hoffman looked to the company man. Our guide informed us that the corner of Lake Street and Wabash Avenue was directly skyward.

The coroner then resumed authority. "There's nothing up there that would explain this down here. If the cause were on the surface, we surely would've noticed it long—"

Vera shook her head to show that's not what she had meant.

I offered, "I think Miss Van Slyke means *between* the surface and here."

The guide stepped forward. "Nothing we know about. This far down, it's mostly clay. I didn't hear about them running into anything any different."

Mr. Hoffman laughed. "Of course, I explored the same possibility, Miss Van Slyke. So far as we can tell, there's nothing between here and ground level that might have washed its way down this far. Besides, I'm told that, except for maybe a bit of water, there's practically no physical substance that could seep through the clay."

I turned to Vera and reiterated, "No *physical* substance. Do we need to return with the two oboes?"

Vera's eyes grew wide before she whispered, "Return? *No!*"

"I don't understand," Mr. Hoffman protested. "Did you say 'two *oboes'?*"

Vera inhaled deeply. "The concrete now prevents us from checking the surrounding soil, and it would be very risky to whoever breaks through the ceiling to take a sample. I'm of the mind, though, that the solution can be found more easily by going back and examining the history of what lies buried at this spot. Now, let's return to the *surface,* shall we?"

Vera immediately spun around and took a step back toward the elevator.

"Now, *hold on!*" Mr. Hoffman commanded, appearing startled by the sound of his own echoes. "Don't tell me you're suggesting that there's some ancient Indian burial ground above us! And that digging way down here has put a *curse* on these men!"

Vera did not turn around. Instead, she put her hand against the wall as if to steady herself.

"A curse cast by an Indian burial ground seems oddly *specific,* Mr. Hoffman," I insisted. "All Miss Van Slyke suggested was that we examine what might be buried above us, be it bones or ruins or even pots left by French explorers. Do you suspect that there's a supernatural cause—or, no, let me ask you this first: did you contact Miss Van Slyke because of her expertise in ghost hunting?"

Mr. Hoffman glanced a few times at the company guide, who turned away. The coroner then tested the strength of one of the rails with his toe. Finally, he confessed, "I was told a man named *Vernon* Van Slyke had skills along those lines!"

Vera pivoted toward us. Her face was ashen now, but the glint of glowing embers shone in her eyes. *"Regardless* of whether you're calling for my skills in solving hauntings or in reporting news, sir, my stance is exactly the *same!* The key to these deaths lies buried directly above us! Now, let's *go!*"

Without hesitation, the company guide led us back to the elevator. Mr. Hoffman stayed two or three steps behind. He did not utter a word.

•

When we were again on street level, Vera tugged me aside. In the new light, her complexion looked waxy. She teetered from side to side.

"Have I eaten lunch yet?" she asked me in a hushed voice.

"Yes, about three hours ago."

"Then I need a *beer.*"

"Now, what's all this?" Mr. Hoffman demanded.

With barely a thought, I stepped between the coroner and Vera. "Miss Van Slyke said she could use a *beer!*"

"Are you serious? A *beer?*"

"That's right," I affirmed pointedly. "And *I'd* like one, as well! Are you going to tell us that a man with the name *Hoffman* doesn't occasionally indulge in a—"

"What *kind* of beer?" he interrupted. He slowly narrowed his eyes.

I searched for a biting rebuttal until I realized—he wasn't debating. I was stymied.

From behind, Vera tapped my shoulder. "I favor ales and porters," she stated, her voice still weak. "But a pilsner might be in order, since it's still afternoon."

"*Excellent* suggestion," Mr. Hoffman replied with a nod. "No one knows local history better than a bartender. I see your investigative methods are top-notch. The corner of Lake and Wabash is just a few blocks away. Shall we hop on a streetcar or walk there?

"If no one minds," Vera murmured, "the walk would do me good."

Mr. Hoffman offered his arm to Vera. As she accepted it, she turned to me with one eyebrow raised. It was my turn to remain silent and a few steps behind.

It was an easy jaunt to Lake Street and Wabash Avenue. There, a passerby directed us to the nearest tavern. Once inside, Vera marched straight to a table, where she sat down and looked around with the grateful grin of someone allowed to live another day.

The bartender appeared from a backroom, no doubt having heard us enter. He was a lanky man with an angular face and very little hair. His green and yellow striped shirt gave him a snake-like appearance. Looking in the direction of Vera and myself, he stopped short.

"Excuse me, folks," he said. "This is a businessman's bar, and I'm prevented from serving women. It's a rule. I recommend the ladies visit one of the restaurants in any of the department stores over on State Street."

Mr. Hoffman put his hands on his hips as if preparing for a Wild West showdown. "Oh, we're not here for pleasure, friend. We're here on Cook County business. I'm investigating a series of mysterious deaths, and these two—they're both cooperating witnesses. Let's bend the rule slightly, and you bring a couple of glasses of *water* for these women. Now, for myself? I'll have *three* beers. Pilsner, if you have it. Bring all three at the same time." The burly coroner then ambled his way to the table.

After all were seated, Vera quietly acquiesced, "Sir? I misjudged you. Can you forgive me for not telling you my correct name from the start?"

Mr. Hoffman snorted. "Oh, I never would've asked for your help if I'd known you're a woman. But you gave me a right good scolding, and I saw you master your fear of being that far underground! You've proved you're not the kind who writes weepy romances with a quill, so to speak, and I suspect the joker who recommended you probably does. Besides, you could also charge *me* with having misled *you*. Your assistant was right when she implied I contacted you more for your ghost hunting than your journalism."

I asked, "Does this mean that you suspect the supernatural is behind these deaths?"

The wooden chair creaked when Mr. Hoffman rested his considerable weight back against it. He sighed deeply. "I lean toward some scientific explanation. Maybe there's some unknown *bacteria* living in the clay. Some kind of *germs*. But, as you said earlier, Miss Van Slyke, investigating that—well, it's like poking a wintering bear."

Vera stated, "Your position requires you to poke that bear if there are any *more* deaths."

The coroner nodded pensively. "If there are any more deaths, I pray the councilmen will agree to take action. Until then, though, all I can do is investigate other avenues." He turned to see how the bartender was doing with the drinks. The last beer had just been poured. Remaining silent, Mr. Hoffman waited while the glass was added to the tray and delivered to the table. "Thank you, friend," he said to the bartender. "You go ahead and finish your work in the back while I interrogate these witnesses."

The serpentine man swiveled his head toward Vera and then toward myself. After cold-blooded consideration of our presence, he took Mr. Hoffman's money and slithered off with it.

The coroner pushed a glass of beer to Vera and one to me. He resumed the discussion. "Now, about those other avenues of investigation. Though none of the tunnel workers will say so on record, a few of them claimed they've heard *sounds* in the tunnels. *Human* sounds. Moans and groans and such. Isn't that one of the telltale signs of a ghost?"

Vera finished a swig of beer and sat upright. Her strength seemed to be returning. "A ghost, yes—or possibly only a reverberation of all that concrete settling. But, tell me, do *you* believe in ghosts, Mr. Hoffman?"

He pulled a handkerchief from his suit pocket and wiped off his hands. "I'm of two minds regarding that topic. As a coroner, I nose around for the physical chain of events that explain death. The *science* of death, if you will. And I have yet to find a magnifying lens that reveals the afterlife. On the other hand, I've walked through the valley of the shadow of death for so long, it's like my own backyard. And a lot of fog drifts around that valley. Sometimes, when I'm investigating a case, my thoughts gets so bunched up that I go down to the morgue and ask questions of the corpses themselves!"

"Oh dear! Have they ever answered?" chuckled Vera.

Mr. Hoffman smirked, stuffing his handkerchief back into his pocket. "Not as yet they haven't. In my way, though, I ache to communicate with the dearly departed almost as much as their loved ones do. And I've heard stories from those loved ones! Stories of seeing or hearing the spirits of those they've lost. Well, let me just say that I do not dismiss the reality of ghosts."

We raised our glasses.

He continued. "Yet why would ghosts be lurking in tunnels far below Lake and Wabash? Now, some of your Eastern cities have cemeteries in the downtown area, but Chicago's too young for that. We didn't pass any graveyards on the way here! Even when the Great Fire swept through this area, all the victims were buried in *outlying* areas, according to the old-timers I asked. Best explanation I could devise was some ancient Indian burial ground."

After savoring another swallow of her beer, Vera replied, "I have a hunch that Indian curses are invented by the Indians themselves in an effort to keep away the white people. Perhaps it's time to call back the bartender and tap into his knowledge of local history."

"Let's finish our beers first," Mr. Hoffman suggested. "In the meantime, what's this business with the two oboes you mentioned down below?"

I let Vera drink her beer while I explained our discoveries that intense guilt tears holes between this and the spirit world, and that those holes cast a violet glow when B-flat and high G are played on oboes. As he listened, Mr. Hoffman's "two minds" concerning ghosts were reflected in his eyes, which narrowed with doubt and then widened with wonder.

At the end of my lecture, the coroner again made his chair creak as he leaned backward. He twisted his beer glass clockwise and then counterclockwise. "Well," he said, "if you've convinced me of anything, it's this: if women succeed in getting the vote, ours is going to be an interesting world."

Again, we lifted our glasses.

And Vera's glass was empty, so Mr. Hoffman called for the bartender. The man appeared holding a broom, disappeared, and returned without it. He unrolled his shirtsleeves as he approached our table. Vera and Mr. Hoffman began to speak at the same time, and the gentleman deferred to the lady.

Vera inquired, "During your time as a bartender here, have you ever heard any unusual tales about the history of this area?"

The bartender turned first to Mr. Hoffman. Once the coroner nodded, the man began to rub his neck. He then made a quiet hissing sound. This was his way of recollecting, it seemed.

Vera prodded. "Especially something having to do with a traumatic death. Or a death kept secret. Perhaps a *murder?* Or a person gone *missing?"*

Mr. Hoffman added. "Possibly something from long ago."

The bartender only continued to hiss.

Mr. Hoffman pursed his lips. Vera shook her head to indicate that she had no further questions.

"All right, friend," Mr. Hoffman said, "thank you for your—"

"Mr. Hoffman, they found that fourth digger! Found him *dead and grinning*—exactly like the others!" The voice belonged to a young woman who stood at the entrance of the tavern. She wound her way quickly through the tables toward us. She was a diminutive, smartly dressed woman, carrying a number of files.

After a harsher hiss, the bartender started to repeat his 'no women allowed' speech—but Mr. Hoffman stood up and halted him.

"No, no," the coroner said. "She's with me, too. Though how she manages to find me, I'll never know."

The bartender threw up his hands and slipped back to his sweeping. Once the offending female had arrived, Mr. Hoffman introduced us to Miss Emily Cowles, a secretary from the Coroner's office.

Regaining her breath, Miss Cowles greeted us each rapidly and then said to Mr. Hoffman, "The fourth tunnel digger was found *dead!* Murray Brandon!"

Mr. Hoffman explained to us, "Murray Brandon worked with the three others. He had been missing from work, and we couldn't track him down."

Miss Cowles continued, "Found his body up in a tree at Jackson Park! Folded over a branch! No unusual marks on the body. He must've climbed up there! He's at the morgue now."

Mr. Hoffman dropped back into his chair. Staring at the glasses on the table, he said, "Brandon was new to the city. He lived at a boarding house on the south side, and his only family is in Indiana. Miss Van Slyke? Would you care to join me tomorrow when I ask around at the boarding house?"

"Certainly," she answered. "In the meanwhile, I'll search for whatever might be haunting these grounds and consult my books for comparable manifestations. I imagine, though, that Catherine Crowe never came across *anything* quite like this!" She turned to face Mr. Hoffman's secretary. "I don't suppose *you* know anything about the history of his neighborhood?"

The woman's head wobbled slightly. "*This* neighborhood? All that comes to mind is Fort Dearborn. It stood near this spot long, long ago. Beyond that, all I know is that they sell souvenir teaspoons with an image of the fort embossed on them. I bought one for my cousin."

"Fort Dearborn?" Vera repeated. "Several years ago, we investigated ghosts at Fort Pitt. We met a gentleman there in Pittsburg named Vitellius Berry. A remarkable man, whose talent for retrieving historical information has been vital to solving subsequent cases. Lida, we must telegraph Mr. Berry to see what he can find out about this Fort Dearborn. Mr. Hoffman, kindly send the time and address for tomorrow's interviews to my office." With no further formalities, she rose and started toward the doorway.

I quickly thanked Miss Cowles for her help and bid them both a good evening before rushing to catch up with Vera.

•

Two pieces of evidence helped Vera crystalize a theory of what had killed the four tunnel workers. The first clue had come from the landlady and residents of the Vincennes Avenue boarding house where Mr. Murray Brandon had resided. Over lunch, Vera and Mr. Hoffman reviewed what their questioning had uncovered.

After ordering a pork cutlet, Vera said, "I'm struck by the final words the residents heard Mr. Brandon say on the last morning they had seen him. He said he was going to 'stop slogging away like an earthworm and start living like a man.' Isn't that the phrase they remembered him using, Lida?"

I flipped through my notes to confirm Vera's recollection. "Yes, and then the landlady described him as an 'admirable specimen of a man.' She recalled that Mr. Brandon went to the Y.M.C.A. almost daily to build up his muscles. She marveled at how much he could eat and added that, at mealtimes, Mr. Brandon would discuss how he didn't mind the digging itself so much as the time he spent down in 'those infernal caves.' I'm not sure whether Mr. Brandon or his landlady described the tunnels as 'infernal caves'."

Mr. Hoffman explained that the corpse of the late Murray Brandon attested to his time spent at the gymnasium. "And that helps to explain why he was the last to die. Brandon's physique was able to handle the increased activity—at least, for a while."

Vera replied, "It's as if whatever infected these men is so hungry for life, it ends up killing its host. A parasite that lives on *life*—but *kills* in the process."

"A *vampire!*" I gasped. Suddenly embarrassed, I stammered, "Well, a—a vampire of sorts. Vampire germs, perhaps?"

Mr. Hoffman sighed. "Now, vampire germs would be an interesting compromise between science and the supernatural." He chuckled without conviction.

Vera remained silent. She even ignored her lunch when it was placed in front of her. I would have worried, but she commenced eating after only a minute or so.

That had occurred on Thursday. The following Tuesday, the second piece of evidence arrived. A familiar face delivered it.

Unannounced, Mr. Vitellius Berry of Pittsburg knocked on the door of Vera's rooms at the Hotel Manitou. My first feelings upon seeing him were less than hospitable. True, we had telegraphed him the previous week, requesting any relevant history he could find regarding Fort Dearborn. However, it would have been more mannerly of him to send a return telegraph or to otherwise inform us that he had come to Chicago in person.

Nonetheless, Vera beamed upon seeing Mr. Berry standing in her parlor. Walking toward him, she cooed, *"You* again!"

"And—and *another* crazy story," he returned in his high voice.

I tried not to watch as they complimented each other's appearance and failed to drop their handshake.

When considerable time had passed, I quietly inquired, "Does your crazy story pertain to Fort Dearborn, Mr. Berry?"

Vera giggled as she quickly fiddled with her hair and pulled at the cuffs of her blouse. She then offered her guest a chair and took one herself.

"Indeed, Miss Parsell, I'm here to report on Fort Dearborn," replied Mr. Berry as he sat. "But—but exactly how it relates to the tunnel diggers' deaths—well, Miss Van Slyke is best qualified to decide that, I venture. My resources were too limited back home, so I decided to come and visit your city's historical society. I've compiled some facts."

Vera leaned forward. "We're eager to hear whatever you've discovered. And we're especially interested in unusual burials in the area of Fort Dearborn."

"I venture that many of these facts will prove valuable, then. And—and, while smallpox was the issue with Fort Pitt, the case of Fort Dearborn concerns cholera."

Vera tilted her head. "Another fort—and another *disease?"*

"That's what makes it *crazy!* But—but you'll see that the two histories are very different." Mr. Berry took a small journal from his pocket and referred to it while speaking. "It was back in 1832 when reinforcements came to join the Fort Dearborn soldiers fighting in the Black Hawk War. They came on the steamship *Sheldon Thompson* via the Great Lakes. On route, some of the soldiers contacted cholera, which had spread to Canada from England."

I said, "Surely, they wouldn't allow a ship carrying a deadly disease to land! Or would they?"

"I'm afraid they did," Mr. Berry replied. "General Winfield Scott ordered that Fort Dearborn be converted into a makeshift cholera hospital. The uninfected soldiers already there were commanded to camp elsewhere. Unfortunately, several civilians— the early settlers of Chicago and the surrounding prairies—had arrived at the fort, seeking protection from the Indian attacks. They also remained in the area. And—and the order to stay clear of the fort was *disobeyed.*"

Vera moaned slightly before lamenting aloud, "Resulting in an epidemic of cholera?"

Mr. Berry lowered his head. "I don't know if the disease spread to the civilians, but one book claims that, among the soldiers, the cholera took about one hundred lives. Years later, General Scott said that, throughout his long military career, he had never felt as helpless and in need of Divine assistance as during that cholera outbreak. But—but it's the *burial* of the Fort Dearborn victims that you'll find significant to your case, I venture."

"Yes," Vera whispered, "the burial."

"Let me read the words of Captain Walker of the *Sheldon Thompson.* 'The earth that was removed to cover one made a grave to receive the next that died. All were buried without coffins or shrouds, except their blankets, which served for a winding-sheet, there left, as it were, without remembrance or a stone to mark their resting-place.'" Mr. Berry looked up and glanced between Vera and myself.

Vera stood and began to pace. "All those lives ended so suddenly, so horribly—dumped side-by-side in one plot of ground." Suddenly, she stopped. "Mr. Berry? Is there a record of *where* these poor souls were buried?"

"It's difficult to say, since the current streets weren't in place at the time. Still, one resident claimed he remembered it being where Wabash Avenue meets South Water Street today."

Vera winced.

"But—" Mr. Berry resumed, "but Captain Walker along with a man named Luther Nichols, a soldier who helped bury the dead and who died in Chicago fifty years later, both place it a bit further south." He closed his journal. "At what is now the corner of Wabash Avenue and Lake Street."

Vera laced her fingers together. "They wanted more life, those cholera victims. As would *anyone* who dies before growing old. The difference is, by absurd happenstance, the unhappy corpses buried near Fort Dearborn got their wish."

I shivered at the thought.

•

"I don't fully understand," said Miss Cowles, the secretary from the coroner's office. "What *is* Miss Van Slyke's theory regarding the four deaths?"

She and I were sitting in one of the hallways of Chicago City Hall. Mr. Berry was with us, too, though he had wandered off to study the building's architectural features. The three of us were waiting for Vera and Mr. Hoffman to finish a meeting with the city council that oversaw the downtown tunnel project.

As Vera herself was likely explaining her theory to the councilmen, I explained it to Miss Cowles.

"All species on Earth," I began, "are imbued with a tremendous drive to *live*. Think of it. From the frozen poles to the ocean depths, from the arid desserts to the smallest gaps between bricks in a city street—we find plants and animals struggling and often *succeeding* in the business of living. It's really very wonderful!"

"A point on which the Darwinists and the religious can *both* agree," submitted Miss Cowles. Though diminutive in size, she was proving to be formidable in intelligence.

I continued, "Now, imagine that this *drive* to live is so deeply engrained—so tightly woven into our being—that it resides even in the very smallest particles of our bodies. Particles that remain even after death."

"What a grand discovery *that* would be. To prove the existence of such particles, I mean. Until such evidence is found, I will listen on the *conjecture* that they exist."

"Thank you," I replied, hoping that Vera had as receptive an audience as did I. "Well, Vera speculates that—whether these particles are natural, supernatural, or wavering on the threshold *between* the two—after death, they are released through the process of decay. They eventually become a part of the soil, just as all bodies become dust over the years. And as rain trickles through the dirt to replenish the water for our wells, these minute particles slowly wash downward. Of course, we would never know the potential effects they might have so long as we remain on the *surface.*"

An elfin grin came to Miss Cowles's face. "But were we to dig tunnels *below* the surface!"

"And were those tunnels to coincide with an unusually dense deposit of these particles, where they might be inhaled or even absorbed through the skin—well, we've seen the results."

Miss Cowles held her fairy grin. It then faded. Finally, she concluded, "It's a conjecture worth studying. If the life-hungry dust motes exist somewhere between the natural and the supernatural, perhaps that concrete barrier has only hampered their descent instead of halting it."

"As I understand it, that's exactly what Miss Van Slyke and Mr. Hoffman hope to convince the councilmen. Previous reports of the same thing happening would help their argument. But how often have people tunneled directly under such a crowded mass grave? Of course, there are vampire legends, which are ancient and widespread. But *this* seems to be a twentieth-century version of such a monster!"

Miss Cowles shuddered at the suggestion, reminding me of my own reaction upon hearing it. As we continued to chat, I discovered I had much in common with this young lady. She was seventeen years old and had only recently started assisting Mr. Hoffman. I told her that that's the age I was when I had first met Vera. She mentioned that some of the coroner's investigations had sparked her interest in chronicling the cases, possibly in the form of fictional detective stories. I confessed to having had similar thoughts with my adventures with Vera. By the end of our conversation, I was calling her Emily, and she was calling me Lida.

Far less congenial was Vera and Mr. Hoffman's meeting with the councilmen, as we soon learned. Vera's tall figure emerged before Mr. Hoffman's burly one. Mr. Berry came rushing back. Emily and I rose to stand beside Vera.

Other than her raised eyebrows, there was no expression on Vera's face. In sharp contrast, Mr. Hoffman's face was burning red, his jaw clenched, and his eyes darting furiously from side to side.

"So—so it didn't go well, I venture?" Mr. Berry inquired meekly.

Mr. Hoffman snarled, "It was an outrage! A *travesty!* It's a sorrowful day when a gang of politicians manages to suppress a mere *attempt* to discover the truth behind these four deaths! No, Mr. Berry, it did *not* go well!"

Mr. Berry cowered behind his own arms. I imagined a wren flailing its wings to avoid the stomping legs of a bull elephant.

"These are not men of *science!*" Mr. Hoffman resumed. "These are not even men with *souls!* Prattling on about mass panic and civic pride and commercial priority!" He railed against the council's decision to thwart any further investigation of Vera's theory. He decried how they had threatened Vera and him with professional ruin should either draw public attention to the Fort Dearborn mass grave.

With a tone of resignation, Vera added, "The decomposed remains of those cholera victims and the bizarre symptoms of the four dead tunnel workers were ruled to be 'an unsubstantiated coincidence.' Coincidence, perhaps, but I believe Mr. Berry substantiated the burial site very nicely."

The two traded smiles.

Mr. Hoffman continued to simmer. "To be honest, Miss Van Slyke, I'd expect you to be much more upset, if not *hysterical,* given how they treated your theory and threatened your reputation as a journalist in this town. How can you *tolerate* it?"

She tilted her head a moment before stating, "One finds ways to cope with constraints imposed by politicians."

Vera placed her hand on my shoulder. I placed mine on Emily's shoulder.

Mr. Hoffman appeared to understand our gesture. With sudden soberness, he slowly straightened his tie. Next, shaking Vera's and my hands, he wished us better luck in the future. The coroner then bid Emily to accompany him back to the office. Turning to depart, he almost crushed Mr. Berry. The elephant apologized to the wren.

At that point, the councilmen entered the hallway, and Vera quickly ushered Mr. Berry and me along the hall to avoid a confrontation.

"It's time for me to return to Pittsburg, I venture," announced Mr. Berry. "Unless I can be of further service, Miss Van Slyke."

Glancing back at the departing councilmen, Vera spoke in a low voice. "I venture there *is* a service you can provide, Mr. Berry, if you can spare another hour or two. It occurs to me that we might have presented my theory to the wrong authority. Do you think you can go to the offices of the Illinois Tunnel Company and pretend to be a historian with an interest in Fort Dearborn?"

Mr. Berry contracted his eyebrows. "Pretend?"

Vera explained, "Tell them that you have a particular curiosity about the cholera epidemic that took place there. Ask if they happened to run into any artifacts—or even any *bones*—while they were digging under the corner of Lake Street and Wabash Avenue."

"But—but no artifacts would have worked their way down as far as—*oooh*. Are you asking me to pretend that I know nothing about the deaths of these four tunnel diggers?"

Vera nodded. "If Lida or I were to do so, we might be recognized. We are prohibited from telling this story, but the men who work in those shafts *deserve* to hear it. Even if they must put the pieces together on their own."

Mr. Berry stopped and pulled us to the side. He chewed his lip. He scratched his balding head. "I worry that I'll prove to be a terrible actor. I fear I'll let you down."

Vera took his hand into her own. "Vitellius? Of course, the decision is yours. But imagine if the concrete provides only a *temporary* shield from those vampiric particles! I don't ask this for myself. I ask it to ensure that no others share the unfortunate fates of those four dead men."

A gleam came to Mr. Berry's eyes. He patted Vera's hand before saying, "I will do it for them. And—*and* for you, Vera."

We did not see Mr. Berry again before he left Chicago. He sent a message, telling us that his editorial duties at *The Pittsburg Daily Canvas* required that he return—but that he *had* found the time to stop at the Illinois Tunnel Company office before leaving.

•

Apparently, Vera's trick had worked. Months afterward, on a chilly Friday evening, she and I recognized the employee who had guided us through the tunnels. He had just exited yet another tavern that was forbidden to women. We stopped to greet the tunnel worker, whose tottering posture suggested he might need some assistance finding a vehicle to carry him home. He thanked us for our kindness.

As we waited for a cab, the tunnel worker confessed that he could not remember us. His eyes widened, however, when we mentioned that he had shown us the tunnels that intersected far below Lake Street and Wabash Avenue.

"Lake and Wabash? Did ya know dat spot's haunted?" he slurred.

"Haunted?" Vera exclaimed, feigning astonishment. "You don't mean haunted down in those tunnels, I hope!"

After a hiccup, the man responded, "Yesh, down in dose tunnels! Ya see, dere were bodies buried at dat corner long, long ago. *Unmarked* graves, mind ya. Lots of 'em! An' de spirits of dose buried—well, dey trickled down, down, *downnnn!* Some say de concrete keeps 'em out—but here's de rub. Here's de rub about *dat* tunnel." His eyes started to wander.

"Do tell us what the rub is about *that* tunnel," Vera urged. "Have there been any odd occurrences there? Have the ghosts trickled through the concrete?"

"We wouldn't know to say!" he insisted. "Oh, dere's track along dat tunnel. But don't none of us ever run a train through it! No, ma'am, we all avoid *dat* innersection whenever possible. And we know ways to *make* it possible."

Vera replied, "And you are wise to do so, sir!"

An available cab appeared, and we helped the gentleman into it. We watched the coach depart, and then Vera turned to me.

"What do you think of that, Lida?" she asked with a ring of pomp. "The tunnel workers *avoid* the intersection below Lake and Wabash. Now, let's see *Vernon* Van Slyke accomplish *dat!*"

We strutted away from the bar's entrance.

KING MIDAS EXHUMED
(1907)

The trouble is that the colored people have still to contend against 'a fierce and formidable foe,' the ghost of a bygone, dead and buried institution.

— Frederick Douglass

On July 9th of 1907, Vera Van Slyke tightened her lips and blinked repeatedly upon opening my birthday present for her.

"How many times have I said I need to replace my poor, old Cathy?" she asked, referring to her bowed, frayed, and yellowed copy of Catherine Crowe's *The Night-Side of Nature; or, Ghosts and Ghost-Seers*. It was the 1850 edition, the first printed in the U.S. Vera then answered her own question: "I say I need to replace it *each* and *every* time I pick it up, don't I?"

I had given her a fresh edition of this enduring book, one published at the start of the new century. "I might've heard you say that once or twice," I allowed. "But I should have guessed why you never went ahead and replaced it. It's too dear to you. I would hardly ask you to replace, say, your *grandmother* simply because she's grown a bit hunched."

Vera smiled softly. "I'll treasure them both, side by side! One was a gift from the man who taught me how to hunt ghosts. The other is from someone who I hope has learned some things about them from me. Perfection!"

We shared a quick caress.

Even so, in my remaining years with Vera, I don't recall her ever consulting that newer edition when she thought Mrs. Crowe might lend a hand with one of our investigations.

"Speaking of ghosts," I said, taking my familiar chair before her desk, "here's a letter in reply to your 'Help for the Haunted' advertisement. Mr. Adrastos wonders if you can use your special knowledge to help him attract customers to his new tavern."

"Tavern?" Vera looked back from the shelf that held her library of the occult. "Do go on!"

I grinned. "Beware. The Trojan horse was a gift from Greece, Mr. Adrastos's homeland! His plan is to attract those customers by—let me read you this part—'calling forth and installing a ghost. Americans love ghosts for feeling as they have a history older than they do.' He's still honing his English, it seems."

Taking her seat behind her desk, Vera said, "The Greek makes a valid point about our lack of ancient history, I suppose. But if he wants to *install* a ghost, tell him he'll have more luck buying a Ouija board."

"I'll tell him that ghosts are like cats. They're real, but they don't come when called."

"See?" she laughed. "I *have* taught you some things about ghosts! Wish him luck with his tavern. It isn't in town here, is it? We *could* reply in person."

I checked the front of the envelope. "Unfortunately, his business is in Philadelphia. A bit far for a beer." I went to the next letter.

"Pennsylvania?" Vera mumbled.

After rechecking the address, I replied, "Yes. Philadelphia, Pennsylvania."

Vera placed two fingers against the side of her jaw. "I was thinking that *Pittsburg* is also in Pennsylvania."

"On the other side, I believe."

"You know, it *is* possible that our Greek's tavern might have some interesting history to it. Philadelphia is an old place despite it being such an *American* city."

I knew Vera was formulating a theory, but it seemed I hadn't learned enough about ghosts to see how they might fit. I tilted my head.

"Our historical researcher in Pittsburg, Mr. Berry, might be curious to see if Mr.—uhm."

"Adrastos."

"Mr. Berry could help discover if, uh—this Greek gentlemen purchased a property with a skeleton or two buried beneath it."

"Not quite the same as a *ghost* or two," I teased. I knew Vera was scheming to visit with Mr. Vitellius Berry, the man whose skills in locating long-buried information had aided a number of our previous investigations.

"I know you don't understand why I enjoy Mr. Berry's company," Vera explained, blushing. "I know he's a funny, little bird."

"A *mouse* comes to my mind." I might have teased too much.

She squinted at me and raised one eyebrow. "Don't be absurd. I've never heard of a bald *mouse.*" She held her expression as a friendly challenge.

Instead of riposting that I had never heard of a bald *bird,* several varieties ran through my head. Suddenly, I cried, "*Eagles!* Fair enough. I cannot say that Mr. Berry calls to mind the image of a bald eagle, but I *will* say that you're owed a birthday gift of your own choosing."

"Excellent! Inform Mr. Androcles we'll see what we can do!"

•

That name had become "Mr. Acropolis" by the time we arrived in Philadelphia the following week. Vera always enjoyed returning to the East. With a sparkle in her eyes, she gazed through the train window as the taut blanket of the Middle West ruffles and rumples into the Appalachians. I sometimes suspected that she regretted having moved to Chicago from New York.

At the same time, I wondered if Vera ever felt at home anywhere. Her residence was the Hotel Manitou, where she also conducted business, granting her the option to relocate by the end of the month. She seemed similarly ungrounded in regard to the times. While very modern in her successful journalism career, she also bristled at the more physical signs of progress, from skyscrapers to subways. "Ghosts went out with gas," claims the novelist Fergus Hume—but not for Vera Van Slyke. Though investigating a haunting was always secondary to probing a political scandal or a workers' strike, Vera would have devoted each week to traversing the globe in quest of supernatural mysteries, could she have financed it.

Mr. Adrastos, on the other hand, was working very hard to make Philadelphia his new home. His ambition had already won him his own business, though he was not much older than thirty and had been in the U.S. only six years. The white of his eyes and teeth contrasted sharply with the black of his irises and heavy moustache. His olive skin added a third color, making his face seem almost like the flag of some Mediterranean nation. It was a friendly nation, we learned.

We met him at his new establishment. It was called The Lyre, according to the hand-painted sign leaning in the window. Inside, polished chrome taps and trim glistened in the low sun of afternoon, and piquant fragrances wafted in from a backroom. After introductions, Vera explained that Mr. Berry was to arrive shortly. She ordered us both beers, which our host laughingly retrieved while dismissing any offer of payment.

He next rushed to that backroom to retrieve a freshly prepared delicacy that he called *dolma*. It consisted of rice and spicy meat wrapped in cabbage leaves. I was hesitant to bite one, though, because it looked like a wet cigar stub. After Vera assured me that it was delicious, I sampled one—and I was reminded that her tastes were broader than mine.

"No more *dolma* for you?" Mr. Adrastos laughed. "Then I made a mistake. I reckoned that, because of your pretty complexion, you must be Greek!"

"No, Lida is Czech-born," Vera explained, "but she does turn very brown in the summer. Maybe you should read your books *indoors*, dear."

Mr. Adrastos explained, "We read, work, and *eat* under the sun in the Peloponnese, from where I am born! When a boy, I learned working in cafes. Many tables outside! In America, though, I sweat inside chophouse kitchens. No good for me, so I worked hard and learned English nights. I think maybe I open my *own* restaurant. But I am told the Americans don't know what is Greek food. Spaghetti, yes. Souvlaki, no. This is why I bought my own *tavern* at a good price."

"And how has business been for you?" Vera inquired.

"Fine, fine." Our client put a finger to the tip of his nose. "But I have a customer who is from Philadelphia since birth. I tell you, he's a *talker*." He illustrated this point by making his hands mimic two ducks squabbling. "One evening, he was telling about the General Wayne Inn over in Merion nearby. This is a very honored building. You've heard of George Washington, I am sure. Have you also heard of Edward Allan Poe?"

"*Edgar* Allan Poe?" I suggested.

"Yes, yes, *Edgar!* Well, the president and the poet *both* slept at this General Wayne Inn. Another person does *not* sleep there. A *ghost!* Some say the ghost might be from your glorious Revolutionary War—a Haitian soldier."

"A *Hessian* soldier?" Vera offered.

"*Hessian!*" Mr. Adrastos accepted. "Thank you, but that is not the moral of my story. This talker, he convinced half my customers to get up and visit the bar at the General Wayne Inn. They all wanted to meet a ghost!"

Vera nodded. "So you decided you need a ghost, too, to attract new customers to *your* bar. That's the moral of your story, correct?"

"Very correct!" Our client leaned forward as if to reveal a secret. "And this ghost doesn't need to be real. But you, Miss Van Slyke—you are a real ghost *hunter*. If people hear that you hunt to *hope* for a real ghost—well, you understand?"

We had been tricked. Mr. Adrastos hadn't summoned us to summon a ghost. He wanted us only to perform an investigation, which would create a sensation about there being a ghostly presence here. This was one of the hazards of ghost hunting, something we had encountered previously. Still, I was fearful Vera would upbraid the man for luring her into such a ruse.

Instead, she burst forth with laughter. She wagged her finger at Mr. Adrastos. He also laughed, though with more reserve.

"We shall perform a thorough investigation, sir," Vera assured him. "We shall use our instruments to seek ruptures between the physical and spiritual realms. We shall have our friend, Mr. Berry, track this location's history." Once her laughter stopped, she added, "And we shall *charge* you for our services."

This last condition had no adverse effect on the businessman. He beamed with his white teeth and dark eyes, extending his hand to shake Vera's.

"And who knows?" he said. "Maybe you *will* find a ghost! One of those soldiers from the Revolutionary War!"

Without warning, a voice from the backroom shouted, "More likely, a soldier from the *Civil* War, I venture!"

The three of us exchanged expressions of astonishment.

Vera stood suddenly. "Vitellius, is that you?"

As if waiting behind the curtain for his cue, Mr. Berry appeared at the doorway. "I let myself in through the back," he said in his high voice. This was his only response to having startled us by entering so unconventionally.

Clearly, Vera didn't mind the breach of etiquette. She scampered to Mr. Berry to grab his hands and share a lingering grin. After a while, Mr. Adrastos looked to me, and I nodded to assure him that he was now free to go meet this man who had stolen into his kitchen. The image of a mouse again came to my mind.

After I had also greeted Mr. Berry, I asked him, "Why do you think the bar is more likely haunted by a Civil War soldier than a Revolutionary one?"

"Not a soldier in *uniform*," he replied enthusiastically, "but—but a layman fighting the abolitionist cause! I arrived yesterday and began researching previous owners of this property. It's been a saloon since the 1830s. Our abolitionist bought the place in 1848. More facts about him are waiting to be exhumed, but his name was Ambrose Petty."

"Ambrose Petty," Mr. Adrastos enunciated as if paying his respects to an ancestor. "Please, could someone explain 'abolitionist'?"

Vera clarified the term and the context. Switching to a tone of girlish admiration, she next asked Mr. Berry, *"However* were you able to discover that a humble tavern owner crusaded against *slavery?"*

"In 1852, he was arrested for harboring *runaways!"* Mr. Berry nearly squealed. "Vera always says that, where there's a ghost, there's guilt. Once I had a list of previous owners, I walked to the other side of City Hall and checked the records of arrest! The only match there was Mr. Ambrose Petty. And—and that was for providing safekeeping for fugitive slaves!"

"You amazing man," Vera cooed.

Mr. Berry's face became a portrait of elation.

I cleared my throat.

The researcher continued, "But—but where might a saloon owner shelter these slaves, I asked myself. Tavern? Wine. *Cellar!* If Ambrose Petty had a cellar to store wine, *that* might have served as a way station on the Underground Railroad, I ventured. Mr. Adrastos, am I correct in assuming that a wine cellar is behind *this* door here?" He indicated the door with pride enough to imply that he had already peeked behind it.

The barkeeper confirmed that wine was among the alcohols he stored below. He bid us to explore the cellar. Indeed, it proved to be large enough to provide a place to sleep during daylight. Other than crates and racks for concealment, however, there was nothing to confirm or disprove that it had been used as a haven for escaped slaves following the Northern Star.

While we were in that cellar, something caught my eye. It is insignificant perhaps, but I was quietly amused by the fact that Vitellius Berry required two steps of the stairway to be the same height as Vera Van Slyke.

At least, that is how I remember the difference between them now.

•

The very next day, the establishment's name changed from The Lyre to The Ambrose Petty Tavern. While Mr. Adrastos painted a new sign for the window, Vera used her journalist skills to spread the story that an investigation for an unquiet spirit led to the discovery of an unsung hero. Mr. Berry, a newspaper editor himself, preferred to burrow through musty records in search of details regarding that hero. I decided to take the opportunity to read Mr. Washington's *Up from Slavery*, which had been published some years earlier. Upon Mr. Adrastos's recommendation, I read this book under the sunny skies of Fairmount Park.

Once it became generally known that our client's wine cellar might have been part of the Underground Railroad, a generation who had only heard tales of slavery and the Civil War came to pay homage to the historical site. Our client grew enamored with his customers' retellings of their parents' and grandparents' stories about the abolition movement or about the War itself.

Occasionally, small groups of colored people arrived and entranced everyone with their family stories of slavery and escape. In some cases, the tales were about the special challenges facing their ancestors who had lived *free*. One evening, we met a gentleman old enough to have been born a slave in Tennessee. Though a man of few words, this sage said, "Folks sketch slavery two ways. One's full of banjos and 'Jim Crack Corn.' In my account, there's a lack of *bandages* for *Jim's cracked calluses.*" Some of the white customers laughed softly. Others remained silent.

"Very polite, the Negroes," Mr. Adrastos remarked one afternoon. He was working behind the bar. "I catch them standing outside, peeking by the window. I invite them to come see the cellar. After, they ask if they can buy drinks. *Many,* I say! They ask which seats are for them. *Any,* I say. Even so, they seem shy to sit."

"They're not used to being so welcomed in this part of the city," said Vera, gazing at one of the mirror-like taps. "Have you had any trouble with your usual customers? Do you still see the gentleman who gave you the idea about the ghost?"

"Oh, that fellow," the barkeeper sighed. He repeated his squabbling ducks gesture. "He says to me I make a mistake to let in the Negroes. I tell him this is the City of Brotherly Love. I tell him, if he likes people to be pale, he should go back to his ghosts." The immigrant shrugged. "I guess he did."

I asked him, "Have *you* personally experienced much race prejudice since coming to this city?"

"Oh, sometimes, I'm on the sidewalks with my countrymen, and we are named *'dagoes'* by men walking there. Greeks here are too few to have our own insult, you understand. Those men, they are scared from the idea we come to take their livelihoods. Many Greeks here do the same to the Negroes, also scared from losing their livelihoods. Is this true with your other Czech immigrants, pretty one?"

I felt myself blush at being so addressed. "Well, we've been coming from Bohemia long enough to be called *'bohunks'* by those who wish we hadn't come at all. Some people say we're not even white people. Not *pure* white, at least. And, yes, many Czech immigrants spurn colored people, too." I felt a strong urge to add, "But many don't! And one *could* write a history of the American struggle to achieve harmony. Along with abolition, I certainly hope Antonín Dvořák's *New World Symphony* will be covered in that book."

Mr. Adrastos smirked in appreciation of my quip about the Czech composer. Vera, however, had remained silent during this exchange. Her averted gaze told she might be ill at ease. I attributed her reticence either to her being a native among newcomers—or, more likely, to this being our last day in Philadelphia.

Once again, Mr. Berry was late joining us at the tavern.

When he did arrive, instead of a surprise entrance, he skulked through the front door. Without a word, he climbed on a stool beside us at the bar. Mr. Adrastos went to the backroom to make a cup of tea, Mr. Berry's usual beverage even in summer.

"You seem out of sorts, Vitellius," Vera said with some alarm. "Is it because we're at the end of another adventure?"

He peered up at Vera and then leaned as if to see where Mr. Adrastos had gone. In a hushed tone, he explained, "Ambrose Petty is not who I thought he was. Should I tell your client?"

"Dear me," Vera replied. "Yes, I think he has a right to know everything we do. Is it something upsetting?"

"It will upset Mr. Adrastos, I venture."

We waited for our new friend to return with the tea.

"I'm sorry," Mr. Berry began, "but—but—but the man for whom you named this bar was *not* an abolitionist. I checked the court records more thoroughly. I double-checked the newspaper archives. Ambrose Petty only *pretended* to be a sympathizer, even attending abolitionist meetings to learn the whereabouts of fugitive slaves."

Vera straightened her posture. Mr. Adrastos contracted his brow and squinted his dark eyes.

Carefully, I asked, "Why did he want to know the whereabouts of fugitive slaves?"

"So—so." Mr. Berry sipped some of his hot tea. "So he could get the reward for returning them. They must have *gratefully* walked right into his trap."

Mr. Adrastos put his fingers to his lower lip before pivoting to face the backroom with its door to the wine cellar.

"Then 1850 arrived," Mr. Berry continued. "The Fugitive Slave Law was passed. All U.S. citizens were made responsible for capturing escaped slaves. The law brought slavery to the North, and some say it was a first step to war. And—and, under the new law, federal commissioners were paid ten dollars for every runaway they returned. Two years later, Ambrose Petty was seen as competition, I venture, so they had him arrested. They used his own ploy against him. He shammed being a liberator of slaves. And they charged him for exactly that."

We shared a span of speechlessness.

Until Mr. Adrastos pleaded, "What am I ready to *tell* them? What am I ready to say to them who come to see the wine shelter? The wine *cellar*, I mean."

Vera slapped the top of the bar. "A newspaper is like a beer. If it's not being held in front of someone's face, it goes flat." She rose from her stool. "Mr. Achilles? You tell them exactly what you've been telling them. Fame is fleeting. Or is it fickle? It doesn't matter. The novelty of your wine cellar will pass, and when it does, you can rename your bar whatever you like."

Despite Vera's heartening talk, we left Mr. Adrastos looking as if the temperance league had visited his business with *axes.* Down the street, I waited while my employer and her diminutive gentleman shared intimate farewells.

Barely two hours after leaving The Ambrose Petty Tavern, Vera and I were boarding the train back to Chicago.

•

Barely two *weeks* later, Vera received the following telegram from Mr. Adrastos:

INVISIBLE HAND THROWNING DRINKS ON ONLY NEGRO CUSTOMERS. PETTY OR OTHER REAL GHOST. PLEASE RETURN. YOUR SERVICES PAID.

Whether those final words meant we had *already* been paid or we would be paid *again* hardly mattered to Vera. She had me dash off a telegram to Mr. Berry, requesting that he join us again. The next day, we were on the train back to Philadelphia.

However, the glimmer that I had seen in Vera's eyes on the previous trip east had been left behind.

"He must have felt *terribly* guilty," Vera lamented as we were crossing Indiana. "Lying about Ambrose Petty being a hero. That poor Greek. I left him in the lurch! Why didn't you stop me, Lida? Once I learned the tavern had belonged to a slave-catcher, I fled like a—oh, why didn't you or Vitellius stop me?"

I was only able to say, "Do you think the ghost might actually be Petty?"

Vera placed two fingers to her jaw, but she didn't seem able to hold her hands still. "Impossible to tell at this point. Yet having his name said so often! Having it printed in the newspapers and on the tavern sign! What if it—what if we indeed *summoned* him?"

"And, if Mr. Adrastos does feel terribly guilty," I speculated aloud, "then the dimensional ruptures *he* brought about might be allowing Petty to reach back into the physical realm."

Vera nodded. "I pray the manifestation doesn't escalate beyond spilling drinks."

"According to the telegram, the spirit can also *see* whose drink it spills."

"*See* or, at least, *sense*. I sometimes think that ghosts perceive *us* in as phantasmagorical a way as we perceive *ghosts*. Some evidence suggests this." Vera scratched at her earlobe. "But other evidence suggests they see us with deeper clarity than our purely *physical* senses allow."

Our train arrived on a Tuesday afternoon. Sending our luggage to the hotel, we hired a taxi to take us directly to the tavern. There, I asked Mr. Adrastos if he could see about having some food brought in for Vera.

She seemed unaware that she had missed lunch.

"How often do you see colored customers?" Vera asked.

"They were here *several* each night," the barkeeper said, shaking his head. "But not as many these last days. I worry that the ghost has words spreading that the Negroes aren't welcome here."

Vera and I spent the next several evenings at the tavern, and to be sure, it was in the company of only white patrons. At a corner table, we sipped beer and kept watch. Mr. Berry's duties in Pittsburg prevented him from joining us until Friday, and even so, his leave was granted with the promise that he would write a biographical article about Ambrose Petty for his newspaper.

It was on that same Friday that we saw three colored customers enter the tavern. A stylishly appareled young couple had brought a more plainly dressed woman, whom they both called Mother. The gentleman asked Mr. Adrastos if they might see the mythical wine cellar. As he guided them to the backroom, the myth was again recited, though the storyteller had a quaver in his voice and a wrinkle in his brow.

"This might be our best opportunity," Vera whispered after the family had returned and settled at a table for some refreshment. "We should move to a table nearer them."

Mr. Berry raised his eyebrows. "That would strike them as a bit irregular, I venture."

"As you say," Vera replied. "Still, if our ghost performs his drink-spilling trick, I want to observe it closely. Let's ask if we can *share* their table."

Mr. Berry's eyebrows rose higher. "But—but that doesn't seem at *all* regular! You do as you wish. *I'll* stay here and—and work on my *article*." He withdrew a pencil and notebook from his pocket with flourish enough to suggest indignation.

Vera was obviously more interested in the colored family, since she walked to their table without a backward glance. As I grabbed our beer glasses, I couldn't help but wonder about Mr. Berry's reluctance to join us. Admittedly, Vera's forthright manner sometimes could be interpreted as rudeness. A prime example is the manner with which she introduced us to that family.

"I'm Vera Van Slyke, and this is Lida Parsell. I noticed that you're black. May we join you?"

I fought an urge to inch myself behind Vera's tall figure. The son reclined to the back of his chair and tilted his head to the side. The mother leaned over to whisper in her daughter's ear, causing the daughter to look at Vera discerningly. The daughter then whispered in the son's ear, causing him to do the same. But this lasted for only a moment. The son then quickly stood and

219

graciously pulled out the fourth chair for Vera. Next, he retrieved another chair from an empty table, and the family made room for me to join them.

As Mr. Adrastos delivered their drinks—along with a pile of bar towels—the family introduced themselves. Cassandra Hebert, the mother, was up from Louisiana to become better acquainted with her new daughter-in-law, Emma. She was a native Philadelphian who worked at the same electric lamp factory as did Cassandra's son, George. He had migrated north years earlier to find employment. And, with it, he found a wife.

Vera asked if they had learned about the tavern's possible role in the Underground Railroad from the newspaper reports about a ghost hunter's inquiry. They replied that, no, they had heard secondhand tales about its historical importance, but that was all. Without specifying that she was the ghost hunter, Vera admitted that she had had a hand in the discovery.

"Well, then, here's a toast to your great find!" Mr. Hebert proclaimed with a Louisiana accent too faded to transcribe.

Vera and the family raised their drinks. I kept a sharp eye on each of the hands holding each of the glasses. The elder Mrs. Hebert's drink returned to the table with no incident. Her son's was next.

Her daughter-in-law had almost put her glass of red wine back when—*against all physical laws*—that glass tipped and lurched toward her! The wine splashed across Emma's neck and bosom as the poor woman yelped and leaped from her chair. The rest of us snatched towels and went to work at dabbing the spill.

"How did—how silly of me," she apologized. "Is there someplace for me to—someplace with water?"

Mr. Adrastos arrived with apologies and more towels. He then escorted her to a place where she could wash herself and her blouse. A customer laughed loudly, and George's head spun as if to identify the culprit. He adjusted his cuffs and resumed his seat. I then noticed the elder Mrs. Hebert was judiciously studying Vera.

She stated, "You said, Miss Van Slyke, that diggin' up the history of that ol' cellar started with ghost huntin'. An' that you were a part of the discov'ry. Now, tell us honest, are *you* that ghost huntuh?"

"Very astute," Vera admitted, bowing her head. "I was hesitant to tell you who I am for fear that it would hinder the manifesta— oh—oh *my!*"

The beer in Vera's untouched glass was *undulating* of its own accord. The glass itself began to vibrate. Suddenly, it slithered across the table toward *Vera!* The glass paused, then levitated, then *flipped* onto her lap!

Rather than standing, Vera became transfixed by the beer soaking her skirt.

Mr. Hebert demanded, "By all that's Holy, tell me what is *happening* here!"

I removed the glass from Vera's lap and grabbed more towels. At the same time, Mrs. Hebert rose resolutely. She marched around the table and pulled Vera up from her seat.

"You come along, Miss Vera. Let's clean you up down in that wine celluh, where there's some privacy." The matron then guided Vera to the backroom.

I found myself with a handful of towels and a very confused gentleman. "We—we were mistaken. About Ambrose Petty," I sputtered. "His being an abolitionist, that is. Petty only pretended to offer help to runaways. To collect the reward, if you follow."

It was clear to me that Mr. George Hebert did *not* follow.

And I wasn't following why the ghost, reported to assault only *colored* customers, had spilled a drink on *Vera*. After a deep breath, I stated, "Your mother is helping Vera. I should see if your wife needs a woman's help, too. Once we're all presentable again, I'm sure Vera will explain everything. At some *other* tavern. Until then, please don't touch the drink you have. Please?"

Mr. Hebert eyed me and then eyed his beverage. He shrugged without looking back at me.

I walked to the backroom, and as I was about to pass the door to the wine cellar, I saw the younger Mrs. Hebert returning with Mr. Adrastos. She grinned sheepishly as she went to rejoin her husband, but the barkeeper stopped and winced.

"Another spill?" he asked.

"Another spill," I answered.

He continued on this way, grumbling something in Greek that I was thankful for not understanding. I decided my best course of action was to check on Vera. Remembering the first victim's sheepish grin, I opened the door gently and descended the steps delicately.

Vera and Mrs. Hebert were conversing behind a rack of bottles, and I thought it best to wait at the bottom step rather than barge in on them.

Their conversation held me in place.

"Your haih," Mrs. Hebert said. "I saw right away that your haih is jus' a little too crinkly, and I whispered as much to the children. They's all shades o' skin, but a woman's haih is where to look. You'da known that if you'da been raised in Louisiana."

"I do have my father's frizzy hair," Vera replied. "And my grandmother's brown eyes."

"She the full black one, huh?"

"Yes. My grandmother," Vera confirmed. "My *grandfather*—he was the Van Slyke—earned his living by captaining a transport ship down the east coast and around the Gulf. From Norfolk to New Orleans, slaves sometimes became a part of his cargo, and he spotted my grandmother on one voyage."

I sat down on the steps. I could hear the agitation squeezing Vera's throat, but I wasn't able to go to her.

Nor was I able to leave.

Mrs. Hebert spoke next. "That's an ol' story, honey. White man thinks he's in love. Says he's savin' some pretty girl from the whip. He can't marry her, though. I bet he kept her stuck in some out-the-way cabin."

"Y-yes," Vera sniffled. "Upstate New York. That's where she bore him a child. But my *filthy* grandfather never acknowledged his own *son!*" She moaned and then found strength in a different topic. "My pa didn't need him, though! He grew up and took care of my grandmother by learning how to make candles!"

"Candles!" Mrs. Hebert repeated with a ring of pride. "We all need help findin' our way through the night. And who was your mamma? D'she explain why yuh pass so easily for white?"

There was a pause before Vera said, "My mother was Irish."

"Well, there yuh go."

"Yes. There you go."

"Let's head back up now, Miss Vera. I do believe I heard some critter down heah."

I knew that I would be caught seated on the bottom of that stairway. I did not care. I felt as though I had learned more about Vera Van Slyke in that single minute or two of conversation than I had in our seven-and-a-half years together.

When the two women came from behind the bottle rack, they halted.

"Least it ain't no rat," chuckled Mrs. Hebert.

"No," I replied, pushing myself up and walking toward Vera. "Only a mouse."

We caressed until a tap on my back indicated that Vera had had enough sentiment.

•

"I think we now know enough to expel this ghost," Vera proclaimed as we returned from the backroom. Her eyes were still reddened from tears, and her skirt was still darkened by beer.

Mr. Adrastos and Mr. Berry had both been waiting near the cellar door, eager to ensure Vera's comfort. Mr. Hebert, however, was at the foyer, eager to take his wife and mother out of this haunted place. His mother gave Vera a silent, meaningful look before bidding her good luck with the exorcism. Without looking back, the kindly woman exited with her family. We assembled around the same table the Heberts had occupied.

"Wooo!" Vera yowled as she sat on the soaked part of her skirt. After a moment of rearrangement, she leaned forward. "We know now that our ghost will interact with myself, and I hope to use that to our advantage. I'm struck by how rude—but *limited*—its actions are. It seems capable of nothing else but tossing drinks at those it dislikes."

"But—but why would it dislike *you?*" asked Mr. Berry.

I placed my hand on Vera's arm.

After only the *slightest* instant of hesitation, she answered simply, "My grandmother was a slave. She was a black woman."

Mr. Berry remained expressionless but sunk backward in his chair.

"As I say," Vera resumed, "I'm struck by the limits of this supernatural lout. To move a glass, though, some manner of *physicality* is needed. I'd like to *latch* onto that ghostly hand. If it's going to behave like a nasty child, let's give it a firm slap on the wrist!"

I entered the planning. "The touch of a ghost can be cold enough to cause blisters. I wonder, Mr. Adrastos, if you have some kind of glove. The thickest you can find?"

"I try the best." He nodded and dashed to the backroom.

"But—but if this is dangerous," Mr. Berry objected, "shouldn't we consider other theories? I'm reminded of our first case together. Unseen hands started those fires in Pittsburg, and an unseen hand tosses these drinks. There, the specter *appeared* to be committing bad acts. When you assured it that its motives were *good*, the guilt was relieved and—and the fires never returned. This could be a similar situation, I venture."

I had never seen a fiercer glare arise in Vera's face than at that moment.

"Burning blankets infected with *smallpox* to save the *wives* and *children* of the enemy," she spit, "is hardly *comparable* to betraying freedom-seeking *slaves* for the *reward!* Are you arguing that Ambrose Petty was simply returning someone's rightful *property?*"

Mr. Berry appeared to realize that he could sink no further into his chair. "No, not that. Not that. What if Petty were looking for forgiveness? What if, in the next world, he learned the error of his ways, and—and hearing himself portrayed as a hero here, he's returned to make certain history would remember him as a *villain?*" A twitch on the side of his mouth implied that even Mr. Berry himself was having difficulty accepting this theory. "I mean to say, what if reminding us of his wrong-doing were his way of apologizing? What if this is the only way he can think of *to* apologize?"

A cloud lowered over our table, but it was gusted away by the return of Mr. Adrastos.

Shrugging, he held out a stove mitten. He explained, "Not the season for gloves."

"It will serve," Vera responded curtly. Working her hand into the mitten, she added, "Now—may I have another beer? My last one spilled."

Mr. Adrastos hurried off. I watched Vera and Mr. Berry attempting to look at one another. They failed at the task. It was a long wait while our bartender made the short trip to the beer tap and back again.

When Vera's beer was delivered, however, very little time passed before our insolent phantom made its presence known. As before, the beer began rippling, though no vibrations were discernable under the glass. As before, that glass slid in the direction of Vera, meandering tauntingly. This time, though, I noticed spots of beer seeming to freeze on the *inner* surface of the glass. The spots quickly took the form of an icy, skeletal imprint of a *human hand.*

And the very instant this possessed vessel jumped into the air, Vera *seized* it! She *seized* the glass as well as the hand holding it. Vera grunted as that glass began to shake and scuffle, pulling then pushing then twisting, the beer sloshing out from it. The stove mitten was already becoming unwieldy, making Vera squeeze harder to retain her grip on the ghostly hand. I felt driven to assist her, but the horrible coldness of the manifestation kept me at bay.

Dimly aware of the other customers drawing closer to our table, I saw Mr. Berry biting his lower lip. I heard Mr. Adrastos emitting guttural cries as if cheering on a boxer. I then perceived that Vera was *losing* that boxing match. The outer cloth of the stove mitten was being shredded, almost crystalized, by the frigid, invisible hand.

"You filthy, *filthy* horror!" Vera growled, her face twisting into an avenging fiend's. "Get out! You *betrayed* them. You turned your back on your own *family.* Your own—the family of *humanity!* Leave this world, and suffer for your sins in the next! *Out!"*

Vera's arm was now lurching forward and back, side to side. Tears of anger were welling in her eyes. Her unprotected hand was rising, the fingers forming the shape of claws. She was obviously preparing to use that hand to double her strength against the manifestation!

At that moment, I realized that Vera could not distinguish between the hand of Ambrose Petty, Slave Catcher, and the hand of Captain Baltus Van Slyke, Slave Shipper. She would have willingly suffered searing pain to punish *either* phantom.

I clutched her free hand just as it snatched for the ghost. She spun to glare at me.

"Let go, Vera!"

It was all I needed to say. Vera released her grip on the manifestation, and the beer glass hurled past Mr. Berry's ear and across the room. It shattered and splashed against the floor a good fifteen feet away. Another customer had narrowly dodged it, and he looked back at us with wide eyes. Only then did I become sensible of the crowd that had formed around the table. For lack of any better response, I suppose, they began to cheer.

They then began to depart, bidding one another goodnight with conspicuous urgency.

Vera slowly removed the now tattered stove mitten and examined her palm. There was some inflammation, but it appeared minor. She looked at the three of us with the bud of a smile.

"I may have dismissed your theory too quickly, Vitellius," she said. "We were in error for painting Ambrose Petty so heroically, and we should let it be known that he was a villain. Whether or not that somehow promotes his penance and lessens his guilt, we'll never know. We *do* know that no longer perpetuating a lie will alleviate Mr. Adrastos's guilt." She displayed her singed palm. "Either way, the severed skin between the dimensions should heal with time."

"I'll change my tavern's title again!" Mr. Adrastos exclaimed. "Not back to 'The Lyre.' This sounds too much like 'The Liar,' you understand? No, I call it *'Clio's'!* Clio is the muse of history! She is the muse for remembering great deeds like this here tonight!"

Smiling, Vera nodded. "And we'll run your biographical article on Ambrose Petty in the Philadelphia papers, Vitellius, instead of just in Pittsburg."

Mr. Berry pried himself out of the back of his chair. He stood, clearing his throat. With gravity, he stated, "I have provided you research for some extraordinary adventures, Miss Van Slyke. You'll have many, many more, I venture. *Without* my help. You see, I didn't mind serving you as any gentleman ought to serve a woman. But—but I had been led to believe that you were a certain *kind* of woman. You deceived me about that."

Vera's spine became rigid, and her lips grew tight. Beside her, I also sat straight and stared hard.

Mr. Berry swallowed before adding, "You are a journalist and can write your *own* article on Ambrose Petty. *Without* my help." He bowed to Mr. Adrastos. He bowed to me.

He gave Vera a final glance before turning around and exiting the tavern. I placed my hand on her arm once more.

Once the front door was shut, Mr. Adrastos eased himself down beside Vera. He fiddled with the tattered stove mitten a long time before speaking. "Please explain something. Mr. Berry said he was foolish to think you are a 'certain *kind* of woman.' Was this meaning one *not* with slave blood?" He crumpled the mitten within his fist. "What is he scared from? Greece had slavery. All over the *world* had slavery! Does the little man forget he probably has slave blood *also?*"

Blinking several times, Vera replied calmly, "He didn't mean *slave* blood exactly. Do you suppose, my friend, that I might have another beer? Mine keep spilling, and I feel as though I'd be grateful for even one drop."

Vera leaned against me, and I counterbalanced her.

"Of course, of course," said Mr. Adrastos as he rose. "I think I understand what he is scared from." Before going to fetch us all beers, the Greek leaned down to Vera's ear. "The little man is scared from your *Amazon* blood!"

Vera managed to chuckle. Once our client was out of earshot, though, she murmured to me, "'*Amazon*'? You're the avid reader. Does he think I have *South American* blood?"

I sighed. "I'll explain it on the trip home."

"Home," Vera whispered amid a deep sigh. "What a pleasant-sounding word."

MONSTRIMONY
(1908)

Ye ghosts, and hobgoblins, and horrible shapes
Ye lions and griffins, ye dragons and apes

— George Watson-Taylor

To Vera Van Slyke, he was always the Professor. It's true that he served as a Professor of Anthropology at a fledgling college in New Brunswick, Canada. However, Vera simply found using his professional title far easier than remembering his full name: Geoffrey Wallace Livingstone Adams.

Via letter, Dr. Adams invited Vera to join him on a ghost hunt in Arkansas. He clarified that the trip would be fully funded with an additional stipend for Vera. As he would be stopping in Chicago on his journey south, he wondered if they might discuss the details of the expedition over lunch.

The mention of lunch convinced Vera that the Professor was a colleague well worth meeting. The three of us gathered at The Foiled Gelding. Despite the expanse of his complete name—which became a veritable litany when followed by his various degrees— Dr. Adams seemed to be a frank and unaffected gentleman. With his accent as corroboration, he told us he had been born and schooled in England. His settling into a teaching position in Canada came after an extensive search for a legendary hairy giant that the native tribes of British Columbia described as walking on two feet and, often, darting *away* on both.

"Tracking these so-called wild men of the woods is my special avocation," said Dr. Adams as his roast beef arrived. "While you've been hunting ghosts in a general way, I've crossed the globe in search of the *maero* of New Zealand and the *sistimite* of Guatemala. Indeed, I almost froze to death in the Himalayas, hoping to spot what the locals there call the *meh-teh*."

After finishing a bite of the potatoes beside her pork chop, Vera replied, "But these creatures you name strike me as the quarry of a zoologist rather than a ghost hunter. My own investigations typically involve mansions, cottages, and theaters. The farthest I travel is to bridges and battlefields in the countryside, not to isolated jungles and mountain ranges."

As if to build suspense, Dr. Adams grinned as he cleaned his spectacles with his napkin. Returning them to his ears, he explained, "One theory holds that the maero, the sistimite, and the rest have survived for millennia because of their highly evolved skill at eluding predators. I, however, ask if they've *survived* at all! But for the occasional footprint or tuft of fur, no definitive physical evidence has yet been discovered. No skulls, no hides, no nests! And witnesses often say these creatures appear and vanish exactly like *ghosts*." He nodded suggestively before readying his knife and fork.

Vera hadn't bothered to swallow the meat in her mouth before mumbling, "Ghosts of *what?*"

Dr. Adams lowered his cutlery. "Ghosts of the missing link! That transitional species between some primordial anthropoid very much like our modern chimp, gorilla, or orangutan cousins—and *ourselves!* Let me ask you, do you believe that *animals* have spirits?"

Chewing, Vera's gaze drifted. She seemed to be either pondering what Dr. Adams was saying or, perhaps, ignoring it outright.

I answered for her. "Some years ago, we investigated a case that revealed that *whales* have spirits. It's sometimes said that a dog or a cat or even a horse loyally stays beside its owner even after its death."

Our visitor set down his knife and fork before clasping his hands. "If *animals* can return as ghosts, is it too much to believe that our prehistoric ancestors can as well? Those who have developed the foundation of human essence, what? If I'm right, *here's* an interesting connection with our most distant relatives! What remarkable things might we learn from them?"

Vera and I looked to one another. She pursed her lips and shrugged, acknowledging the possibility of antediluvian ghosts. Dr. Adams then let us digest the notion while we nibbled at our meals.

The moment that Vera raised a finger, however, he interrupted.

"I presume you're going to ask me about *guilt,*" he said. "Yes, I know about your theory regarding strong feelings of guilt ripping the tissue between this world and the next. Combining your prerequisite for ghostly manifestation with my own theory is exactly why I hope you'll accompany me to Arkansas. You see, there've been newspaper reports of a creature that's half-ape and half-man spotted east of the Ozarks! Granted, these articles treat the sightings as the folly of country bumpkins. However, what if you're able to use your methods to establish the presence of guilt? *Enough* guilt to open a dimensional doorway! Well, wouldn't *that* lend credence to my theory that these creatures are spectral?"

Vera squinted at the man. "I've never gone public with my theory regarding guilt and ghosts? Kindly inform me how *you* know about it."

Dr. Adams drank some water. He rearranged his napkin. Finally, he grinned. "This expedition is being financed by an individual whose social circles cross with a gentleman familiar with your ghost hunting. A gentleman, I believe, who resides in Pittsburg, what?"

Vera sat upright and spun her head to face me. I gently touched her arm.

Turning back to our visitor, I said, "Do you mean *J. Horace Ritchie?* It strikes me that Mr. Ritchie's wealth might put him in the same social circles as someone eccentric enough to fund an expedition in search of phantoms." I glanced back at Vera.

She eased her posture.

Dr. Adams uttered, "Yes, 'Ritchie' does, in fact, sound rather like the name that—that, uh, had been mentioned to me."

Vera persisted. "And *who* mentioned that name, Professor? If I'm to join you on this expedition into darkest Arkansas, shouldn't I know *who's* paying my passage? Hmm, Professor?"

Again, Dr. Adams cleaned his spectacles. "I can tell you that's she proven to be a stalwart champion of occult research. She's funded many of my earlier trips—and I certainly don't wish to endanger any *future* travels. As such, I must respect her wish to remain anonymous."

Vera grew mute. She stared at Dr. Adams. He slowly reclaimed his silverware.

Putting that silverware down again, he implored, "Come now, doesn't the prospect of encountering the ghost of the missing link have a certain irresistible allure, Miss Van Slyke?"

Exactly as she had upon being introduced to the possibility of such a ghost, Vera pursed her lips and shrugged. She then conceded, "I've never been to Arkansas before."

•

Within the week, our train arrived in a bustling town with the interesting name of Paragould, Arkansas. Dr. Adams had chosen this location based on the sightings of what witnesses had termed an "ape-man"—at least, according to those snide newspaper articles. Once we were settled in our hotel, the Professor made arrangements for a driver to take us out to a rural general store frequented by those witnesses and, as needed, to the cotton farms or timber camps where they worked.

We met the driver the next morning. Averse to ceremony, he insisted on being called Stan. His stubbly cheeks and dusty shirt were in keeping with this philosophy of informality.

Once Stan had gotten our buggy to the outlying road, he said, "Now, I ain't saying these folks are lying, and I ain't saying they *ain't* lying. See, this here ridge we're on—called Crowley's Ridge—it's *old!* Long before Jesus walked, they say it was a narrow island with the Mississip flowing on one side and the Ohio on the other. A *plateau* of sorts. So who knows if there ain't some ancient apes still loitering about?"

For the remainder of the trip, Stan and Dr. Adams expounded upon firsthand observation versus hearsay, the local flora and fauna, and the variances between their respective dialects of the English language. Stan was clearly impressed when the Professor suggested that using "ain't" is far more consistent than saying "I *am* not," "he *is* not," and "they *are* not." Both gentlemen merrily agreed with Vera's proposal that we replace that fickle verb, not just with *ain't,* but also with its positive form, *ai.* I rode silently, delighted by how the playful poetry of my companions blended with the music of innumerable birds.

The mood changed, however, once we arrived at Hooper's General Store. Stan tended to the horses as the three of us entered the mercantile. Inside, we found a wizened woman stooping behind a display of liniments and poultices. We announced our interest in the ape-man.

She ascended and pointed a talon-like finger at us. "We sure as *sheep* don't need any more blasted newspaper reporters in here! My own husband saw what he saw! As did two more folks! I will *not* abide any more mockery from the likes of y'all!"

Vera stepped forward, ready to respond, but she shut her mouth, probably owing to her being a newspaper reporter. Dr. Adams first bowed to Vera and then to the vexed shopkeeper. He grinned.

"Good woman, I assure you we are *not* from any of those detestable newspapers." He spoke serenely, letting the polish of his English accent glisten. "Quite the opposite. I am an *expert* in these sightings, and I hope to *confirm* what your husband and the others witnessed. My name is Adams, good woman. *Doctor* Adams. Am I correct in assuming that you are Mrs. Hooper?" He pulled a handkerchief from beneath his vest and began to clean his hands.

After confirming who she was, Mrs. Hooper continued the conversation with less venom. "Y'all are an expert?"

"An expert," Dr. Adams assured her.

"Not a newspaper reporter?"

"Oh, most definitely not one of *those.*"

Yet again, Vera pursed her lips and shrugged.

"Well, then," Mrs. Hooper declared, "y'all arrived too *late!*"

"Too late? Why too late, good woman?" Dr. Adams quickly stuffed his handkerchief back beneath his vest.

The good woman looked around as if to ensure that no one else would hear what she had to say. "Each of the three who saw the monster says it was stomping around *one* spot and one spot *only.* They saw it by a homestead that belongs to a man name of *Micah Clark.*"

Mrs. Hooper's volume was diminishing, so we stepped closer.

"Nice enough fellow, this Micah Clark. But he lives and works all *alone.* Does some blacksmithing. Hires hisself out during harvest. We sell honey from his hives." She pointed to a supply of jars.

We stepped closer still.

"Now, this Micah Clark also makes his purchases here on occasion. Since that wild man of the woods showed up, Micah's bought *doilies.* Fine *chocolates.* And other such *dainties.* Didn't put two and two together, but then he was in here not twenty minutes ago. He done something my husband and me saw as powerful suspicious." She raised her talon again but lowered her voice even more. "That man Micah Clark bought hisself several yards of *gingham!* Enough gingham to drape a barn door, I reckon!"

Dr. Adams pivoted to Vera and me with his head at a tilt. Vera's blank expression suggested that she was feeling uncooperative due to the jibe against reporters—or she was as stymied as the Professor.

I explained, "Gingham is a fabric often used for sewing draperies. And dresses. Purchasing a *lot* of gingham implies, if not drapes for a barn door, then for a particularly *large* dress. Can I assume, ma'am, that this struck you as suspicious because Micah Clark lives as a *bachelor?"*

She nodded slowly, clawing the side of her nose.

Dr. Adams rubbed his neck, presumably still unable to follow the chain of implications. Vera, on the other hand, stepped in front of him.

"You're not suggesting—or *are* you?" she stammered.

"What I'm suggesting," whispered Mrs. Hooper, "is that Micah Clark has taken hisself a wife. And that wild man of the woods ain't no ape-*man.* No, she's an ape-*woman!"*

•

Vera asked if we could speak with Mrs. Hooper's husband, since she had named him as one of the witnesses of the wild man— or woman—of the woods. The shopkeeper explained that, immediately after Micah Clark's suspicious purchase of gingham, Mr. Hooper hurriedly organized a meeting of his fellow church deacons. Mr. Clark belonged to the same church as the Hoopers, and duty demanded that the deacons ascertain whether or not the solitary bachelor truly had strayed from the path of decency. I withhold the name of this church for the sake of respect and for a touch of mystery.

Mrs. Hooper gave Stan directions to the church, noting that if the deacons hadn't assembled there, they would be at the minister's cotton farm across from the adjacent graveyard. After a brief ride, we located the rustic chapel. It consisted of only one room, and instead of pews inside, we discovered benches painted black. Among those benches sat three gentlemen.

They stood as Dr. Adams introduced himself and promptly made it clear that he had expertise in exactly what the deacons were confronting. I knew Vera well enough to know that acquiescing to the Professor's authority would test both her composure and her digestion.

A man whose age and apron suggested he was Mrs. Hooper's husband remained quiet, as did a much younger man plagued by twitches. The church's minister was the Reverend Mr. Orson F.

Burnett, a tall, steel-haired man whose loose jowls and coal-black suit gave him a funereal air. It was he who spoke for the assembly.

"Your arrival is a blessing, Dr. Adams," said Mr. Burnett. "We welcome you. However, because of the deviant nature of the topic at hand, I'll have to insist that your wife and daughter there wait outside. For the safety of their souls."

Vera and I both turned to look behind us. We must have realized simultaneously that *we* were being referred to as the wife and daughter of Dr. Adams. *Ours* were the imperiled souls!

Vera was struck speechless. Perhaps that was another blessing. I grabbed her elbow and dragged her out of the church and back to the buggy. She stumbled the entire way because she never stopped facing that assembly of deacons, even after we were outside of the church again.

Upon regaining her voice, she declared, "Well, I can honestly say that I've now been to Arkansas! The *audacity* of these rubes!"

Stan cleared his throat. He struggled up from riders' seat in the buggy, where he had apparently settled for a nap. Vera glanced in his direction, her cheeks coloring. She now took *my* elbow and escorted me to the shade of a nearby oak.

"I am not *old* enough to be your mother!" she insisted. "Well — *barely* old enough!"

I laughed. "But look at the intrigue of our situation, Vera! We're investigating the possibility of a marriage, if that's the right term, between a man and a missing link! A *female* missing link! Possibly, the *ghost* of a female missing link! Oh my, wait until I tell this to Rick! He *adores* following our adventures."

"I have serious doubts about the Professor's theory regarding antediluvian ghosts," Vera spit. "And exactly who is *Rick?*"

"Oooh," I responded. I tapped my fingertips together. "Haven't I told you? Rick Bergson's come back from Alaska. Uhm — some months ago."

Vera sighed heavily. I realized I would have to tell a story I'd narrated to her several times before.

"Rick is Eric Bergson. You met him years ago, when he assisted in our discovery that playing B-flat and high G on oboes illuminates any ruptures between the spirit and physical realms. Some while after that, he courted me. This was interrupted, though, by his going to seek his fortune in Alaska. Do you remember any of this?"

"The quest, yes, but the hero is hazy."

"Well, he continued to court me by letter, always intending to return to Chicago. I wrote back, sometimes describing our investigations of hauntings. He finds them to be delightful, and he's encouraged me to record our exploits in a more formal way."

"And he's returned to Chicago now, you say?"

"Yes. Yes, he has." There was more I wanted to say. For some reason, however, this did not feel like a fitting moment. I confess that I had felt the same urge to delay my confession on several previous occasions.

We sat down under the oak tree. I was not sure if the sneer lingering on Vera's face was meant for the deacons *alone.* Instead of speaking to each other, we listened to Stan's snoring amid the clamor of birds and insects.

Eventually, Dr. Adams emerged from the church. He scanned the churchyard while wiping his spectacles. Vera and I stood to signal our location.

"Progress!" he shouted as he walked to us. "The minister's devised a plan. He and Hooper will coax Clark out of his house for an evening of cards. This will allow me to roam the property after dark. That younger deacon will let me share quarters with him for the remainder of the night. He's also offered to take me to interview all the witnesses in the meantime."

Vera nodded. She nodded even though it seemed as if the very man who had sought her aid were now the one debarring her from the investigation.

Dr. Adams continued, "I'll ask *you* to return tomorrow with your oboes to check for dimensional ruptures if warranted. Let's confirm that we've got something authentic *before* exploring how it might have arrived here, what? I'll fetch my Kodak, my flask, and few other things from the buggy. Stan can then take the two of you back to the comforts of civilization." He chuckled.

To my surprise, Vera yielded to the Professor's plan without a quibble. In fact, she accompanied him to the buggy to ensure that our oboes were not blocking his own equipment. She suggested we all reconvene at nine o'clock the following morning at the mercantile. Vera went so far as bid him to beware of Clark's beehives during his hunt.

"Back to Paragould, Miss?" asked Stan as he helped Vera and me into our seats.

"One detour first," she answered. "We must return to Hooper's General Store to purchase ourselves a grand picnic lunch!" More privately, she stipulated, "We'll send the bill to that anonymous benefactress of ours."

Stan climbed into position to take the reins.

Vera called to him, "I should have said *two* detours. We'll also ask Mrs. Hooper for directions to Micah Clark's homestead. We've got our oboes. Let's stay until dusk to conduct our own part of the investigation, what?"

•

At sunset, Stan halted the horses a fair distance from Micah Clark's property, since we were acting clandestinely. Vera and I assembled the oboes. According to his habit, our driver stayed with the buggy as the two of us walked the rest of the way.

"We can assume Mr. Clark will be out playing cards," I said, "but what if Dr. Adams hears our instruments?"

"We'll have to risk it," Vera answered. "Keep your high G low to the ground, and I shall likewise flatten my B-flat." She giggled at her own quip.

I was finding this affair less humorous. I was not as convinced as my companion that whatever lurked in this wooded area was more malarkey than monster. It being dusk, the throng of birds seemed to be madly shouting a warning to any living creature that would heed it. A chill shook me as an evening mist rose and the last of the sun dropped from sight.

As the birds were trading shifts with the frogs and crickets, Vera pointed to a cabin that must have belonged to Mr. Clark.

She whispered, "Would he have left a lamp burning?"

"I certainly would have! Otherwise, I might never find my way home in this darkness!"

Vera seemed to ponder my point before putting a finger to her lips. Almost as an orchestra conductor does, she gestured that it was time to play our well-rehearsed notes.

The steady wheeze of two oboes in a dark and desolate wood only exacerbated my anxiety. I followed Vera as she meandered onto and around the property. At times, we glimpsed flashes of the holes that guilt tears between this world and the next, edged with violet as our resonance teased them into the visible spectrum. However, those holes were too few and too scattered to suggest much supernatural activity.

If there were a monster here, it was one born of nature.

Nonetheless, Vera and I continued to drone on in harmony. Our serpentine march must have looked like some pagan ritual for the lost. Fortunately, only an owl observed us, displaying silent respect on a branch close to the cabin.

That owl swooped off and away, though, when footsteps rustled behind us! Footsteps rustling *toward* us! I hit a tooth as I jerked the oboe from my mouth and crouched for cover behind Vera.

With me clutching her, we managed to swing around — finding a *rifle* aimed at our heads!

"Good evening," Vera responded genially. *"Mrs.* Clark, I presume?"

A young woman lowered the rifle from her shoulder and her angled head. Her eyes darted quickly between the two of us. However, a grin gradually overtook her lips. She nodded in reply to Vera's question, and hers became a very pretty face. Despite it being framed by dark, straight hair, that face was almost as round as the full moon behind it.

Mrs. Clark positioned the rifle as if it were a shepherd's crook. "Y'all just about made me soil myself! All this talk of an ape-man, I was thinking that noise I was hearing was its *love* call! What in blazes you ladies *doing* out here?"

"Would you mind if we explained all that inside?" Vera asked. "The mosquitoes are a bit thick tonight."

Fifteen minutes later, we were drinking ginger ales with Mrs. Micah Clark. Only a month earlier, she had been Miss Alicia Hoch, the daughter of Otto and Greta Hoch. Mr. Clark met the family while working on their farm during a previous harvest.

"So your new husband bought the doilies and candies and, uhm, gingham for *you*, correct?" Vera asked.

"That's right." Quick to smile, our hostess shook her head. "So *much* gingham! I told him to get enough for a dress, but he's never bought cloth before. Wanted to make me happy, bless his heart."

That mystery solved, I wondered aloud, "Why didn't you simply go to the store with him? Or why didn't he ask Mrs. Hooper how much would be needed for a dress?"

Mrs. Clark slumped in her chair. "Oh. Well. That. I'm a bit of a *secret* for the time being." She examined her ginger ale and then took a hard swallow. "You see, Mike and the minister are working on a way to let the folks here know about me without them getting all riled up."

Vera cocked her head. "Riled up?"

"Without just up and telling them," explained Mrs. Clark, "that the boy's gone and married a *Catholic!*"

Had Dr. Adams been lurking close enough at that moment, he would have wondered why there were three women inside bachelor Micah Clark's cabin guffawing loud enough to frighten away a dragon.

Dabbing the mirth from her eyes, Vera relaxed her smile long enough to say, "You say the minister knows your secret? That gloomy man who expelled us from his church to protect our souls? What's his name again, Lida?"

"Orson Burnett. The Reverend Mr. Burnett gave us the impression he might be the *first* to object to your marriage."

"Aw, he's just an old scarecrow, the minister is," explained Alicia Clark. "More hay-filled than hateful. He stops by regular, easing Mike's worries that his falling in love with a *papist* will make him an outcast from the congregation. About where I caught you blowing them clarinets, that's where Mike paces back and forth, back and forth."

Vera turned to me and winked. This explained those few violet holes we had spotted.

"Mr. Burnett also comes here to ask me all manner of questions about the Roman Church, too. He's real curious what beliefs the Protestants share with my folks, but he hasn't had much chance to sit and chat about it. Honestly, y'all could invite every Catholic in this state, and there still wouldn't be enough to throw a barn dance."

"Has he tried to convert you to Protestant doctrines?" I asked.

"Of course, of course. That's his duty, after all. I told him, though, that converting me will be like asking a rabbit to take a vow of celibacy." Mrs. Clark smiled. "Still, I reckon he's working on some scheme to win me over. That's his way."

Vera tapped gently on her ginger ale bottle while repeating, "Like asking a rabbit to take a vow of celibacy. I'll have to remember that one. However, my dears, it's a fair ride back to the hotel. We'd be wise to go while there's light enough. The signalman has strong arms, but the moon does get heavy."

"But the moon does get heavy," our hostess recited, snickering. "I call that a pretty good swap, Miss Van Slyke."

•

According to plan, Vera and I were back at Hooper's General Store at nine o'clock the next morning. The scene was very different, though. Some people were waiting on barrels. Some were standing in groups. Some more were entering or exiting the mercantile.

In other words, a *mob* was forming.

Stepping down from the buggy, Vera asked, "Did *we* cause this somehow?"

Before I could advance a theory, the younger deacon we'd seen the previous day rushed up to us. He twitched a few times before speaking.

"Weren't y'all with Dr. Adams yesterday? He told us you're not his wife and daughter. Still, weren't y'all with him just the same? Because he's *gone!* He was supposed to meet me at a particular time and at a particular place. But he never showed. I had a cot all set for him. But he never showed. I waited! I searched! He's *gone!*"

Vera patted the man's shoulder. "Not to worry. The Professor has survived jungles, deserts, and mountains. I imagine he'll endure Arkansas."

"I waited! I searched!" the nervous deacon insisted.

I then spotted the Reverend Mr. Orson F. Burnett approaching the crowd. I pointed out his tall figure to Vera, and she walked forward. I thanked the young deacon, doing my best to assure him that Dr. Adams would be found in good health.

The rumblings of the crowd swelled as the minister neared.

"People!" he bellowed. "Let's display a semblance of *order!* What is this I'm hearing about our friend Micah Clark?"

"Married a monster!"

"Cohabitating with a she-gorilla!"

"It ain't *natural*, Reverend!"

"Wants to dress her up in a *dress!*"

This last statement stirred a stew of laughter, skepticism, and outrage among the mob. Someone rushed toward the minister, carrying a crate. Once it was properly placed, Mr. Burnett stood upon it and used his hands to hush the crowd.

"Friends? Who hatched this tale?" he said. "It's *true* that Micah Clark got married a few weeks back, but—"

"Married to a giant monkey!"

"Ain't *natural!* Buying all that gingham!"

"Mr. Hooper seen it, and so did the others!"

The minister again hushed the crowd. He declared, "Exactly what was seen, well, it's not for me to say. I *have* seen Micah's wife, though. While she's a right sturdy woman, it ain't very neighborly to call her a giant monkey!"

This time, the laughter outweighed the other sounds from the crowd.

"I sent someone to fetch the two them!" he continued. "Now, I wonder who it was started this cockamamie story." He scanned the crowd, and he appeared to stop on Vera. Sure enough, he pointed directly at her. "Was it *you*, stranger? Did you listen at the door yesterday when I asked you to wait outside the church?"

With an edge of irritation, Vera replied, "No, sir! I am sorry to disappoint you!"

"Well, then you Yankee women ain't as *reliable* as Southern gals!"

Again, the laughter increased.

Vera put two fingers to her jaw. After a moment, she leaned down to my ear. "Was the man *planning* to start this rumor?"

Considering the notion, from the corner of my eye, I noticed Mrs. Hooper slip furtively back into her store.

At that exact moment—as if by design—a horse with two riders came around the corner. In front was a strapping, young man with a full beard and dark eyebrows. Embracing his waist from behind was the pretty, round-faced woman with whom we had shared ginger ales the previous night.

And both Mr. and Mrs. Clark were *beaming*.

"Ladies and gentlemen," Mr. Burnett announced like a circus ringmaster, "I am most pleased to present to you—our good friend Micah Clark and his lovely bride, Alicia! And you know what? From the looks of her, if she's only *half* human, maybe that other half is *angel!*"

Amid cheers and applause, Mr. Clark slipped from his saddle to help his wife to the ground. The two braved handshakes, hugs, and hollers to reach the minister.

Once the crowd had begun to settle, Mr. Burnett resumed his place on the crate. He struck a pose by placing one hand on his hip and the other over his heart. "There is one thing you should know about our Alicia here. She was born and raised in the Roman Catholic faith!"

The mob suddenly fell silent.

"But I've found her knowledge of Scripture to be admirable. I've confirmed her love for our Lord and Savior. And besides—as we've learned so very, very well today—Micah sure as sheep could've picked *a lot worse!*"

The crowd burst into jubilance and celebration.

Vera tugged me out of the crowd. She said something that I could not discern in all the commotion. The young deacon had remained by our buggy, biting his thumbnail. Stan was waiting beside him.

Vera addressed the deacon. "Sir, your present duty is to welcome that new bride to your community. Go! Go revel amongst your people!"

The deacon twitched a few times before trotting off.

Vera then turned to Stan. "Weren't we told that the minister's cotton farm is near the church?"

"Across from the graveyard beside it," he affirmed.

"We need to go there before this jamboree fades."

Once we were on our way, I asked Vera to repeat what she had said a moment earlier.

"Ah, that! I said, 'Misjudge *not*—lest ye be misjudged.' At first, I took our clergyman to be a man of narrow vision, just as he assumed we would listen outside his church door. I now hope to verify that his ken is far-reaching enough to have led his flock toward accepting that sweet Catholic woman." She turned toward the passing scenery before grumbling, "That is, accepting her well enough before relentlessly laboring to *convert* her."

True to form, Vera validated her assumption shortly after our arrival at the minister's farmhouse. In a rear shed, we found a construction made of chicken wire and cotton, painted in the same black as we had seen on the benches in the church. When placed upon a man's shoulders—especially, those of a tall man—the contraption would create the illusion of a hulking, ape-like creature. From a distance, a witness's imagination would supply the eyes, the mouth, and all the other realistic details.

"This will remain our secret," Vera said. "Are all we agreed?"

I nodded. Stan, who had at last found some interest in our investigation, continued to lift and walk the ape-man costume.

"Are we *all* agreed?" Vera scolded.

"I ain't going to tell anybody!" Stan declared. Placing the costume over his head, he added, "We *all* need monsters. They make it easier to love our neighbors."

Vera crossed her arms before surmising, "A fitting moral to the conclusion of this case."

"Vera?" I said.

"Yes, my dear?"

"We still don't know where Dr. Adams is."

"Very astute. I spoke prematurely."

•

By that afternoon, Stan had located Geoffrey Wallace Livingstone Adams. While surveying Micah Clark's homestead the previous night, the world traveler had taken a wrong turn and consequently become lost in the woods. Nonetheless, we were back to the hotel in Paragould while the sun still hovered well above the horizon. Dr. Adams washed his face, changed his suit, and attended to a few other necessities before he treated us to dinner. At the hotel restaurant, Vera and I took turns recounting our private meeting with Alicia and her very public introduction to the community.

Unlike the rabbit striving to remain celibate, we upheld our vow to never divulge our discovery in the minister's shed. Even so, Dr. Adams admitted to being doubtful about the ape-man sightings here. Based on his interrogations and observations—as well as the scarcity of dimensional holes that Vera and I had discovered—he attributed the sightings to a calculating hoaxer. Or, perhaps, a prowling bear.

After our meal, Dr. Adams said, "Let's make this our final evening here. It would be charming to mark the occasion, but I didn't sleep a wink last night. I ask for your permission to retire early for tomorrow's long train ride north. I do fear, though, I'll have nightmares about Mary, Queen of Scots, and Guy Fawkes. Both of them *Catholics* against the Church of England, what? An unsavory end for both."

Vera explained that, anticipating his need for a good night's rest, she and I had discussed possibly drinking a farewell beer. His company would be missed but not required. Dr. Adams bowed and headed toward his room.

However, I noticed he left an envelope with the desk clerk before disappearing.

"If you wait here a moment, *I* might solve a mystery, too!" I told Vera. I next strolled to the front desk and said to the clerk, "A moment ago, Dr. Adams kindly dropped off my letter for tomorrow's post. May I check to see if I addressed it correctly?"

Without the slightest compunction, the desk clerk complied with my ruse.

I had to *struggle* to mask my shock at seeing the recipient's name. I'm certain I had blanched when I returned the letter to the clerk. Without thanking him, I coughed, "It—it's fine."

Vera was waiting for me by the front door, her back toward me.

"Vera!" I hissed as I rushed to her. "I have—I have something important to tell you! Something that might be *upsetting* to you!"

She spun to face me. "No! No, you mustn't get married! I'm sure this Eric—Rick—Bergstone is an upstanding fellow! But, *no, you must not get married! You simply mustn't!*"

"P-Pardon me?"

"You are betrothed to the fellow back from Alaska, aren't you? Isn't that what you were about to tell me? Isn't that what you *failed* to admit under that oak tree beside that church?"

"*No!* I mean—well, yes. Yes, I *am* going to marry Rick Bergson. But what I was going to tell you was—wait one moment! *Why* mustn't I marry Rick Bergson?" I felt dizzy.

Vera sniffed twice. "I need a beer! Let's go get a beer! *Two* beers. And one or two for yourself. As many as you like!" She bolted through the hotel door.

Fortunately, there was a tavern nearby. The bartender said he only served women accompanied by gentlemen. He agreed, however, to let us wait there for our husbands and to please them by having their beers already at the table. This same trick had worked in several states prior to Arkansas.

In a private nook, I sat beside Vera and admitted, "All of the subterfuge on this trip makes me wonder if I haven't traveled back in time to my years in the Spiritualism racket."

Vera was in no mood to grin, though. She stared forward, pouting.

I offered, "Let's start with my marrying Rick Bergson."

Vera squirmed in her chair.

"I've been meaning to tell you about my engagement for quite a while now. But I knew it would be an adjustment for you. Tell me what it is that bothers you most about my getting married?"

Vera squirmed again. "I'll have to learn yet *another* name! What was the name you used when I defrauded you as a medium?"

"Ludmila Prášilová."

"But you told me your true name was *Lucille Parsell!* But that wasn't your *real* true name, was it!"

"My real true name is Ludmila Prášilová."

"But your family called you *Lida!* And then you asked me to call you *Lida* instead of *Lucille.* And I eventually learned to call you *Lida* instead of *Lucille.* Now, you'll be taking on *another* name? It's *cruel!*"

"You'll still be calling me Lida. That is, I hope you will."

Her squirming lessened. "You'll still work for me, then? You'll still be my assistant?"

I sighed. "Well, nooo. Rick is buying his own music shop. I'll be helping him there. At least, at first. But I'll still be in Chicago! I'll still be available for investigations of ghostly phenomena! Rick loves to hear about our mysteries, so I don't think he'll mind. I promise I'll still be Dr. Watson to your Sherlock Holmes!"

Vera muttered, "Perhaps, but Dr. Watson would never go off and get married!"

I patted her hand. "You really ought to read those tales sometime, Vera. Speaking of doctors, though, shall I tell you the name I saw on the letter our Dr. Adams left at the front desk?"

Vera pursed her lips and shrugged. It seemed to have become a habit with her.

"The name is Madeline Morley! I checked the city, too, and yes—she lives in Boston! I imagine the envelope contained Dr. Adams' report on this case. That's our mysterious benefactress! Madeline Morley!"

"Who?"

I needed a swig of beer. "Roderick Morley was the millionaire who hired me to conduct a séance at his mansion in Boston nine years ago. The very séance where you defrauded me! The very séance that ended with the distraught Mr. Morley taking his own life!"

Vera jolted upright. With her eyes opened wide, she nodded. She took a sip of her beer before saying, "That *is* interesting! And you're suggesting this Madeline Morley must be related to the millionaire. His cousin, perhaps—or his sister?" A twinkle came to her eyes.

"Roderick Morley was enthralled by the occult! And someone inherited all his money! If it's his cousin or sister, she's spending it in the way that he would have wanted."

The great solver of mysteries touched two fingers to her jaw. "Yet why would she expressly withhold her name from us? Lida, do you think this woman blames me—or possibly, the two of us— for her relative's suicide?" Vera pressed her palms together. "Lida,

do you suppose this Madeline Morley remains in the shadows—
because she's out to *avenge her family?*"

Slowly, we raised and touched our beer glasses together.

"We can only hope, Vera," I granted. "We can only hope."

BEYOND THE GREAT BEYOND
(1909)

[W]ith this living substance in my grasp, with its body pressed against my own, and all the bright glare of a large jet of gas, I absolutely beheld nothing!

— Fitz-James O'Brien

Vera Van Slyke never had to sign her messages to me because they were easily identifiable by their content. An example is the note that read:

I've been contacted by M.M. Empty coats are dancing in Milwaukee. Lunch?

The dancing coats were certainly a point of interest. Still, I was more intrigued by the first line, which indicated that Madeline Morley had communicated with Vera. Over the preceding year, Vera had made discreet inquiries to confirm that this woman supervised a foundation dedicated to occult research, from astral projection and psychometry to sea serpents and fairies. We also knew that the benefactress was aware of Vera's study of ghostly phenomena. Despite their mutual interests, Vera had been respecting Miss Morley's wish to maintain a certain distance.

We assumed that wish was related to her brother. Toward the close of the 1890s, Roderick Morley had entrusted much of his wealth to a psychic advisor. This advisor was then *murdered* under mysterious circumstances. Being accused of committing the crime only added to Mr. Morley's desperate desire to solve it. He arranged to reveal the true culprit by contacting the murder victim's *spirit* with the help of a young medium. The subsequent séance was dramatically revealed to be a sham, though, due to a journalist who had made defrauding mediums her special crusade.

That same evening, the distraught Roderick Morley ended his own life with a gunshot. His wealth eventually passed to his sister, who created the foundation to promote her brother's otherworldly interests. Meanwhile, the journalist took pity on the medium—and Vera and I became good friends.

And she promptly introduced me to the truth regarding ghosts.

A full decade later, as I rocked on an elevated train, I contemplated my role in that tragic séance. I realized that my guilt had since eased. Those ghosts had quieted.

In keeping with that feeling of denouement, once I left the train and came upon Vera, she appeared like an illustration from the last page of a novel. In the cold air of Chicago in December, Vera stood as if frozen across the street from where we had regularly met for lunch. Her head was held back, her mouth was slightly open, and her breath turned to frosty smoke. I turned to see that the shingle announcing The Foiled Gelding no longer hung in front. In its place was an enormous sign heralding JAKE'S EATERY.

"Look," she uttered, "they've changed the name. Someone's bought the place, I guess."

I stood at her side. "They still serve food. But are you still hungry?"

Turning her head, Vera only needed to raise an eyebrow to let me know I had asked a very silly question. By the time we had crossed the street, we were giddy to discover what changes had been made to the menu.

After we had settled at our table and ordered our food, Vera's actions reminded me how the preliminary niceties of conversation always bored her. Instead of inquiring about my five months of married life, she handed me the letter from Miss Morley and began to summarize its contents. She was as systematic as I had been when employed as her assistant.

"After explaining the goals of the foundation," Vera began, "M.M. asks if I might investigate a case of empty coats that *dance!* The owner of a secondhand-clothing shop, his wife, and their employee all witnessed the coats dancing in the shop's stockroom. News of the manifestation reached one of the foundation's local agents, but M.M. says that my experiences better qualify me for the case. If I accept, I will receive a stipend upon the foundation's receipt of my written account of the investigation."

Perhaps to counter my earlier contemplative mood, I felt like teasing. I put the letter down between us and nodded before saying, "Rick and I are doing well. The new music store already has had several customers."

After blinking twice, Vera replied, "I'm pleased. But can you imagine coats dancing with nobody in them? Nobody *visible*, that is! That's the most distinctive part of the manifestation. The employee quit working there after she *bumped* into one of the ghosts! She described it as a 'hard ghost.' A *hard* ghost!"

"Rick wonders if we should reduce the number of pianos to make room for more phonograph cylinders and discs, but I'm not sure I agree."

"A difficult decision. You know, Harry Escott told me about his own encounter with a hard ghost! Not really a ghost at all, he said. Instead, it was an *invisible* creature that he managed to bind with ropes! I never knew if his encounter involved too little opaqueness or too much *opium.*" She snickered.

"Pianos, after all, have been popular far longer than phonographs."

"Very astute. Will you be able to join me for a few days in Milwaukee? It's surely not anybody's first choice for a winter sojourn, but it's barely more than an hour's train ride from Union Station." A twinkle came to her eye. "Adequate time for you to tell me all about married life and the music store and the phonograph-versus-piano question."

Vera had earned my sincerity. After giggling, I replied, "I'll have to check with Rick first, but he says he never wants to hinder any of our investigations. In fact, speaking of phonographs, he used a home-recording device and two other phonographs to make a record of two oboes playing a B-flat and high G. It plays steadily for two minutes, and he thinks it could improve our method of checking for the violet holes."

Vera smiled but contracted her eyebrows. "Very innovative of him. Yet won't lugging one of those awful machines instead of two oboes be more cumber—"

"We'd only need to bring the cylinder," I interjected. "It's not hard to borrow a phonograph these days. This secondhand-clothing merchant might even have one in his shop! Hopefully one that plays cylinders instead of discs. Now, do these coats dance to *music*—or in silence?"

Vera's eyebrows rose. She snatched and quickly reviewed the letter before reading aloud: "'The coats mimicked the waltz that Mrs. Bartowski and Miss Sawyer danced during breaks from their repair work.' Vera searched the letter some more. "Yes! It says 'Mrs. Bartowski noted that Strauss was playing during the manifestation'."

"At least the ghosts have good taste! Vera, this doesn't seem like much of a haunting! *Hard* ghosts that mimic *waltzing?* Do you think Madeline Morley might be sending us on a fool's errand? It's been ten years, but she *does* have reason to begrudge us our role in her brother's suicide."

"I had exactly that concern. And so did *she!* M.M. closes by confessing that she *did* harbor ill will towards me immediately after her brother shot himself. However, learning that my battle against Spiritualists has been matched by my efforts to help the haunted sweetened that bitterness. She then worried that *I would assume* she harbored ill will towards me. That's why she took her time contacting me. It strikes me as a believable story."

"Yes," I muttered. "A *believable* story. But is it *reliable?*"

After we had finished our lunch and settled on details for the trip north, I rode the elevated train back home. I again found myself dwelling on my life as a Spiritualist medium. I remembered having learned time and again that *any* story is believable—so long as its listener is poised to believe it.

And I wondered if my dearest friend were poised to believe a story about her being forgiven for having any role at all in the suicide of Madeline Morley's brother.

•

As we stepped off the train in Milwaukee, Vera's earlier comment about this city not being anybody's first choice for a winter sojourn came back to nip me on the nose. We scurried into the station where passengers and porters alike were stomping, cursing, and laughing to banish the bracing cold. All I could think of was how I had packed far too few mufflers, mittens, and other woolens.

Her eyes gleaming, Vera scanned the depot. "Given this city's reputation for breweries," she sang, "I'm eager to sample several new beers while we're here!"

Vera wasn't oblivious to the cold, however. It simply wasn't a hindrance to her. This became clear after we had checked into the Blatz Hotel. She explained that it would be smart to begin the investigation by speaking with Miss Sawyer, the woman who had made physical contact with the frightful manifestation and promptly ended her employment with the secondhand-clothing shop.

"Ordinarily," Vera reasoned aloud, "we might have difficulty finding this witness, since she'd be out searching for a new position. But these frigid temperatures suggests we'll find her at home."

After shivering on streetcars for twenty-five very long minutes, we confirmed Vera's hunch. We met Miss Amelia Sawyer at a working-class boardinghouse on the city's south side. Her room there was tiny, providing only enough room for a bed and a bureau with one of its drawers missing. Miss Sawyer was short, rosy-cheeked, and maturely proportioned for a woman probably under twenty years of age. She left Vera and me to stand while she stretched across her bed as if she were royalty. The brashness of this gave me the impression that she had gumption enough to eventually rise above her current financial situation.

"The *Mrs.* Bartowski is a good gal," said Miss Sawyer. "The *Mr.* Bartowski, though—well, he's an old fuddy-duddy. But not *too* old. You ladies might appreciate the fact that he's built like the mighty Sandow. Gus Bartowski's got the broadest shoulders that I have *ever*—well." She snorted. "Let's just say he's more *fuddy* than *duddy*."

Vera looked at me. I shrugged.

"Kindly tell us about the manifestation," Vera said. "I understand you referred to it as a *hard* ghost."

Miss Sawyer nodded while pinching some of the ends of her chestnut hair for close examination. "After the *Mrs.* Bartowski and me'd finish repairing a pile of coats, I'd drag her up to get the blood flowing again with a dance. Of course, given their music, it was always a hoity-toity dance."

I asked, "What kind of music do they enjoy?"

"Oh, Beethoven and Mozart and that fiddle-faddle. The *Mr.* Bartowski doesn't allow any Billy Murray or Ada Jones! Nothing with any razzle-dazzle."

With contracted eyebrows, Vera put two fingers to her jaw. "If I understand you, the fuddy-duddy's fiddle-faddle taste in music explains why you chose the hoity-toity *waltz* instead of a dance with more razzle-dazzle?"

I tightened my lips.

"You got it," replied Miss Sawyer matter-of-factly. "And *that's* when the coats started waltzing, too! Four or five of them! Scheesch, I swear I'd been blown to the Land of Oz! But as soon as *we* stopped dancing, those *coats* stopped dancing! They just hung in the air like some levitation trick performed by Houdini himself!"

Vera gave me a wink before turning back to ask, "How long did they hang in the air?"

"When the music stopped, they dropped straight to the floor. We started the record up again, but the coats stayed there on the floor—until *we* started dancing again. Then they jumped and flapped and began to waltz all over! The Mrs. ran to the sales floor to fetch the Mr. But *I* figured we were being flimflammed. Strings from the rafters or such. I kept right on dancing, moving closer. And *closer*. And *closer still!*" Miss Sawyer's eyes drifted toward the tiny room's only window.

Glancing at that flimsy window, I noticed that two triangles of ice had formed on the sill in both corners. Nonetheless, I knew that something *else* had distracted Miss Sawyer.

Softly, I inquired, "Is that when you bumped into them? Is that when you felt the hard ghosts?"

Miss Sawyer kept her gaze aimed at the icy window. "Yes. But I didn't bump into them. They all came toward me. *They* bumped into me, and everything went harum-scarum! That's when I knew we weren't being flimflammed. *Scheesch,* there was something in those coats! Something with *skin* on it and *bone* beneath!" She glared at the window. "And something there that looked like nothing there at all!"

"Were they *cold?*" I asked. I was thinking of ice being solid but transparent.

Miss Sawyer spun her head to face me. "They were warm! Almost *cozy!* That's when I knew I had to quit working there! Ladies, does that make any sense at all?" She then suddenly faced Vera.

Vera nodded to assure Miss Sawyer that her reaction made *perfect* sense.

The young woman pushed herself up into a sitting position as we changed the subject to the history of the secondhand coats. She was only able to tell us that Mr. Bartowski had purchased them from a man whose livelihood was acquiring large quantities of discarded clothing and selling them to small shops throughout the

Middle West. She could tell us nothing about where these coats had originated or this drummer's method of finding the castoffs in bulk.

We thanked Miss Sawyer and wished her well in finding new employment. Before leaving, I asked for her recommendation of a nearby restaurant. I then mentioned to Vera that the cold must have made me very hungry for a hot lunch. Rather than reply, she drifted into a state of contemplation that was very familiar to me. I remained silent as we traveled to the restaurant.

Not until two bowls of steaming stew were placed before us did Vera speak.

"Despite our young witness's *hurly-burly* vocabulary," she began, "I have an inkling that she refrained from saying something about her interactions with her dance partner's husband. That curious mix of disdain for the man and admiration for the muscle. Did you sense that, too?"

I tore some bread. "Yes, I did. But aren't some French novels better left at the bookstore?"

Vera's eyes widened. "I couldn't have phrased it better myself, Lida! Yes, we shall leave that book unopened. Our mystery involves ghosts made of skin and bone. I honestly have no idea what that poor girl encountered. What *was* it?"

"I don't recall anything in Catherine Crowe's book similar to this, but you mentioned that your mentor dealt with something similar. Could we be confronting the same phenomenon that Harry Escott did?"

"Possibly," she mumbled.

Vera then stared at me with one eyebrow raised. She stared at me long enough to unnerve me.

Finally, I understood. "Yes, Vera," I acquiesced. "I've begun to study Crowe's book about ghosts. Since settling into married life, I guess I've also started to miss the years I spent with you."

My companion shook out her napkin before stating, "Well, it hardly gives you permission to *become* me! Making that metaphor about the French novels! And lunch was *your* idea, my dear! Shall I let *you* pay the tab?"

•

The Bartowskis' secondhand-clothing shop was next on our list of stops. Rushing in from the cold, we discovered the sole occupant of the sales floor to be a woman mending a heap of clothing. Her hair, pulled back austerely, was blonde with streaks of white. She looked up to reveal a face with sharp features and alabaster skin. Her polite grin suggested welcome, but the narrowing of her eyes implied suspicion. Seemingly, she hadn't anticipated many customers braving the low temperatures that day.

My companion charged ahead of me. "I'm Vera Van Slyke, and this is my—my *former* assistant, Lida Parsell."

"Lida Bergson," I corrected.

"Lida Bergson," Vera repeated. "Can I assume that you are—uh—"

"Mrs. Bartowski," I assisted.

Vera's assumption was correct. A closer look revealed that Mrs. Iris Bartowski wore a crucifix over a light gray frock, almost as if she were dressed for Sunday services. I had some difficulty combining the woman's reverent countenance with the image of her waltzing playfully with Miss Sawyer.

Vera explained that we had come to investigate the dancing coats, the mere mention of which made Mrs. Bartowski shudder. Upon learning that we might be able to eliminate the manifestation, though, the seamstress readily recounted her ghostly experience. Doing so, she escorted us to see the large stockroom in the back, where repairs were typically handled.

"While you can *look*," she stipulated, "you mustn't play any music. I enjoy Strauss and Chopin, but since those devils appeared, I'm not so certain even *that's* decent."

"*Devils?*" Vera repeated with a ring of derision.

To avoid offending our witness, I quickly asked, "Can I assume, then, that you share your husband's disdain for Tin Pan Alley music?"

"My husband!" Mrs. Bartowski spit. With her own strain of mockery, she added, "My husband can't tell ragtime from a requiem!"

I saw Vera's head list sideways. I felt certain that she was recalling Miss Sawyer's claim that the *Mr.* Bartowski was the fuddy-duddy who favored symphonies over razzle-dazzle.

Wandering a few steps through the room's boxes and racks of clothing, Vera asked, "Did we miss him today? Your husband?"

"August knew we'd do poor business due to the freeze, so he left early. Said he's hoping to pick up a load of clothes at an estate auction."

"It's a *chilly* afternoon to hold an auction," I replied, not intending to sound doubtful.

Still, Mrs. Bartowski muttered, "Yes, well. Sometimes, all he returns with from his so-called *auctions* are a red nose and a sore head the next morning." She turned her own head down to rub her knuckles. "I spoke rashly. His vices are *my* burden, not *your* concern."

I gently touched her arm. Meanwhile, Vera stretched high to examine the rafters and stooped low to study the floor. This inspired me to do some probing of my own, and I quickly spotted the phonograph that presumably had been playing during the manifestation. My experience in the music shop helped me identify it as an Edison Fireside, a model that would play the cylinder I had in my valise.

I faced our witness. "I respect your wish that we don't play any music, but I have a recording that will help us confirm that something supernatural has occurred."

Mrs. Bartowski shrugged. "You wouldn't have to confirm that if you'd seen those coats dancing. I tell you, the *Devil* has a hand in this!" She moved her head from side to side. "But you go ahead and play your record. I—I'll be in front, thank you!"

With some haste, our hostess returned to her mending, and I told Vera that we were free to experiment with Rick's recording. Rarely pleased with technological progress, she responded with a sigh of consent. As I slid the cylinder onto the phonograph, she found the switch for the lights.

I wished my new husband could have joined us in marveling at how well his idea succeeded! As soon as the two oboes sounded—one playing B-flat, the other playing high G—the workroom blossomed with wavering, violet circles. Each glowing circle marked a rupture between the physical and spirit dimensions, a breach shifted into the edge of visibility by that precise harmony of oboes. Each circle hovered and drifted with the grace of sea life.

More like *oil* on the sea, though, some of the violet holes merged with others. We had observed this before, but Rick's sustained recording allowed us to notice something new. Some of the largest holes, four to five feet in diameter, seemed to reach a point at which they trembled momentarily before bursting into a myriad of tiny holes. After spreading in all directions, those holes then repeated the cycle of coalescing with others.

We had watched these bursts occur twice when Vera commanded, "Shut off the recording, Lida. We know the consequences of physical objects passing through those holes, and I don't like them scattering in my direction. I'd rather *not* become crystalized dust today."

I lifted the needle of the phonograph, and Vera switched on the lights. We sat down on stools that probably had been used by Miss Sawyer and Mrs. Bartowski. We let our experience settle.

"Wasn't that beautiful?" I whispered.

"A great advance in our investigations. But so long as those holes are within the visible realm, they pose a danger to us. Regretfully, it seems as if *every* technological stride forward sidles us closer to the cliff."

I smirked. "Which one of the Wright brothers do you imagine is the *Devil?*"

Vera chuckled before changing the subject. "More to the point, those beautiful holes were made by a concentration of stabbing guilt. Again, I feel as if some mystery surrounds the *husband.*"

261

"His drinking?"

"That or something to do with the pretty employee who had admired his broad shoulders. I'm wont to believe that those hard ghosts passed into our dimension because the door was opened from *this* side."

"You've taught me that, in most cases, ghosts haunt the living because something haunts the ghost, and these ghosts don't seem to be haunting anyone!"

Vera nodded slowly. "They've come only to dance."

"Or to show that they *can* dance. Miss Sawyer mentioned that, after imitating the first waltz, the coats only resumed dancing once she and Mrs. Bartowski began waltzing to the music *again*. What if these beings are not just invisible to us but also *mute* to us? What if this is their way of—"

"*Communicating* with us?" Vera exclaimed, sitting suddenly upright.

"And showing that they're *intelligent!*"

Vera grabbed my elbow forcefully. She stared at me, holding her gaze slightly above my eyes. She held this pose until I pried her tightening fingers from my arm.

She declared, "These are not *ghosts!* At least, not the ghosts of anything that's ever lived here on *Earth.*"

"*My gracious!*" I gasped. "Vera, if they're not from Earth—if they're not from here, then—have you read about the canals on *Mars?* An astronomer named Percival Lowell says they were built by a highly advanced race. Do you—you don't suppose—" I ended my sentence by furrowing my brow.

"If I had to guess, my dear, I'd say these entities hoping to communicate their grasp of music and movement came from a place far more distant than Mars." She inhaled deeply and stifled that breath some time before releasing it. "I suppose we'll need to ask the wife about sources of guilt. If we can alleviate the guilt, we can at least shut the door."

We continued to sit in silence for a while. Neither of us wanted to shut that door too quickly.

As it happened, the only information relevant to guilt that we were able to extract from Mrs. Bartowski concerned her worries about the coats that she and Miss Sawyer had been fixing. The drummer who sold them had a policy of never divulging the background of his merchandise. Nonetheless, the two seamstresses had to wash out stains that seemed to be raw coal, soot, and possibly blood. They speculated that the coats might have come from a mining disaster. Indeed, only one month previous, over 250 men and boys had died when fire and fumes surged through a coal mine in Cherry, Illinois. News of the catastrophe had spread rapidly.

Mrs. Bartowski lamented, "It's the *uncertainty* about those coats that makes me worry it's profane to profit from them! If we knew they'd come from those fallen miners, well, maybe a priest could come bless them. In our way, we clothe the poor, after all! Let some good come of those coats. But—but we simply don't know!"

Vera explained, "We'll have to coax the drummer who supplied them to break his rule. I suppose he travels a lot, but do you have his name and a stable address?"

"My husband handles that part of the business. He should be in tomorrow. Unless, of course, he's off to another of his—*auctions.*"

"I understand," Vera replied softly. "I know casting out these *devils* is important to you, ma'am. Perhaps, your husband could visit *us* this evening if it's convenient. And not too cold. We're staying at the Blatz Hotel downtown. Will you remember that name? Blatz is also the name of a brewery here, isn't it?"

"Oh, I'll remember," she replied. "Everyone in this city knows the name Blatz."

On the streetcar ride back to the hotel, Vera said, "Miss Razzle-Dazzle doesn't strike me as someone wracked with guilt. However, that devout woman *does*. She might be the key, but I'm of the mind that some of her husband's regrets ought to be unveiled, too."

"Well," I said through chattering teeth, "he *is* a drinker, isn't he? Perhaps *that* could help us unveil some of his regrets."

"Are you suggesting we get him drunk?" Vera laughed. "My, but aren't you the little *devil*, Lida Parsell!"

I was too cold to correct her.

•

Our luck was with us. Mr. August Bartowski came to our hotel that evening. Vera discreetly elbowed me upon our greeting him. The nudge was not because our guest's shoulders brought to mind the mighty Sandow, as Miss Sawyer had suggested. To the contrary, Vera was prodding me to notice how very *ordinary* Mr. Bartowski was in appearance. He was neither large nor small, neither muscular nor scrawny. Thinning, brown hair fell over his unremarkable brow. Light eyebrows sheltered his unimpressively hazel eyes. A conventional moustache topped his indistinctive mouth and chin.

After introductions, Vera said with her typical directness, "I see your nose is florid, sir. Have you been celebrating the approaching Yuletide with an ale?"

"Uh, no," Mr. Bartowski answered. "The freeze is to blame for that. I probably would have stayed at home if I hadn't also wanted to buy an opera ticket across the street."

"An opera ticket for your wife?" I asked.

"Uh, no. She enjoys her symphonic music, but I attend the opera on those rare occasions when I can afford it."

Vera cocked her head. "So you *can* tell ragtime from a requiem? Your musical tastes aren't limited to, say, the polka?"

"Uh, no."

Vera began to stare at the man.

I promptly offered, "Speaking of Yuletide ale, would you care to join us for some beer here at the hotel bar? It'll be our treat, and while we ask our questions, you could savor the warmth."

"Do you women drink beer?" he asked innocently.

Still appearing to be baffled by our guest, Vera uttered, "Perhaps not as much as we ought."

Mr. Bartowski nodded politely. "I find my limit is two glasses. Uh, yes, it would be nice to be out of the cold for a while."

We strolled to the hotel bar. Once our beverages had arrived, Vera asked Mr. Bartowski what he could tell us of the manifestation in his stockroom. He explained that he had only glimpsed the conclusion of the ghostly event, but his descriptions accorded with those of his wife and the former assistant. Recounting the strange scene affected him emotionally—but only with very measured fear and perplexity. At the same time, he sipped his beer at regular intervals.

Vera's glass and mine were emptying more quickly than his.

I introduced our theory that the entities he had seen were attempting to communicate with us as best they could. Here, he expressed what I can only describe as *tranquil astonishment.*

He commented, "You're saying they're invisible to us, but we're not to them. And, unless they don't have speech, we can't hear them—though they *can* hear us."

"Very astute," Vera said. "Through manipulating the coats, these beings conveyed their ability to see us and to hear at least the *rhythm* of our music. Nevertheless, if they're natives of our physical dimension, wouldn't we have met them long ago? I'm fairly certain they come from some distant realm, entering through dimensional ruptures caused by intense feelings of guilt. Now, how I learned of these ruptures will take a good deal of explanation. Lida, would you mind fetching another round of beers?"

Mr. Bartowski declined another drink at that time, pointing out that his glass was only halfway empty. I returned with a second round for Vera and myself, though. At that point, we regaled our guest with a series of stories. We opened with how we discovered the violet holes. We next narrated tales of ghostly fires igniting of their own accord, the spirits of whales netted by a sea captain's knotty past, an Irish immigrant convinced he was Chinese, and vampire-like particles filtering through the soil of downtown Chicago. After every adventure, the vaguely mechanical man expressed his tranquil astonishment and took another sip of beer.

That is when Vera leaned toward Mr. Bartowski and said, "Your wife mentioned you attended an *auction* this afternoon. Did you get some good clothing at this afternoon's *auction?*" Clearly, she had decided that it was time for the unveiling.

"Uh, yes," Mr. Bartowski answered. "I was able to get some very nice dresses at a good price."

"Well. Good. Good for you," replied Vera, pursing her lips. "That's good. Well. Who's ready for another beer?"

As all of our glasses were now empty, Mr. Bartowski went to the bar.

I took the opportunity to tell Vera, "Methinks he doth protest too *little*. I'm not sure this man has any regrets or—or even much personality at all! It's as if Miss Sawyer and Mrs. Bartowski each have painted one for him in order to make him—well—*visible!*"

"We all perceive others through two small windows. Perhaps that's especially the case with this translucent man." A mood for metaphors seemed to have risen in Vera because she added, "To be sure, the crystal of a watch can be harder to crack than a peanut. But he said his limit is two beers. Let's see what happens once he's well into that second glass."

After returning with more beer for us all, Mr. Bartowski continued to incrementally sip his while we discussed such matters as his wife's theory that the coats had come from a mining disaster, the drummer's reasons for not revealing how he acquired his merchandise, even the directional advantages of living in cities that sit on the shore of Lake Michigan.

Vera and I were almost finished with our *third* beers while Mr. Bartowski had reached midway through his *second.*

With a decided lean to the left, Vera said, "Mr. Bartowski? I got your name right, didn't I? Excellent. Earlier, I was shpeaking about how *guilt*—terrible *guilt*—punches its fist through the dimenshional membrane. Remember that?"

"Uh, yes."

"Now, is anyone among ush *without* guilt?"

"Uh—no."

"Nooo," Vera repeated, using a raised finger to help counterbalance herself.

"I am not without guilt," I announced, more to my glass than to my companions. "My own mother made me pretend to be a Spiritualist medium for *five* years, and I'm not certain I've ever fully forgiven her for that. Having to bamboozle those poor people who only wanted to speak with their dearly departed made me *abhor* my own mother. *Abhor!* My own *mother!* I am not without guilt." I raised my glass as if to toast. If I recall correctly, I also yawned.

"No, Lida ish not without guilt. With me, it was my grandfather. Yet I don't feel any guilt about that—he treated my father and my grandmother monshtrously. Do you know why I am not without guilt? Lida hasn't pretended to communicate with shpirits for ten yearsh! Yet I've shpent a lifetime pretending to be *white!*"

Seeing Mr. Bartowski's eyebrows rise slightly, I pointed out, "Vera's grandfather was Dutch, and her mother Irish. But her grandmother was a colored woman from—where was it, Vera?"

"She was born here in the United Shtates, but she told me she had been worked all over the Shouth. You know? I get fidgety shtaying in one place for too long. Maybe I inherited that from her. Along with my hair. Now. What wush I talking about?"

"*Guilt!*" I exclaimed with conviction.

Vera looked back at me and grinned. Next, her eyes moistened. "I'm shorry I haven't shown more interesht in your marriage, my dear."

I reached my hand across the table, and Vera held it in her own for a sweet minute. I forget now which one of us was clearheaded enough to resume the scheme to unveil Mr. Bartowski's regrets.

"And do *you* harbor any feelings of guilt, Mr. Bartowski?" asked one of us.

"Uh—it's probably best I walk you back to the lobby, so you ladies can go up to your rooms. Business will be slow again tomorrow most likely. I'll give my wife the day off, and maybe we can get those ghost-beings to communicate again. Do we have a deal?"

As I chronicle these events, I struggle to remember what happened next. All I can say with certainty is that my dreams that night involved Mr. Bartowski dancing amid several hard ghosts, his figure swirling like smoke among the others.

•

Somehow, the next day, we remembered Mr. Bartowski's invitation to elicit the invisible entities to communicate again. Thinking back now to the *results* of that experiment, however, makes me gravely wish we had forgotten his invitation.

Though I couldn't fathom how, that day was even colder than the previous one. After a hearty breakfast, we stalwartly rode the streetcars back to the secondhand-clothing shop. True to his word, Mr. Bartowski had granted his wife a respite from her mending. If our plan worked, she also would be saved from again witnessing the abomination of empty coats dancing.

Our host made no mention of Vera's and my indulgence of the prior evening. I like to think it was the gentlemen in him, but I know this might be my own attempt to paint him a personality. He did supply a pot of tea for us, though, in the stockroom of his shop.

He also returned to the sales floor after only a few attempts of our experiment. Starting with "The Blue Danube," Vera and I waltzed in our best approximation of how Miss Sawyer and Mrs. Bartowski had done so. We danced and danced through the entire music collection. As our failures were mounting, Vera even started to loudly plead with me to come dance, projecting her lines like an actress on stage. She directed me to voice reluctance and to make the sign of the cross over my heart before accepting.

"Wait one moment," I protested, "why haven't you cast *me* in the role of Miss Sawyer? I'm younger than you!"

"And prettier, too—but you're the only available *Mrs.* here, aren't you!" Vera retaliated, adding a playful sneer.

Eventually, our inability to lure the hard ghosts into manifesting took its toll. We sat down on the two stools to rest and to reconsider our tactics. Vera hunched in her seat, her two fingers on her jaw. I took advantage of the tea.

All of a sudden, Vera snapped her fingers. "We need to make a telephone call!"

"*You?* A telephone call? I'm not certain you'll be able to find a 'phone in *this* neighborhood, and it's too cold to—"

"I'm hoping the telephone is in your valise," Vera replied.

It was only an instant or two before I realized she was referring to my husband's recording of the oboes.

Vera explained, "We know how to shift the dimensional ruptures into our visible spectrum. We also know those holes are always visible—well, *perceptible*—in the spirit world. But who knows if our tugging on them might not send out a few ripples across the ether. I believe they're calling it *wireless.*"

One never needed to paint a personality onto Vera Van Slyke. Hers came readymade in vibrant, unexpected hues.

She walked to the light switch. "Let's make absolutely certain they catch our signal. This time, we'll risk letting Rick's cylinder play to the very end," she said, illustrating that her difficulty with names vanished whenever her mind was operating at its fullest.

I prepared the cylinder, started the machine, and put the needle in place. Vera shut off the lights. We stood perfectly still as the violet-rimmed holes again performed a ballet that far outshone our earlier waltzing. I tried to peer through the holes that swirled close before me, but only absolute dark appeared beyond.

The holes hovered close to our skin and clothing, but they stopped and then reversed direction before making actual contact. Nonetheless, I knew that pushing a physical object, such as a pencil, through the hole destroyed that object. This is why I moved with acute sluggishness when I heard a rustling coming from Vera's direction.

Once I had pivoted my head far enough, I saw she had inserted the end of a clothes hanger into one of the larger holes. She was scrutinizing how it had come back transformed into something like quartz. She next blew on that crystalized end of the hanger, and sparkling flecks cascaded to the floor.

"Always fascinating," Vera mouthed more than spoke.

The beautiful pageant vanished as the recorded oboes ceased to play. Vera switched on the lights, and my eyes took a moment to adjust.

And my *heart* took a moment to adjust to the sight of five empty coats levitating in the area where we had been waltzing! The coats shifted slightly, not as if they were on strings, but as if they were worn by *people*. People with no *seeable* corporeality. People who were standing patiently.

"Vera?" I said, discovering that I was unable to lift my arm to point.

From the corner of my eye, I saw her turn back from the light switch. First, she turned toward me. Next, she followed my gaze toward the impossible tableau.

"Lida?" she responded. "I imagine our guests are awaiting some music."

With trembling hands, I managed to remove Rick's cylinder and replace it with "La Serenata Waltz." I started the machine and put the needle in place.

If the descriptions given by our three witnesses hadn't prepared me, I suspect I might have succumbed to fits of laughter. The empty coats were, in fact, *dancing!* I felt my way back to a stool and steadied myself against it.

Vera, on the other hand, followed Miss Sawyer's lead by swaying in place and then inching toward the coats. Remembering that the entities halted when the music stopped, I reached back toward the phonograph. I readied my hand to lift the needle or, if need be, swat it off the cylinder's groove. Meanwhile, Vera danced closer.

And she danced closer *still*.

I heard her giggling as the coats moved toward her. One bumped her but quickly withdrew. It brought to mind an eager puppy wishing to play with an alert cat. Whether Vera was bedazzled or *bedeviled* by this gesture, I am not sure. I do know that she raised her arms into the position of a dance partner. She then waited to be accepted.

Almost with the nervous hesitations of a schoolboy, another of the coats approached her. The left arm of the coat extended toward Vera's shoulder, and Vera carefully lowered it to her waist. The right arm then moved toward her upraised hand.

Vera's head lolled in my direction, her eyes and mouth expressing utter enchantment. She swallowed before finding the resolve to describe what she was discovering. *"Warm*—but not shaped like us. Shoulder feels ridged. Arms move as if they have additional joints. The hands are—the hands are without digits." While still dancing, she was manipulating her right hand to blindly detect what she was holding.

Vera then began to scream. I had never before heard Vera *scream.*

But *Vera was screaming!*

I saw her yank herself away and double over. My hand shoved the phonograph off its table to crash on the floor. All of the coats spun in a flurry.

And still *Vera was screaming!*

The coats flew in various directions, being shaken off and hurled away. One almost slapped against me, and my bob to dodge it caused me to topple from the stool. As I regained my footing, I heard Mr. Bartowski charge into the room.

And *still*—*Vera! Was! Screaming!*

I arrived by her side at the same moment as Mr. Bartowski. Vera was shielding her right hand deep within her middle. There was blood on her dress and on the floor.

"Lie down, Vera! *Lie down!"* I commanded. "Sir, can you bring something to stop the bleeding? Anything at all!"

He ran somewhere. I helped Vera down to sit on the floor, and balancing on one knee, I wrapped my arms around her. Her face was pallid, her eyes filmy with tears. Amid cries, she struggled to lift her hands—the left clutching the right—above her head. She was doing what she could to diminish the bleeding.

Reaching above myself, I snatched a blouse from a rack and fought to free it from the hanger. Wrapping the sleeve around

Vera's right forearm, I used the hanger to twist the sleeve tighter and tighter against the artery.

Only then did I see that Vera's blood-covered hand was missing its last two fingers. They appeared to be severed at the knuckles furthest from the tips. Stupidly, I searched the floor for them as I cradled my friend, whose cries turned to groaning.

Mr. Bartowski hurried back. At a moderate volume, he uttered, "Uh—uh, we only have basic emergency supplies. But, uh, there's a doctor two streets over. I'll fetch him. Uh, I'll fetch the doctor. I'll be right back with a doctor."

As he dashed out the backdoor, a gush of cold air entered and washed over the two of us. The air roused Vera enough for her to focus on my face.

She licked her lips several times before mumbling, "The hard ghosts. More lobster claws than human hands." Passing into unconsciousness, she added, "Should've had lunch first. Don't I always say lunch before—"

•

Severed fingers are a routine business in an age of mechanized factories. The hospital staff sutured and bandaged Vera's two stubs with great efficiency and almost no curiosity. They did not ask for details when I told them that her accident had been caused by a sewing machine. After all, I wanted them to concentrate on their surgery instead of what had befallen their patient.

Within a matter of days, Vera was back in her rooms at the Hotel Manitou. I began to visit her regularly, bringing her meals and helping her adjust to household chores. Once again, I was serving as her assistant.

One morning, Vera was sitting behind her desk. Her hand was still bandaged, but her color and strength had rebounded entirely. She asked me, "Did you happen to see a somewhat languorous woman heading out as you came in today, my dear?"

"The one who moved as if she were sleepwalking?"

Vera nodded with a raised eyebrow. I gave it some thought.

"Nooo!" I exclaimed.

"Yes."

"Madeline Morley?"

"M.M."

"Good heavens! It's as if I've seen Santa Claus! That is, if Santa Claus were melancholic instead of jolly."

Vera chuckled. "After reading the bloody finale of my report on Milwaukee, she hopped onto the next train west from Boston. She seems like a good-hearted woman. She brought me a gift!" Vera held up a book titled *The Diamond Lens with Other Stories*, by Fitz-James O'Brien. "Both cases that Harry shared with this O'Brien fellow are included. M.M. had assumed he might have shared them with me, too, when he was mentoring me. It appears she knows far more about *me* than vice versa."

"Despite her gift, I hope you'll forgive me if I withhold my verdict concerning M.M. a while longer," I stated, Vera's scream still echoing in my memory. "But did she have any news regarding the Bartowskis?"

"Her agent in Milwaukee reports no subsequent sightings. Of course, the secondhand man now joins his wife in refusing any music at all to be played—but I have a strong hunch that whatever manifested there has been frightened away for good." She lifted the book. "It would be too bad, wouldn't it? I was just skimming over Harry's account of his encounter with one of the invisible beings."

"Things didn't end much better that time, did they?"

Vera winced. "He captured the thing and naively *starved* it to death. M.M. says her foundation preserves Harry's plaster cast of the thing. I'd always wondered if that were real or the writer's embellishment." She rose, bringing the book with her. Stepping toward her occult library, she laughed, "The tale ends with Harry leaving for a place *from which he might not return,* according to O'Brien. Isn't that a particularly dramatic way to describe Cleveland?"

I grinned. Vera added the book to the others on the shelf. She then gently ran the remaining fingers of her right hand over the spines of those books.

Still facing away, she declared, "The Morley Foundation has offered to sponsor me for a year's travels through Europe and, especially, the British Isles. I'm to devote myself to studying their ghosts and seeing if my theory about guilt is still validated. It's an attractive proposal, don't you think?"

I remained silent, watching Vera wander back to her chair.

"It *sounds* attractive," I said at last, "but was the loss of *additional* body parts mentioned during the negotiations? Oh, forgive me. That was rude. I—I am—I'm somewhat adrift here."

Vera smiled gently as she used her left hand to raise a letter opener, which she immediately placed back down. "There wasn't much in the way of negotiations." She peered up at me.

"I'm glad you'll be staying, then," I said with little confidence.

"No," she clarified. "I'll be informing the hotel management that I'm leaving at the end of the month. I've lived in these rooms for almost a decade. And in this *country* my entire life. It's high time for me to see what it's like somewhere else." She faced me directly. "I *accepted* the offer."

I swallowed—and then stood. I paced—and then retook my seat. Leaning across Vera's desk, I took her pen and a slip of paper. "I'm writing down my name and address. I hope you'll write to me on occasion."

The point of the pen became blurred. One of my tears fell on the desk. I set down the pen.

Clearing my throat, I whimpered, "I can't—I don't seem able to write my own name."

Vera reached for the pen with her bandaged hand. She then remembered to use her better one. "Let me assist you, then," she whispered.

She wrote on the slip of paper, spun it around, and slid it toward me.

Vera had written: "My dear."

POSTSCRIPT

Let me end at the top. When I opened the box holding my great-grandaunt's manuscripts, the first document I saw was a letter. It begins to explain what motivated Lida to chronicle the supernatural investigations she had shared with Vera Van Slyke. That letter, dated July 28, 1918, was addressed to Mrs. Lida Bergson and signed by Chaplain Raymond J. Rice. The chaplain offers his condolences for the death of Pvt. 1cl. Eric "Rick" Bergson, whose life was lost in battle at Soissons, France.

The letter goes on to praise the soldier's patriotism, his sacrifice, and "his continual efforts to bolster the spirits of his company through music and story." The chaplain concludes by saluting Lida's devotion to her husband, mentioning the numerous letters she sent him. A single sentence especially caught my attention: "Rick never failed to delight us by passing along the accounts of little Vera and those ghostly mysteries you sent to him."

It is feasible that the manuscripts I edited had gone to Europe and, somehow, made their way back. I'm more inclined to think that, at the same time as she mailed her husband letters, Lida wrote these fuller and more formal "ghostly mysteries" as his welcome-home gift. It seems as if she had abandoned the project on receiving word of his death. This is suggested by the disheveled way the pages had been placed in, of all things, a wooden box designed to display seed packets. It is also hinted at by the occasional missing title or epigraph (which I did my best to furnish).

Perhaps more important is the chaplain's mention of *little* Vera. Of course, the chronicles beneath his letter describe Vera Van Slyke as being tall, almost six-feet in height. My genealogical research has confirmed that my great-grandaunt had a *daughter* whose maiden name was Vera Rose Bergson, born in 1910. However, I have not been able to locate contact information for any of her descendants. One day, I hope to get the opportunity to ask them if they recall Vera Rose's mother ever mentioning any additional experiences with Vera Van Slyke. In that regard, the book you are about to close is my message-in-a-bottle to them.

In addition, we know that Vera wrote at least one report for the psychical research society administered by Madeline Morley. What if there were more than one report out there, waiting to be reclaimed?

But those are both dreams of the future. At present, all I know for sure is that one more chronicle came in the seed-packet box that I inherited from my great-grandaunt. Its length prohibited including it with this volume. The narrative details Lida's very first encounter with Vera at the Morley mansion in 1899 as well as their 1903 investigation of the *two* ghosts that lingered there. Lida titled this narrative *Guilt Is a Ghost*. My next project will be to edit this book-length chronicle.

While living, Vera Van Slyke touched the life of my ancestor. It seems her spirit will be prodding *me* to share her stories for some time to come.

First, though, I think I'll have lunch—and perhaps a beer.

Tim Prasil

This is the only known photograph of Vera Van Slyke (seated) and
Ludmila "Lida" Bergson, née Prášilová, aka Lucille Parsell.

ABOUT THE AUTHOR

Tim Prasil writes fiction, plays, and the occasional limerick. He also researches quirky genres of fiction from the 1800s and early 1900s, from occult detective fiction to tales of sinister hypnotists. From this research, Tim edits entertaining and informative anthologies.

In 2017, he started Brom Bones Books as a publishing "cottage" for his work. Visit brombonesbooks.com to learn about Tim's upcoming projects. The site also has a page titled "The Life and Ghosts of Vera Van Slyke," which reviews the verifiable history underlying many of the cases chronicled in this book.

One more thing. *Tim Prasil* rhymes with *grim fossil.* Flattering, aint' it?

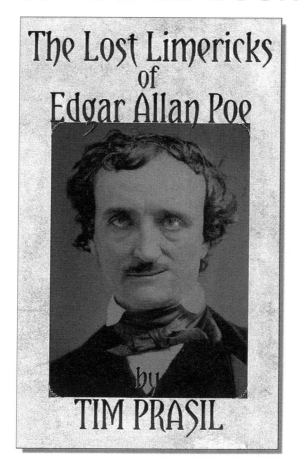

The Lost Limericks
of
Edgar Allan Poe

by

TIM PRASIL

On a hot summer day, a man in a heavy coat sold Tim Prasil a manuscript of 100 limericks purportedly penned by Edgar Allan Poe. Prasil has never been able to prove or disprove the true authorship. Is it possible that the gloomy author dabbled in writing limericks? Decide for yourself as you page through these silly, spooky, and sometimes serious glimpses at Poe's work, his life, and his world.

Visit www.brombonesbooks.com for sample limericks and more information.

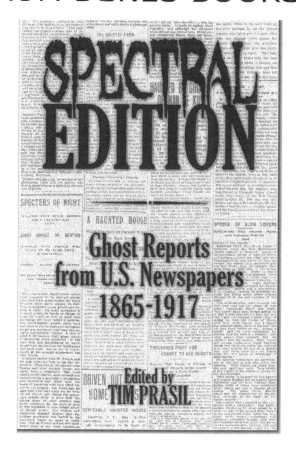

78359795R00175

Made in the USA
Middletown, DE
01 July 2018